Destitution Intensified

By

James Gervois

Argus Enterprises International, Inc.
New Jersey***North Carolina

Destitution Intensified © 2012. All
rights reserved by David Jervis

A-Argus Better Book Publishers, LLC

For information:
A-Argus Better Book Publishers, LLC
9001 Ridge Hill Street
Kernersville, North Carolina 27285
www.a-argusbooks.com

ISBN: 978-0-6156268-6-4
ISBN: 06156268-6-5

Book Cover designed by Dubya

Printed in the United States of America

'Germany – May, 1945'

The barbed-wire gate swung shut behind the Bedford truck as the driver lurched forward, the gears howling in protest as he attempted to change up. Pushing the rear canvas flap to one side, Dieter glanced out, feeling another punch to his kidneys as the truck dropped into a pothole. Grimacing with pain, he noticed how many men there were; sullen, dishevelled, apathetic and starving; sitting, lying and standing, glancing disinterestedly as the convoy of prisoners passed.

The truck came to a juddering halt as the inexperienced driver hit the brakes.

'Raus! Get out! Schnell! Schnell!'

Dieter heard the shouts and the sound of hobnailed boots coming towards the rear of the truck. A head appeared, the British Tommy glaring up at him as he took the tailboard pins out, dropping it with a loud crash.

The soldier unslung his .303 rifle and pointed it at the truck occupants. 'Get out! Raus! Schnell! You effing German bastards!'

Dieter tried to lower himself to the ground, landing heavily and wincing. The shrapnel wound to his calf was still very painful, worse now after the ride to Munsterlager from Wiesbaden, some three hundred kilometres away. It had taken two days to make the journey and they had only stopped once for food, some watery soup and a piece of stale bread. Dieter felt the last rays of the May sunshine penetrating his greatcoat, easing the stiffness from his body.

'Get in line…come on, you Nazi shits, get in line!' The young Tommy seemed to be enjoying his moment of power.

More men scrabbled out from the truck and Dieter noticed the same happening further along, mentally noting that there were twelve trucks in the convoy. He smiled wryly to himself, thinking this is the pride of the Wehrmacht, Germany's once all-conquering army, now reduced to a rabble of vagabonds.

'Into line! Into line! Schnell.' The deep voice belonged to a Sergeant Major, walking towards the men.

'Im reihe und glied,' Dieter shouted out.

The men started to shuffle into lines, their backs to the trucks. Dieter, standing in the middle line watched as the British soldiers started to take a head count, checking against lists they obviously had on clipboards. He glanced along the line in front of him, noticing that, like himself, most of the men had removed their identifying badges and badges of rank, their uniforms tattered and torn. Like himself, everyone sported straggly beards, unkempt long hair and looked filthy.

The Sergeant Major, his chest puffed out like a strutting rooster, started his tirade. 'You are Prisoners of War and will behave accordingly. Here, at Munsterlager, we pride ourselves on discipline and you will always obey orders given to you by British personnel. Superior forces have defeated you and now, you will live with the consequences. You are scum! Your leader...Hitler, has killed himself,' The Sergeant Major paused.

Looking rather red in the face, Dieter thought.

'You will march to the huts you are assigned to and strip off. You are all filthy and need delousing. You will parade tomorrow morning. Corporals! Get them moving.'

British soldiers started yelling at the men along the lines. There was utter confusion as nobody understood what they were supposed to be doing or what the Sergeant Major had said.

Dieter had understood. 'Ab marsch, in die Richtung,' he said, pointing towards the wooden huts in the distance. 'Wir sollen dahin maschieren und uns ausziehen.'

The rifle butt hit Dieter hard, between the shoulders, knocking him to the ground. A hobnailed boot smashed into his back, catching his spine, causing him to yell out in pain.

'Get up you Kraut bastard! Nobody gave you permission to speak. Move.'

Two other Germans helped Dieter to his feet, supporting him between them. He glanced over his shoulder, seeing the young Tommy standing there, ready to use his rifle butt again, his face contorted with hatred.

Moving around the cellar, Brigitte was careful not to tread on the sleeping bodies lying on the floor or bump into the more fortunate neighbours who sat on chairs or lay on crates. The air was stale and stank of rotting potatoes, urine and humans who had not washed for some time. The heat from so many bodies was oppressive. The pale glow, coming from an old, oil-wick lamp, cast murky shadows across the cellar but barely helped Brigitte to find her way. She felt an outstretched arm against her thigh, easing her way around it as she came to the child's cot where her baby was making his quiet sobs, chewing vigorously on an old piece of cloth.

Brigitte took the turnip from under her coat and felt under the baby's rugs, finding the knife she kept hidden there. She cut a chunk out of the turnip and started to chew it, the sharp, strong taste in her mouth making her grimace.

'Can't you sleep?' a voice whispered close to her.

Brigitte looked across at her friend, Gisela, the plump, blonde haired daughter of the postman and his wife who use to live in the apartment above hers. 'Trying to chew this...for the baby,' Brigitte replied. 'Do you want some?'

Gisela gave an involuntary shiver and pulled a face. 'That is awful but...yes, I'm so hungry. Will Heinz eat it?'

'Wait and see. He'll eat anything.' Spitting her mouthful into a tin can, Brigitte carved another piece from the turnip and, cutting it in half, passed a piece to Gisela.

'Where did you find it?' Gisela asked, trying not to gag.

Brigitte smiled. 'None of your business. What I can say, I had to walk a long way to find it. That's why I'm so late getting back. Thanks for keeping an eye on Heinz.' She untied her scarf and shook her head, releasing her long blonde hair.

'Ever since those bloody British bombed us out of our homes almost two years ago, we've had to struggle to survive,' Gisela said with anger. 'Why did they pick on us here in Hamburg?'

Placing an arm around her friend's shoulder, Brigitte pulled Gisela towards her. She remembered the July '43 bombing; five nights of sheer terror when the city had burned down. She had even seen the asphalt on the roads in flames. The neighbours had christened the event, 'The Catastrophe' and it had been. The firestorms stopped people breathing; literally tens of thousands had perished. Somehow, Brigitte had survived but her parents, two streets away, had not. And days before the raids began, Brigitte had been ecstatic, rushing round to her parents, telling them the wonderful news that she was pregnant.

'Gisela, I know it is confusing, especially when you are only sixteen, but we are not the only ones to have suffered. Most of our cities have been bombed...that is the price we pay for being at war.' Brigitte spat another mouthful into the tin.

'We will win. We will still overcome,' Gisela said, standing up. 'As long as our Fuhrer is alive, we shall succeed.'

Brigitte patiently cut another piece of turnip, placing it in her mouth. 'Didn't the Hitler Youth teach you anything? Have you seen outside? Have you seen the British soldiers? From what we know, the Russians have overrun Berlin. So, where is Hitler? Some say he has fled to South America.'

Gisela looked down at the floor. 'Lies,' she said under her breath. 'Anyway, how old is Heinz now? He's teething...isn't he?'

'He's sixteen months and yes, he's teething,' Brigitte replied, annoyed with herself for having snapped at her friend. She knew she should be careful, especially as Gisela had been a youth leader and would still report people to the authorities, should some sort of normality return. Somehow, Brigitte doubted that it would.

Gisela looked across, a slight sneer in her voice. 'Do you know where your husband is?'

'God knows,' Brigitte replied. She knew that most people around here did not accept her claim that she was married. Most assumed she had fallen with Heinz from a passing fling, a one-night stand. Well, that was probably right, Brigitte thought. No sooner had she married than her husband was ordered to join his unit and they had only managed the one night together. 'We have far more problems to concern us than worrying about things we can't change. If he's alive I'm sure he will find me.'

'Well, you're young enough, I suppose, to get another man,' Gisela joked.

'Cheeky. I'm only twenty-three so...' Brigitte stopped, spitting into the tin. 'Anyway, I'm not interested in other men. Heinz is my only concern.' Grabbing a small bottle of water she had boiled earlier, Brigitte poured it over the masticated turnip, stirring it with a spoon. She leant over the side of the cot and, picking Heinz up, cuddled him in her arm, spooning the thin gruel into his mouth. Heinz's face puckered at the first taste but his eyes were already seeking out the next spoonful.

The Franconia II slipped her moorings and eased away from the Hull quayside at first light. Standing at the stern rail, Colin looked down at the water churning up as the powerful screws started to push the vessel forward, moving it quickly into the estuary. He turned round and looked up at the sky, seeing the sun rising, casting its light across the water, feeling the excitement building up in his stomach. He was on his way, crossing to Bremerhaven and then onto somewhere called Bad Oeynhausen where the British Army had its headquarters. As a newly recruited member of the Control Commission, Colin was looking forward to getting to Germany and helping to rebuild it. *Far more fun than going up to Oxford to read law,* he thought, especially as he had just missed out on the war.

'Time for breakfast, lad,' the man next to him stated in a broad northern accent. 'If you hang around, it'll all be gone, knowing those greedy buggers up ahead.'

Colin looked at the men pushing and shoving to get through the door into the lounge. 'I suppose you are right.'

The man and Colin joined the group ahead, taking a tray apiece and helping themselves to the bread as a chef passed each of them a plate with fried sausages, black pudding, scrambled eggs and fried tomatoes. Colin made his way to a spare table and sat down, the man sitting opposite.

'This is all rather good,' Colin said. 'I wonder where they get it all from seeing as how we have been rationed.'

The man laughed. 'Take it you're with the Commission...so am I. From now on, we get what we want...no rations for us. By the way, I'm Bill...Bill Thornton.'

Colin smiled, shaking the extended hand. The man was obviously in his forties, he thought, judging by the thick matt of greying hair. The man's face was round, one could say chubby, but the sharp, blue eyes were alert, darting round the room, noticing everything. 'Colin Forsyth-Patterson but I just use the Patterson.'

Bill nodded. 'Did you know this was a famous cruise liner? Cole Porter's played in this lounge. Wouldn't think it would you, looking at it now? It's been a troop ship for the past few years and they stripped out all of the luxury fittings. I hear this is its last voyage before going back to the yards for refitting.' Bill paused, taking a mouthful of black pudding. 'Anyway, lad...sorry, Colin, what's your story?'

'My story?'

'Aye, where're you from?'

Colin smiled. 'My family live near Harrogate and my father owns some cotton mills in Huddersfield. I've just finished school and...when I was asked by one of my father's friends if I wanted to join the Commission, I jumped at the chance.'

'Well, you look a tall, well-built lad to me but I think you may be in for a bit of a shock once you get over there,' Bill replied.

'That's rugger and athletics at school...I was captain of both teams,' Colin added, slightly self-consciously. 'What about yourself?'

'Oh me? That's a long story,' Bill shrugged, munching on a sausage. 'I was in the police force, in Richmond. Now't much going on except trying to nab black marketers and, as most of those on the force were involved in the racket, not much point in that. So, when I heard about the Commission back end of last year, I applied. Reckon it's got to be more…well, exciting than sitting at home with the wife and three squawking kids.' He shovelled some scrambled egg into his mouth. 'Surprised me how easy it was to get in but, suppose they need people like me, use to dealing with criminals and the like.'

'As a policeman I assume you were exempt from military service?' Colin asked.

'Not fit enough for the army,' Bill chuckled. 'That's why I've got three young 'uns. Told I had flat feet, couldn't march when I applied at the beginning. Well, their loss, not mine.' He wiped his hand across his mouth. 'How come though, a young lad like you got in?'

'I speak German, well enough to get by. Always seemed to have an affinity for languages and we had a very good German master at my boarding school.'

'Aye, we'll need a lot like you. Can't speak a bloody word myself. Well, Heil and Zeppelin. What..?'

Colin could not contain his laughter. 'Zeppelin is an airship.'

Bill burst out with a raucous laugh. 'See what I mean? Anyway, you've read the instruction books…no fraternisation. We've got to regard all Germans as dangerous. They're all guilty and we've got to keep them in their place.'

Colin frowned. 'I think that's a bit strong. We know that in this country some supported Mosley, others supported Communism. Some even supported Hitler. It doesn't make everyone bad.'

'You've got a lot to learn, lad. Remember our orders. You've got to keep clear of all Germans – men, women and children. You can't walk with them, shake their hands, visit their homes, play games etc. etc. You can't fraternise.'

'So how are we supposed to help with the reconstruction of Germany if we aren't permitted to discuss things with them?'

'That's not our concern. That's up to the politicians and generals. The likes of you and me...we do as we're told.' Bill wiped his plate with the remains of his bread, burping loudly. 'If you've got any sense, you'll take every opportunity that comes along, take whatever you want and come home a wealthy man. That's my advice.'

Colin frowned again. 'I don't think that's right, Bill. I am not going to Germany to line my pockets, so to speak. I'm going there to help.'

'They're all Nazis. What do you think they would've done if the boot was on the other foot,' Bill snapped back. 'For starters, they'd probably shoot your old man, being a factory owner and all that. Got a sister?'

'Two, as it happens.'

'Well, they'd get raped. I tell you, these people are sub-human.' Bill leaned backwards, fixing Colin with his stare.

'You're absolutely right. Those effing Nazis, all of them, need to know whose boss,' said the burly man at the adjoining table. 'And I intend to make sure they quickly understand that.'

Colin looked across at the man, surprised at his intrusion. He looked back at Bill, unsure what to say. He knew, instinctively that if these two were representative of the majority then the Germans were going to suffer badly.

'Time we made a move, we've got a lecture in what used to be the smoking room,' Bill said, getting up from the table.

Colin did the same, following Bill out of the lounge.

Men shivered in the cool evening air as they stripped off. The British soldiers were yelling orders, incomprehensible to most and Dieter watched as each man was given a towel, razor, bar of soap and herded into the grey, single story building in front of them. He eased off his tunic and vest, feeling the pain between his shoulder blades where the rifle butt had landed. Undoing his belt, he lowered his trousers and pants, sitting down on the grass to undo his boots. Carefully, he removed them and his trousers, trying not to dislodge the filthy bandage around his calf.

'Come on, come on...we haven't got all day,' the British corporal shouted at him.

Feigning ignorance, Dieter eased himself up.

'Get that off!'

Dieter looked at the corporal, seeing that the man was pointing at the bandage and Dieter, after frowning and looking puzzled, lowered himself to the ground, undoing the bandage. When he eased it off his leg, momentary pain shot through it as the bandage pulled at the wound. A quick glance showed it was at least clean. Grimacing, Dieter got to his feet and ambled forwards, feeling the warmth of a trickle of blood running down the back of his leg.

As he walked through the door a man in a dirty white coat shook DDT over him, making Dieter cough and, before he realised what was happening, another man had stuck a needle into his backside, injecting him. Dieter did not bother to ask what it was for and followed those in front of him towards the large washroom. Men were passing a pair of scissors to each other, hacking at their beards and hair. The long, concrete troughs were full of water and Dieter started to wash himself, feeling invigorated as the cold water cleansed him. He lathered the soap in his hands and attempted to wash his hair. Then he got the scissors and trimmed his straggly beard, eventually using the razor. He eased his leg into the water, carefully bathing his wound, seeing a small amount of blood coagulate in the water and float away. When he was satisfied, he towelled himself down, feeling as though he had come alive again. Leaving the building, he dropped the towel, razor and soap into the boxes provided, noticing the vigilance of the guards making sure no man took anything with them. It would be difficult, Dieter thought, standing naked.

'Schnell! Schnell! Over there.' A Tommy pointed towards a long wooden hut where an orderly queue was forming. Dieter walked forward slowly. The loud smack across his back made him wince and stumble forward. He glanced over his shoulder, seeing the Tommy grinning towards his friends, the canvass rifle sling dangling in his right hand.

Once inside the hut, Dieter was given underclothes, woollen socks, a pair of green woollen trousers and matching tunic top and, to his surprise, a decent pair of leather boots. He pointed at his leg, indicating it needed bandaging and the emaciated man behind the counter hawked and gobbed at him, the saliva landing on Dieters chest. Dieter turned away, joining the others, putting the clothes on. At least he felt clean, felt human again, after weeks in the filthy clothing he had just discarded. Outside, he saw the men being lined up and joined one of the ranks, turning and walking towards a group of long huts behind a barbed wire fence, some two hundred metres away. They soon reached the huts and Dieter estimated groups of fifty were split off and ordered into each hut. He went up the four steps into the one the Tommy indicated and entered the hut, seeing the wooden bunks lined up in rows, the smashed wood burning stove in the middle and the smell of excrement in his nostrils made him gag. Dieter made his way past others and saw the door leading to what was, judging by the overpowering smell, the latrines. He forced himself forward, looking through the doorway, seeing the filth of the place. He turned back and found a bottom bunk near the back wall, slumping down. He noticed the crude engravings on the boards beside him, making out the odd Polish word.

'Made us wash after delousing and then…then they stick us in this filthy pigsty,' a voice said from the top bunk opposite. 'Who left it like this?'

Dieter was momentarily startled. This was the first time anyone had spoken since he had got onto the truck. 'I think it was Polish POW's,' he replied. Others in the hut started to talk to those nearest to them.

'They should have been made to clean up their filth,' the man retorted.

Dieter shrugged. 'Maybe they had other things on their minds.'

'Anyway, we'll soon be out of here, once we've been processed and then, its home, here I come,' the man said.

Dieter shrugged. 'I wouldn't be so sure. It could take some time before we are released.'

The man got down and sat on the bunk opposite, stretching out his hand. 'I'm Hartwig Nadel.'

'Dieter Barth.' Dieter shook the man's hand, noticing his blond hair and blue eyes, in contrast to his own dark brown hair and green eyes. The man looked about the same age as himself, twenty-five.

Hartwig smiled. 'How long have you been captured?'

'I'd estimate three weeks but as some Tommy took my watch, I'm not certain.'

'I got taken two weeks ago, down near Metz,' Hartwig said. 'Bloody unlucky, I tell you. I'd got clean away from Brest and virtually reached the border when the truck I was hiding in got blasted off the road by a fighter. Still, I was the lucky one, the rest were killed or badly injured.'

'British or Americans?' Dieter asked.

'Americans but they handed me over to the British at Koblenz.'

Dieter leaned back against the wall. 'Who were you with?'

'You ask a lot,' Hartwig replied, 'but give very little in return.'

'Who were you with?'

Hartwig looked at Dieter's eyes, drilling into him. He looked down. 'The 266 Infanterie-Division.'

'Where did you serve?'

'All right, I'll tell you,' Hartwig said, obviously annoyed. 'I joined in May '43, based in Stuttgart and then went to Normandy last June, fighting alongside the 352 Infanterie. Some of us got sent to St. Malo to support the garrison and then we were ordered to fall back towards Brest. What about you?'

Dieter smiled. 'Me...I'm an enemy stooge.'

Hartwig looked shocked, the colour draining from his cheeks. He stared at Dieter.

'Thanks for all the information,' Dieter said.

'But...but, you can't be,' Hartwig spluttered.

'Why not?'

'Well, I saw you in the washroom and then getting the clothing. You can't be.' A frown set in as Hartwig continued to stare. 'But, you do understand English.'

'What makes you assume that?' Dieter asked, raising an eyebrow.

Hartwig shrugged his shoulders. 'When we arrived, I heard you shout out to the men, telling them what the Tommy had said.'

'How observant.'

Hartwig stood up and started to walk past Dieter.

'Don't believe everything you hear,' Dieter said, placing his hand around Hartwig's wrist. 'The point I am making is that you are obviously a decent chap but you have to be more careful what you say to strangers as there will be stooges planted in these camps to root out SS, Nazi sympathisers and others.'

Hartwig sat down again. 'You're not a stooge?'

Dieter laughed. 'Would I tell you if I were?'

'Don't suppose so.'

'The Americans captured me at Blankenheim after my tank was destroyed. They gave me basic field treatment on my leg and then took me to a field hospital where I stayed for five days before being sent, along with some twenty others across to Koblenz and the British.'

'Who were you with?' Hartwig grinned.

Dieter smiled and nodded. '2 Panzer Division...joined in '43, just in time for the Kursk Offensive.'

'So we both joined around the same time,' Hartwig replied. 'But...what about your English?'

Dieter leaned back again. 'My mother is English and I spent time in England before the war.'

'Are you going to tell them that?' Hartwig nodded towards the door.

'Prefer it if you keep that between you and me, at least for the time being,' Dieter replied.

Hartwig nodded. 'I was trained here. Can't remember this camp though.'

'Likewise,' Dieter said. 'I think it was four months, out on the ranges. Used to be a beautiful place - Luneberg Heath and Fallingbostel. Didn't Goring have his hunting lodge around here?'

'Yes, I think he does...well, did. Plenty of forests around and they must be full of wild life.'

'If I remember correctly,' Dieter continued, 'there was a POW camp near Belsen for the French and Belgium prisoners and later, the Russians. It's probably still in use.'

Hartwig coughed, looked round and lowered his voice. 'I've heard it said it was turned into a concentration camp for the Jews. Apparently the British have just liberated it and they found more than sixty thousand people there, starving to death.'

A loud hooter went off outside the hut followed by soldiers yelling, telling the men to leave the huts and parade outside.

'No wonder we're getting a harsh reception,' Dieter replied. 'Better do what the Tommies want.'

Chapter Two

The battered Morris truck made slow progress along the road from Bremerhaven to Bremen. Squashed in the canvas-topped cab between Bill Thornton and a cockney, lance corporal driver, Colin could not take his eyes off the road. It was cluttered with people going in both directions, most looking like vagabonds, carrying whatever they could. There was a mixture of carts and trailers; some hand drawn, some horse drawn, a few tractor drawn. All of them were laden with people, usually children and the old, and all types of belongings – furniture, bedding, pots and pans, crates, pictures, clothes – everything appearing to be suitable for a bonfire. What surprised Colin even more was the look on the people's faces. Everyone looked haggard, their eyes almost lifeless. It was not what he had expected. Occasionally they passed groups of men who cheered them, laughing and shouting. The driver explained that they were probably freed slave workers.

'Cor blimey, look at 'at,' the corporal shouted as he double-declutched to change down, the engine whining.

Colin stared at the huge mounds of rubble on each side of them. 'This is Bremen?'

'Yep. Took a pasting, just like all the other German towns and cities. Serves 'em right is what I says. Jerries don't deserve no better. Got our own back for the East End.'

'Agree with you, lad,' Bill said. 'There's hardly a building intact. In fact haven't seen one yet. Only loads of graffiti. See that wall over there,' Bill pointed through the screen, 'it says *See Germany and Die* in perfect English. What do you make of that lad?'

'You will also have seen the others,' Colin replied. 'Look at that one – *Sieg oder Siberien*, or that one – *weg mit Hitler*.'

Bill puffed on his cigarette. 'Don't understand what they mean.'

'One says 'Down with Hitler' and the other, 'Victory or Siberia', Colin said. It's just propaganda but I'm surprised with the one about Hitler.'

'Ah, it's all beyond me, mate,' the corporal said.

Colin coughed. 'Look at the people. They're…they're scavenging. Look, look at that woman over there, she's picking wood out of the rubble and putting it into that pram.'

The corporal chuckled. 'You ain't seen the rest, mate. Wait tills we get to Hannover. Now that's what I call real bombing.'

'Watch out!' Colin snatched at the wheel, the corporal resisting him as the truck knocked an old man across the road.

'One less Jerry to worry about, mate.'

Bill chuckled. 'One more who won't want feeding.'

'Stop the truck! We must see if he is injured,' Colin shouted above the whine of the engine.

The corporal shook his head. 'No way, mate. You want to start a riot. Stop around 'ere and you're liable to wind up dead yourself.'

Colin put his head back and closed his eyes, sickened by what he had seen since leaving the ship. He reflected on the lectures they had received with the extensive lists of Do's and Don'ts. Do give orders; be firm; immediately discipline. Don't make requests; be kind; be put off. What he had been told about the Germans seemed appalling. His German master at school, whilst strict, had always seemed to be a decent person and a very good athlete, as far as Colin was concerned. Now, the visual impact of the Allied bombing and the state of the people caused Colin to wonder if he had made the right decision. Such was the obvious chaos, he didn't know how he could begin to help.

The truck lurched and bumped over debris as the corporal fought the wheel, cursing, causing Colin to look ahead. A woman was pulling what looked like a toboggan, something glinting on it in the sun.

'Stop the truck,' Bill shouted as they drew level. He opened the door and jumped down, the woman turning, a look of terror on her face. She let go of the cord and cringed, putting her hands to her face. Colin leaned over and saw Bill pull the sacking off.

'Well, well, what have we got here then,' Bill shouted. 'Looks like a little gold mine. There's candelabras, some wine goblets, napkin rings and...a jewel box. Think we'll be taking this, no use to you,' he said to the woman.

'You can't, it's not ours,' Colin shouted, starting to get out of the cab.

'Wouldn't do that, mate,' the corporal said, grabbing Colin's arm.

Bill started placing the oddments inside the sack. 'Who said it's hers. She's stolen it anyway, bet me life on it.'

'You don't know that,' Colin shouted.

Bill climbed back into the cab, placing the sack between his feet. 'Let's get moving. Don't want any trouble...do we.' He looked at Colin menacingly. 'Say no more about this if you understand what I mean.'

The corporal engaged the clutch and the truck lurched forward, leaving the woman standing, staring after them as they drove away.

Watching the small group of men coming down the forest track towards him, Cyrek Rutkowski could see that there were another four newcomers in the group.

'Wicus! Wake up, you idle slob.' Cyrek kicked the man lying on the ground.

'What! Can't a man get some rest?' Wicus Sobczak groaned, stumbling to his feet, wiping his eyes. He glared at Cyrek. He was not frightened of any man but Cyrek was different. A tall, dark haired man with beetled brows and glaring eyes who came from Krakow. He had been a lumberjack before the war and was as powerful as an ox. But it was not his physical presence that made Wicus wary, it was Cyrek's sudden changes in mood, from reasonableness one moment to extreme rage and violence the next.

Cyrek pointed at the approaching group. 'Take the four they've found and check them out.'

Wicus nodded, collecting up his rifle and baton. He strolled amiably towards the group, smiling, joking with the men he knew, telling them to get food and drink for the newcomers.

Watching Wicus chatting to them, Cyrek sat down. He trusted Wicus, especially after Wicus had saved him in the camp – Stalag XIB, near Fallingbostel. When he had first been captured, back in 1940, he had been too rebellious, too young at nineteen, to accept the treatment dished out by his German captors. He had been beaten to within an inch of his life and, thanks to Wicus taking huge risks, bringing him food and drink whilst he was held in solitary confinement, he had managed to survive. With more and more prisoners arriving and then large numbers of Russians, the camp conditions had become atrocious. There was no fresh water, little in the way of food and disease, especially typhus, was rampant. Whilst they still had some strength, Cyrek and Wicus determined that they would escape. Encouraging others, they stormed the barbed wire fences during a pitch-black night, using their straw palliasses to protect them as they went over the wire, catching their German guards by surprise. Of the fifty or so men who charged, only Cyrek, Wicus and four others made it into the forest, the rest being shot where they stood or captured shortly afterwards.

Due to the size and density of the forest, it had been easy to evade capture, not that the German's seemed too determined to find them. With a plentiful supply of rabbit, hare, pigeon, wild boar, pheasant and dear plus berries and fruit, the Poles had not only survived but had regained their strength. The occasional raid on a village or farmhouse had furnished them with an assortment of weapons, clothing and suitable materials to make waterproof shelters. Their camp, deep in the forest and next to a fast flowing stream, now had a look of permanence about it.

The sound of a man crying out in pain caused Cyrek to look up. Wicus was standing over the man, hunched up on the ground, clasping his stomach. Wicus bent down and whispered to the man, the man replying. Cyrek smiled. Trust Wicus to sort them out, he thought. Wicus may be short but he was wiry and powerful and Cyrek admired his bravery. He also knew Wicus enjoyed interrogating others; could see the look of satisfaction in Wicus' eyes when he had a man, or woman, at his mercy.

Wicus grabbed the man's hair and hauled him to his feet. 'Nazi lover!' He spat into the man's face and then hit him hard in the stomach, letting him fall to the ground. Wicus turned to Cyrek. 'Was with the Waffen SS…trying to get away, pretending to be a slave worker. What shall I do?'

Cyrek drew his hand across his throat.

Pulling his bayonet from his belt, Wicus walked behind the man. He grabbed his hair and pulled the man's head back, exposing his throat. The bayonet blade was pulled hard and fast across the man's throat. Blood spurted and Wicus kicked the man hard in the back, the man falling forwards, gasping and moaning. Wicus wiped the bayonet on the man's coat and turned, smiling, towards the other three newcomers.

'Spare some…if you can,' Cyrek shouted across to Wicus, other men in the camp turning back to whatever they had been doing before Wicus' show.

The sound of the cellar doors being eased open immediately awoke Brigitte. She had slept fitfully, her stomach gnawing and griping throughout the night but weariness had overcome her and she had slept soundly for the past few hours. She eased her body into a sitting position, wiping the sweat from her brow and looked around, seeing others starting to move, people hacking and spitting, drinking thirstily from a variety of containers, bottles, even a flower vase. Hardly anyone spoke. She nodded at Frau Eichel, who used to live in the flat next door and smiled. Frau Eichel was a large, plump woman who had kept to herself. She was a widow in her mid fifties and she had lost both her sons during the war.

'Good to see you managed to sleep,' Gisela said.

Brigitte looked round, seeing Gisela cradling Heinz. 'Oh. Thank you…has he been too much trouble?'

'Only bawling his head off for the past couple of hours.' Gisela smiled. 'Think he's too tired to keep it up.' As if he had understood, Heinz started wailing again.

Reaching under her bed, Brigitte felt for the tin with the turnip gruel. She knelt down and looked under the bed, moving the cardboard box containing all her worldly possessions to one side. There was no sign of the tin.

'Shit! Someone has stolen the gruel.' Brigitte looked round at those people nearest to her, looking to see if anyone showed any signs of guilt. She was met by blank stares, indifference.

'Try him with this,' Frau Eichel said, holding out a hard-tack biscuit. 'It will soften if you warm up some water.'

'Thank you.' Brigitte took the biscuit and put it into her dress pocket. She looked around and saw a fire being lit near the far wall, the smoke drifting up and out through a ventilation slat. She poured some water into a tin and made her way across the cellar, soon returning. Breaking the biscuit into the warm water, she stirred it into a runny mix and then spooned it into Heinz's mouth. He gulped it down as fast as she could feed him.

'My, my, he is hungry,' Gisela said, buttoning up her skirt. 'Do you want me to feed him?'

Brigitte passed Heinz across and went to the makeshift wash area. Someone had curtained off a corner and there were two tin baths and some washing tins placed on trestles. Other women were trying, as best they could, to wash themselves, Brigitte smiling at their attempted modesty. She unbuttoned her dress and removed it, followed by her bra and pants. Standing naked, she used a piece of cut-down towel and some soap, washing herself thoroughly. It made her feel better as she towelled herself dry. But the hunger would not go away. She washed her pants and bra, combed her hair and clipped it up on top of her head. Dressing in clean underwear, she pulled her dress on and made her way back to Gisela. She hung her washing over the end of the bed, wondering if it would still be there when she returned.

'I'm going to get some water Gisela and then I'm going out for food.'

'Can't I come with you?' Gisela pleaded. 'I'm fed up being cooped up in this damn cellar.'

Brigitte sighed. 'You know what we agreed. For you to go outside at the moment would be extremely risky. The soldiers may take advantage of you. Until order is restored, it is best if you stay out of sight. I'll take responsibility for food and water, you look after Heinz.'

'So you're safe? Why shouldn't they pick on you?' Gisela replied petulantly.

'Don't be daft. I'm a married woman, a mother,' Brigitte snapped back. She knew however, that it made no difference, she always had to be careful.

Picking up the two wooden pails, Brigitte made her way out through the cellar door, walking through the adjoining two cellars, both full of people and as hot as the one she had left. Thankfully, Brigitte thought, someone had the foresight to build these large cellars to act as air raid shelters otherwise, with the bombing, there would have been very few survivors. She walked up the wide flight of stairs and emerged on the street, looking across at the huge pile of debris and rubble, all that was left of the building where she used to live. She walked along the street, heading for the standpipe a block away, her stomach grumbling.

As she turned the corner, she saw the car parked ahead, an Austin 'Tilly' she thought it was called. Beside it were four soldiers, talking to a man inside. She continued walking, looking down.

'Allo, love. Fancy some cigarettes?' one of the soldiers called out. 'A little favour and I can take care of you.'

'That's all you could manage...a little one, mate,' one of the others said, the men laughing at each other.

'She'd make a good screw I'm telling you...look at those tits,' the first soldier replied.

Brigitte kept walking, feeling the nerves gripping her stomach, her heart beating faster. Obviously, what they were saying was not complimentary, probably crude. She turned into a side alley and reached the garden square, joining the queue for the standpipe. Nobody spoke, everyone locked up with their own thoughts. When she reached the pipe she cranked the squeaky lever, slowly filling each pail. She set off, feeling the weight of the pails, walking carefully so as not to spill the water. She noticed the old man in front of her, struggling with two buckets, breathing heavily as she reached him.

'You're from our cellar, aren't you?' Brigitte asked.

The old man paused and glanced at her, his eyes glazed. 'Yes. I've noticed you.'

They turned back into the street and Brigitte immediately saw the soldiers standing on the pavement ahead, the car had gone. She was thankful the old man was with her. They walked on, approaching the soldiers, both of them looking downwards. The old man stepped onto the road to walk round the soldiers who made no attempt to step aside. Brigitte followed him.

'Looks like they're a bit heavy for you old fella,' one of them said.

The old man looked at him. 'I'll manage,' he replied.

'Naw, we'll help you.' A soldier stepped in front of the old man and reached down, grabbed one of the buckets and then proceeded to pour the water onto the road. The other bucket was also taken and emptied. 'There, should make it a bit easier for you.' The soldiers burst out laughing.

The old man picked up the buckets and started walking. 'One day you will regret that.'

'Piss off you old sod before I get annoyed,' a soldier shouted. 'Like your woman though, thinks I'll be having her later.'

The old man and Brigitte kept on walking, Brigitte surprised that the man had spoken English – she hadn't understood what had been said. She heard the hobnailed boots running up behind her and a hand roughly groping her bottom.

'Yea, was right, no knickers,' the soldier shouted back to his mates. 'Fancy some chocolate, darling?' he whispered, Brigitte determined to continue walking. He squeezed her breast then let go, turning round and walking away.

Brigitte almost collapsed when she reached the entrance to the cellars. She was shaking all over, perspiration lined her face.

She looked at the old man. 'Thank you.'

'For what?' the man replied.

'For being there. Without you I'm sure they would have got nasty.'

The old man smiled. 'All beer talk. You just have to ignore them, they're animals.'

Brigitte held out one of her pails. 'Here, take this.'

'No. No, I can get more later.' With that, the old man set off down the stairs.

'Welcome to 'annover,' the corporal shouted over the noise of the engine.

Looking through the cab window, Colin was appalled at the sight in front of them. Hardly a building was intact - walls missing, floors at strange angles, water dribbling from burst pipes, not a window with glass and everywhere, mounds of rubble, masonry, splintered wood, shards of glass and smashed belongings.

The truck ground on, following the track cleared by bulldozers. The corporal stopped the truck as they approached a large building that seemed to be reasonably intact, just the end wall missing. 'This is where we stop for the night. You two had better go inside and report. I'll take care of your stuff,' he grinned.

Bill looked across at him. 'Don't get any ideas, lad. I know what's in the sack...anything missing when I get back and you'll regret we ever met.' Bill opened the door and got down, Colin behind him, stretching after the long ride, feeling the chill of the evening air. Colin dusted down his navy uniform, noticing that Bill did not seem to care. They walked up the steps and into the building.

Bill strolled across to the soldier sitting at a desk. 'Control Commission...Bill Thornton and Colin Patterson...told to report.'

The soldier continued writing, ignoring Bill as Colin joined him. The soldier looked up. 'Yes, what do you want?'

'Told to report,' Bill replied.

'Wait there.' The soldier bent down then eased himself upright, using crutches to support himself, his left leg swathed in bandages. He moved across the hall, disappearing through a door on the opposite side. A moment later, the door opened and the soldier emerged, accompanied by a young looking officer.

'Lieutenant Dewar. Understand you're with the Commission but nobody told us to expect you.'

'We're only passing through,' Bill replied. 'Need a bed for the night.'

The Lieutenant smiled. 'You'll be lucky old man. No beds available around here unless we kick a German family out of their home.'

'That won't be nec...' Colin started to say.

'Sounds all right to me,' Bill cut in. 'Food wouldn't go amiss either.'

Dewar's smile faded. 'OK, follow me.' He placed his hat on his head and set off for the front door.

They walked along the street and turned the corner, entering a road where the houses were mainly intact. Colin noticed a few people who scuttled away as soon as they saw them coming. Dewar went up to the front door of a house and rattled the doorknob. The door eased open and a young girl peeked shyly round the edge.

'You speak English?' Dewar asked.

'A little...please?'

'You are to leave this house in thirty minutes and only take with you what you can carry. Do you understand?'

'Please?' the girl replied, frowning.

Colin stepped forward and repeated Dewar's instructions in German.

The girl slammed the door shut, shouting for her mother. Dewar drew his pistol and used the butt end on the door. The door opened again and a tall, beautiful woman stood, glaring at him, taking a long puff on her cigarette.

'Was wollen Sie?'

Dewar looked at Colin. 'Tell her.'

Colin repeated what Dewar had said to the girl, feeling himself blushing. The woman glared at him, taking another puff on her cigarette, defiance in her eyes. She snappily told Colin that this house consisted of five older women and twelve children and asked him where they were supposed to go at this time of day.

Repeating what she had said to Dewar, Colin added, 'this is not necessary, we can stay in the building we just left. It's only for the one night.'

'Rubbish!' Dewar looked at the woman. 'Tell her this house has been requisitioned by the British Military and she has one hour to get out.'

Shamefaced, Colin relayed his instruction. Dewar turned sharply, almost knocking Colin over and marched back along the street, Bill and Colin behind him.

'Good to see you are exercising your authority,' Bill said. 'Need to teach these Nazis where they stand.'

Dewar did not reply.

They arrived back at the large building that used to be the Rathaus, the Town Hall and waited for a while, eating in what used to be the canteen, Colin and Dewar talking about the war and the chaos and confusion that Dewar had found in this part of Hannover. Bill had slipped out when he had finished gorging himself, returning a while later having found the corporal and told him where they were staying.

The three of them went back to the house and Colin noticed that Bill had somehow managed to equip himself with a Webley Mk IV revolver, complete with belt and holster. He didn't ask where it had come from. The door was open with no sign of the inhabitants. They walked in and Colin was immediately impressed with the tidiness and cleanliness of the rooms as he walked around. It was the same in the bedrooms, every bed made, nothing out of place. He heard Dewar bidding Bill goodnight and departing along the street, the front door closing. Colin sat on the bed, undid his laces and removed his boots. He then lay back and promptly fell asleep.

Chapter Three

A gnarled looking Major stood in front of the lines of prisoners accompanied by a scrawny man in striped jacket and trousers. The gleam of light reflecting from the round, silver knob on the end of his swagger stick, flickered in Dieter's eyes. He also noticed the sergeant major and the other British soldiers standing to attention, obviously wary of the Major. The sergeant major bellowed out, calling the prisoners to attention and Dieter promptly complied, others following his lead.

The Major spoke. 'You POW's will set to and clean your billets. Over there are carts with buckets, brushes and brooms. Your billets will be inspected in two hours time and there will be no sleeping until they meet my standards. Do I make myself clear.' He turned to the scrawny man who then repeated what he had just said in German.

'Ein Schweinestall,' Dieter blurted out.

'Bring that man here!' the Major bellowed.

Two soldiers pushed through the lines, making straight for Dieter, grabbing him by the arms and pulling him forward. Dieter stood in front of the Major, looking him in the eyes.

'What did you say about schwein?' the Major asked. 'Did I hear you say they are not fit for pigs?' The scrawny man interpreted. Dieter nodded.

The Major scowled, his cheeks started to flush. 'I've been to Belsen and seen what you lot have done. Thousands of bodies, lying like logs, piled high. Hundreds dying every day, starved to death by your comrades. I've found the Medical Officer who enjoyed experimenting on live human beings. And you stand there saying these billets are not suitable for pigs!' The Major was breathing hard. He waited for the interpreter to repeat what he had just said. Dieter looked down, shocked and sickened, ashamed of his race.

'Wir sind Wehrmacht, wir wussten nichts davon,' he said apologetically.

The interpreter translated.

The Major looked at the knob on the end of his swagger stick. 'Well, now you know. I don't care if you were the army, you're all scum. Get to work.' The soldiers on each side of Dieter shoved him back into line and the sergeant major started shouting out orders, the men going to the carts, collecting the brushes and buckets and returning to the huts.

For most of the day and well into the night the prisoners worked, men gagging as they emptied the latrines, maggots wriggling in the excrement, flies everywhere. The soldiers had been back three times and each time had decided more had to be done. Dieter and Hartwig wiped their brows, scrubbing the hut floor yet again.

'Do you think he was telling the truth?' Hartwig whispered.

Dieter nodded. 'It explains why we have been treated like lepers since we got here. How would you react if you were in their shoes?'

'I'd probably want to kill the perpetrators,' Hartwig replied. 'But we didn't do it. We were fighting for the Fatherland. For sure, I witnessed some atrocities along the way but...not on that scale.'

'As far as the Tommies are concerned, we're all the same. It means that until they calm down, we will all have to be very careful.' Dieter kept on scrubbing.

Cupping his hands to his mouth, Wicus Sobczak let out a bird call, hearing the reply from Cyrek. He moved carefully forward, making sure he did not snap any twigs, as he crawled closer to the eleven men sitting around a low burning fire in the clearing. Wicus knew the Forest Langeloh like the back of his hand having spent the last three years since his escape, living and surviving in it. He could hear the men talking quietly to each other, dressed in a mixture of uniforms from the Wehrmacht and the Waffen SS, their weapons left near a bivouac. Wicus smiled, he was going to enjoy this, killing more Germans.

Another bird cry came from his right and Wicus stood up, firing his Schmeisser submachine gun, spraying bullets across the clearing. He heard the rattle of the machine gun from his right and then, silence. Cyrek walked into the clearing, covering the soldiers lying on the ground, Wicus joining him.

'Short work. Weren't prepared, were they? That one over there is injured and he's alive,' Cyrek said, pointing at the soldier on the ground. He strolled over to him, other men now emerging from the forest, looking at the bodies on the ground, starting to check pockets and take everything of value.

Cyrek kicked the soldier lying at his feet and the man looked up at him. 'You're only a boy. How old are you?'

'Sixteen.'

Cyrek turned to Wicus. 'Wicus, we've got a youngster over here.'

'Your Polish?' the boy asked, his eyes widening in fear.

Wicus had now come over, standing beside Cyrek. 'What are you doing here?' Wicus asked.

'We were beaten back by the British near Luneberg and when they broke through our lines, most of us scattered. I managed to get into the forest and then came across this lot a couple of days ago.' The boy attempted to stand up but winced in pain, sitting down. A trickle of blood was forming beside his boot. 'Got winged near my ankle.'

Wicus stepped closer and kicked the boy's leg, making him screech out in pain. Cyrek's arm thumped across Wicus' chest. 'Wait! Tell me boy, if the British are this close, where is the bulk of the Wehrmacht?'

'You haven't heard,' the boy said between sobs. 'The German army has surrendered, the Fuhrer is dead and the Russians have taken Berlin.'

'Good God!' Cyrek and Wicus looked at each other, standing frozen, struggling to comprehend what the boy had just said.

Wicus broke the silence. 'When did all this happen?'

'During the past week or so,' the boy said.

'The war is over! The effing war is over!' Wicus shouted to the others in the clearing. Men stopped their thieving and stood, all looking across at Wicus. 'The effing war is finished...we can all go home!'

Everyone started hugging each other. Men started sobbing, kissing, mumbling, shouting. Someone fired his sub machine gun into the air.

'Stop that!' Cyrek bellowed. 'You don't know who else is around here.'

One of the men shouted across to Cyrek. 'Better come over and see this one,' pointing at the man groaning on the ground.

Cyrek slowly walked across and looked down at the man clutching his side, blood covering his hand. Cyrek noticed the SS flashes. 'What is your name?'

'Bekowski,' the man replied, gritting his teeth.

'Polish?' Cyrek squatted down beside the man.

The man looked into Cyrek's eyes but did not reply.

'Where from?'

'Katowice.'

Cyrek smiled. 'I'm from Krakow.'

The man grimaced.

'How long with the German's?'

'Since 42.'

'Lads, we've got a fellow countryman here,' Cyrek said, standing up. 'Only trouble is, he's one of them. One of the shits who joined the Nazis, joined the SS.'

Men started to gather round, Wicus pushing his way through. Aiming deliberately, Cyrek kicked the man hard in the side where he had been shot. The man yelled out.

The man spat towards Cyrek. 'We are members of Werwolf. You will pay dearly for this. Other groups in the forest will find us and track you down. They will...'

The man's scream rent the air as Cyrek's boot rammed into the man's wounded side.

'Strip him and stake him,' Cyrek ordered, pushing past his men and back towards the boy, Wicus by his side.

Reaching the boy, Cyrek squatted down. 'Have you seen any others in the forest?'

'There are many who hid here but I've not come across them,' the boy replied.

'You say the Russians have taken Berlin. How did you know?'

'We heard it on the radios before the British attacked us.'

Cyrek stood up, frowning, thinking. 'All right Wicus, you can do what you like with him.'

Turning away, Cyrek went across to the SS man, now stripped and staked out on the ground. 'You are a traitor to our country.'

The man just stared at Cyrek. Cyrek squatted down, drew his dagger and, holding the man by the jawbone, stuck it into his eye, ignoring the man's scream as he did the same to the other eye. 'Leave him for the crows, they will finish him off.'

A scream from behind a bush made Cyrek look round. 'I think Wicus is enjoying the boy. Wicus! Wicus! Get on with it, we're leaving.'

Wicus appeared, smiling, buttoning up his trousers.

'Do you have any food? I have an infant and he is starving.'

'Very good, you are improving your English daily,' Professor Ostermann replied, smiling at Brigitte, his eyes lighting up.

Brigitte smiled back. Since the incident with the soldiers, she had spent as much time as she could with the Professor, the old man who had refused her offer of a pail of water. She felt privileged as he rarely spoke to any of the others in the cellar and she knew most were frightened of him. Rumour had it that he had been an adviser to Admiral Donitz and a trusted member of the Nazi party. Brigitte never asked, she was just pleased that the Professor seemed to take a delight in teaching her English.

'He won't keep quiet,' Gisela said, interrupting Brigitte, holding Heinz in her arms, trying to soothe him.

'Sorry Professor, I will have to go,' Brigitte said.

The Professor nodded, closing the book on his lap. 'It is important that you always put motherhood first and look after that infant. He is your future and ours. He and others like him are the future of Germany. Go, go...do what you have to.' He waved his arm, ushering them away.

Brigitte and Gisela made their way back to their beds.

'I have to go out,' Brigitte said. 'I must find more food. That's why Heinz is so miserable and he's teething. Look.'

Gisela looked down at Heinz. 'Oh! Yes, he's got front teeth coming. I won't be putting my finger in his mouth much longer, will I?'

'Not if you want to keep it,' Brigitte said, laughing.

'I have to come with you,' Gisela pleaded. 'If I stay cooped up in here any longer I think I will go mad.'

Brigitte, putting her coat on, paused. 'I'm not sure. I think it is too risky.'

'Please, please. I must get outside.'

'All right. Put Heinz on the bucket and then we will go,' Brigitte said. 'But hide your hair under this beret.'

Gisela whooped with joy. She placed Heinz on the bucket and quickly put her coat on, securing her hair as instructed. She turned back towards Brigitte and flinched as Brigitte started to rub mud across her face.

'What are you doing?' she mumbled.

Brigitte smiled. 'Trying to make you look old and dirty. Don't worry, it's only dust and water...it'll wash off when we get back. Now, let's get Heinz dressed and then we go.'

The bright sun caused them to squint as they emerged from the cellar. Taking the pathway between two blocks, they made their way through the bombed ruins, seeing others gathering whatever they could find, loading carts and wheelbarrows, filling boxes and sacks. They reached the street and Brigitte peered round the corner, seeing a long queue outside the bakery shop. She knew she had to go to the Ratheus soon and register so that she could get her ration coupons but others had told her that it was so chaotic there was no point going until the British had got organised.

With Heinz tied to her back, Brigitte and Gisela were soon at the outskirts, avoiding any troops they saw along the way, seeing the green fields beckoning. They made their way along the road, turning off into a tree-lined lane, noticing the summer flowers emerging. The warm sun was making them both hot, Gisela removing her coat. Walking for another two miles, Brigitte turned into a farmyard, putting her finger to her mouth.

'Be careful. This is usually deserted...the owners left months ago,' she said to Gisela. 'The barn has got potatoes and turnips. Stay here with Heinz and I will go and get some.'

'Do I have to,' Gisela moaned. 'There's nobody here.'

'We have to be careful...now stay here.' Brigitte walked round the corner of the stone building, listening and looking for any sign of others. She reached the end of the building and, holding the wall, peered round the corner. The barn stood across the yard, its large doors closed. She walked quickly, easing the door open and slipping inside, letting her eyes adjust to the gloom. Since her last visit, Brigitte could see that others had been here, the pile of potatoes was only half what it had been. She took the sacks tucked into her belt, opened the first one and started to fill it, picking potatoes as quickly as she could. With two half-full sacks, she dragged them across to the door and then went to the heap of turnips, again half filling a sack. Working quickly, she wiped her arm across her brow. Then she heard a cough. Spinning round she peered into the gloom, her heart beating furiously. She stood up and stared at the stall in the corner. Looking around, Brigitte saw an old potato fork lying on the floor and she walked slowly towards it, picking it up. She slowly approached the stall.

Fighting her instinct to run, she forced herself to peek over the top. She let out a sigh.

'What are you doing here?'

Crouched against the opposite wall were three young girls, fear on their faces, staring at her, petrified.

Brigitte put the fork down and walked round to the entrance. 'Where are you from?'

'We…we are going to Elmshorn,' one of them managed to stutter.

'It's all right, I'm not going to harm you.' Brigitte smiled. 'But why are you leaving the city?'

The girls stood up, Brigitte seeing that they were between ten and fourteen.

The eldest approached her. 'These are my sisters. We are trying to get to our grandparents. They have a farm near Elmshorn. We reached here last night and…well, it seemed safe so we hid in here.'

'Where are your parents?'

The girl looked down, tears running down her cheeks. 'They're dead,' she mumbled.

Brigitte stepped forward, placing her arms around the girl, feeling her sobbing against her. They stood like that for quite some time, Brigitte thinking about her own parents. The sisters joined them, all clinging together.

'How?' Brigitte asked.

The girl looked up. 'They were collecting wood and I was told that someone nearby fell into a bomb crater. My parents went to help them and…and then an unexploded bomb went off.'

Easing their arms from her, Brigitte stepped back. 'Do you want to come with me, back to the city?'

The eldest girl shook her head. 'No. We have to go to my grandparents.'

'Well, if you insist but you must be very, very careful.' Brigitte smiled. 'Do not walk along the roads, stick to the fields and, if you see anyone, hide in the hedges.'

The girls nodded.

'Have you got water?'

'Yes, those bottles over there,' the girl said, pointing.

'Take care and God bless you.' Brigitte gave each of them a hug and then, collecting her sacks, made for the door. She quickly reached Gisela.

'Where have you been?' Gisela demanded. 'I was starting to think something had happened to you.'

Brigitte told her about the three girls as they set off.

Making their way along the road towards Osnabruck, Colin was feeling excited that they would soon arrive at HQ in Bad Oeynhausen. After four days in Hannover doing nothing while they waited for transport, he was pleased to be out in the country. He had been amazed by the amount of baggage Bill had collected but when he had asked what it contained, Bill had just told him to mind his own business.

Grinding to a halt, Colin looked at the imposing building in front, noticing the half dozen or more Humber Snipe staff cars parked neatly outside and an assortment of other vehicles. Montgomery was probably inside, he thought, wondering if he would meet the great man.

The sentries at the entrance eyed Bill and Colin carefully, checking their papers before letting them enter the building. Once inside, they were soon introduced to a young woman wearing the uniform of the Women's Auxiliary Air Force who took their papers and gave them to a clerical assistant before taking them back outside, jumping into a Jeep and whisking them off to Lubbecke. Colin, sitting in the back, noticed Bill attempting to charm her but, to no effect. As they entered the small town, Colin was pleased to see that most of the buildings were intact and even noticed some of the locals smiling and waving at them as they passed, so different to Hannover. They pulled up in front of a large house, surrounded by reels of barbed wire, the WAAF explaining that this was where they would be working. She waited while Bill unloaded all his baggage and then, promptly drove away.

Making their way inside they were ushered into a large room, a captain sitting at an old table, strewn with papers and bulging files.

'Welcome gentlemen,' he said, without looking up. Colin and Bill waited. Bill looked out through the window, Colin studied the captain, seeing the thinning grey hair and the way the captain's tunic hung off his slight shoulders.

Putting his pen down, the captain looked up and leant back in his chair. 'Well gentlemen, you are some of the first to arrive and I'm glad to see you. As members of the Military Government, you will find your work cut out. We have to bring administrative order to the Germans under our command and that means, we control everything they can and cannot do. You will be shown your billet shortly and when you have sorted yourselves out I look forward to seeing you in the briefing room. You will receive your orders then. My adjutant…well the woman outside, will tell you where to go. Any questions will be answered at the briefing session. Now, I have to get on with my work. Oh, you…get yourself armed.' The captain pointed at Colin.

Not sure whether to salute or not, Colin looked at Bill, the pair of them turning round and heading for the door.

'One last thing,' the captain called out. 'Get your rank braid sown onto your uniforms.'

As he closed the door, Colin looked at Bill. 'What rank braid?'

Bill shrugged his shoulders. 'Don't know but I'm not objecting. Perhaps she will tell us.' He nodded towards the middle-aged woman sitting at a table, surrounded by papers and filing draws.

The man squirmed, his face ashen, biting hard on the wooden spatula. Hannelore Gerber paused for a moment, wiping her arm across her brow. She looked at the two men, one each side of the man lying on the table in front of her and nodded to them. They tightened their grip on their comrade. Hannelore, using tweezers, dug deeper into the man's thigh. She dabbed at the blood obscuring her view. She knew she had to get the bullet out if the man was going to survive. She thought she felt it, carefully manipulating the tweezers. On the fourth attempt she felt them grip the bullet and with a sigh of relief, she extracted it. She poured iodine into the wound and then squeezed it shut, reaching across and picking up her needle. Within minutes she had stitched the wound up and bandaged it.

'That was painful, yes?' Hannelore said, removing her white coat.

The man nodded and gave a slight grin. 'Worse than childbirth, Doctor.'

Hannelore laughed. 'A mere bee sting in comparison. Now, you will have to go. I can't let you stay here. You should get rid of those uniforms...the British won't take kindly to them, especially with the SS flashes.'

The men looked at each other. 'You're right Doctor but, we haven't got any other clothes.'

'Here, in Buchholz, there are plenty of houses who have lost their men. Go to them and ask for civilian clothing then...then disappear into Hamburg. There is so much chaos, nobody will know who you are or where you came from.'

Helping the wounded man to stand up and supporting him between them, the men made their way to the door.

'And don't let him walk far...not until the wound has healed up,' Hannelore said. 'Here, take these and change the dressing every day. You can wash them out.' She passed the wrapped bandages to one of the men.

'Thank you for helping me,' the wounded man said.

The men turned into the street and disappeared into the night. Hannelore shut the door and locked it, leaning back against it. She could feel the tiredness throughout her body. How many more will come, she thought. Without anaesthetic and a dwindling supply of medicines and bandages, she would not be capable of helping many more. She made her way up the stairs knowing she should clean up the surgery but, for once, it could wait until the morning.

'Hello Mother, have you eaten?' Hannelore asked the frail woman sitting darning.

'I thought I'd wait for you.'

Hannelore sighed and walked across to the dresser, pouring herself a large cognac. 'We have some of that venison left that Herr Schaltz gave us and I have some potatoes and vegetables. Will that do?'

Her mother nodded. 'Wouldn't mind a glass.'

'Oh, of course.' Hannelore poured her mother a cognac and then went into the kitchen and prepared the meal.

It all tasted very good and the two women sat back, each sipping their cognac.

'You shouldn't keep taking these wounded men in.'

Hannelore looked at her mother. 'Why not? They need my help. That is what I trained for. I cannot select whom I will or will not help. I am a Doctor.'

Her mother shrugged. 'If you'd married Welf when he asked you…'

'Mother, not that again,' Hannelore cut in. 'If I'd married Welf what would have become of you? You wouldn't have travelled to America…would you?'

'No. But you could have married somebody else…a man to look after you,' her mother replied. 'You had plenty after you when you were training and your still young enough to attract the right man now.'

Hannelore stood up, drained her glass and started to gather up the plates. 'Mother, you cannot live in the past. Today is today…we have to adapt to the conditions we now find ourselves in. I'm going to bed.'

Walking alongside the barbed wire fence, Dieter noticed the few clumps of grass struggling to grow in the muddy compound. He could see where previous incumbents had dug out shallow holes and erected dilapidated shelters, where primitive latrines had been dug, a log beam still in position, making Dieter wonder who the previous prisoners were. He looked up, noticing the machine gun tower ahead, glancing across the compound, seeing a tower on each corner, estimating the distance at around five hundred metres between each one. What was the point of escaping Dieter thought. Without papers, where would one go?

'Shit!' Hartwig shouted, causing Dieter to look round, seeing Hartwig struggling to get out of a shallow trench.

Dieter laughed. 'Literally. You've slipped into a latrine.'

'Shit, shit,' Hartwig snapped, 'thought I'd seen the last of this after those effing Tommies made us clean that effing hut until you could eat your food off the effing floor.'

Dieter waited for Hartwig to reach him. 'What food?'

'You're right, what food. All they give us is a quart of watery soup…if that's what it is and rock hard, stale bread.'

Hartwig stared down at his filthy boots. 'We've got to get out of here soon…haven't we?'

'The British will take their time,' Dieter replied. 'Why should they rush. There must be thousands walking around, now that they've liberated all of our former prisoners – Dutch, French, Italians, Polish, Russians, Yugoslavs and…and Jews. And God knows who else.' Dieter pointed to a group of people outside the compound. 'See that lot, in striped uniforms? They are Jews.'

'Christ. They don't look too healthy, do they?' Hartwig replied.

Dieter grimaced. 'They are the ones who survived, the fittest. Now you can understand the Major's reaction.'

'Yep.' Hartwig sighed. 'Anyway, when we do get released I'm going to get home as fast as possible. I haven't seen my wife for two years or my baby son. He'll be walking now and talking.'

'Didn't know you were married.'

'Use to carry a picture around with me but it was taken off me as was my identity card,' Hartwig replied. 'Should see my wife. She's beautiful, blonde…got lovely legs. She was the best athlete in her school, before this war started. I only hope she is all right.' Hartwig went quiet.

They carried on walking, both lost in their own thoughts, Dieter sure his wife was still alive, determined to find her once he was discharged.

The sound of trucks caught their attention. 'Look at that. There must be twenty or more,' Hartwig said, pointing at the convoy pulling up at the compound gate. 'Won't be much room left when they get in.'

Dieter watched as men started to climb out of the trucks, estimating there must be at least five hundred. The compound was already full with at least four thousand held captive. If this carried on Dieter could foresee problems arising.

Chapter Four

Incessant rain, day after day, only made matters even worse for Brigitte. She was aware that she was losing weight and that her strength was ebbing away. Queuing for food, clutching her coupons, seemed to take longer as each day passed and frequently, the baker or the butcher did not receive supplies, leaving those waiting frustrated and fractious. Brigitte had seen how people reacted when there was a rumour of supplies. A vehicle had been seen backing into a butcher's yard and the crowd in front of the building had been alerted, smashing through the shop and rushing into the rear yard. The butcher had tried to stop people but someone had hit him over the head and when Brigitte found him, the poor man was almost dead. The shop had been totally wrecked and she later heard that there had only been two small cases of pork on the vehicle. Brigitte had also noticed that there were increasing numbers of people offering food for cigarettes or jewellery.

Yesterday had been one of the better days when Brigitte had managed to get some rations – some coffee substitute, sugar, coarse-ground grain and four bread rolls – enough for her and Heinz to last three days, with care. But there was no way of knowing if further rations would be supplied. Standing in the sheeting rain, five abreast, she had heard someone say that all German resistance had stopped and that the Allies had issued a Proclamation, stating that everyone had to obey the Occupation authorities immediately and without question. They had the right to 'shoot to kill' anyone who disobeyed them. They were not allowed to travel more than six kilometres from home or use the telephone and someone jokingly asked where was home and did anyone know of a telephone line that worked. On her way back to the cellar, Brigitte had noticed that the soldiers now on the streets seemed to be different – generally older, dressed in different uniforms and hostile.

'This is good,' Gisela said, taking another spoonful of the sweet porridge Brigitte had cooked. 'Can you make it again?'

Brigitte sighed, placing another spoonful into Heinz's mouth. She was thankful that Gisela shared her rations with them but knew Gisela had little or no idea how precarious their existence was. 'If we get more grain and sugar, yes.'

'Can we go out?' Gisela asked, placing her empty tin on the floor. 'Someone came in a short while ago and said it had stopped raining, the sun was shining.'

Frau Eichel coughed, causing Brigitte to turn. 'Go on, it'll do you some good. You came in yesterday soaked and you need to get your coat dried. I'll look after the infant.'

Are you sure?' Brigitte asked. Frau Eichel nodded and Brigitte handed Heinz across to her. 'Come on then Gisela, let's go and see what we can find.'

They reached the street and immediately Brigitte felt better, the sun's rays warming her. Setting off towards the outskirts, passed the skeletal buildings and along well worn tracks over the mounds of debris, they soon reached the fields. Brigitte started to collect nettle leaves, urging Gisela to help her.

'But I haven't got any gloves…they sting,' Gisela complained.

'Use the sleeves of your coat,' Brigitte replied, demonstrating with her hand tucked inside her sleeve. 'These will make a nourishing soup and, if we pick plenty, tea.'

With her sack half full, Brigitte straightened up, easing the stiffness in her back. 'Look, over there, dandelions. I think we can do something with those. Let's pick some.'

Gisela moaned. 'I'm too hot and, I'm tired.' She removed her coat and lay down on the grass. Brigitte looked down at her and then did the same.

'Do you think your husband will…will find you…if he's still,' Gisela paused, 'still alive?'

Brigitte closed her eyes. With hunger constantly gnawing at her, Heinz to take care of and the struggle to find food every day, she had not thought about her husband, somehow pushing him to the back of her mind, concentrating on the needs of the moment. She could see his face with the lovely smile and the dark, wavy hair. With the warmth of the sun, she could almost feel his arms around her. Tears started to well in her eyes. She sat up, taking her handkerchief and blowing her nose.

'Did I upset you?' Gisela asked.

'No, no. I'm sure he will find me.' Brigitte stood up. 'I'm going to pick those dandelions. I'm sure Frau Eichel will know what we can do with them.'

Setting off across the field, Brigitte was soon busily picking. She paused and looked across the field to where Gisela was still resting, realising that the lie of the land hid her from view. The sun continued to warm her and when she found a cluster of mushrooms, she thought God was looking down on her, picking them carefully and placing them in her sack.

Gisela's scream startled Brigitte. Now what, she thought. I bet she's seen a grass snake or hedgehog. Another scream told Brigitte she was wrong. She ran back across the field as fast as she could, hearing further screams. Then she saw them. Six armed men were grouped around Gisela who was standing, clasping her coat tightly to her chest. Brigitte shouted at them, as she pushed past two of the men, hugging Gisela.

'Was wollt Ihr?'

Brigitte looked at each man, seeing their unshaven, dirty faces, their filthy clothes and despaired at the look in their eyes. Lust and hatred. She repeated her question.

A man approached her and stared at her, looking her up and down, stripping her with his eyes. Brigitte regretted not having her coat on.

'You can have these,' she said, holding out her sack.

The man leered and stepped forward, taking the sack and tossing it aside. He smacked her hard across her face with the back of his hand, Brigitte letting out a yelp, tasting the blood from her lip. She stepped backwards, falling over the man squatting behind her and then the men pounced.

One of them kicked her hard in the side, catching her hip-bone and as she doubled up, hands grabbed her arms and body, forcing her onto her knees, pushing her head forward. Hands pulled her dress up and ripped her pants down and she knew what was going to happen. She felt the man kneeling behind her, pushing his erection against her, roughly entering her, thrusting hard. Tears poured down her cheeks, obscuring her vision as she heard the screams of Gisela. Brigitte tried to look across but someone grabbed her hair, pulling her head backwards. A man stood in front of her, waggling his member, trying to push it into her mouth. She felt the man behind come inside her, grunting and then he withdrew. Another man immediately replaced him. The man in front of her walked away and then she heard a loud smack and Gisela stopped screaming. She looked across, seeing a man underneath Gisela and one on top, both raping her at the same time. Gisela's face was covered in blood where a rifle butt had hit her. She lost count of how many times the men took turns with them, the evening sun fading below the horizon.

Within two weeks of arriving at Bad Oeynhausen, Bill Thornton had got himself well organised. With his honorary rank of sergeant major in the Commission, Bill had easily got to know the military NCO's in the Mess, made good contacts in the Officers Mess and knew who to contact in the Commission. He had also realised the true value of cigarettes and chocolate, whisky and rations, before others had even thought about them. Offering to buy any man's surplus, as he liked to call it, had soon resulted in Bill accumulating a large stock of items on credit and now he needed to turn them into cash.

The Morris truck was half full by the time Bill had loaded it and he set off for Osnabruck. As he had been given the job as Commission Assistant in the town, he had the right to drive to and from as often as he wished. He had quickly made the acquaintance of an army sergeant based in the town who had, over a bottle of whisky, disclosed that he had good connections with some Americans down in Cologne and that any 'surpluses' could be lucrative. Bill drove cautiously along the road, observing carefully any groups walking along, glancing across at his recently acquired Sten gun, lying on the seat next to him. He had heard of vehicles being attacked or forcibly taken by the numerous groups of ex POW's and foreign labourers who were making their way home. He certainly didn't want to come across such a group or, for that matter, a military roadblock.

Skirting the centre of the town, Bill drove down the road leading to the bar where he had agreed to meet, checking his watch and seeing that he was a few minutes early. He smiled to himself as he reversed the truck into the yard beside the bar. He waited.

'Back it further in till you see the other truck then back up to it,' a voice said, catching Bill by surprise. He hadn't seen the sergeant come from behind and stealthily walk along the side of the truck. 'We don't want others to know our business...do we?'

Doing as he was told, Bill manoeuvred the truck, backing up until the tailboards met. He got out and started helping to transfer the cartons and boxes, sweating and puffing. Within minutes the load had been transferred and Bill handed the sergeant the list.

'Here you go,' the sergeant said, peeling off a sheaf of notes and handing them to Bill. 'There'll be more of that, a lot more, if you can keep the supplies coming.'

Bill started to count the wad in his hand.

'Better be on your way now,' the sergeant said, 'before anyone comes snooping. You can count it later.'

Bill climbed into the cab and set off, heading for the Rathaus. He could feel the excitement running through him. From what he had just pocketed, he knew he had made at least three times the amount of money he would be paying out.

Placing his hand on Wicus' arm, Cyrek shook his head. He stared across at the swarm of men, milling around the railway trucks in the goods yard, stumbling and fighting, yelling and swearing. Their prime target appeared to be a tanker car. Hidden behind the hedgerow, Cyrek glanced to each side, seeing his own men waiting for his command. Ever since they had left the comparative safety of the forest, Cyrek had been on edge. They had forcibly taken three trucks from others they had ambushed on the roads leading to Luneburg and increased their cache of arms and ammunition. Also, the group now consisted of twenty-two, including two Yugoslavs and a Ukrainian. Cyrek and Wicus had argued over returning to Poland, Cyrek eventually convincing Wicus that, as it was overrun by the Russians, it would be best to stay in Germany for a while and see how things turned out.

'We can clear that lot,' Wicus said. 'We're armed.'

Cyrek looked at Wicus. 'Caution my friend...and patience. Let's just watch for a while.'

'Someone's managed to open the tank valve, look,' Wicus shouted.

Men were kicking, punching and screaming, climbing over each other to get to the tank. They were using anything that could hold the gushing liquid; shoes, tins, hats, buckets, cans, bottles; even their cupped hands. Some tried to drink directly from the tanker, others started drinking from the puddles spreading around it. Cyrek sensed his men were getting restless.

'Wait! We don't need to expose our position for...for the unknown,' Cyrek said. 'You two, take a look but leave your guns behind.'

He watched his men scrabble down the embankment and run across to the melee. They easily forced their way through and then Cyrek saw them gesticulating madly, could see that they were shouting to those around them but he couldn't hear what they were saying. He saw his men force their way back through the throng, running towards him.

Breathless, one of them shouted up to him. 'It's methyl alcohol. It's poison but they won't listen.'

'Get up here,' Cyrek said. He turned to Wicus. 'Fortunate I'd say, wouldn't you?'

Wicus grinned. 'You're right. Just as well we didn't get there first. We could go over there and start shooting. Might save a few.'

Shaking his head, Cyrek gave the order to move on. His senses numbed by what he had experienced during the past five years and with no regard for others, he was unconcerned with the men who were poisoning themselves.

Looking at the growing piles of papers on his desk as he walked into the office made Colin wish he were still in bed. It was a beautiful summer's day and the heat inside the pre-fabricated offices was already rising. To be outside, doing something, was Colin's immediate desire. Removing his hat, he slumped down onto his chair, picking up the nearest file. Scanning through the contents he could see it contained requests for travel permits, fuel and food movement permits, medical supplies and housing accommodation requests. Colin closed the file and took the next one. He did not think about the consequences of his actions, the effect it would have on the individuals and groups waiting for permission. He did not yet fully understand the level of control the Commission had over the subjugated people under its command. Opening the next file, he started thumbing through case notes on internees, POW's and others under investigation. This was more interesting and Colin looked at the file cover, seeing that he was being asked to translate the German notes into English – not his strong suit, he thought. Picking up a sheet of blank paper, he took the first case file and started working.

Around mid morning, the office now baking even with all of the windows wide open, Colin stood up, stretching himself. The door opened and the captain strolled in. Colin stood to attention.

'Good morning Sergeant Patterson,' the captain shouted out, 'got a job I want you to help me with. Stand at ease man.'

Colin relaxed. 'Yes Sir.' He waited, expectantly, seeing Captain Manson glancing over the shoulders of two women secretaries, both German, who were furiously working away.

'Right Sergeant, we're off to Hamburg...within the half-hour so, get your overnight bag packed. Meet me in front of the Officer's Mess.' Captain Manson turned and left the room before Colin could ask any questions. Grabbing his beret, he set off to get his bag.

With the breeze through the window, Colin was enjoying the drive through the countryside in the Austin 'Tilly'. Captain Manson was telling him about his wife and their children, how his eldest son had been killed in Egypt and his youngest son was recuperating in hospital after arriving back injured, from Normandy. Their daughter had joined the WAAF and was now working in London, something secret she had said, which Manson was obviously proud of. He had been working in the civil service but, once the invasion had started, he had been dispensed with, a point that obviously still rankled, judging by the way his face flushed and his hands tightened on the steering wheel. Then he found out that the Commission was desperately seeking people and of course, he was immediately accepted. As far as he was concerned, this job would last him for the rest of his working life.

'You mean we will be here for a number of years?' Colin asked.

Manson chuckled. 'It'll take twenty or more years to get this place back to something normal, some even say fifty years. 'Mark my words Sergeant, you'll be my age before you leave Germany.'

The thought depressed Colin. He had reckoned on a couple of years then back to England and university. He started to tell Manson who assured him that he would be permitted, probably, to do as he wanted, dependent upon the circumstances at the time.

Within three hours they had reached Bremen. Travelling through the city, Colin could see that it had not noticeably changed since he had past through a few weeks before. The ruined buildings and piles of debris were still there. He saw a chain of women, passing bricks to each other and

Manson told him they were starting to clear up the city and commence building, the women working to get their rations. Manson drove on, telling Colin that they should be in Hamburg within the next two hours.

The sudden jolt of the car woke Colin up, making him yawn.

'Been cat-napping?' Manson asked.

'Must have.' Colin looked through the dusty windscreen, seeing more bombed out buildings. 'Where are we?'

'Outskirts of Hamburg…soon be at our destination.' Manson slowed the car down, coming to a stop. 'Need a slash.' He eased himself out and walked across the road, urinating against the wall opposite. Colin joined him, feeling the weight of his Webley pistol hanging from his belt.

'Where are all the people?' Colin asked.

Manson looked around. He walked across to the car, popped the bonnet and removed the distributor cap, placing it into the boot, behind their luggage. 'Come with me, I'll show you.'

They followed a well-trodden path over the debris and reached another street, the captain pausing and looking around. 'Ah, there it is.' Manson pointed at some steps and, when they got closer, Colin could see that it was the entrance to a cellar. He followed the captain down the stairs into the gloom. The foetid smell grew stronger with each step and Colin pulled his handkerchief out, holding it to his nose. As they passed through a set of steel doors, Colin's eyes widened. The huge, gloomily lit room in front of him was full of Germans. Old men and women sitting in rows of chairs and benches of all types, knitting, reading, talking, sleeping. There were some women feeding their children, others preparing what little food they had, others playing cards. There was a variety of made up furniture, old tables and some beds but certainly not enough room for everyone to lie down.

Suddenly, Colin was aware that everyone had stopped what they were doing, everyone was staring at him and Manson. His hand gripped the butt of his pistol. The captain walked on, motioning Colin to follow him. They reached the end of the cellar and went through a doorway, entering another cellar just as large, just as full of people. Manson told Colin that there were probably three or more cellars beyond this one and Colin was relieved to see him turn and head back towards the exit. Colin could see the haggard look on the faces of the people he passed, their poor clothing and the effects of starvation.

Reaching the outside, Colin breathed deeply, sucking in the fresh air, his face pale and sweat pouring down his cheeks.

'Now you know where the Kraut's are,' Manson said, 'underground.'

Colin shook his head. 'That is awful. They can't survive like that for long. What are we going to do? How can we help them? There must be accommodation somewhere…surely?'

Manson coughed. 'They're the lucky ones, the ones who survived the bombing offensive. Heard tell we dropped more bombs on Hamburg in July '43 than the Jerries dropped on us during the entire war. Killed more than forty thousand in two nights and God knows how many were injured.'

The two of them walked in silence back to the car.

Chapter Five

Hartwig coughed, shaking under the coat lying over him. He noticed Dieter pushing his way through the throng of men, trying to avoid stepping on the bodies that littered the floor, clutching a tin tray and can tightly to his chest.

'Here you are, drink this.' Dieter put his arm around Hartwig's shoulders, easing him up and holding the can to his lips. Hartwig tried to resist but was too weak. 'You must drink otherwise you will die. The dysentery will pass, then you will recover.' Dieter wasn't sure about this but he had to give his friend hope.

Hartwig sipped at the water, drinking it as fast as he could manage. 'Where did you find it? From the latrines?'

Smiling, Dieter shook his head. 'Rainwater... uncontaminated. It's pouring outside but it still takes ages to get a can full, even with the tray to help.'

When Hartwig had finished the can, Dieter lowered him gently down and pulled the coat up to his chin. He made his way outside and started to gather more water, watching the men around him. There was no fresh clothing available now for the newcomers and de-lousing had stopped, the men living in the clothes they arrived in – filthy, tattered and torn uniforms; shoes and boots worn out, stuffed with newspaper; dirt encrusted dressings. And this was once our proud, all conquering army, Dieter thought.

During the past few weeks the camp had taken in thousands more prisoners. The entire compound was full and conditions had deteriorated rapidly. Typhus, diphtheria, dysentery and no medical supplies meant that, every day, men were dying, their bodies being piled near the gate, the swarms of flies gorging themselves. The water supply trickled spasmodically and food, consisting of the odd sack of grain, potatoes and turnips, arrived infrequently. The smell of urine and faeces covering the compound no longer affected Dieter, he hardly noticed. The majority of the men slept in the open, Dieter considering himself fortunate that at least he had a place in the hut and that his calf wound had healed up cleanly. As for the camp's condition, the Tommies did not seem to care.

Drinking from the can, Dieter saw the Commandant arriving at the gate, surrounded by his soldiers. Dieter went inside the hut and placed his tray and can under Hartwig's trousers, rolled up and being used as a pillow, then set off for the gate.

'This cannot continue,' Dieter said, 'unless you intend all of us to perish.' He was standing inside the gate, looking through the wire, facing the Major. He waited for the interpreter.

The Major turned away. 'Not a bad idea,' he joked with his men.

'Ihr seid alle Morder!' Deiter yelled.

The interpreter spoke to the Major, causing him to turn and look at Dieter. 'A murderer! Arrest that man and bring him with me.'

The gate eased open and two soldiers came up to Dieter, taking him firmly by the arms and leading him out and along the road towards the row of huts ahead. He was roughly pushed through the door of a small hut, seeing the one bare room and the single, naked light bulb hanging from the ceiling. Buckets of water were lined up along one wall and the floor was covered in stains – blood by the looks of it. There was a wooden table, three chairs and, in the middle of the room, some sort of stool with straps across the top and a board with two holes, Dieter unsure what it was. A tall, tin cabinet completed the furnishings.

'Sit down,' one of his escorts ordered, pushing Dieter towards a chair. Dieter did as he was told.

Behind him, Dieter heard the door close and footsteps approaching, the Major, his interpreter and a bull of a man, wearing uniform with sergeant's stripes on his sleeves, walked to the opposite side of the table. The Major sat down.

'I will not tolerate insubordination under any circumstances and you will be punished accordingly. Give me your name, rank and service number.'

Waiting for the interpreter, Dieter looked at the sergeant, seeing the sadistic look in his eyes.

Dieter gave his details and then continued. 'Under the Geneva Convention all POW's are entitled to basic rights and this…'

'Rights! Rights!' The Major exploded, his face going bright red. 'Don't talk to me about rights you…you Nazi scum!'

The interpreter grinned.

So, the Major understands some German, Dieter thought. 'This camp is a disgrace to the British army, men are dying of starv…'

The slap across Dieter's face stopped him talking.

'You effing Kraut…shut up! Ten lashes sergeant and make them good ones. These scum have got to be taught discipline.' The Major stood up and Dieter heard him leave the hut.

Dieter, wiping his lip, looked at the sergeant, seeing the glint in his eyes. The sergeant nodded to the soldiers behind Dieter and they immediately took him by the arms, yanking at his coat, pulling it off. They tore his shirt off, pushing him forward, towards the stool. They pushed him across the top of it, securing his hands through the holes in the board, pulling the leather straps tight across the back of his neck and across his thighs.

The sergeant stood in front of Dieter, having removed his tunic and rolled his shirt sleeves up. 'You're goin' to like my whipping block sonny.' He walked out of Dieter's view and went to the tin cabinet, unlocking it. Dieter knew what was coming.

The hiss of the whip through the air, followed by the pain across his back, forced Dieter to gasp for air, realising the loud scream had come from himself. He blacked out after the fifth blow, coming to when cold water was splashed in his face. Through bleary eyes he glanced at the sergeant as the soldiers undid the straps and hauled him upright, his back on fire. He could feel the blood trickling down, feel the weakness in his legs, unable to stand without support, realising he had wet himself.

The sergeant came towards him, his face right in front of Dieter's. 'Don't think you'll want more of my cat-o'-nine-tails sonny. Don't ever speak to any British military personnel unless they've asked you a question first. Understand?'

When the interpreter had finished, Dieter nodded. The punch from the sergeant hit him on the jawbone and Dieter fell to the floor, unconscious.

For the past fortnight, Brigitte had not managed to get any sense out of Gisela. The girl had laid on her bed, hunched under her coat, her haunted eyes barely registering Brigitte's presence. Since their raping, Brigitte had forced herself to carry on looking for food, responsible for Heinz and his wellbeing. She had bathed Gisela and herself as carefully as she could, feeling the pain in her vagina where the men had abused her and knowing Gisela had suffered even worse. She had tenderly bathed and bandaged Gisela's face where she had been hit by the rifle butt, fearing that the cheekbone may have been broken. Frau Eichel, who at first had shouted at them for being so late, then realising from their distraught appearance that something had happened, had become very friendly, doing what she could to help and keeping Heinz amused. Frau Eichel had sat down with Brigitte, craddling her in her arms, letting Brigitte cry until she could cry no more. She had gently asked what had happened and Brigitte had only told her that the men were French, refusing to talk about what they had done.

Clutching her ration coupons, the cards that had been christened 'Death Card', being the lowest level and entitling the person to around one thousand calories a day, Brigitte looked at Gisela, leant forward and kissed her on her brow and then set off for the stairs. She knew she would have to queue for at least half the day in the hopes that she would get something for Gisela, Heinz and herself.

Outside, the sun was shining, lifting Brigitte's spirits slightly. She made her way towards the bakers, seeing others coming back, some clutching bags tightly to them, others carrying pales of water. Brigitte could see the long queue ahead, her heart sinking. She joined it and started talking to the woman in front of her, finding out that the British were calling for labourers to work on the rebuilding of the city.

'Would that entitle us to better rations?' Brigitte asked.

The woman smiled. 'Go to the Rathaus tomorrow morning...early mind you, and get your name on the lists. Once you are registered, they give you a new card, maybe level three and then you get more rations.'

'Assuming they deliver the supplies to the shops,' Brigitte retorted. 'Anyway, what are we expected to do to get these?'

The woman looked around, lowering her voice. 'Once you are registered, so a friend of mine has told me, you don't actually have to do anything, nobody checks up.'

Brigitte smiled. 'Do you think the British are that stupid?'

'Could be true,' the woman said, shrugging her shoulders. 'Look out, her come the Tommies.'

Feeling a grip of fear in her stomach, Brigitte turned round, surprised to see a soldier within feet of her.

'Like some real coffee or, maybe some chocolate?' the young soldier asked her, smiling. 'Even got cigarettes.'

Brigitte lowered her head and turned away.

'Suit yourself, love, there're plenty of others who'll only be too thankful,' the soldier said.

They reached the counter and Brigitte handed over her cards, the woman behind stamping them. She passed across six small rolls, Brigitte placing them in her sack. Bidding the woman in the queue goodbye, Brigitte stepped outside, intent on setting off for the butcher. As she reached the end of the road she became aware of footsteps behind her, hobnailed boots on asphalt. She stopped and turned round.

'Remember me, love?' the young soldier said, smiling. Another young soldier stood beside him.

In her broken English, Brigitte asked them what they wanted.

The two soldiers looked sheepishly at each other. 'We could let you have cigarettes and food for...' The soldier blushed.

Brigitte turned her back to them, her mind in turmoil. She could see her husband, her baby Heinz, their home before the bombing. She could see Gisela, dependent upon her, feel the puny rolls in her sack, the gnawing in her stomach. She could see the Frenchmen, raping them.

'Wie viele Zigaretten?' Brigitte demanded, turning back to the soldiers.

They looked surprised.

'Vell, how many und food?'

'A pack,' one of them blurted out, 'and we've got some tins of bully beef, potatoes and vegetables.'

His friend kicked him on the shin. 'Steady...that's all our lot.'

'Me see,' Brigitte replied.

'Not here, not in the open,' the young soldier replied.

Brigitte turned. 'Kommen with me.' She walked round the corner and saw the bombed out building opposite, noticing part of the rear wall still standing. Walking across the road, she led the soldiers behind the wall, seeing the piles of debris and a small area of grass where a garden had once been. Reaching it, she stopped, indicating to the soldier to open his rucksack. He immediately slipped it from his shoulders, opened it and tipped the contents out. Taking her sack, Brigitte placed eight tins into it and two bars of chocolate. 'Der Zigaretten?'

The soldiers looked at each other. 'Give her the pack then,' the taller one said to his mate.

The pack was handed over, Brigitte quickly placing it inside her sack. She unbuttoned her coat and lay it on the grass. She turned away from them and, lifting her dress, pulled her pants down, kicking off her shoes. She then lay down on the coat.

'Blimey,' the taller soldier said, swallowing hard. He took off his belt, unbuttoned his trousers and knelt down between Brigitte's legs, pushing his trousers down his thighs and pulling her dress up. He fumbled with her womanhood, staring at it and then he pushed himself into her. Within three or four thrusts, he released his seed, grunting. His mate followed him and came almost immediately. Quickly, they buttoned up their trousers, thanked her and ran off.

Laying in the sun, Brigitte felt dirty, her tears running down her cheeks. After a while, she cleaned herself up and got dressed, making her way back towards the cellar, feeling the weight of the tins in her sack, realising that what she had could keep her and the others from starving for the coming few days. And she had a whole pack of cigarettes.

Lying in the ditch, Cyrek watched the group of around thirty men approaching his position, beside the Luneburg to Hamburg road. He let out a low whistle, hearing Wicus' response from the opposite side. Studying the men, Cyrek could see that they were all young and malnourished, probably slave labourers on their way home. He noticed that a few had rifles slung over their shoulders. Six men were struggling along, pulling a four wheeled trailer behind them and further back was another cart with a horse in the traces. The group started to pass him and Cyrek waited, hidden behind the tall grass. When the last cart was level with him, he let out a loud cry and, jumping up, ran onto the road. Men appeared from both sides, catching the group by surprise.

A shot rang out and Cyrek flinched, looking along the column. He saw some of the travellers running off the road and into the trees, his own men firing and setting after them. Cyrek ran forward, grabbing the horse's bridle, shouting to his men to keep their positions. The travellers started gabbling to each other, Cyrek unsure what language, unable to understand. Then there was a fusillade of shots, forcing Cyrek to duck under the horse's head. He saw a number of his own men fall, realising that the shots had come from the trailer ahead. Cyrek reached down to his belt, took a German stick grenade, unscrewed the metal cap at the bottom of the handle, pulled the porcelain bead and lobbed it towards the trailer, yelling out a warning as he did so. The explosion ripped the trailer to pieces, causing the horse Cyrek was holding to lunge forward, its eyes bulging with fear, trampling on Cyrek's foot. Cyrek yelled out. He pulled his pistol, placed it against the horse's head and pulled the trigger. The horse dropped where it stood. Spasmodic shooting came from the trees as Cyrek tried to make sense of what had just happened.

He hobbled towards the smouldering trailer, firing his pistol at any man lying on the ground who moved. He could see the bodies of a woman and four children lying in the bottom of the trailer, the debris of food sacks and belongings all around them. His own men were finishing off any survivors, Cyrek yelling out for Wicus. Then he spotted the metal trunk in the bottom of the trailer. Clambering up, Cyrek cursed the horse, feeling the pain in his foot, grabbing at sacks and cans, throwing them onto the ground. He moved towards the trunk, shifting the sacks partially covering it and bent down to take a closer look. Someone coughed behind him and Cyrek whirled round, his pistol levelled. A child amongst the sacks tried to duck back behind them. Cyrek aimed and fired, hitting the child in the top of the head, killing it instantly. He turned back to the trunk and fired at the padlock, smashing it. Hauling up the lid, he looked inside and pulled the rug covering the contents to one side. The gold coins glittered in the sun. Cyrek pulled the rug back and closed the lid, his eyes gleaming. One of his men came running up, asking him to come immediately, Wicus was hurt.

Easing himself down from the trailer, Cyrek hobbled after the man, seeing Wicus on the ground, surrounded by the men. He pushed through them and knelt down beside Wicus, lifting his head onto his lap.

'Where does it hurt?'

A dribble of blood ran from Wicus' mouth, running down his chin. 'Can't feel. Can't feel anything. In my back.'

Easing Wicus over, Cyrek could see the bloody hole in Wicus' jacket, just to the side of his spine. He eased Wicus onto his back. 'You'll live my friend. We'll get you to a doctor.' Cyrek stood up, issuing orders to his men. Wicus was carefully lifted and placed in one of the trucks whilst others ransacked the trailer and the cart, removed the clothing and footwear from the bodies, collected all the arms and ammunition they could find and loaded everything onto their trucks. Cyrek had overseen the removal of the trunk and had it placed in his truck, noticing how his men struggled under the weight.

They drove off, heading towards Hamburg, Cyrek turning left onto a narrow road. Within a couple of miles, they came to the village of Buchholz, slowing as they reached the centre. The village appeared to be deserted but Cyrek knew better. He ordered two of his men to break into the house nearest to them and ask the people inside where the nearest doctor was. Reloading his pistol, Cyrek watched as his men smashed down the front door. They quickly came out, dragging a middle-aged woman by her hair. Cyrek got down from the truck.

'Where is a doctor?'

The woman in front of him stared in defiance. Cyrek smashed the butt of his pistol across her face, seeing one of her teeth fly out, the woman screaming and falling to her knees. She mumbled something, pointing at the house opposite. Cyrek kicked her hard in the ribs, thankful that he hadn't used his damaged foot. He hobbled across to the house and thumped his pistol butt against the door. He heard someone approaching from the inside and waited, hearing the lock turning and a bolt being drawn. The door eased open and Cyrek rammed his shoulder against it, the tall, attractive woman inside stumbling backwards, her dressing gown falling open, revealing her night-dress.

'I want the doctor,' Cyrek shouted. 'Where is he?'

The woman looked at him, pulling her dressing gown around her then pointing at herself. 'I am the Doctor.'

Cyrek leered. He turned round and shouted to his men. 'I have an injured man. You will help him.' He pushed passed the woman and walked along the dim corridor, entering the room at the rear. The woman followed. His men came in, carrying Wicus, who was unconscious, between them. Cyrek lounged against one of the tables and watched as the woman pointed to the table in the middle of the room. She eased Wicus over and looked at the jacket.

'You have to help me to get his clothes off,' she said, looking at Cyrek.

Moving towards the table, Cyrek had understood what she wanted and told his men to help. They removed Wicus' jacket, shirt and vest.

Looking at the wound, Hannelore knew immediately how serious it was. The bullet had entered through the rib cage, narrowly missing the spine but had not exited the body. The man was bleeding from the mouth, indicating that his lungs could be filling with blood. She took a bottle of iodine and, using a swab, cleaned around the wound.

Gesticulating, she asked the men to grip the unconscious man's arms and legs. When she was satisfied, Hannelore used her tweezers and started to locate the bullet. She winced when she hit the man's ribs, seeing his body twitch. Taking a scalpel, she sliced the wound open further, pulling back the flesh, mopping at the blood. She went in deeper, wiping her brow, looking and feeling for the bullet. She was about to give up when the tips of the tweezers closed around a hard object and Hannelore tightened her grip, pulling slowly. She held the tweezers up and looked at the deformed bullet, breathing a sigh of relief.

'Your comrade may be lucky,' she said. 'The bullet wedged between his ribs and has not penetrated into the lungs.' Getting a needle and using more iodine, Hannelore set about stitching the wound.

Throughout the operation, Cyrek had studied the woman. She was certainly elegant – tall and fair skinned with a good figure.

'You will have to change this bandage every day until the wound has healed,' Hannelore said, looking at Cyrek.

Cyrek nodded. 'Take him upstairs and put him to bed,' he instructed his men. 'Then hide the trucks and find yourselves accommodation. We stay here for a few days.'

'You can't take him upstairs,' Hannelore said. He's not in a fit condition to be moved up there. Also, you cannot stay here. The British patrols come every day.'

Walking across to Hannelore, Cyrek took her by the elbow. 'We'll take care of the Tommies. Now Doctor, I have a problem with my foot that needs your attention.' He shoved Hannelore towards the doorway, grinning at his men as he passed. Hannelore turned to protest but the slap across her face stopped her. 'Upstairs Doctor.'

The room was clean and tidy, a large bed against the wall. Cyrek could see the rumpled sheets and blankets where the doctor had been sleeping. He shoved the woman hard, pushing her onto the bed and turned, closed the door and jammed a chair against it. Undoing his belt, Cyrek sat down and started to unlace his boots, easing them off. He removed his sock and looked at his foot. It was swollen and bruised. 'What can you do for this?' The woman got up from the bed and crouched down, looking at his foot.

'I will get some bandages and liniment from downstairs and dress it,' Hannelore replied.

Standing up, Cyrek undid his trousers and let them drop to the floor, pulling his pants down, his erection standing proud. 'You can firstly administer to this.' He grabbed Hannelore's hair and forced her to take him into her mouth, hearing her gagging. After a moment or two, he pulled her up, kissing her hard on the lips. He squeezed her to him, feeling her trying to resist and then he shoved her backwards, across the bed. Cyrek moved quickly, yanking Hannelore's dressing gown open and ripping her night-dress apart. Breathing heavily, he straddled her, looking at her heaving breasts, pinching her nipples, enjoying the whimpering sound she made. He eased himself backwards and forced his knee between her thighs, excited by the sight of her pubis, the curly blonde hair masking her womanhood. Cyrek hadn't had a woman for a long time. He forced her legs apart, pinching the inside of Hannelore's thighs, making her groan in pain and then he stroked her entrance with his thumb, feeling the shivers running through her body. He licked his thumb and eased it between her lips then, suddenly, he thrust it in hard, hearing Hannelore yelp. He lowered himself on top of her and guided himself inside, moving slowly, almost lovingly as he felt the warmth and increasing moistness clinging to his member. Continuing to thrust, Cyrek nibbled Hannelore's nipples, resisting the urge to bite them too hard. He moved his face up to hers, seeing the tears running down her cheeks, his thrusting quickening. He tried to kiss her but she turned her head to the side, annoying him. He gripped her jaw and forced her head back, kissing her lips, feeling his moment arrive.

Chapter Six

Taking a long pull on his cigarette, Bill looked through the windscreen, along the street ahead of him, the tension building in his stomach. He glanced again at the entrance to the bar some fifty yards away, waiting for the Americans to arrive, knowing they would soon be here, having seen his contact, the sergeant, go in a short while before. He thought about the cargo he had in the back of the truck and what it was worth. Since his last two trips, getting food, cigarettes, alcohol and chocolate from the men around Bad Oeynhausen had been easy. Word had spread quickly that Bill was the man to see if you wanted to make some extra money and Bill had obliged, offering what appeared to be good prices for the items the men offered. Bill chuckled to himself. If only the idiots knew what their cartons of cigarettes or bottles of alcohol were really worth on the black market, they would be amazed. He could make a profit of two hundred percent on everything he sold. Now, Bill wanted to meet the Americans and cut out the sergeant, the middleman, realising there was more money to be made dealing direct. He took another pull on the cigarette and then threw the stub into the street, glancing nervously at his watch. He had agreed to meet the sergeant in another fifteen minutes and time was getting tight, he would have to drive to the rendezvous.

He heard the vehicle coming from behind, glancing in the wing mirror and seeing a Jeep approaching. Bill slid down in his seat. The Jeep went passed and swung into the curb, outside the bar. Two Americans got out, glancing each way along the street, not seeing Bill inside the truck. They strode into the bar. Bill opened the cab door and jumped down, walking towards the bar entrance. He looked behind him and could see nobody watching his movements. He went inside.

'Hello,' Bill said, looking at the sergeant. The two Americans were sitting with their backs to him, both looking round quickly.

'What're you doin' here?' the sergeant responded, anger in his face.

'Saw you coming in and thought I'd join you,' Bill replied, feigning innocence. 'Hello Gentlemen, I'm Bill...nice to meet you.' Bill stuck out his hand, the Americans, a little surprised, shaking it. 'I'm a sergeant major with the Commission HQ...provide the sergeant here with a few bits and pieces from time to time, if you know what I mean. Now, what's that you're drinking?'

'American beer. Here, have one.' The American passed a bottle to Bill.

'I told you where to meet,' the sergeant snapped, 'so why didn't you go there?'

Bill ignored the question. 'Understand you Gentlemen are in need of...of goods down in Cologne.' Bill looked at the two Americans, wearing open necked shirts and corduroy trouser. One was short and compact with closely cropped fair hair and cold blue eyes, the other tall and rangy with curly brown hair and a permanent smile. Bill could see that they were studying him closely, making him feel slightly uneasy. The sergeant started to say something when the short American held up his hand.

'So Bill, what makes you think you've got something of interest to us?'

Undoing his tunic buttons, Bill pulled out a sheaf of paper and passed it to the American. 'That's what's available today, depending of course on...on the prices being offered.'

The Americans, their heads together, studied the pages, the sergeant unable to see what they contained. 'Think there's some bits here of interest,' the rangy American said.

'Yeah. Could be some interest,' the other added.

'That's my shipment,' the sergeant snarled.

Bill grinned. 'It's mine...mine until I sell it.'

'Boys, boys. No need to fall out, there's plenty of opportunity for all,' the lanky American interjected. 'Suggest we all go to the rendezvous and see what's what.' He stood up and walked towards the door, the others following.

Outside, the Americans told Bill to follow them, the sergeant getting into the back of their Jeep. Bill ran to his truck, climbed into the cab and started the engine, relieved that the meeting had gone much as he had hoped. He could feel the sweat on his back as he eased the truck into gear and set off after the Jeep.

They reached an old warehouse building, the sergeant jumping out and opening the large front doors, the Jeep and truck driving inside. The Americans climbed into the back of the truck and undid some of the boxes, checking the contents, nodding to each other. They, helped by Bill and the sergeant, quickly emptied the truck, stacking the contents in the warehouse.

'Here you go Bill.' The lanky American held out a handful of dollar notes as he slid off the tailboard.

Bill frowned. 'How am I suppose to use those?'

'Easy. Take them to your cashier, he'll change them into whatever you want.'

'You've got to be bloody joking!' Bill complained. 'I can't go in and change this amount of money without thirty thousand questions being asked. How much is here?'

The lanky American thought for a moment. 'Let's say four to one of your British pounds. That makes...let's see, you've got about two thousand four hundred pounds there.'

Bill almost fainted. 'Jesus! But I can't have your dollars. I need pounds. I have to pay in pounds.'

'Wait a minute.' The lanky American and his shorter colleague walked some distance away, talking out of earshot. They came back. The American held out his hand. 'Give me the dollars.'

Bill did as he was told, noticing the short American counting out a stack of notes

'There you go Bill, make you happier?' the American said.

Bill looked at the notes and smiled. 'A pleasure doing business with you Gentlemen. When do we next meet?'

The sergeant, who had stood quietly in the background, coughed. 'This time next week, same place.'

Bill nodded, smiled, shook hands with the Americans and, getting into his truck, set off. He did not like the look on the sergeant's face as he pulled out of the warehouse.

Sitting in the car beside Captain Manson, Colin watched the convoy of lorries pulling into the newly erected compound, next to the Rathaus in Hamburg. He could see the armed soldiers behind the wire, facing a huge crowd of Germans, waiting to get their rations, the rations that would mean the difference between life and death.

'Done a good job Patterson,' Manson nodded, looking at the last truck pulling in.

Colin smiled. 'Thank you Sir.'

Manson looked across at him. 'Don't know how you managed to get this lot in such a short time my boy but...well done.'

'I was fortunate that a shipment of food and other essential items had just arrived in Antwerp. I managed to get Hamburg part of the allocation.' Colin opened the car door and got out. He leaned against the vehicle, watching as the trucks were organised into lines and the Germans were allowed into the compound in orderly queues. He felt tired having worked ceaselessly since the last time he had been here. He knew he had been lucky. He had been working in his office, getting nowhere, when the young WAAF driver he had briefly met earlier, strolled in. They had started talking and he had found out that she was called Mary Shipton. Her primary job was driving one of Montgomery's Generals and, when he did not require her, she undertook other assignments. She had invited him to join her for lunch and whilst eating, Colin had told her about his visit to Hamburg. Mary assured him that she would mention this to the General and, a week later, Colin received a call, telling him that there were limited rations available. He had worked very quickly, making sure he secured the allocation and today, it had at last arrived.

Manson stepped out of the car. 'It'll barely feed a few thousand. We need a convoy like this every day if we are going to save the majority of these Krauts.'

'It's a start Sir,' Colin replied testily, immediately regretting his tone.

Manson continued to look at the people. 'What concerns me is winter. In a few months time, we'll be in the thick of it and, if the weather is bad, thousands will perish.'

'We have to make sure there is a continuous and regular supply Sir. Without it...,' Colin paused. 'Without it, the Germans could rebel.'

Manson nodded. 'Then we'd be forced to shoot them. Hamburg's not the only city you know. We've got the same problems all over the British zone. Bombed out cities from Hamburg in the north to Dusseldorf and Cologne in the south. And all points in between. Every day there are tens of thousands more people coming into the zone – returning German soldiers, those fleeing from the East, those passing through. God alone knows who else. '

'We have to try Sir, we have to.'

'I suppose so Patterson. But would the Krauts have treated us any differently if they had successfully invaded us?' Manson asked. 'Anyway, I need a couple of dozen more like you, then we will start to get somewhere. By the way, where's that Thornton fellow?'

Colin shrugged his shoulders. 'Don't know Sir.' He hadn't seen Bill for days and the last time he had, Bill only seemed to be interested in taking the cigarette cartons Colin had in his locker.

'Right, we'd better make tracks,' Manson said, getting back into the car.

Scraping the small mound of masonry out of the way, Brigitte stood up, stepping to one side and letting Frau Eichel past, coughing as the dust in the corridor caught her throat. Frau Eichel tried the key and unlocked the door, pushing it slowly open, the hinges creaking. Brigitte, looking over Frau Eichel's head, could see the dark hallway ahead and the women entered the apartment. Brigitte pushed open the door on her right and walked into a small living room, the three upholstered chairs covered in dust, debris and glass. She went through the other two rooms, seeing the beds and opened the last door, almost stepping into fresh air. Brigitte clung to the door handle, pulling herself backwards, staring down four storeys to the pile of bricks and debris that once made up the rear wall.

'Are you all right?' Frau Eichel called out.

Brigitte shut the door. 'Yes...yes, I'm fine. But don't open that door. There's nothing behind it.' Brigitte went back to the living room, brushed off one of the chairs and sat down, Frau Eichel doing the same.

'Do you think this will do?' Frau Eichel asked. 'It was my nephew's but he moved to Gustrow, south of Rostock and farms there. With the Russians now occupying that area I'm not sure if he is all right or if he has perished...'

'I'm certain he would want you to live here,' Brigitte cut in, seeing the tears welling in Frau Eichel's eyes. 'He may return and with you here at least nobody else will take it over. We can cover the windows as none of them have any glass intact and we can block up the door at the back. It is most kind of you Frau Eichel to suggest that Gisela, Heinz and I live here with you.'

Frau Eichel waved her hand. 'Nothing of the sort. I wouldn't feel safe on my own and...and I'm not sure I could provide for myself.'

Brigitte smiled. She knew what Frau Eichel was implying. Since her episode with the two Tommies, Brigitte had started to bring back more and more rations, keeping Frau Eichel and the others reasonably well fed. It was now causing Brigitte concern as others in the cellar were becoming envious and, in some cases, downright rude, calling her names behind her back. Moving into this apartment would provide a lot more space and, hopefully, get Gisela out of her despair. 'Shall I go and get the others and bring our belongings here?'

'Good idea,' Frau Eichel replied, 'and whilst you are gone, I'll try and get this place cleaned up a bit.'

Descending the stairs, Brigitte left the building, careful that nobody saw her emerging. She walked along the street, noticing the trees on each side, most reduced to splinter wood and the burnt out cars, rusting in the damp September air. As she turned the corner, she almost bumped straight into four soldiers, one of them grabbing her arm, saving her from falling over.

'Bit of a hurry lass?' he said.

Brigitte frowned, regaining her composure. 'Pardon...I don't understand.'

'Papers. Where are your papers?' the soldier with corporal stripes on his arm demanded.

Brigitte handed over her identity card, recently acquired from the Rathaus, stating that she was a labourer.

The corporal looked up and handed her the card. 'Trummerfrauen? A rubble lady?'

Nodding, Brigitte put her identity card back into her pocket.

'Then why aren't you working?' the corporal asked. 'We'll have to take you to the compound and hold you.'

Brigitte understood. 'No, no, you don't understand. I've just visited a sick friend. I'm going back to work.'

The corporal looked her up and down, a grin on his face. 'Well, if you be nice, maybe we can overlook your absence from your place of work.'

'For not going to the compound?' Brigitte asked.

The corporal looked at the other three and nodded slowly.

'No. All four of you or the compound?' Brigitte shook her head, then forced herself to smile. 'Maybe you have cigarettes and some chocolate?'

The men all nodded and, within minutes, the group had stepped of the road, behind the wall of a bombed out house. Three of them had taken Brigitte against the wall and then they had left, leaving her with some tins, bars of chocolate, their cartons of cigarettes and, making Brigitte smile, two pairs of stockings. Packing the items into the sack she always had tied to her belt, Brigitte made her way back to the cellar.

'Ow! That stings.'

'Shut up! Hartwig replied, coughing, his weakened body hunched over Dieter's back. 'You're lucky I got this salt at all.'

Dieter turned slightly. 'It must be almost healed up by now.'

Hartwig shrugged. 'You didn't see your back when those bastards threw you, unconscious, into the compound. It was flayed. Luckily for you, Igor saw you, came and got me and we carried you back to the hut.

'And your jaw was not broken, fortunately,' Igor Szadinov said.

Dieter sat up and smiled, rubbing his jawbone. He looked at the two men as they sat down opposite. He studied the Russian, a lean man wearing spectacles, his hair thinning, his cheeks sunken, noticing the empty sleeve of the coat where Igor had lost an arm. Igor had joined them a month before having served in the Wermacht as a doctor. He had been badly injured and captured by the Germans near Stalingrad in 1942 and, because of his skills, offered the chance to join the Wermacht, serving on the Western front.

'Thanks to you two I am still alive,' Dieter said, 'but I can't see any improvement in our conditions. The compound is holding at least three times the number of men it should have and the food supply is woeful.'

Hartwig coughed again. 'Seems to me there are no more men coming in.'

'And they've changed the guards,' Igor added. 'Look like old men and invalids.'

'Is the major still here?' Dieter asked.

Igor nodded. 'Still strutting round the perimeter, ordering his men about.'

Dieter looked down at the floor. 'We've got to do something. Sitting here is waiting to die.'

'They must let us out soon,' Hartwig said. 'There's no reason to keep us confined like this. We are hardly a threat. Look at me, skin and bone and my teeth are falling out.'

'The longer we stay here, the weaker we become. Soon, we won't have the strength left to stand up let alone walk,' Dieter snapped.

'I know how you feel,' Igor said, 'but I would advise patience.' He leant forward and lowered his voice. 'Some are planning to break out but I think that is almost certain death. It would be for me. The Tommies would send me back to Russia and I know that I would be shot as a deserter or, probably worse, sent to the Siberian labour camps.'

Breathing out heavily, Dieter slumped back against the wall, flinching as his back stung. 'We've got to do something. I think we...'

The sudden yelling of men outside stopped Dieter talking. He and the others inside the hut made their way outside. Thousands of men were shouting and cheering, Dieter trying to see why. The sudden burst of machine gun fire caused him to look across the compound. Dieter froze, staring almost in disbelief at the scene in front of him. Men were running through the mud, pushing against the barbed wire fencing, falling over each other, scrabbling at the wire, bullets ripping through them as both guard towers opened fire. A mound of bodies started to build up, others using them to get over the top, falling to the ground outside, most perishing as the machine guns continued to fire. Dieter turned round and pushed his way past the men crowded behind him, making his way back inside the hut, shaking with anger.

Exhausted, Hannelore watched through the window as the three trucks, bluish smoke trailing behind them, made their way out of the village. Her body started heaving, her stomach going into spasms and she ran into the kitchen, throwing up into the stone sink. She leant over the sink, retching for some minutes before standing up and, taking a cloth, wiping her eyes and mouth. Then she remembered her mother, running along the corridor and up the stairs, entering her mother's room, seeing the back of her mother's head, her hair matted.

'Mother. Mother, it's me,' Hannelore said, walking round the bed.

Her mother buried her face in the pillow, refusing to look at her.

'Mother, please, you have to get up. We have to wash ourselves and clean up,' Hannelore said, pleadingly. Her mother ignored her. Hannelore burst into tears, the nightmare they had been through, flashing through her mind.

When she had first treated the wounded Pole, she thought they would be thankful and leave but their leader, the man who called himself Cyrek, had decided to stay a while. After the first night raping her, he had encouraged his men to find accommodation in the village, his friend Wicus being placed in the spare bedroom, next to her mother's. Her mother had protested when she first saw the men in the house, despite Hannelore's pleas for her to stay in her room and two men had carried her mother upstairs, her mother screaming as they had forced themselves upon her. Cyrek had forced Hannelore to dress the man's wound and feed them, threatening her if she ever demonstrated disobedience that he would kill her mother. Hannelore had become his slave, doing whatever he wanted. She had quickly realised that he was a psychopath, verging between almost childlike tenderness to extremes of sadistic behaviour. His size and physical strength had both fascinated and terrorised her. He had taken her whenever he felt inclined, enjoying debasing and humiliating her. He had also taken her mother on a few occasions. After seven days of hell, this morning they had decided to leave.

Wiping her tears, Hannelore stood up, realising that she had to put what had happened behind her, she had to think of the present and the future, she had to be strong both for herself and her mother. She went downstairs and heated a kettle of water on the range, pouring the hot water into a large, round earthenware bowl. She added some cold water to the bowl and then, with a towel and soap, carried it back to her mother's room.

'Mother, get up,' Hannelore ordered, as she removed her clothes. Stripped off, Hannelore looked at herself in the dressing table mirror. She could see the teeth marks around her nipples and on her breasts and buttocks, the bruising on her breasts, neck, stomach, inner and outer thighs and across her back and buttocks and the messy scab on her belly where the Pole had enjoyed using his dagger to brand her. Hannelore shuddered and started to carefully wash herself, wincing at times and feeling the pain shoot through her when she washed between her legs where the Pole had abused her.

Finished, she put on clean underwear and a blouse and skirt, brushing her long hair and fastening it up into a bun at the back of her head. She turned towards the bed and took hold of the top of the sheet, wrenching it out of her mother's grasp, pulling it off the bed. Her mother shouted out, screwing herself up into the foetal position. Hannelore could see the dried blood that covered the lower sheet and what remained of her mother's night-dress. She had to remain determined.

'Mother, get up!'

Her mother cowered in the bed, whimpering.

Hannelore reached across and grasped her mother's arm, pulling her round, forcing her to stand up. Her mother stood unsteadily, refusing to look at her as Hannelore, using scissors, cut the night-dress off. Hannelore suppressed a gasp. Her mother's body, like her own, was covered in bites, bruises and cuts. She started to wash her mother as gently as possible, feeling her mother's pain, sharing her mother's shame.

Watching the train chug past, smoke billowing from the funnel as it struggled to climb the gradient, Walbert counted the trucks. He could glimpse the people inside but could not tell if they were soldiers or civilians. He saw the Russian soldiers riding on the truck roofs, their rifles slung casually across their shoulders, the hatred rising inside him, making him duck down behind the ridge. He looked across at his younger brother Ernst, seeing his ashen face. He realised he had to look after his brother, that it must be more difficult for him, at twelve, to come to terms with the death of their parents.

'Can we catch a train Wally?' Ernst asked. 'I'm so tired and I want something to eat.'

Walbert slid across to his brother. 'I know you are hungry Ernst but so am I. It will be dark soon and then, if we find somewhere to hide, I can go and get some food for us.'

'Why did they do that to Mutti and Vatti?' Ernst pleaded. 'Why did those soldiers have to...to kill them?'

Walbert placed his arm around Ernst shoulders, feeling him sobbing into his chest. He closed his eyes. The day on the farm had started like most days, his father getting him out of bed at six o'clock and both of them going to do the milking and feeding the animals before breakfast. At breakfast, Walbert as usual complained about Ernst, wanting to know when he would start doing his share, being only two years younger than himself. His mother always gave the same reply - because he was much bigger and stronger than his brother, ignoring Walbert's reply that he was the same at twelve. After breakfast, the boys had been sent to clean out the pigsty and whilst they heaped the muck onto the wheelbarrow, they had heard the noise of approaching vehicles. Walbert went to see who was approaching, seeing four military vehicles pulling up in the yard, soldiers getting out. He ducked back inside the pigsty, telling Ernst to stay still, the pair of them watching their father stroll across to the man with a pistol. They could not hear what was being said but suddenly, the man hit their father across the face, knocking him to the ground then starting to kick him. Their mother ran out of the house, shouting and was grabbed by two of the soldiers and thrown down. One of them appeared to be pulling at her clothing, others gathering around, obscuring Walbert's view. He saw his father try to stand up and then the man with the pistol pointed it at his father's head and fired. Walbert pushed Ernst down, stopping him from seeing any more. He could hear his mother screaming and pleading but the soldiers around her only laughed and seemed to be joking. He saw one soldier doing up his trousers, wondering what was happening. Then the soldiers dispersed, a number going into the house, others heading towards the buildings, towards them. Walbert had grabbed Ernst arm and gone to the back of the sty, pushing the pigs out of their way. He had lifted the wooden slats and pushed Ernst into the manure trench, following close behind and pulling the slats back into place. The smell was awful, both gagging, Ernst protesting, Walbert hissing at him to be quiet. The soldiers had come in and herded the pigs outside, the pigs shrieking in protest. A shot rang out, followed by another, the bullet splintering the wood above their heads, both of them petrified. They stayed in the trap, listening to the pigs shrieking as they were being loaded onto the vehicles and the noise of glass breaking and wood splintering. Then they heard the vehicles start up and drive away.

They had lay in the filth for some time, Walbert listening for any sound breaking the unnatural silence. He pushed the slats out of the way and stood up, helping Ernst out of the trench. He had crept across the sty to the open door, Ernst clinging to him, peering out. There was no sign of the soldiers, only his parents lying in the yard. He had run across to his mother, aghast at the sight of her, lying in a pool of blood, her arms and legs spread-eagled, her clothes ripped apart. He vomited, turned and pulled Ernst to his chest, trying to stop him seeing their mother. He had told Ernst to turn away, going back to his mother and through his tears, pitifully pulling at her clothes, trying to cover her up. Then he had gone across to his father, seeing the blood drying in a pool around his head, his father's face almost peaceful with just a small hole in his forehead. Walbert and Ernst stood in the middle of the yard, holding each other, both crying, Ernst urinating.

The noise of an aeroplane, flying low, caused Walbert to turn and run towards the house, through the smashed door, Ernst following him. They barely noticed that the house had been ransacked, furniture smashed, belongings strewn across the floor, drawers emptied. The plane had disappeared and Walbert had forced both himself and Ernst to carry their dead parents in the wheelbarrow to the orchard where they had dug a shallow grave and buried them. Walbert had gone back into the house and, taking a sack, had found some food items left behind by the Russians. He had forced Ernst to join him and wash, putting on clean clothes. He had gone to his father's secret cubby-hole, behind his parent's bed, taking a small bundle of money. He had also found the addresses of his father's house and great-aunt's house in Hamburg, written on a card, placing it in his rear pocket. Finally, the boys put on their Sunday best boots, each taking a thick coat and, as they left the house, Walbert took his father's shotgun and a box of cartridges. Walbert knew his training in the Hitler Youth would help him to look after Ernst and get them to Hamburg.

Chapter Seven

Itching his neck where his collar chafed, Dieter felt his finger nail catch one of his scabs, causing him to curse under his breath. He spooned the thin gruel into his mouth and took a bite of the hard-tack biscuit, feeling his stomach aching and knowing that this food was not going to reduce his constant, overwhelming feeling of hunger. He thought about his wife, how she might be surviving, if she were alive or dead. He shook his head, realising how the war had affected him, how he could even think about his wife being dead and yet feel little or no emotion. With death being ever present during the fighting and now a daily occurrence at the camp, he realised how immune he had become, how his senses had been completely dulled by what he had experienced. If life was so cheap, he pondered, why was he so determined to survive this hellhole and return home, return to whatever might be left. He wanted to see his wife, feel her body against his - that intimate togetherness, shared by those in love.

'Das ist Schweinefutter,' Hartwig protested, belching loudly, breaking Dieter's thoughts.

Igor coughed. 'Better than nothing.'

'Well, at least since the attempted breakout, the Tommies have slightly improved the daily ration, pigswill or not,' Dieter said, looking at Harwig.

'It is still not enough,' Igor stated in his usual, quiet manner. 'I can see the number of men suffering from hunger oedema increasing every day and, as you both know, that is only one step from death. The numbers actually dying are increasing each week.'

Hartwig belched again. 'You really know how to cheer people up, Igor.'

'I only tell what I see,' Igor replied.

'A Doctor's viewpoint.' Dieter stood up and stretched. He went through to the ablutions and noticed the water was dribbling out of a pipe, using it to clean his can and spoon, shaking them when he had finished. As he walked back, easing his way past the crowd of men in the hut, he suddenly heard Hartwig's raised voice. Dieter pushed forward, seeing Hartwig desperately trying to hold onto his can, another man trying to wrench it from his grasp.

'Leave him alone,' Dieter shouted, 'it is not your can.'

The man let go, Hartwig falling backwards against a bunk. The man turned to face Dieter, his face flushed with anger. 'If you know what's good for you, you won't interfere.'

He turned back, facing Hartwig. Dieter came up behind him and placed his arm tightly around the man's throat. The man brought his elbow back sharply, Dieter ready for it, moving to the side and squeezing harder. The man was strong and Dieter could feel his own energy fading but he maintained his grip, feeling the man's attempts to fight him weaken as he fought for breath. The man stopped struggling and Dieter released him, the man leaning forward, coughing, struggling to regain his breath.

'Leave us alone,' Dieter ordered, breathing heavily.

The man looked at Dieter, his anger and hatred clear on his face. 'You idiot! You don't know whom you are dealing with. I will make sure you suffer for this.' He turned and pushed his way through the men, out of the hut.

'Thank you, my friend,' Hartwig said, coming up to Dieter. 'What an oaf.'

'That oaf was ex-Gestapo in my opinion,' Igor said.

Dieter breathed in. 'He can be whatever he likes. In here, we are all prisoners, no matter what we were before.'

'True, true,' Igor replied, 'but I would suggest we keep well away from the likes of him.'

'This will do very well,' Cyrek said, glancing at Wicus. 'Get all these people out and we can then unload our trucks. Make sure they take nothing of any value with them.'

Wicus shouted to his men and they started to herd the people out of the cellar, dealing brutally with anyone who showed any signs of protest. Cyrek watched, dispassionately, as old men and women were kicked, punched and hit as they tried to make their way up the stairs, his men wrenching any suitcases or boxes they were carrying from their hands, emptying the contents and checking through it. A baby was yelling nearby and Cyrek could see that two of his men were raping the mother. He walked over to the baby, picked it up by its legs and smashed its head against a concrete pillar, tossing the dead infant to one side. 'Schnell! Schnell!' he shouted, indicating with his rifle for people to hurry.

A young woman caught his eye. She was dressed in a shabby and torn coat with her hair tied up in a headscarf, helping an elderly man to walk. Cyrek walked over to her, seeing the fear in her eyes as he approached. He pulled the headscarf away, seeing her long, blonde hair fall about her shoulders, matted and dirty. He reached out and unbuttoned her coat, the woman standing rigid and proud. Her dress was filthy but he could see she was slender. He ordered her to wait, telling the old man to get out. When the woman protested, Cyrek grinned at her then slapped her hard across the face. The old man hobbled away, not looking back, heading as best he could for the stairs. Cyrek took the girl by the wrist, pulling her behind him. He saw a blanket strung across a corner of the cellar and, pushing it aside, saw the bed behind it. He pulled the woman forward, forcing her to lie, face down on the bed. Pulling her dress up he ripped her pants down and proceeded to rape her. She never made a sound. When he had satisfied himself, he buttoned up his trousers and went back to the stairs, thinking she was much like the woman doctor he had taken in Buchholz. At least she had saved Wicus, who now joined him as they made their way up to street level.

'How many do you think were in there?' Cyrek asked.

Wicus shrugged. 'Could've been a hundred or more…smelly bastards, weren't they?'

You think you smell any better?' Cyrek joked, thumping Wicus on the arm. 'Look over there…must be the tower of St. Michaelis church.'

Wicus looked in the direction Cyrek was pointing. 'We should take a look, bound to have something of interest. Anyway, where are we?'

'Think this is Balcluinstrasse and that is the Elbe flowing past.' Cyrek pointed at the river. 'We're in the St. Pauli area of Hamburg and this cellar will be a good place for us to work from. We can hide a lot of stuff down there. Now, let's get the trucks unloaded. We'll start looking around tomorrow.'

Just off Balcluinstrasse was Erichstrasse where Frau Eichel was cooking a pot of goulash on the wood burner, singing quietly to herself. Gisela entered the kitchen, holding Heinz in her arms.

'Mmm. That smells absolutely fantastic,' she said, 'when can we eat?'

'Not until it is well cooked and when Brigitte comes.' Frau Eichel looked at her sternly, then smiled. 'You are getting better by the day and so is Heinz, look at the smile on his face.'

Gisela sat on a chair by the table, moving Heinz onto her knee. 'At least we are getting plenty of food, thanks to Brigitte. I don't know how she manages to get so much. I thought our daily rations were for small amounts but we have plenty of potatoes, turnips and parsnips, meat and bread. And I love the chocolate we have sometimes, especially that American candy.'

'Hello everybody,' Brigitte said as she entered the kitchen. She placed her sack on the table and started to pick items out of it. 'I got these today,' she said, holding open a bag of plumbs. 'Try one, they're delicious.'

Gisela bit into a plumb, the juice running down her chin. 'Lovely…where did you find these?'

'The black market?' Frau Eichel stated, raising a questioning eyebrow.

Brigitte nodded. 'With cigarettes you can get almost everything you want. I even found myself looking at some dresses and shoes...hardly worn, almost like brand new.'

Gisela looked at Brigitte. 'Can we get clothes? Oh, I would love to have a new dress.'

'You've perked up a lot. Must be living here and getting a reasonable amount of food,' Brigitte replied, noticing how Gisela's face was starting to fill-out again, her eyes losing the dark circles around them.

'How do you get the cigarettes?' Gisela asked.

Brigitte saw Frau Eichel turn back towards the stove. 'Well, let me see. I...'

'Get the plates Brigitte,' Frau Eichel called out, 'it's ready to serve.'

Placing plates on the table and cutting some bread, Brigitte sat down, watching as Frau Eichel ladled out the goulash. Brigitte cut some meat into small pieces and passed a bowl across to Gisela who started to spoon it into Heinz's mouth, careful to make sure it was not too hot for him. They all started eating.

'I'm fed up with these rags I wear,' Gisela said between mouthfuls. 'Can't we go tomorrow and get some new clothes?'

Frau Eichel looked sternly at her. 'Be thankful girl you've got a full stomach. Brigitte can't go buying dresses and the sort for you. She needs to make sure there is enough food for Heinz first.'

'It's all right,' Brigitte said, placing her hand on Frau Eichel's arm. 'I don't think it would be a good idea just yet to be seen wearing good clothes Gisela. The streets are not safe so where would you wear such items?'

Gisela pouted. 'If I had good clothes, I would go outside. I'm fed up being cooped up in here like a chicken. I want to go out.'

Brigitte took another mouthful of the goulash. 'This is wonderful Frau Eichel.'

'If you won't take me then I will go out by myself,' Gisela said, determined to get an answer.

Looking down at her plate, Brigitte thought for a moment. 'Would you like to come with me on the train to Kassel?'

'Are you sure?' Frau Eichel said, the concern unmistakable in her voice.

'Why Kassel?' Gisela asked, frowning.

'To visit the farmers and get sufficient food to help us through the winter,' Brigitte replied. 'We can get off before Kassel, probably at Paderborn.'

Gisela put Heinz on the floor, letting him crawl towards the large chair. 'But we've got plenty of food. I want a dress,' she pleaded.

'Food first!' Brigitte snapped. 'Wearing your old clothes will not attract attention to you. Do you want attention? Do you want soldiers to look at you? You know what can happen.'

Gisela burst out crying, pushing her chair back and running from the room. Frau Eichel placed her hand on Brigitte's. 'She is so young. She doesn't understand.'

'Well, it's time she started to learn what is going on,' Brigitte retorted. 'How does she think I get all this food? By smiling sweetly?'

'I know, I know,' Frau Eichel said soothingly.

'Sorry.' Brigitte was annoyed with herself for losing her temper. 'Shall I go to Gisela?'

'Leave her be,' Frau Eichel said. 'Now, how about a second helping?'

Just as he was getting to grips with organising essential food shipments and overcoming the resistance by military personnel to handing over this responsibility to the Control Commission, Colin was called in to Captain Manson's office.

'Sergeant Patterson, take a seat,' Manson said, not looking up from the document he was studying. 'Need you to visit the Military Governor at...at Nienburg. Says he's got a problem with the Burgermeister, needs someone who can translate. Got the WAAF driver waiting downstairs so, off you go.'

Standing up, Colin hesitated. 'Is that all he wants, Sir?'

'If he wants you to help him sort out a problem, then that's what you will do.' Manson waved his hand, dismissing Colin.

During the one-hour drive to Nienburg, Colin enjoyed both the beautiful countryside along the Weser river valley and glancing frequently at Mary Shipton. She told him about the General and some of the people she had met whilst she had been in Germany, confiding in him that she was being pestered by a young lieutenant whom she did not like. Colin had suggested she might like to come to the cinema with him and she immediately agreed.

Pulling up outside a large house on the outskirts of the town, Colin got out of the car and made his way up the steps. Before he could pull the bell-chain, the door opened and a man appeared, nodding and ushering him inside. Colin looked around the entrance hall seeing the large, oak staircase leading up to the first floor and the magnificent gilt mirrors adorning the walls. The furnishings were elaborate with large paintings dominating the far wall.

'You must be the interpreter,' a tall, lean man said, walking across the hall towards Colin, his highly polished riding boots, tinkling spurs and riding whip in his hand, catching Colin's attention.

Colin saluted. 'Yes Sir.'

'Captain Blinkey...come this way.'

Blinkey shouted to the man who had met Colin, telling him to organise drinks and food and to get the Burgermeister. They entered what appeared to Colin to be the library, again extremely well furnished with bookshelves covering two walls and a massive mahogany desk placed in the large bay window. Blinkey indicated for him to sit down in one of the sumptuous leather chairs, going to the opposite side of the desk where he eased himself into what looked to Colin, almost like a throne. There was a light knock on the door and the man appeared, accompanied by two women, each carrying silver trays laden with food, the man carrying a tray of silver pots, china cups and saucers.

'Help yourself,' Blinkey said.

Colin stood up and took a plate, filling it with a selection of food. The man asked if he would like tea or coffee, Colin opting for the coffee and returning to his chair. 'This is a magnificent building Sir. Was it like this when you arrived?'

Blinkey looked at him. 'Good God no. I've had to acquire the furnishings from the local area. Man's got to live with what he is accustomed to. Also need to show these Krauts what the British way of life is all about.'

'The food is very good Sir,' Colin responded, surprised by what Blinkey had just said and his arrogance. 'I understand you have a problem with the Burgermeister Sir.'

Before Blinkey could answer, there was a knock on the door and Blinkey, very loudly, told the person to enter. A small, rotund man stood in the doorway, clutching his hat nervously between his hands, breathing heavily and sweating slightly. He bowed towards Blinkey and also to Colin. Blinkey beckoned him forward, raising his hand when the man was some ten feet from the desk.

Blinkey looked at Colin. 'This is the Burgermeister. You will translate, word for word what I say. Do you understand?'

'Yes Sir.'

'As the duly appointed Military Governor for Nienburg, you Burgermeister, will do precisely what you are told.' Blinkey paused for Colin to translate. 'You will requisition china, crystal glassware, silver and gold cutlery, embroidered table linen and silver and gold goblets from all of the houses in the town and surrounding area.'

Colin looked at Blinkey, his mouth open.

'Get on with it man,' Blinkey shouted. Colin translated, seeing the Burgermeister reach for his handkerchief and dab at his brow.

'Da ist nichts mehr, mein Herr. Sie haben schon alles ganommen. Die leute haben nichts mehr zu geben und fullen sich in ihrer Manschanwurde angegriffen,' the man replied. Colin translated.

Blinkey's face flushed. He took a sip of his coffee. 'Rights! Rights! You have no effing rights. You have been conquered. You will do what I say otherwise you will be imprisoned immediately and most of the town with you. Do you understand? Now, get out and be back here tomorrow morning with what I want. Don't tell me there is nothing left'

Stammering slightly, Colin spoke to the Burgermeister.

Halfway through, Blinkey shouted at him. 'If you don't translate exactly what I have said and in the same tone, you will face military disciplinary charges.'

When Colin had finished, the Burgermeister bowed and backed out of the room.

'Got to teach these Krauts whose boss,' Blinkey said. 'That man has singularly failed to deliver. He's been deliberately obstructive and I will stand no more. You can go.'

Leaving the room, Colin could feel himself shaking, not with fear, with anger. He walked towards the front door, seeing the man who had first let him in. They stepped outside and Colin turned to the man.

'Why has the Burgermeister got to supply all of these items to the Governor?'

The man shrugged. 'To keep the shipments going.'

'What shipments?'

'I don't want any trouble,' the man replied, turning towards the door.

Colin grabbed his arm. 'You won't get into trouble, I promise you.'

The man searched Colin's eyes, deciding he could be trusted. 'He has a truck loaded every week and sent to Antwerp...the black market. Every week we have to box up all sorts of valuables, carpets, works of art...whatever he thinks is suitable. He has five men working all the time in the barn at the rear of the house and, if anything goes missing, he takes it out on the women in the house.'

'How many women are here?' Colin asked.

'He keeps at least a dozen at any one time. Supposedly for cooking and cleaning but he abuses them constantly. When he has finished with any of them, he kicks them out and gets others.'

Shaking his head in disbelief, Colin grasped the man by the shoulders. 'This will stop. I promise you, I'm going to stop this.'

Turning away, Colin went down the remaining steps and got into the car, ignoring Mary's questioning as to why he was so upset.

The brief squeal of the rabbit alerted Walbert and, getting to his feet, he walked along the hedgerow, squatting down and seeing the snare had done its work. Picking up the struggling rabbit, he hit it hard across the back of its neck with the edge of his hand, killing it instantly. He made his way back to where Ernst was lying, sleeping under his coat. Dawn was breaking and Walbert started to make a small fire, sure it was safe as they were in a hollow, surrounded by trees. He blew and fanned the fire, seeing it quickly catch, placing twigs on it, followed by old branches he had broken the previous evening. He fanned the smoke, trying to dissipate it as much as possible, not wanting anyone, who may be nearby, seeing it. Satisfied, he used sticks to make a rudimentary frame above the fire, hanging a can of water over the flames and then set about skinning and gutting the still warm rabbit. With the water boiling, he dropped portions of the rabbit into the can, waiting patiently as the rabbit cooked.

'You must know exactly when to wake up,' Walbert joked, as Ernst sat up, rubbing his eyes. 'Rabbit for breakfast.'

Ernst stood up and stretched. 'Where did you get it from?'

'Stupid. I caught it a short while ago.' Walbert stuck his dagger into a piece of meat and passed it across to Ernst, taking another piece for himself. 'We'll keep some for later along with the apples and pears we took from home.'

Ernst started to cry.

'Eat up as we have to keep moving,' Walbert said sharply. 'We can't dwell on the past...we have to get to Hamburg. The longer we take to get there, the greater the chances of getting caught.' He stood up, taking a long swig from the water bottle. 'I'll go and fill this up.'

Crouching down next to the stream, Walbert watched as the bottle refilled, trying to stop himself from remembering the death of his parents a week ago. He knew he had to concentrate now on getting safely to his great-aunt and so far, by staying away from roads, houses and people, they had not faced any problems. He just wished Ernst would stop crying every time home was mentioned.

The unmistakable clanking of tank tracks, accompanied by the deep roar of an engine, broke Walbert's thoughts. He quickly screwed the cap onto the water bottle and scrabbled up the bank, reaching Ernst who was just standing, transfixed. He kicked earth over the dying fire, shouting at his brother to get his belongings, Walbert picking up his coat, sack and shotgun. The boys scrambled down the bank and into the stream, Walbert leading the way as they ducked under the low branches, intent on getting as far away as possible. Walbert could feel his heart thumping as he waded forward, trying to keep his coat, sack and gun out of the deepening water. He saw a ditch coming into the stream and clawed his way up it, ignoring the briars and nettles pricking and stinging his hands and face. Glancing over his shoulder, he could see Ernst following. Walbert stopped, breathing heavily.

'Are you all right?'

Ernst nodded. 'That was a lucky escape.'

Walbert listened. 'There are more tanks and, I think, trucks. Can you hear them?'

'Sound as though they are near where we camped.'

'You're right. I hope they don't see the fire otherwise they will be on to us.' Walbert eased himself up, straining to see over the bank. 'We can't go much further down the stream…it's getting too deep. We'd better carry on up this…'

The sudden silence of the tank engines, followed by the shouting of orders, stopped Walbert talking. He placed his finger to his lips, Ernst nodding and then started to creep further along the ditch. They made steady progress, following the ditch as it turned ahead. The cover was getting thinner and Walbert prayed the ditch would lead them to woods, somewhere where they could hide.

A vehicle started, revved up and then set off, Walbert pausing and listening intently. It sounded as though it was coming directly towards them. Walbert stumbled forward, seeing the ditch start to straighten, another ditch coming into it, the vehicle getting closer. He started to panic, looking to each side, pushing the undergrowth to the side. Then he saw it. A culvert over the ditch joining theirs, some fifty feet ahead. He turned and grabbed Ernst's wrist, pulling him along. They reached the culvert and, ducking down, crawled inside it, just as the vehicle came to a halt above them. They could hear men's voices, Russian, Walbert thought, obviously looking along the ditches. A cigarette butt hissed as it hit the water in front of him and then he heard the vehicle move off. He leant back against the side of the culvert, taking deep breaths, uncertain if any soldiers had been left behind to guard the ditches.

Chapter Eight

Whistling as he drove along, Bill reflected on his morning's activities. Stopping in Herford had resulted in the truck
being filled to capacity. He glanced across at the passenger
seat and footwell, seeing the cartons stacked there, no spare
space left. When he had stopped in his usual street, the
Krauts had soon appeared, offering him fur coats, jewellery,
candlesticks, paintings, antiques, watches, clocks, cameras
and other items. Bill had exchanged their offerings for tins
of soup, fruit, meat, sweets; for bottles of whisky, gin,
brandy; for cigarettes - maybe two cigarettes for a watch,
four for a camera. The trade had been fast, Bill having to
shout at times to stop people pushing forward, trying to load
the truck as quickly as he could. He had to admit to himself
that he would not know a genuine antique from something
made twenty years ago or know the worth of a particular
piece of jewellery. What he did know was that he would get
good money for most of what he carried and that it had cost
him very little. This trade was proving to be even more lucrative than providing the Americans with the excess rations
the soldiers supplied him with at Bad Oeynhausen.

Bill reached for his cigarette packet, opening it with one
hand, taking one out and placing it between his lips. He
pulled his Zippo lighter, a present from one of the Americans, from his tunic breast pocket, flicked the lid open and
thumbed the flint, lighting his cigarette and drawing in
deeply. Shoving the lighter back into his pocket, he could
see the bend ahead, changing down as he approached, the
road disappearing between the trees. He turned the corner
and double de-clutched, dropping down a gear as the road
descended, hearing the truck engine whine as the truck tried
to speed up. The descent was steep and Bill was relieved to
see the road level out, a shallow ford appearing ahead. Just

as he started to drive through the water he saw a battered kubelwagen placed across the road where it started to wind up the opposite side of the valley. Bill frowned, glancing across the cab, realising his sten gun was buried under the cartons, causing him to curse. He threw his cigarette out through the window and slowed to a stop, hunched over the wheel, studying the car ahead.

A glint of metal in his wing mirror caught Bill's attention, a man was stealthily approaching the driver's door. Bill rammed the truck into gear and hit the accelerator. Ahead of him he saw the sergeant from Osnabruck appear from behind the car, levelling his sub-machine gun at the truck. Bill continued, changing up, seeing the man alongside the driver's door, grabbing for the handle. Bill swerved towards the man, seeing him jump away, smacking into a tree. In the same instance, the cab glass shattered causing Bill to duck down as a stream of bullets screamed past his head, piercing the canvass behind him. Bill gripped the steering wheel in fear, seeing the sergeant jump out of the truck's path and then Bill felt the shudder as the truck struck the car, spinning it to one side. Bill kept his foot hard down on the accelerator, going round the next bend, the engine screaming in protest, Bill certain that the sergeant would appear at any moment, standing on the running board, firing his gun.

Reaching the top of the hill, Bill was relieved to see the road straighten out, open fields on either side. He changed up and drove as fast as he could towards Osnabruck, glancing frequently in his wing mirrors, relieved to see that nobody was pursuing him. His breathing slowed down, the thumping of his heart diminished and Bill pulled out his handkerchief, mopping his brow. Nervously, he lit another cigarette, inhaling deeply. He had never been shot at before and he could feel his legs and arms shaking.

As he approached the warehouse, Bill tried to calm himself down. He saw the doors open as he drew level and he swung the truck inside, coming to a halt.

'Jesus! What happened to you?' a familiar American voice asked.

Bill opened the door and looked down at the short American. 'Your sergeant friend shot at me. Almost effing killed me!'

'What are you talking about?'

Getting down from the cab and taking the cigarette offered, Bill looked at the American, studying him. 'You didn't know...did you?'

The American frowned, his lanky colleague coming up to them. 'Wow! Looks like you had a bit of bother.'

'About ten miles away the sergeant set up a road block and tried to stop me getting here.' Bill took another drag. 'When I drove forward, the effing sod shot at me. What I'd like...'

'Not us guys,' the short American cut in. 'Why would he do that?'

'What I'd like to know is how did he know where I was coming from,' Bill continued. 'As for why...that is obvious. He wanted to rob me.'

Lanky looked at his colleague. 'Always thought the guy was a bit of a jerk. Anyway Bill, you're here now so let's take a look.'

The three of them lowered the tailboard and climbed up, the Americans going through the load, never showing any sign other than mild interest. Bill emptied the passenger side and brought the cartons round to the back.

'Some bits here of use Bill but also quite a bit of junk. We'll give you two and a half for the lot.'

Bill kept a straight face, nodding. 'All right.'

Shorty handed over the money, Bill quickly stuffing it inside his tunic.

Lanky placed his arm around Bill's shoulders. 'If you want to make serious money Bill, there are a few things we could do with.'

'Such as?'

'Well, let's see. If you can get diamonds and precious stones, there's good money there,' Lanky replied

Bill shrugged. 'And where the bloody hell am I supposed to find those?'

Shorty smiled. 'If you keep alert chum, you'll be surprised.'

'We would also pay well for medicines,' Lanky said. 'Penicillin and insulin in particular. Suggest you have a chat to your MO or medical orderly when you get back.'

Bill stuck out his hand and smiled. 'See what I can do. Meet you here next week?'

The Americans shook his hand and nodded. 'Look after yourself Bill. Suggest you keep away from men with guns,' Lanky said, laughing.

Much as she had hoped, to Hannelore's dismay, life had not returned to some sort of normality since the Poles had left. Her mother did not say anything to her about the Poles but she knew her mother held her responsible for what had happened. Neighbours likewise hurried past when she was out in the street, lowering their heads. Few had visited her surgery except those out of necessity, mainly the women and girls who had been raped by the Poles. Even in her surgery, whilst inspecting and advising them, Hannelore could feel their hostility towards her. And now, the British had arrived, requisitioning a number of the houses and forcing families to move in with others. An English Captain had taken over two of the upstairs rooms and there was a constant stream of soldiers coming and going. Hannelore thought this was a blessing in disguise but, even though she tried to explain this to her mother, her mother remained insular and fearful that the British would behave the same as the Poles.

Cleaning the surgery, Hannelore heard a rap on the door, causing her to turn round.

'Doctor, I'm sorry to disturb you but I would like your advice please.'

Hannelore looked at the young English Captain, his hat clasped between his hands, smiling at her. She was thankful that she understood what he said having learnt English whilst at Medical School. 'How can I help, Captain?'

The Captain suddenly looked unsure of himself and Hannelore could see him blushing.

'Captain. I am a Doctor.'

Coughing, the Captain looked at her. 'It's rather a delicate matter. I have an itch well, more like a rash around my private parts.'

'Shut the door, come over here, drop your trousers and lie on the couch,' Hannelore ordered, suppressing a smile. The Captain moved forward and did as she instructed.

Hannelore quickly inspected him then went to the sink and washed her hands. When she looked round, the Captain had already done up his trousers and was standing in front of the door. 'You have venereal disease and you need penicillin to effect a cure,' Hannelore said. 'The trouble is, I do not have any penicillin left.'

'What about mercury. I thought...well, I've been told that is what is used,' the Captain replied.

Hannelore laughed. 'Mercury and the umbrella? How old fashioned. No, get me penicillin and I will have you cured quickly.'

The Captain placed his hand on the doorknob, opened the door, then paused. He coughed again.

'Is there something else?' Hannelore asked.

'Yes. I think you should inspect all of my men,' the Captain replied.

'Get me penicillin first, sufficient to cure everyone. Oh, and when you get the penicillin, can you get me insulin, iodine, bandages and lint cloths.' Hannelore turned and continued to clean the surgery, hoping she was going to be busy during the coming days. Damn what the neighbours think, she said to herself.

Pulling his coat tighter around him, Dieter shivered in the autumnal air. The queue ahead of him was getting slowly shorter and he could see the men at the tables, just inside the hut entrance, busily writing down the details of each POW. Igor and Hartwig stood in front of him, Hartwig excited, sure that release from the camp was imminent. Dieter tried to share Hartwig's enthusiasm but knew he would only believe it when he walked out of the camp a free man. That day could not come soon enough. The situation was deplorable; men crowded inside the compound with no protection from the weather, lying in their own faeces and urine; no medical attention for the injured and dying, the smallest cut turning septic; no clean sanitation, living in absolutely filthy, disease ridden conditions with a pitiful daily ration of food. Dieter knew he had lost considerable weight and strength, knew that a harsh winter would finish off the majority of those held in the camp. At least Hartwig's belief that they would soon be making their way home was something to cling to. Dieter decided to push his pessimism aside as he reached the doorway.

Leaning against the doorframe, Dieter listened to the questions being asked by the men sitting behind the tables and noticed the soldiers standing nearby, alert and ready for any trouble. The questions were simple and direct, the questioners refusing to reply to requests for more information concerning release. Dieter noticed the young boy next to an officer, translating the replies, thinking his German was quite good. He could see Igor becoming more and more agitated as the questioning progressed.

Suddenly Igor got to his feet and started shouting. 'That is a death sentence! If you send me back to Russia, I will be shot on arrival! Please, please, let me stay in Germany.'

The man at the desk looked on impassively, explaining that he had no alternative, his orders were clear. All Russians had to be repatriated, irrespective of status, who or what they were.

'I will not go! I refuse to go! I am a doctor, a doctor of medicine. I am of more use here,' Igor yelled. 'You need doctors and I can help. Please...please...don't send me to my death.'

The man behind the desk nodded towards the soldiers and two of them came up behind Igor and grasped his shoulders. He was taken out through the back of the hut, screaming, shouting and struggling. The British took no notice, Dieter feeling a chill pass down his spine, trying to think what he could do. Hartwig stood up at the next table and lowered his head, refusing to look at Dieter as he passed him.

Dieter walked to the table where Igor had been and, as instructed, sat down. The boy asked him for his military details – service number, name, rank, regiment, Dieter replying, his mind still thinking about Igor. He was asked where his home was, what he had done during his service years, replying perfunctorily, with the minimal amount of information as possible. When he had finished, the man behind the desk indicated he could leave. Dieter stood up.

'Gestapo! He's Gestapo!'

The man at the desk looked towards the doorway, Dieter turning round at the same instance, seeing the man he had prevented from robbing Hartwig of his can, pointing directly towards him.

'He was at Oderblick. Near Slubice. One of the camp guards. I'd recognise him anywhere,' the man claimed, his pointing finger trembling. 'Gestapo! The revolting pig!'

Before Dieter could fully comprehend what the man's accusations meant, he felt his arms pinned, a soldier gripping him tightly on each side. 'No! No! He's lying. I've never been to Oder...whatever the place is.'

'Take him immediately to Bad Nenndorf,' the man at the table ordered, scribbling furiously on Dieter's notes.

'Ask him where he has been. He's Gestapo, he's the one you need to question,' Dieter said. He noticed Hartwig standing in the doorway, a look of horror on his face. 'Tell them Hartwig...tell them what happened. For God sake man, tell them,' Dieter shouted. Hartwig lowered his head and, turning, pushed his way past the men behind him.

The soldiers wheeled Dieter round and took him out through the rear door. They roughly bundled Dieter into a waiting truck, joining him on each side and the truck set off.

As she had thought, the queue for the train was already forming and Brigitte was thankful she had got to the station before four o'clock, finding space on the platform in the chill morning air. She looked at Gisela, wrapped in an old coat and wearing a brown woollen hat, her hair tucked up underneath. Like herself, Gisela would not attract attention, merging with those around them. Brigitte noticed an old wooden trunk and walked over to it, sitting on one edge, indicating for Gisela to join her.

'It's going to be a long day, if not two,' Brigitte said.

Gisela puffed out her cheeks. 'Don't see why we are here. We have plenty of food and you can always get more.'

'We've discussed this,' Brigitte snapped. 'Our supplies of potatoes, vegetables and meat are diminishing rapidly and there are no indications that the British are going to ship in any more. We have to be ready to survive the winter.'

'Have you got the tickets?' Gisela asked, a note of hope in her voice.

'Yes.' Brigitte noticed Gisela's downcast look. 'About the only thing you can buy with our marks. I've heard there is a new name for what we are going to do. It's called 'hamstern', you know, foraging for food.'

Gisela looked away, disinterested and Brigitte decided it was pointless trying to talk to her if all she wanted to do was sulk.

Around nine o'clock, a train pulled into the platform, with some ten carriages and a dozen or so goods wagons. Brigitte pushed forward, along with everyone else, managing to force her way inside one of the carriages, Gisela right behind her. They managed to get a seat and very soon the carriage was packed solid with people. Brigitte could see people outside, climbing onto the roof, others finding handgrips wherever they could as they stood, precariously, on the running boards along the sides of the carriage. Brigitte stood up and lowered the carriage window, three people immediately clinging to the inside of the frame edge. The whistle sounded after a considerable delay and the train started to move slowly forward. Brigitte smiled to herself. If anyone wanted to inspect her ticket, they'd have great difficulties reaching her.

The train made reasonable progress and, somehow, Brigitte managed to doze as the train lurched along, Gisela asleep with her head on Brigitte's shoulder. It stopped at Hannover where hundreds more people tried to find somewhere to get onto the train. With the heat of bodies squashed together and the rising temperature outside, Brigitte could feel the perspiration forming on her brow, her body becoming sticky. The train moved forward, eventually arriving at

Paderborn where many people got off, much to Brigitte's relief. Then it set off again, stopping at various small stations as it made its way towards Kassel. As the train emerged from the deep valley, Brigitte saw the fields on either side widening out and she decided they would get off at the next stop. The train started to slow and Brigitte told Gisela to follow her as she forced her way through the people to get to the door. The train stopped at Warburg and they got out, Brigitte setting off at a rapid pace, Gisela complaining behind her, wanting to know why she was in such a hurry.

'It's dark soon and we have to get to the farmers before they have got rid of everything,' Brigitte replied, 'before this lot get there first.' Walking quickly, Brigitte and Gisela were soon out into the countryside, walking along the bank of the River Diemel, approaching an isolated farm. As they entered the farmyard, an Alsatian started barking, startling them, Brigitte relieved to see that it was tethered to a post by a long chain.

'Stop there!' A portly man appeared at the doorway to the barn, a shotgun hooked over his arm. 'What are you doing here?'

Brigitte smiled. 'We have come to buy some food from you.'

'Ain't got any spare for the likes of you. Now, be off, before I let the dog loose.'

A noise behind Brigitte made her turn round. A large woman stood watching her, her arms folded across her ample chest, her apron dirty. 'What you got to trade?'

'We've got money,' Brigitte replied.

'And other things,' Gisela added. Brigitte glared at Gisela.

'Show us what you got...money's not worth anything,' the woman said.

Brigitte undid her coat, taking her sack from her belt. She opened it and brought out a carton of cigarettes. 'These are worth...'

'Know what they're worth, girl,' the woman cut in. 'What else?'

'What have you got to offer?' Brigitte replied, her jaw tightening.

The woman nodded towards the barn. 'Let 'em have a look.'

Gisela and Brigitte turned, Brigitte picking up her sack as they walked towards the barn. The portly man went inside making his way towards the rear, nodding in the direction of a stall. Brigitte looked inside, seeing a large mound of new potatoes.

'We've got them and roots in the next stall. Beyond that there's cabbage,' the woman said.

'Have you got any meat?' Brigitte asked.

The man looked at her suspiciously. 'Might have a bit we can spare. Now, what's you got?'

For the next hour or so, Brigitte haggled and bargained with the farmer and his wife over every single item. So many potatoes for a cigarette, a piece of pork for half a bottle of whisky, a bar of soap for three cabbages. The farmer did, begrudgingly, let her have four small sacks to put the food into. By the time they had finished it was virtually dark inside the barn.

'May we stay here for the night?' Brigitte asked, mindful that it was almost curfew time.

The man shook his head. 'No.'

'We've got a spare pigsty next to the house...if you want to use it,' the woman said.

Picking up a sack in each hand, Gisela doing the same, Brigitte followed the woman to the pigsty. She bent under the low roof and was surprised to see that it had been cleaned out, fresh straw scattered on the floor. 'This will be just fine. Thank you. Just one more request. Could we have some water?'

The woman nodded. 'Get you a pail.' She walked off, heading towards the house, the man following her, obviously not pleased that she had let Brigitte and Gisela stay.

Brigitte could hear them arguing inside the house then the woman reappeared, carrying a pail of water and a metal scoop. She came across to them. 'Be sure you're gone before sunrise. He's not use to strangers.'

Chapter Nine

Slumping down on his chair, Colin removed his beret, looking at the increasing stack of files gathering on his desk. Even though three other people had recently arrived, the work never seemed to diminish, there were always more reports to be completed, letters to be written and signed, permits to be issued and a constant stream of forms to be filled and returned to HQ. Colin was convinced that the reasons for so much chaos was down to the simple fact that everyone spent more time shuffling paperwork than actually getting on with their jobs. Bureaucracy was compounding and damaging what was already a horrendous situation.

'Busy then?'

Colin looked up and saw Bill Thornton standing in the doorway, lighting a cigarette. 'Where have you been? I could do with your help in getting through this lot.' Colin pointed at the paperwork on his desk.

Bill laughed. 'Far too busy, lad, just popped in to get your cigarette ration.'

'You smoke too much,' Colin replied, bending down behind his desk and picking up two cartons of cigarettes. He handed them to Bill.

'Have you visited any of the internment camps?' Colin asked.

'No. As I said, I've got my responsibilities over in Osnabruck...they keep me busy all the time.' Bill took a puff on his cigarette. 'Don't need to go near places like those. Anyway, why do you ask?'

'They are terrible,' Colin said. 'There is no detailed questioning of the prisoners, nobody seems interested in finding out where they come from, who their relatives are, what are their circumstances. And the conditions are atrocious. The men are emaciated, their clothing is nothing better than rags and they are filthy.'

Bill dropped his butt end onto the floor, stamping on it. 'They're only Krauts. That's all they deserve. They should think themselves lucky we give them any bloody food.'

'They are human beings,' Colin replied. 'When I was at Munsterlager the other day, a Russian doctor was being transported back to his homeland, despite his protests. Nobody cared.'

'Poor bugger,' Bill said, with feeling. 'Heard the Ruskies shoot all returning POW's out of hand on the basis they shouldn't 'ave surrendered in the first place.'

'Precisely! If we know that is going to happen then we should investigate a man's background more closely.' Colin stood up and walked across to the table near to the door, helping himself to a mug of water. 'He doesn't deserve to be treated like that. Then there was another chap. Seemed decent enough to me. Just finished and, as he got up, another POW claimed he was Gestapo. The chap was marched off and bundled into a truck without any chance of defending himself.'

Bill smiled. 'Devious buggers those Gestapo types. Seem all right until you dig deeper, then they get nasty. Where were they taking him?'

'Some place called Bad Nenndorf.'

'Never heard of it,' Bill said. 'Anyway, they'll get the truth out of him, one way or t'other. Got to go…take this truck load of stuff to Herford.'

Colin looked at Bill. 'Where's Herford?'

What? Sorry, meant Osnabruck…get confused with all these places with funny names.' Bill turned and left the office, relieved Colin had not been looking at him.

Taking a file from the top of the stack, Colin opened it and started to sign off a sheaf of travel permits, documenting each one's reference number in a ledger and laboriously detailing the route. He decided that he would complete this file before stopping for lunch.

A light cough caused him to look up, breaking into a smile as he saw Mary Shipton standing in the doorway. 'Hello. What are you doing here?'

'I've got the afternoon free and thought...well, I wondered if you could take time off and come for a drive,' Mary replied, returning Colin's smile.

Colin looked at the file in front of him and promptly closed it. 'Of course, I'd be delighted. Shall we get some lunch?'

'I've already packed a hamper.'

Colin picked up his beret. 'Organised. I like that. Where are we going?'

Mary's eyes widened. 'A mystery. I'm sure you will like it.'

Making its way slowly through the ruins and piles of debris still littering the road, the BMW R75 motor bike and sidecar came into view, closely followed by an American Chevrolet C15 truck. Cyrek could see the Tommy in the sidecar, holding onto the machine gun and the Tommies in the truck cab. Cupping his hands to his mouth, he made a low whistle and waited for the truck to pass his position at a crossroads. The motor bike and sidecar went passed, turning right towards the docks. As soon as it had turned, Wicus lurched into the road, apparently drunk, causing the truck to stop, the driver leaning out of the cab, yelling at Wicus. Cyrek moved fast, reaching the driver's door and pushing his pistol into the driver's jawbone, pointing with his free hand for the driver to turn left. The driver froze, his eyes widening in horror. The Tommy next to him looked just as startled then Wicus was on the running board, yelling at the man to leave his sub machine gun on the floor. The Tommies did not understand what was being shouted at them.

Opening the driver's door, Cyrek grabbed the man's tunic and hauled him out, throwing him to the ground. He got into the driver's seat and rammed the truck into gear, hauling on the steering wheel, setting off along the road in the opposite direction to the motor bike and sidecar. Wicus clung on then he fired at point blank range, the Tommy's brains and blood splattering across the windscreen. The truck bounced over the debris as it made its way forward, Wicus shouting and cursing at Cyrek, trying to get into the cab, the soldier's dead body preventing him. The truck touched the edge of a bomb crater as Cyrek wrenched at the wheel, causing Wicus to lose his grip and jump backwards, rolling into the crater, the truck almost toppling. Cyrek saw the motor bike and sidecar catching him up in his wing mirror. He heard the bullets pinging off the underside of the truck as the machine gun opened fire. He carried on, waiting for the bike to get closer. When he was sure the bike was close enough, he slammed on the brakes, the truck juddering to a halt. Cyrek picked up the sub machine gun from the floor and jumped from the cab. He ran towards the rear, firing at the two Tommies on the bike, killing both of them before they could take aim.

'You maniac! You almost killed me,' Wicus shouted, breathing heavily as he approached.

Cyrek grinned. 'Knew you'd be all right. Should have got in quicker. Let's go.'

Wicus grabbed the dead soldier's body and dragged it out of the cab, leaving it on the ground where it fell. He climbed into the cab and they set off, Cyrek skilfully driving the truck through the narrow streets, back to the cellar. He parked the truck in the yard behind the remains of the building they now occupied, getting out and strolling to the back where Wicus joined him. They undid the canvas flap, dropped the tailboard and climbed into the back, looking at the cargo of boxes, cartons and furniture. Some of Cyrek's men appeared, standing at the tailboard.

Cyrek forced one of the wooden boxes open. 'Looks like the Tommies are clearing quite a bit of good stuff out...look at this.'

Wicus peered round. 'Gold and silver...cheeky buggers.'

Cyrek gave instructions and very quickly, his men were emptying the truck, taking everything down into the cellar.

'Fortunate that young Tommy you caught last week told you about this little business,' Cyrek said.

Wicus grinned. 'Cried like a baby he did. There's a shipment like this goes to the docks every other week. Some British general sending it back to England. We can do well...let the Tommies collect it, then we take it.'

'We'll have to be careful,' Cyrek replied. 'After this, it won't be so easy. They'll guard it more carefully. How did you catch the Tommy anyway?'

'Oh, he was shagging one of our frauleins and then refused to pay. I enjoyed having the little lad to myself for an hour, then I drowned him.'

Cyrek laughed. 'The truck's empty so I'll drive it away from here and dump it. You make sure the cargo is correctly sorted and stored. We've got some trading to do tomorrow.'

Sitting astride the tree branch, Walbert looked each way along the road that passed beneath his position. No vehicles or people were in sight but Walbert was unsure what to do next. He could see the glint coming off the water in the distance and was sure it was the Schweriner See where his father had taken them on fishing trips. He studied the ground between himself and the lake, noticing that it was flat and marshy with little cover. If anyone came along the road whilst he and Ernst were walking towards the lake, they would easily be seen. To attempt it at night could be very risky as he would not be able to pick out the marsh and they could get stuck in the mud or even worse. Also, they had not made good progress since leaving the farm. After the scare with the Russians, they had lain in the culvert for the whole night, both frightened to venture out in case there were Russians above them. It was not until later the following day when, stiff and damp, Walbert had crept out and climbed the bank, finding that the Russians had gone. Since then, they had been even more cautious, Walbert refusing to light a fire, living off what they picked and what they carried with them.

There was a noise behind him, causing Walbert to look round. 'When are we going to get down from this tree?' Ernst asked. 'I'm stiff, cold and hungry.'

'Just be patient. I need time to think,' Walbert replied.

'I want to get down now.' Ernst complained. 'Nothing's come along here for hours. Nobody's around as far as I can see.'

Walbert pursed his lips. 'All right! Collect your back pack and we'll climb down, me first.'

Making his way back along the branch, Walbert gripped the trunk and started to ease himself down, his foot stretching for the branch below. When he was secure, he reached up, taking Ernst back pack and letting it drop to the ground. He helped Ernst swing over the branch above and started to guide Ernst foot to the branch he was standing on. Then he heard the noise, the low whine of engines in the distance.

'Wait! Get back up onto the branch,' Walbert ordered, his brother doing as he was told. The noise of the vehicles increased as they got closer and Walbert eased himself round the trunk, looking along the road. Then he saw the first truck, a large red flag flying from the bumper. The truck went roaring past below him followed by at least twenty others, Walbert clinging to the trunk, hardly daring to look. The engine sound subsided and Walbert checked the road both ways.

'All right, let's go,' he said, looking up at Ernst. The boys climbed down the tree and darted across the road, rolling into the shallow ditch opposite.

'Can we eat?' Ernst asked.

'For goodness sake, not now! We have to find somewhere to hide, then we can eat.' Walbert stood up and, crouching, walked along the ditch.

Ernst shuffled along behind. 'Where are we going? The lake's over there.'

'I know it is but we can't just walk straight towards it. Anyone passing would see us,' Walbert snapped. 'Just keep low and follow me.'

The boys followed the ditch alongside the road for at least two miles before coming to a track leading towards the lake. There were clumps of reeds on either side and Walbert could see that the ground was uneven, providing some cover from the road. He set off along the track, his brother complaining behind him. As the reeds got thicker, Walbert started to relax. He could see a dense clump of reeds ahead and he walked off the track, stumbling through the thick, matted grass and thistles until he was behind the reeds. He immediately saw what he had been looking for, a small hollow between two large clumps of reeds.

'We can rest and eat here Ernst. Here, let me help you with your backpack.' Walbert eased the pack from Ernst and placed it on the ground. Ernst slumped to the ground as Walbert undid their packs and took out the bags of food and wrapped meat. They both ate quickly, Walbert insisting that Ernst drink plenty of water from his bottle. Noticing the light, Walbert realised it must be late afternoon and that the lake was still at least two miles away. He leaned back against the earth mound behind him, wondering what he would do when they reached the lake. He must have dozed off.

The noise of a vehicle, very close, startled him. Walbert placed his finger to his lips as he looked across at his brother rubbing his eyes. He grabbed the backpack and shoved their bags and wraps inside it, quickly fastening it. Looking round, he could see an animal run disappearing into the reed clump and started to elbow his way forward, forcing himself deeper inside. He could feel Ernst hands doing the same behind him. When he felt that they were well hidden he stopped and tried to turn round to face his brother but found it impossible, the reed stems being too thick. He forced himself up until he was standing, just making out the track they had been walking along as the reeds swayed in front of him. The truck had stopped close to them, two other trucks doing the same. Men in Russian uniforms jumped out of the trucks and started to shout out orders.

Walbert felt Ernst tugging at his trousers, waving his hand, warning him to stay still. Some thirty men, filthy and dishevelled, spilled out of the trucks, the soldiers pointing their rifles at them, shouting at them. The men started digging some yards from the track and Walbert wondered what they were doing. The soldiers hit any man who appeared to slow down. They seemed to be digging a trench but why here, Walbert thought. After about an hour and with the light fading, the soldiers shouted at the men who promptly stopped digging. Walbert watched as they lined up along the side of the trench, facing towards it. The soldiers stood behind the men and then, to Walbert's horror as realisation dawned, the shooting started. Walbert lowered his head, shivering. He glanced up and saw a soldier with a pistol walking along the trench, shooting men in the head. Walbert vomited, spraying the reed stems in front of him. He lowered himself to the ground, his brother realising this was not the time to ask questions.

The bare walls stared back at Dieter, their secrets hidden, giving no indication of what had happened to those who had been locked in the cell before him. He shivered, feeling the chill of the wind blowing through the missing pane of glass in the window, high up on the opposite wall. He looked at the concrete floor and the battered pail in the corner that served as his latrine and was now overflowing. He glanced across at the wooden bench and its broken boards where he tried to get some sleep, the single electric light in the ceiling casting a dull glow. He felt the draught coming under the heavy steel door that was only opened once a day when a tin can of watery soup was placed inside the cell. He clasped his hands around his body, trying to retain some warmth, cursing the Tommies, wondering how long it would be before they came to get him.

Since leaving the internment camp at Munsterlager, nobody had spoken to him. The soldiers who accompanied him talked among themselves, Dieter feigning ignorance of what they were saying. There talk had been about getting home to their families before Christmas, how much money they were making out of the black market and how easy it was to get German women to satisfy their needs for a bit of chocolate. Dieter had felt the anger, misery and frustration building up inside him, wondering if the British were treating his wife in the same way. On arrival at Bad Nenndorf, he had been stripped naked, pushed through a cold shower and then, still wet, shoved into this cell, his clothes thrown in behind him except that the Tommies kept his coat and boots.

Using a button from his tunic, Dieter had managed, using a lath on the bench, to mark each day as it passed. He reckoned he had been in the cell for almost three weeks and he was determined to maintain his discipline of marking the lath, despite his lack of sleep. Throughout the nights, the single light remained on but this was not what concerned Dieter most. It was the sounds of men being forced along the corridor outside, the yelling and shouting of the guards and the screams of men being beaten and tortured. Every time a man screamed out, Dieter's disturbed sleep would be broken. He found himself pressing his hands against his ears but this did not stop a man's pitiful screaming from reverberating through his brain. Dieter tried to prevent himself from thinking about what was being done, trying to keep a picture of his wife in his mind but to no avail. The screams always won, bringing him back to reality, making him tremble, knowing that his time would come.

'Don't move...just relax and lie still,' Hannelore said, as she carefully eased her hand forward, concentrating on finding the right spot before pushing the surgical needle sharply upwards. The young girl, lying on the couch, tensed again, letting out a low moan, her mother looking on, gripping her hand.

Standing straight, Hannelore smiled down at her young patient. 'That's it! You will feel pains and start to bleed heavily during the next few hours. Then you will feel a little weak for a few days but after that, you should be all right. There will be no baby to worry about.'

'Thank you Doctor,' the girl's mother said, helping her daughter to get up and put on her pants.

Hannelore nodded. 'If the bleeding does not stop after four hours, come and get me.'

The woman and her daughter left the surgery and Hannelore cleaned up, hoping they would recover from their ordeal. The girl was only thirteen and Hannelore had carried out the same procedure on her mother the week before. Hannelore knew how relieved she had felt when she menstruated after the Poles had left. She leaned back against the

table realising that this was the tenth abortion she had under-
taken in as many days and she was sure there were others to
come. She was certain a number of women were refusing to
acknowledge that they carried Polish bastards and, for them,
there would be little she could do. A polite knock on the
surgery door made her look round.

'Yes.'

The captain appeared. 'I have something you requested.
May my men bring it in?'

Hannelore nodded and watched as the men entered the
surgery, placing six large cartons on the floor. As the men
left, Hannelore placed the first carton on the couch and
opened it. 'Well done! Where did you get this from?' she
asked as she placed the bottles of penicillin on the table.

'You shouldn't ask and you don't need to know,' the
captain replied, winking and smiling. 'The other cartons
have wound dressings and an assortment of bandages and
splints. That carton is full of iodine and there are a small
number of insulin bottles in that one.' The captain pointed at
the relevant cartons.

'Well, well, Captain. I think that deserves a drink. I
have dandelion wine or herb tea. Which would you like?'

The captain smiled at Hannelore. 'If you start my
treatment now, afterwards I would be delighted to join you
for a drink.'

'All right,' Hannelore replied, 'drop your trousers and
pants and get onto the couch.' She turned away, smiling to
herself, pretending she had not noticed the deep blush on the
young man's face.

Scratching his body as the lice and fleas indulged themselves, Hartwig looked round the hut, seeing others doing
the same. He knew he was starting to lose his mind, the urge
to run to the fence and climb it, knowing such an act would
mean certain death, became stronger as each day passed.
The lack of water and food had reduced him to skin and
bone, his coat hanging off him. And now he had to live with
his shame. Every day since Dieter had been dragged away,
played on his mind. He had not spoken out in defence of his

friend, had not supported him, had not tried to speak to the Tommies to explain why the spurious allegation had been made. Also, there was the loss of Igor.

After leaving the hut when Dieter was taken away, Hartwig had been walking beside the fence, feeling disgusted with himself for what he had done. He had approached the gate and stopped, along with a large group of men, watching a truck backing up. Then he had seen Igor being escorted towards the gate, pleading with the soldiers around him to let him remain in the camp. The gate had opened and as the group reached the truck, Igor had suddenly ripped himself free from his escort and started running along the outside of the fence. Men around Hartwig had started to cheer him, yelling at him to run faster, urging him on, Hartwig joining in. He had seen Igor stumble and force himself on, struggling in his weakened state, to reach the trees at the far end. Then the machine gun had started firing, Hartwig and those around him, watching in horror and silence as the bullets flicked up the mud, closing in on their target, Igor falling as the bullets ripped through his back. The Tommies had laughed, picking up the lifeless body and throwing it into the back of the truck.

Men were shuffling out of the hut, Hartwig joining them, as they lined up for a roll-call. He heard his name being called out and stepped forward, a soldier pointing at the gate. Hartwig and five others made their way forward, Hartwig seeing a table being placed just inside the gate. He waited, wondering what was going to happen next.

'Nadel, Hartwig…step forward,' the officer at the table ordered.

Hartwig stepped towards the table, stopping in front of it.

'You are Nadel?' the officer asked, reading out Hartwig's service number and rank. The Jewish interpreter waited for Hartwig's confirmation.

The officer looked up, staring straight at Hartwig. 'I have your discharge papers here,' he said, waving a document in front of Hartwig. 'However, you will sign this document before you are released.' The officer held out a pen and continued. 'You undertake not to tell anyone, no matter who it may be...family, friends, acquaintances, the press...particularly the press, about what you have seen and experienced in this camp. If you do, you will be rearrested. Do I make myself absolutely clear?'

Hartwig barely heard what the interpreter was saying, his mind in turmoil, the only word he had heard clearly being 'release'. He took the pen, nodding, signing the document in front of him. The officer then handed him the discharge papers and Hartwig stuffed them into his pocket.

A soldier came up to him, and pointed towards the gate. Hartwig walked forward, the gate opening as he approached, Hartwig walking through. His heart beat faster as he started to walk along the muddy track, passing the huts on either side, not daring to look at them, staring straight ahead. Hartwig felt the papers in his pocket, sure that he was not dreaming, waiting for the machine gun to open fire. He passed the last hut and stumbled as the track started to drop down, following it round a bend, seeing the woods on either side. Hartwig reached the woods and slumped down on a fallen branch, the warmth of his urine running down his legs. He started to moan, then sob, his head on his arms, folded across his knees, not believing that, at last, he had been released, that he had survived the camp.

Chapter Ten

Dipping the cloth into the warm water and then wringing it out, Brigitte carefully touched her swollen face, noticing the scabs across the back of her hands and the fingernail hanging from her little finger.

'Let me help you,' Frau Eichel said, taking the cloth from Brigitte and very gently dabbing Brigitte's face. 'You've got bruising and you will definitely have a black eye but, apart from that, there doesn't seem to be any more physical damage.'

'My finger hurts the most. Can you get rid of the nail?'

Frau Eichel looked down at Brigitte's hand, taking it in her own. 'Look away.'

Brigitte let out a low moan, feeling the stab of pain as Frau Eichel yanked the nail off, quickly dipping the finger into the bowl and then winding a strip of clean linen round it, tying it. 'That's better,' Brigitte said.

Nodding, Frau Eichel continued to bathe Brigitte's face. 'What happened?'

'Gisela and I had managed to get four sacks of food, which we had to carry and drag back to the station. We managed to get on a train, standing in the corridor and we were making steady progress, passing through Minden when the train stopped.' Brigitte took a long sip of water, then continued. 'Tommies had boarded the train and were just going through everyone's belongings, confiscating food, valuables, everything.'

Frau Eichel looked at Brigitte. 'Why? They don't need the food.'

'I know. Anyway, I could see them coming and I managed to get two of our sacks out through the window and drop them down beside the track. Gisela started crying and I told her to shut up. When the Tommies got to us, they could see we had two sacks which they opened and then tipped the contents out through the window, despite my pleading with them, telling them I had a baby to feed.' Brigitte paused. 'The soldier nearest to me told me that they had been given orders but, I must say, he did seem to be embarrassed about it. When the soldiers moved into the next carriage, I clambered out of the window and started to refill the sacks. The trouble was, others were intent on getting the food and I had to fight like a demon. I screamed out at Gisela to take the sacks from me as I got them but the stupid girl was sitting on the floor crying. Another woman helped me, pulling the sacks into the carriage.'

Frau Eichel shook her head. 'She really is a stupid girl. I blame her parents for spoiling her. Her father doted on her, buying her whatever she wanted, never asking her to do anything in return. That was all right until he got sent away to serve in the Volksturm and her mother disappeared shortly afterwards. Never could quiet understand that and I certainly wouldn't ask Gisela. Anyway, how did you end up with all these cuts and bruises?'

Brigitte sipped her water and took a deep sigh. 'I'd just about filled the third sack when the train started to move forward and I tried pushing it up the side of the carriage for the woman to take it. Just as her hands reached the sack, I tripped on a sleeper and fell over, narrowly missing the carriage wheels. I rolled away from the track and knew I'd smacked my face, hands and knees against the cinders and you know how rough they are. Then I panicked, getting up as quickly as I could, fearful that I would be left behind. I ran alongside the train and tripped again, landing heavily. I was winded and could see the train gathering speed, knowing, after all our efforts, I was going to be left behind. Then a man jumped off the running board and helped me to my feet. He almost threw me onto the train...well, the running board and I clung on until the train stopped at Nienburg.'

'You poor girl.' Frau Eichel said, looking up as she dabbed Brigitte's shins. 'Did you manage to get into the carriage again?'

Brigitte shook her head. 'It was far too crowded. I had to hang on to the outside all the way to Buchholz. It was very cold and my fingers and hands were stiff and numb, my body ached all over and I could feel the blood trickling down my face and legs. But I knew I had to get back...get back to Heinz.'

'And what happened to Gisela?' Frau Eichel prompted.

Wiping a tear from her eye, Brigitte sighed. 'At Buchholz I managed to get inside the carriage I had been clinging to but it was at least four or five carriages from where I had left Gisela. I tried to make my way through the throng but only managed to get as far as the adjoining carriage before we arrived here at the Hauptbahnhof. As soon as the train stopped I got off and ran along to the carriage I thought Gisela was in. I eventually got into the carriage but there was no sign of Gisela or our sacks. I asked people if they had seen her but nobody had. I ran out of the station and looked along the road. I don't know where she is or what happened to her.'

Patting Brigitte's knee, Frau Eichel stood up. 'She'll turn up. Probably got off at Buchholz. You know how stupid she is.'

'I hope you are right.' Brigitte leant forward, staring at the floor, feeling suddenly very weary. 'And I haven't even managed to bring home any food.'

'At least you are here. There's always tomorrow,' Frau Eichel said, as she made her way towards the kitchen.

Slipping his hand underneath Mary's skirt and feeling the tops of her stockings, her soft flesh warm to his touch, Colin suddenly felt very hot, perspiration running down the side of his face. Lying on the rug, Mary looked up at him, her eyes closed, her lips parted, moving her hips against his hand. Colin struggled with his free hand to loosen his tie and unbutton his shirt, feeling his heart racing. He gave up, lowering his lips to Mary's, kissing her passionately, pushing his tongue into her welcoming mouth. Then his hand felt her panties, feeling the mound of her womanhood, the softness of her lips. He stopped suddenly, getting up and unbuttoning his trousers, pulling them and his pants down to his knees, stumbling and falling on top of Mary. He yanked at her skirt, pulling it up and clumsily tried to pull her pants down.

'Wait! Wait. Haven't you forgotten something?' Mary said, smiling at him, staring at his erection.

Colin looked puzzled. 'What?'

'Just a minute.' Mary leant across to her bag and fumbled inside it, pulling out a small packet. 'You need one of these. We don't want babies, do we?'

Taking the packet, Colin took out a condom and looked at it, not sure what to do next.

'Put it on,' Mary whispered, nuzzling his ear, her warm breath encouraging Colin.

'I'm not...well, I haven't...'

Mary giggled. 'This is your first time? Give it to me.' She took the condom and rolled it on, then she pulled her pants down, lying back on the rug.

Colin's eyes bulged at the sight of Mary's womanhood. He fell on top of her, trying to push himself inside. Mary moved her hips and, using her hand, guided him in. Colin thrust forward, groaning, feeling the tightness of Mary, feeling his orgasm coming.

'Oh God. Oh God. Oh...this is...'

Mary kissed him hard on the lips, moaning, encouraging him, feeling his ejaculation.

They lay motionless, Colin breathing heavily, realising for the first time in his life, what it was like to make love to a woman. He felt ecstatic, he felt like a real man, he felt he had met his one and only love. He kissed her on her lips, her cheeks, her eyelids, her ears. He felt so close to her. He wanted to hold her in his arms forever.

Mary squirmed underneath him and Colin rolled off, lying down beside her.

'I've wanted to do that ever since we went on the picnic three weeks ago,' Colin murmured. 'I haven't thought about anything else. I've...I've just thought about you ever since we kissed that first time down by the river. I just can't...'

'I know what you are trying to say,' Mary cut in. 'I have also spent a lot of time thinking about you. You are so caring and considerate. You really are a nice person.'

Colin raised himself on his elbow, leant over and started to kiss Mary on the lips, her arms going round his neck. He broke free of her embrace. 'I think I'll use that other one in the packet.'

When the cell door opened and three Tommies entered, Dieter was almost relieved. The past weeks, being held in solitary confinement with nobody coming into the cell or talking to him, was starting to affect him. He knew he was starting to hallucinate, starting to imagine another person was present, starting to hold conversations with himself.

'Christ! The filthy bugger, he's crapped all over the effing floor,' one of the soldiers said. 'We'll have to teach the Jerry some manners.'

Dieter stood, swaying slightly, looking uncomprehendingly at the Tommies.

One of the soldiers stepped forward. 'You disgusting little Nazi. Come...come with us.' He walked behind Dieter and pushed him towards the door.

'Essen...Wasser und Essen, bitte?' Dieter asked as he stumbled forward.

'What's he say?'

'Don't matter. Just take him to the interrogation room,' his colleague answered.

Entering the corridor for the first time since he had arrived, Dieter could see the line of cell doors on each side, firmly closed, no doubt others being held behind them in similar conditions. The sudden pain across Dieter's lower back forced him to his hands and knees, gasping. The unexpected kick from a hobnailed boot caught him in the stomach, making him retch. Apart from his own groans, Dieter was aware of the laughter of the Tommies.

'Get up! Get up you effing Nazi bastard!' one of the soldiers screamed at him. Dieter struggled to get to his feet, clawing at the wall, eventually standing up. He felt a push from behind and staggered forwards. He glanced at the man nearest to him, seeing the hatred in his eyes and the length of heavy rubber tube dangling from his hand. One of the Tommies walked in front of Dieter, opening a door and indicating for him to go in. The room was large with a table near the far wall, three chairs placed behind it. Two officers and a sergeant sat looking at Dieter as he entered. In the middle of the room was a three-legged stool and nearer the door another table with metal loops bolted to each corner.

'Sit down' the officer said, indicating the stool.

Dieter frowned, feeling a shove in his back from one of the soldiers. He sat on the stool and looked at the men in front of him. The thin-faced officer started to ask him for his name, rank, service number, regiment and other basic details. Again, Dieter looked baffled. The sergeant translated, using poor German and Dieter answered the questions, waiting for the sergeant to tell the officer. Dieter knew he held a considerable advantage if he maintained his feigned ignorance of English as it gave him time to formulate his answers. He noticed the younger officer writing down what was being said in the folder in front of him.

Thin-face asked him where he had served, in which campaigns, under whose command and when and how he was captured. Dieter answered truthfully.

'Tell me about your time at Oderblick,' Thin-face said, his sharp blue eyes studying Dieter carefully.

The sergeant translated, Dieter trying to remain calm before stating that he had never been to Oderblick and did not know where it was.

Thin-face nodded. The blow across Dieter's back sent him sprawling across the floor, curling his body up defensively as the Tommies started kicking him as hard as they could. He felt the kicks against his spine and shins, the ones on his arms, bent round, protecting his head.

'Stop!' Thin-face ordered, the soldiers backing away, breathing heavily. Dieter lay still, hearing the footsteps of the sergeant as he approached. The sergeant pushed his arm to one side and painfully grasped his ear between his sharp nails, pulling Dieter to his feet. The sergeant stared into Dieter's eyes, then spat into his face before yanking him across to the stool and forcing him to sit.

Thin-face continued. 'We know you are formerly a member of the Gestapo guard and that you committed acts of atrocity against those prisoners under your supervision. Admit to this and provide me with a full account of your actions.'

'Whoever provided you with this information is lying,' Dieter replied after the sergeant had translated. 'I am…was, a sergeant in the Wehrmacht, attached to 2 Panzer Division. I have no idea what…'

The swish of the rubber tube, striking Dieter across the side of his head, knocked him senseless. As he lay on the floor, he was aware of more blows raining down on his body and then he felt hands around his wrists and being dragged out of the room and back along the corridor, his knees and feet scraping against the rough floor. He noticed a metal grating in the floor as he was dragged over it, seeing water flowing some five feet below. He was dragged into his cell and left on the floor. Suddenly, a bucket of cold water was thrown over him, bringing him fully to his senses. Another bucket followed, drenching him completely. A ragged piece of cloth was thrown in his face and he was ordered to clean his cell. The door slammed shut and he heard the key turning in the lock.

Easing himself into a sitting position, his body starting to shake as the damp and cold penetrated, Dieter looked at the soaking floor. He realised that this was the start of his interrogation, that more pain was to come. He crawled across to the bench and got onto it, trying to unbutton his shirt. He knew he had to get his clothes off and let them dry out otherwise he would catch pneumonia. His body ached all over and he could feel the bruises swelling up on his back. He knew he could not survive for long taking this level of punishment. He knew he had to do something before he was too weak, physically and mentally.

Gagging on the sock that had been shoved into her mouth, Gisela could not scream. Her tears flowed down her face and the handcuffs around her wrist cut into her flesh as she lay, face down, across the bed. The man behind her pushed his fingers inside her, laughing and then she felt him enter her, thrusting hard, satisfying himself. He withdrew and another man took his place. Gisela lost count of how many men had her, praying this torment would end, praying that she would die. Eventually, she fainted.

When she came round, there was no light, the room in total darkness. She eased herself onto her back, realising that the handcuffs had been removed, gently touching her wrist and grimacing. She could feel the pain and stickiness between her legs and the soreness inside. How had this happened, she asked herself, thinking back to the time when she had got off the train. She had seen people taking the sacks of food and knew Brigitte would be angry with her, deciding to get back to Frau Eichel's before Brigitte in the hope that Frau Eichel would protect her from Brigitte's wrath. As she ran from the station, she saw a man across the street start to run after her and, panicking, she had turned into a side street, running as fast as she could. The man had soon caught up with her and had grabbed her arm, stopping her. He had asked her why she was running, speaking quietly to her, his accent clearly not German. She had cried and he had gently put his arms around her, soothing her. She had told him what had happened and he had said he could help her, that it would be best if she went back to his home with his family where she could stay for the night. He would provide food and go with her tomorrow to see Brigitte. Gisela had agreed.

Walking along the streets, the man had laughed and joked with Gisela, telling her that she was very beautiful and that he could get her some nice clothes to wear. They had approached a cellar entrance and when Gisela looked unsure, the man had smiled and taken her hand, leading her down the stairs. Only when the steel door closed and as Gisela's eyes adjusted to the dimness of the large room did she realise that the cellar was full of men, lounging around, some looking at her, others disinterested. A very tall man had approached her, grinning, introducing himself as Cyrek.

Gisela was terrified, the flickering light from the lamp cast shadows across the man's face and beetled brow, his long dark hair enhancing the menace of his appearance. He had led her across the room, sitting her down at a table and asking if she would like something to drink. Gisela had managed to nod and the man who had walked with her brought a glass tumbler of brown coloured fluid and placed it in front of her. He introduced himself as Wicus. Gisela had tasted the drink, screwing up her face as she swallowed the bitter fluid, feeling it burn her throat. She had pushed the glass away but then, the man called Wicus, had picked it up and, leering at her, insisted she finish it as it was impolite to refuse. Gisela had shaken her head and he had grabbed her hair, forcing the glass between her lips, forcing her to drink it. Two more glasses had followed and Gisela had felt her head swimming, realising she was seeing double. When the man Cyrek had lifted her up in his arms, she had not resisted. She did not resist when he had laid her on a bed and started removing her clothes. She had not resisted when he had taken her. Only the next morning, when she awoke and immediately vomited, had she seen the teeth marks on her breasts, reminding her of what had happened. Since then, she had been kept in this room.

Getting up, Gisela felt her way towards the wash stand, a glimmer of light starting to penetrate the darkness. She poured water into the bowl and started to carefully wash herself, feeling the tenderness around her vaginal lips, the soreness of her anus. She went back to the bed, using a blanket to dry herself. She could not see any of her clothes. Shivering, she climbed onto the bed and wrapped a blanket around herself, clinging to her knees, wondering what was going to happen next, when these men would be done with her, would they ever let her go. Gisela could feel the tears rising in her eyes, her mouth quivering as she started to cry, wishing Brigitte would come and find her.

Chapter Eleven

Slamming the cab door shut as he sat on the seat, Bill Thornton reached into his breast pocket and took the black notebook out. He opened it, pulling the pencil from the spine and entered the amount of the sterling postal order he had just collected from the field cashiers office. He glanced at the running total column and smiled broadly, seeing that he had already sent home four thousand pounds within six months, more than he could earn in ten years before the war. Bill knew he was going to be a very rich man by the time he had finished his service in Germany. The Germans were desperate for cigarettes and he was happy to supply them. He could sell a packet of twenty for at least two pounds, sometimes as much as five pounds and they only cost him three pence a packet, that's when he had to pay for them. Fools like Colin, and there were still plenty around who gave away their rations, lowered Bill's average cost to below two pence a packet. It was the same for the bottles of whisky and gin – Bill could get from twenty to thirty pounds a bottle. It was easy money if you knew how to go about it and Bill now had a good network going.

Glancing at his watch, Bill started the engine and set off, lighting a cigarette. He left Osnabruck, driving towards Munster, feeling the tingle of anticipation in his stomach increasing as he drove along. As he reached the town, he saw the barrier ahead, smiling to himself as a corporal waved him down. Bill handed over his identity card and the letter confirming his meeting with the Burgermeister to detail the requisitioning of houses. The corporal waved him through, Bill grinning, pleased that his forged letter had passed. With access to the right letter headed paper and with the amount of confusion around, it was simple for him to type out letters and sign them off using a false name.

Bill saw the jeep parked outside a butcher's shop and pulled in behind it. He felt the Webley in its holster and leaned across the cab, pushing the Sten gun under the passenger seat. Glancing in the wing mirrors then looking along the street, Bill was satisfied nobody was watching. He got down from the cab and strode into the butcher's shop. A ruddy faced man looked up and nodded towards the door at the rear, Bill going through.

'Hi Bill. Glad you made it,' Lanky called out as he stood up. He shook hands with Bill.

'Who are they?' Bill pointed at two men lounging near the back of the room talking to Shorty.

Lanky grinned. 'It's OK Bill, they're friends.'

'So, what's the meeting about?'

'In a hurry?' Shorty asked as he came over, also shaking Bill's hand. 'Have a drink.' He held out a bottle of beer and Bill took it. 'That shipment you brought last week...it was good. The insulin made a good price so here's your take.' Shorty passed a large brown envelope to Bill.

'Now Bill, we gotta ask if you can help us,' Lanky said. 'We've got a few shipments that need to be taken up to Lubeck and, as you know, our papers wouldn't cover us.'

'So, we thought our buddy Bill could help us,' Shorty cut in.

Bill frowned. 'What's in the shipment?'

Shorty smiled. 'Usual Bill...unwanted soldiers rations. But we've got this contact up there who's telling us there's more money to be made. That's more for us and more for you, if you catch my drift buddy.'

Pausing, Bill thought for a moment or two. 'Supposing I can fix the paperwork, when do you want this doing?'

'Next week. In Osnabruck,' Lanky said, placing his arm around Bill's shoulders. 'We can then swap your shipment with ours and go our own ways.'

'But I may not be able to get the paperwork sorted by then,' Bill said.

Shorty moved and stood in front of Bill, staring at him, Bill suddenly feeling uncomfortable. 'Bill, here's a little bonus. I'm sure that will make sure everything is in order.'

Shorty placed another envelope in Bill's hand. 'We'll see you next week.'

Lanky walked Bill to the door, shook his hand and went back into the room. Bill walked quickly through the shop and got back into the truck. He tore open the second envelope and looked inside, his eyes bulging. Leafing through the notes, he reckoned there was at least a thousand pounds. He stuffed the envelope inside his tunic top and set off.

Glancing discretely across at the captain, over the top of her wine glass, Hannelore noticed how fine his features were, his blond hair flopping over his forehead, his moustache covered by the froth from the beer he was sipping, making Hannelore smile. She noticed his powerful arms and his bulging thighs, surprising herself as she realised she was becoming attracted to this man, the man who had walked in a few weeks before and commandeered her home. However, he had always been scrupulously polite and as considerate as possible, leaving his room clean and tidy. Even Hannelore's mother had been won round, fussing to offer him tea or coffee whenever he returned. His presence certainly made Hannelore feel more secure and she hoped that he would stay for some time, especially as he brought the added bonus of extra food and other rations. She had heard reports that there were still many gangs of men – forced labourers, former POW's, displaced persons and those evading capture - roaming the countryside and preying on the small villages and towns. Hannelore had dealt with the men of the captain's company - most of them, including the captain, well on the way to being cured of the venereal disease they had arrived with.

'This is rather a good beer,' the captain said. 'Is it local?'

'It's a pils and yes, it is brewed nearby.'

The captain stood up. 'I think I've been rather impolite Doctor. I should have introduced myself earlier but we are under strict orders not to fraternise with the locals…if you understand what I mean. I'm Captain Jagger…James Jagger.' He walked across to Hannelore and stuck out his hand.

Hannelore shook his outstretched hand, feeling the power of the man. 'Hannelore Gerber. Little late for introductions Captain Jagger. After all, I have seen rather a lot of you and your men,' she joked.

Jagger blushed slightly. 'Well…well, be that as it may. You are a Doctor.'

'Sit down and enjoy your pils Captain.' Hannelore wiped her finger across her top lip, indicating to Jagger that he should do the same.

Jagger burst out laughing when he looked at his finger, seeing the froth. 'I must have looked a fool.' He sat down.

'Have you been in Germany for long?'

'I came over at the beginning of the year, couple of months before the surrender,' Jagger replied. 'Wasn't at the front line, had other things to do.'

Hannelore was intrigued. 'Such as?'

'Can't say.' Jagger snapped, seeing Hannelore flinch. 'Sorry, I didn't mean to upset you Doctor.'

'Please…please call me Hannelore.'

Jagger smiled. 'Should have a shipment arriving tomorrow and I've requested a few extra items, both medical and other. I think you will be pleased.'

'You have been very kind to my mother and myself already Captain. Whatever we receive we are extremely grateful for.' Hannelore decided to change the subject. 'Do you miss your family?' Jagger's jaw muscles tightened. He looked at Hannelore and she could see the hurt in his eyes.

'What I have seen during the past few months has shocked and disgusted me,' Jagger said, after a long pause. 'The absolute devastation of your country is almost beyond comprehension. Before I had witnessed the damage we have done to Germany, I came here with revenge in my heart. Now, I realise that we are mere pawns in a game played out by madmen. War is ridiculous. It is stupid and what does it ever achieve in the long run? After the last war, the war to end all wars we were told, within twenty years, it all started again.' Jagger shook his head. 'Crazy. And now, we are expected to pick up the pieces and carry on as normal as possible.'

Hannelore sipped her wine. 'I have heard about the damage to our cities and I've visited Hamburg. During the war Goebbels and his propaganda ministry never told the truth. Yet I saw what happened to Hamburg. It was awful.'

'You asked if I missed my family,' Jagger said. 'Yes...every day I think about them.' He lowered his head, his voice barely audible. 'My wife and son were killed in Coventry during a bombing raid.'

Hannelore stared at him, her mouth agape. 'I'm...I don't know what to say.'

Emptying his glass, Jagger stood up. 'Think I'll go to my room.' He walked out.

Another bucket of cold water was thrown into the cell, splashing across the concrete floor, the soldier yelling at Dieter to start mopping it up. Dieter staggered to his feet, feeling his body protest, feeling every bruise the Tommies had inflicted. Of more concern at this time was the fact that his feet had lost all feeling, his toes were permanently white with blotches and no matter what he did, he could not get them warm. Dieter had seen men suffering from frostbite in Russia and he knew his toes would soon be affected. He walked across the wet floor and using the rag they had provided, started to mop up the water, squeezing the rag over the bucket. At least, Dieter thought, my clothes have dried out and it is not as cold as it could be. He had soon filled the bucket, returning to the bench and grasping his feet between his hands, rubbing and massaging his toes before pulling on what remained of his socks.

Dieter heard the voices of the men as they came along the corridor, his stomach tightening, praying they would pass his cell, blotting out the thought that some other poor unfortunate was going to be taken. The jangle of keys followed by the lock on his door being turned, caused Dieter to feel panic for a few seconds, then he forced himself to take a deep breath, calming himself.

'Get up you Nazi shit,' the Tommy shouted as he entered the cell. Come, come.' He gestured towards the door.

Standing up slowly, Dieter moved towards the door, hobbling on his feet. As he passed the soldier, the man stamped on his foot. Dieter yelled out, falling to the floor, clasping his damaged foot, tears running down his cheeks. Hands grabbed his arms, roughly lifting him up and dragging him out into the corridor. He was taken to the interrogation room where the thin-faced officer was sitting at the table and forced to sit on the stool. The officer started by asking the same questions as the last time, Dieter answering.

Thin-face looked at him, almost pityingly. 'Tell me how you became a member of the Gestapo.'

Dieter listened as the sergeant repeated the question. 'I have told you and I will keep on telling you, I am not and never have been involved with the Gestapo. I can tell you exactly where I have been on active service for the past three or four years and, as I have told you...'

The rubber tube hit Dieter hard across the neck, knocking him to the floor, gasping for breath. The Tommy nearest to him aimed a kick at his groin, catching the inside top of his thigh, Dieter curling up to protect himself. Hands again grabbed him and lifted him onto the table behind him, his arms and legs being manacled to the corners. The sergeant came across, grinning at Dieter, then attaching metal hoops around his calves. He started to do something, similar to turning a screw, Dieter could not quite see what. Then Dieter felt the pressure on his shin bone, the metal point hurting. Walking round the table, the sergeant did the same with the other hoop, Dieter feeling the sweat coursing down his face, forcing him to blink, trying to clear his eyes.

'Tell me what your duties were at Oderblick,' Thin-face asked.

'How many times have I got to tell you. I have never been to this place, I've...' It took Dieter a moment to realise that the scream was his own. The pain from his legs exploded in his brain as the shin screws penetrated the skin, biting into his bones. His breath was coming in short spurts.

Thin-face continued. 'Tell me what your duties were. If you continue this pretence...continue to lie to me, then I can assure you, you will suffer a lot more pain.'

The thought flashed through Dieter's mind to tell them whatever they wanted to hear, admit to anything so long as they stopped this torture. He immediately knew such an admission would be a death sentence. 'I cannot confess to something that I have not done.'

'We have witnesses who have identified you as Gestapo and that you were at Oderblick,' Thin-face replied.

Dieter breathed out. 'They are lying or they are mistaken. I don't know...' The screws were turned, the pain unbearable as the metal pins started to grind into his bones.

Thin-face appeared, looking down at Dieter. 'I have given you every chance to tell me what I want to know. I'm starting to lose my patience with you.' Thin-face walked away.

The sergeant appeared, still grinning, then suddenly a wet cloth was placed over Dieter's face and held down firmly, preventing Dieter from turning his head. He fought for breath, the cloth preventing him. He struggled, his mind in confusion, telling him he was going to die, his brain screaming for oxygen. He lost consciousness.

Even with a cool November breeze, swirling the dust into their eyes, the women felt warm, handing each brick and stone along the line as they cleared a building site of debris. It was nearing the end of a long day and Brigitte was looking forward to getting home and bathing, removing the filth from her face where the dust had stuck to her moist skin. Her eyes were sore from specks of grit and she could feel the stiffness already in her back, across her shoulders and through her arms and legs. There was little time to look around as everyone had to concentrate, receiving a brick in the left hand, transferring it to the right and passing it on. There was no time to stop and the overseers kept the women working for three hours at a time, allowing a fifteen-minute break then carrying on. Brigitte knew she would dream through the night of passing brick after brick, never stopping, getting faster. It was monotonous work but at least Brigitte had a ration card that provided her with larger quantities than before. It was still not enough to live on and there were frequent supply failures resulting in people going hungry for days at a time. Most people looked malnourished, their faces gaunt and their eyes dull and sunken.

A loud blast on a whistle startled Brigitte and she dropped the brick in her hand, as did all the other women in the chain. Goodness knows how many bricks and stones had been moved during the day Brigitte thought as she scrabbled down from the pile of debris she had spent the day standing on. She moved at a quick pace, keen to get to the bakery before it closed. She soon reached the end of the street and turning the corner, she was pleased to see that the queue was only short.

Taking her place, she waited, noticing the people coming out of the bakery, clutching bread under their arms. A young man in front of her glanced round, grimaced and spat into the gutter. Brigitte smiled to herself, thinking she must look like an old hag. Looking round, Brigitte saw the approaching Tommies, four of them, her heart beating quicker. She lowered her head, looking at the heels of the man's shoes in front of her. The Tommies arrived by her side, one of them reaching out and placing his hand under her chin, pushing her head up. He looked at her face, sneered and moved on. They stopped further down the queue, looking at a girl of about sixteen Brigitte thought, as she watched surreptitiously. The girl tried to look away but the Tommy grabbed her by the arm and yanked her into the street. He asked for her papers and the girl handed them to him. He glanced at the document, handed it back and asked if she wanted chocolates or cigarettes. The girl, obviously not comprehending, nodded her head. The Tommy grinned at her, suggesting she had to offer something in return, the girl looking terrified and bewildered. The Tommies started to push the girl backwards and forwards between them, making crude jokes and suggestive remarks. Brigitte glanced at the men in the queue, some old, some her age, some youths. Not one of them was looking, all of them looking down. Brigitte felt the anger rising inside; the men of Germany were broken and spineless. She knew many had been through horrendous experiences but she did not believe this could be used as an excuse. So had the women and children.

'She doesn't understand you,' Brigitte said, stepping towards the Tommies.

They stopped pushing the girl and looked at Brigitte, slightly astonished. 'What's it got to do with you?' one of them asked. 'Bugger off before I sort you out.'

'Nah. She ain't worth it, mate...effing old bag...wouldn't fancy fraggin that, me dick might drop off.' All four Tommies roared with laughter.

'The girl does not understand what you mean,' Brigitte persisted. 'Please leave her in peace.'

'In peace...you mean whole?' one of the Tommies asked.

Brigitte frowned. 'Sorry, I don't understand you.'

The Tommies laughed. 'Eff off you stupid cow,' one of them said, approaching her. Holding his rifle in his left hand, Brigitte saw him clenching his right fist, swinging at her. She managed to turn her head as his fist skimmed past, causing her to stumble back onto the pavement. Brigitte turned away and walked back to her place in the queue. Surprisingly, Brigitte felt calm inside even though her heart was beating faster. The Tommies shouted out a few abuses and then they decided to move on, leaving the girl to rejoin the queue. Brigitte saw the girl nod her thanks, smiling back at the girl.

Leaving the shop with two small loaves of bread tucked under her arm, Brigitte started to walk home. She thought about Gisela, wondering what might have happened to her. Frau Eichel had told Brigitte to stop worrying, she was sure Gisela had found someone to stay with in Buchholz who was looking after her and that sooner or later, she would turn up. Brigitte was not as certain.

As the light rain fell, Hartwig remained motionless, watching the rabbits skit about on the opposite bank, nipping in and out of their burrows, sniffing the air, wary of predators. He could feel the dampness of the earth beneath him but it did not affect his concentration, his eyes fastened on the snare placed in front of a hole that Hartwig was sure was in use. When a rabbit came running out and the snare caught it round the neck, Hartwig was on his feet, running across the clearing, rabbits scurrying off in all directions. He grabbed the squealing rabbit, held its rear legs and smashed its head on the ground, silencing it. After a few death kicks, the rabbit hung limp in his hand. He removed the snare, tucking it into his belt and set off back towards his campsite.

'What do you think of that?' Hartwig said as he approached a man hunched over a fire.

The man looked up, nodded and smiled. 'It will keep us going for a day or so. Pass it over and I will skin it.'

Hartwig handed the rabbit to the man and sat down on a log, removing his boots. He helped himself to some water and held his hands out, warming them, watching the man as he quickly skinned and disembowelled the rabbit, cutting it into chunks and placing two legs, the heart, liver and kidneys into a can of water then hanging it over the fire.

The man stood up. 'Keep an eye on it...don't let it boil over,' he said, nodding towards the can. 'I'm going for a walk.'

Watching the man as he disappeared into the woods, Hartwig smiled to himself. When he had left the camp, he had spent the following day stumbling around the forest, not knowing what he was doing, where he was or in which direction to head. He had been so weak he had fallen many times, struggling each time to regain his feet. Eventually, with no water or food, he had fallen and lost consciousness. When he came round, he had found himself here, in a small clearing. A man, who never introduced himself, had offered him some food and Hartwig had greedily eaten it, suffering stomach cramps and vomiting shortly afterwards. The man had told him that he could only eat small amounts, that he had to wait for his body to adjust to food again. During the next week, Hartwig had followed the man's advice and had managed to eat a little more each day, suffering from bouts of diarrhoea but his strength was returning as he managed to walk further without feeling dizzy or nauseous. The man had provided a change of clothes, Hartwig washing in the stream running close by and, even though the water was cold, he had bathed each day, getting rid of the lice and flees. With his clean clothes, his hair cut and his beard removed, Hartwig felt like a new man. He knew he needed to find some decent boots and then he would be ready to continue his journey.

The hissing of water broke Hartwig's thoughts, making him get up and lift the can from the fire. He looked inside and, using a sharpened piece of wood, he picked out one of the legs. Blowing on it he took a small bite, realising it needed a little longer before it was ready. He put it back into the can and placed the can back on the fire.

Hearing footsteps behind him, Hartwig turned, seeing the man approaching, carrying a turnip. 'Where did you find that?'

The man sat down and started to cut the turnip into pieces. 'About a kilometre away the forest stops and there are fields. Found it there.'

'Well the rabbit is about done…shall I take it off?'

The man nodded, tasting a piece of the turnip. 'Can eat this as it is.'

The two men sat opposite each other, eating in silence, Hartwig enjoying the flavour of the rabbit but not the turnip. He forced himself to eat everything, sipping the water from the can and feeling satisfied.

'What are you going to do?' the man asked.

'I have to make my way to Erfurt where my family live,' Hartwig replied. 'Probably go via Magdeburg.'

The man shook his head. 'Wouldn't try that.'

'Why not, it's the most direct route.'

'If you want to meet the Russkies, yes,' the man said. 'Suggest you stay west of Wolfsburg, heading for Frankfurt, then chance your luck turning east towards Erfurt.'

Harwig frowned. 'Are you telling me the Russians control Erfurt?'

The man nodded.

'Shit!' Hartwig felt the fear grip his stomach as he thought about his wife. He had heard the stories going round the camp about the Russians and how they had treated German women. 'How do you know this?'

'I just do. The Russians have the provinces of Sachsen Anhalt, Thuringen and all land east under their control.'

'But that's half of Germany,' Hartwig protested.

The man nodded. 'A fair piece I'd say.'

Hartwig sat in silence, thinking through what he had just heard. 'I will have to leave tomorrow. I must find my wife and...and my son.'

'You will need some of these,' the man said, taking a wad of Reichmark's from inside his coat. He took a quantity from the wad and offered them to Hartwig.

'I can't take your money,' Hartwig said. 'I can't repay you. You've already saved my life.'

'Take them,' the man insisted. 'They are not worth much but it should be enough for you to get a train ticket to Kassel.'

Hartwig took the notes and tucked them into his pocket. 'What will you do?'

The man grinned. 'Stay here.' He turned away from Hartwig and pulled his coat around himself, lying down.

With the embers glowing, Hartwig did the same, thinking about tomorrow.

Chapter Twelve

The sudden flapping of bird's wings startled Walbert and Ernst as they walked along, the partially concealed moon throwing an eerie light across the flat, featureless landscape around them. Ernst nervously snatched at Walbert's arm.

'This place frightens me Wally. Can't we go another way?' he asked.

Walbert stopped walking. 'Do you want to end up like those soldiers we saw...in a hole in the ground?'

Sniffling and rubbing the tears from his eyes, Ernst shook his head.

'If I'm right,' Walbert said, 'we are getting close to the Schaalsee. That's why those birds took off...must have been seagulls or ducks or something like that.'

'What does that mean?' Ernst asked. 'When are we going to get to Hamburg?'

Walbert looked at his brother, his face dark in the dim light. 'You have done very well Ernst. I know it's been a long walk but we won't be many more days now before we reach our great-aunt.'

'I'm hungry,' Ernst whined, 'and why do we have to always walk at night? I can't see a thing.'

Walbert sighed. 'Oh, Ernst. We've been through this countless times. It's too dangerous to walk in the daytime. There are people moving in all directions...you've seen them and we...'

'They can't all be bad or Russkies,' Ernst cut in.

'And you can tell? Just by looking? Who is who?' Walbert snapped.

Ernst lowered his head. 'Well, I'm fed up. And my feet hurt.'

Walbert started walking forward, trying to see the ground beneath his feet, testing each step, waiting for his foot to sink into the mud. The boys carried on in silence, the only sound they could hear was the sound of the light wind through the reeds. Walbert tried to maintain a westerly direction but every time he felt the ground softening, he deviated, trying to stay on the firmer ground. He could just make out a mound ahead of him and he walked up it, stopping as he reached the top. He was certain the blackness stretching out in front of him was the lake. He sat down and opened his sack, taking out the last of the dried fruit he had taken from home.

'Have some of this,' Walbert said as Ernst sat down beside him. 'I'll leave the shotgun and the sack with you whilst I go and see where we can cross the lake.'

'Don't leave me,' Ernst said, obviously alarmed.

Walbert smiled. 'I'll be quicker if you stay here. I won't be gone too long.' He eased himself up and went down the mound, disappearing into the long reeds. The ground was getting softer as he moved carefully forward, sucking at his boots. He continued, coming to the edge of the reeds, splashing the water at the edge of the lake. Bending down, Walbert cupped his hands and took a few mouthfuls of the brackeny water. He started to walk along the edge, the water soon lapping at his knees. It was too dark for him to make out the far side and too cold for swimming in, not that Ernst could swim any distance anyway, he thought. Suddenly, his foot sank, forcing Walbert to throw out his arms as he plunged into the water. He kicked out, trying to turn back, feeling for the bottom, his thick coat weighing him down. He started to panic, flailing at the water, trying to get to the reeds lining the shore. He coughed as he took in a mouthful of water, disappearing underneath then surfacing and kicking out. His hands grabbed at the reeds in front of him and he tried to pull himself forward, feeling the softness of the silt beneath. Holding onto the reeds, Walbert managed to slowly haul himself through them, eventually resting on the mud, breathing heavily. He started to crawl away from the lake edge, fearful that, at any moment, he might start to sink into the mud. The ground started to get firmer and Walbert chanced standing, shivering with cold in his wet clothes. He stepped cautiously forward, finding a way through the reeds, then he started to call out for Ernst. No reply. Walbert stopped, knowing he could not have gone too far along the treacherous shore, setting off in the direction he thought would lead him back to Ernst. The thickness of the reeds hampered his progress, the tallness prevented him from seeing where he was going. Moving in a zigzag way, Walbert could feel the panic starting to rise within him, forcing himself to think rationally. Every few steps he stopped and shouted out, listening intently for Ernst reply. Carrying on, he stumbled onto a muddy track running parallel to the lake and immediately turned in Ernst direction, walking quickly. The track started to veer away from the lake but Walbert was sure he would come across the path he had taken earlier. After a mile or so, Walbert started having doubts. He could see the faint glow of the dawn in front of him and realised that he was heading away from the lake. He knew he had to turn back, that he had to find his brother and that he should strip off his wet clothes. He turned round and stumbled along the track, wiping the tears from his eyes, hoping Ernst had not moved. As he approached a bend in the track, he heard men's voices ahead, forcing him to look to both sides, seeking a way off the track and into the reeds. He saw a slight gap and darted into it, pushing his way forwards, just before the men approaching would have seen him. He sank to his haunches and waited for them to pass. A dog barked and the men's chattering stopped. Walbert froze as he heard the dog pushing through the reeds. The dog reached him, sniffing at his clothes, then started barking again, backing away from Walbert. The men shouted at the dog and eventually, it stopped barking and disappeared back through the reeds. The men walked on, laughing and joking, Walbert shivering with cold and fear. He did not understand Russian.

Slamming the door shut behind him, Colin let out a long breath. He unbuttoned his coat and removed his beret, feeling the water running down the back of his neck, under his collar. He shook his coat, letting the water drip on the floor and glanced round, seeing the rain sheeting down outside. Another wet day Colin thought, wondering when this incessant rain would stop. He walked into his office, nodding at the two men who had joined him as they looked up from their work. Colin hung his coat and beret up, then sat down, pulling the red bound folder towards him, opening it and glancing at the first page. He sat back and looked up at the ceiling, then stood up and walked across to the coffee urn, helping himself to a mug. He went back to his desk and again glanced at the folder. It was no good; all he could think about was Mary.

Ever since the day they had first made love, Colin had craved for Mary. Whenever she had to go off on her duties, he felt a hollowness inside, a desperation to run after her, a feeling of always being hot and sweaty, of nervous agitation and mental turmoil. He knew he loved her with every part of his being but was never sure of Mary's feelings towards him. Every time he saw her again he would feel a rush of adrenalin, the excitement in his stomach. He had tried to explain his feelings but Mary had laughed, telling him that he should not get so serious, that life was for living. Whenever they were together and had the opportunity, they would make love, Mary always insisting Colin wear protection. They had almost been caught in the act a few days ago when Colin had managed to convince Mary that nobody was around late in the evening when she had found him in the office. Colin had turned the lights off and Mary had provocatively bent over his desk, letting Colin slide her skirt up, over her hips, pulling her pants down and taking her. He was nearing his climax and Mary was moaning when the light in the hallway came on. Colin had quickly buttoned up his trousers, Mary pulling her skirt down when the light in the office came on and Captain Manson stood looking at them, a quizzical look on his face. He had said little, Colin knowing his face had gone bright red, his hands crossed in front of his crotch, the bulge in his trousers obvious. Manson had asked Mary to take him to the Mess, leaving Colin frustrated. That had been the last time he had seen Mary and now he was becoming desperate, longing for the moment when he could take her in his arms and kiss her, tell her he loved her, feel her smooth body against his.

'Have you got that report for me?' Manson asked Colin as he strode into the office.

Colin stood to attention. 'Yes Sir.' He handed the folder to Manson.

Manson tucked it under his arm. 'Let's go.'

Grabbing his coat and beret, Colin joined Manson, wondering where they were going, following him outside. There she was, Mary, sitting behind the wheel of the Humber car, looking the other way, Colin feeling his heart miss a beat. He reached for the rear passenger door handle to open it for Manson.

'No...think I'll sit in front,' Manson said. 'You can get in the back.'

Colin was instantly irritated and disappointed with Manson's irregular behaviour - officers always sat in the back. He got in, Mary bidding him a curt good morning.

'We're off to see that chap you visited a month or so ago,' Manson said, flicking through the file. 'That Captain Blinkey up at Nienburg. Got problems again with the Burgermeister.'

'Yes Sir,' Colin answered, hardly taking in what Manson had said, his eyes riveted to the rear-view mirror, desperate to see some form of acknowledgement from Mary's eyes, some sign that she knew he was there. Her eyes concentrated on the road ahead, the wipers flashing back and forth, clearing the rain beating down. Manson started talking to her, asking her stupid questions about her job, joking with her. Colin looked at the back of Manson's head, the thin grey hair barely covering it, feeling the jealousy boiling up inside him. He tried to ask Mary a question but Manson cut him off, talking before Mary could answer. Mary's eyes never looked in the rear-view mirror, they were either glued to the road or looking across at Manson. She smiled frequently and giggled, encouraging Manson to continue with his inanities. She even started flirting with him. Colin sat, stony faced in the back, seething with anger. Didn't she know this man was married, that he had children older than her, that he was decrepit.

The car slowed as Mary approached the large house, Colin surprised that they had arrived so quickly. Manson got out, Colin doing likewise, flashing a look of anger at Mary when she glanced round at him. The man Colin had seen before ushered them inside and led them to Blinkey's study.

'Come in, come in.' Blinkey stood up and walked around his desk, shaking Manson's hand. 'Do sit down Captain. Would you like tea, coffee...something stronger?'

Manson asked for tea, Colin standing just inside the room, listening to Blinkey telling Manson about his problems. A tap on the door behind him caused Colin to glance over his shoulder, seeing the portly Burgermeister standing there, his hands playing nervously with his cap. Blinkey beckoned the man forward, holding up his hand when the man was halfway across the room. A woman came in and placed a large silver tray on the table near Blinkey's desk, pouring out tea and coffee and offering sandwiches to Blinkey and Manson. Colin was offered a cup of tea and a sandwich, the Burgermeister stood still, totally ignored. The woman left the room.

Wiping his mouth with a napkin, Blinkey looked at Manson. 'I've tried very hard to be a good Military Governor here Manson. Tried to get these people organised...to help themselves...you understand.'

Manson nodded. 'Can't have been easy.'

'Absolutely! These Jerries don't know when they're lucky. They've got some rations arriving, houses are being repaired so most have shelter and they all have sufficient clothing. Yet this man here, this elected representative,' Blinkey said, pointing at the Burgermeister, 'continues to ignore...no, refuses to obey my instructions.'

Manson looked round at the Burgermeister for the first time. 'Can't have that. He has to obey...to the letter, all instructions you issue.'

Blinkey nodded. 'Think I should tell him that if he continues being obstructive, he will be shot.'

Manson looked at Blinkey, pondering. 'Not sure we can do that. Have him detained yes but...shot? Well, could threaten him, might get him to realise the gravity of the situation.'

Colin coughed. 'Sir, surely the people have already given you everything they possess?' Colin looked at Blinkey who smiled back.

'You're young man is too soft,' Blinkey said to Manson. 'Give these people an inch and they...'

Both men laughed.

'Tell the Burgermeister that failure to carry out my orders for the collection of all valuables and possessions, other than those items that are essential to the people...clothing but not fur coats, a few pots and pans etc., are to be brought to the house. Failure to do so will result in him being put before a firing squad.' Blinkey leant back, looking at Colin.

Looking at the Burgermeister, Colin translated, seeing the fear in the man's eyes. The Burgermeister pleaded with Colin, asking him to explain to the captain that he had already taken everything of value, that there was nothing left to take.

'See! See what I'm up against,' Blinkey shouted when Colin had finished.

The Burgermeister started talking, telling Colin that the captain had frequently raided every house in the town, had searched through them, that he knew there was nothing left, that he had already shipped everything out. Colin translated.

'What does he mean, shipped everything out?' Manson asked.

For the first time, Colin noticed Blinkey looking slightly uncomfortable. 'You are aware of the problems we are having throughout the occupied territory with the black market,' Blinkey said, Manson nodding. 'Well, the only way to stop people trading is to stop them bartering their possessions. I'm proud to say that, around here, there is no black market. I've shipped their possessions to a colleague in Bremen who has them secured in a compound until we have broken the back of the black market. Then we should be in a position to undertake reparations.'

'I understand,' Manson said, nodding. 'Commend-able...you're actions.'

'What about the abuse of the local women?' Colin asked.

Blinkey's jaw tightened and his face flushed. Then he forced a laugh. 'You've been listening to local gossip...you fool.' He looked at Manson. 'These Jerries will say anything to make us look bad. The local women are treated with re-spect and I'd have any one of my men arrested if I found out they had acted in an improper manner.'

Manson turned and looked at Colin. 'Nobody asked you for your opinions or views Sergeant Patterson. You are here to translate only...do you understand?'

Colin nodded.

'Now tell that wretched little Kraut that if he does not do as requested by Captain Blinkey, he will be shot.' Man-son turned back towards Blinkey as Colin told the Burger-meister, seeing the poor man sway, a look of total despair on his face. He left the room and Colin waited whilst Manson and Blinkey continued to talk, eat and drink.

The soldier thrust quicker and harder, Gisela trying to avoid his slobbering kisses as he pulled her hips tighter against him, groaning as he came. He withdrew, grinning at her.

'You have cigarettes?' Gisela asked, looking at the Tommy.

The soldier buttoned up his trousers and picked up his rifle. 'Don't think you were that good luv. Think I've changed me mind...maybe next time.' He turned to walk away, through the gap in the wall where a window had been, stepping over the bricks and splintered timber.

'Cigarettes...you must give,' Gisela pleaded.

'See you darlin'...next time,' the soldier replied, as he stepped back into the street.

Gisela stumbled after him. 'Cigarettes...you promised cigarettes.'

The soldier suddenly doubled up, Wicus emerging from a doorway, dropping a piece of timber. Wicus bent down and lifted the soldier to his feet, pushing him back past Gisela, into the derelict building, snapping at Gisela, telling her to pick up the rifle. He grabbed the soldier's hair and pulled his head back.

'You promised the girl cigarettes. Where are they?'

The soldier looked frightened. 'I've...I've only got a few in me pocket,' he stammered.

Wicus unbuttoned the tunic pocket and took out a pack of cigarettes, tearing it open. 'You have three cigarettes here. You have my girl and you only have three cigarettes!' Wicus smashed his fist into the soldier's face, breaking his nose.

Stifling a scream, Gisela looked on, seeing the blood pouring down the soldier's mouth and chin. She watched, mesmerised, as Wicus suddenly had a long dagger in his hand, cutting the soldier's tunic open, then ripping the man's trousers down. Wicus forced the man onto his knees and, to Gisela's horror, forced the dagger into his backside. The soldier started to scream but Wicus forced his face down, into a muddy pool of water, the soldier struggling to breathe. The struggling diminished and Wicus groaned, a look of satisfaction, even ecstasy, on his face, Gisela vomiting.

Wicus stood up, wiped his dagger on the dead soldier's tunic and slid it back into its sheath. 'Next time, you get the goods first...before you let them have you,' he snapped, punching Gisela hard on the arm. 'You stupid bitch,' he said as he pushed past her. 'Now get back to work.'

Cleaning herself as best she could and then taking a small mirror from her handbag, using the light from a bakery across the street, Gisela reapplied her lipstick and set off along the pavement, knowing that Wicus was somewhere nearby, shadowing her, watching her every move. She went towards the Atlantic Hotel, seeing the imposing building, its lights blazing out. There were a lot of people outside, mainly in uniforms, making their way into the crowded foyer, the strains of music filtering through the air. Gisela saw three Tommies staggering towards her, their arms around each others shoulders, one of them taking a long swig from a bottle of brandy. As they approached, she forced herself to smile, pulling her coat to one side, showing her legs and the short skirt she was wearing.

One of the Tommies looked at her, smiling. 'How much darlin' for a bit of fratting?'

Gisela frowned but retained her smile. 'Cigarettes...you have cigarettes?'

'Yeah,' one of the others answered. 'How many for all of us?'

'All of you? Um, a carton?' Gisela stammered.

The soldiers looked at each other, said something Gisela did not hear and burst out laughing. 'Yeah. Carton for your services,' the tallest one said. 'Come with us.'

One of the soldiers put his arm around Gisela's waist and walked away from the hotel, the other two following behind. They entered a house and climbed the stairs, entering a room on the second floor. Gisela could see that it was reasonably tidy except for soldier's clothes scattered around. One of the soldiers went across to a gramophone and started it. The music was different to anything Gisela had heard before.

A soldier unbuttoned her coat and removed it, looking appreciatively at Gisela's figure. Then he grabbed her and started, drunkenly, to dance with her. He started to kiss her, Gisela trying to turn away. The tallest one came across the room, pushed his colleague away and, taking Gisela by the hand, started to dance.

'This is jazz...have you heard it before?'

Gisela frowned, shaking her head.

'Have a drink and relax, we aren't going to hurt you,' the soldier said, moving away from her and pouring a glass of brandy. He held it out and Gisela took it, taking a long sip, then shuddering as she felt the hot liquid going down her throat. She took another sip and smiled, feeling less frightened.

The soldier started to show her how to dance and, between sips of brandy and his encouragement, Gisela started to enjoy herself. The glass was refilled at least three times, Gisela smiling and giggling. The soldier took her by the hand and led her into the adjoining room. Gisela saw the single bed, momentarily causing her to pull back. The soldier smiled at her, something in his eyes giving Gisela confidence. He took her in his arms and started to nuzzle her neck, then kissing her cheeks and forehead. He kissed her gently on the lips and Gisela could feel his body against hers. She started to respond, kissing him back, his tongue tickling her lips then slowly entering her mouth. Gisela moved her arms, placing them around his neck, pushing against him.

Suddenly, he broke away from her, pulling his tie off and unbuttoning his shirt. 'You can wash over there,' he said, pointing at a large jug and bowl standing on a table.

Gisela went across to it and poured water into the bowl. She carefully pulled her pants down and washed herself, conscious that the soldier was watching every movement she made. When she turned round she gasped. He was lying, naked on the bed, her eyes focussed on his manhood. He laughed and got up, came across to her and, taking her hand, led her back to the bed. Gisela lay down and the soldier lay beside her, kissing her on the face, neck and lips. His hand fondled her breast and then he unbuttoned her blouse, pulling the flimsy shift aside, lowering his head and kissing her breasts. His hand started to stroke the inside of her thighs and worked its way towards her womanhood. Gently, he started to stroke her moistening lips, prodding carefully at her opening, Gisela feeling herself becoming aroused. He nibbled her erect nipples, playfully swirling his tongue around them and then he moved down the bed. He started to kiss her mound, his tongue darting in and out, sucking and nibbling. Gisela could feel the intensity starting to build in her stomach, thrusting her hips up to meet his tongue, desperately wanting him to enter her. She had never known sex like this before, never had a man so gentle and considerate. She felt her orgasm contracting inside her, yelling out, gripping the man's hair, holding him tightly to her.

Breathing heavily, Gisela wiped the perspiration from her brow, her whole body tingling, her first orgasm surprising her with its intensity. The soldier stood up and Gisela saw him roll a condom on, before he eased himself between her legs and slid, easily into her. She gripped him to her, kissing him passionately, feeling him moving slowly in and out, responding to him. She could feel another orgasm starting, crying out, contracting around him, feeling him pumping into her, both of them suddenly motionless.

With the first signs of daylight peeking round the blanket covering the window, Gisela awoke with a start, momentarily unsure where she was. An arm lay across her breasts, the soldier sleeping beside her. She eased herself out of the bed and started to dress.

'Trying to creep out?'

Gisela spun round, startled, seeing the soldier propped up on an elbow smiling at her. 'I have to go.'

He got out of the bed, unaware of the effect his nakedness had on Gisela, pulling on his pants and trousers. 'You were wonderful,' he said. 'Can you come back?'

Frowning, Gisela explained she did not understand.

The soldier smiled, talking and indicating with his arms, what he meant, Gisela laughing, nodding her head. 'I come back...yes. You have cigarettes?'

The soldier laughed. 'I have cigarettes.' He went out of the bedroom, Gisela continuing to dress and then pulling her coat on. 'Here you are.'

Gisela looked round. The soldier held out a large carton of cigarettes, Gisela taking them and, spontaneously, kissing him.

'You also deserve these,' the soldier said. He held out a pair of stockings and a bottle of brandy.'

Gisela's eyes widened. 'Thank you...thank you.'

Leaving the house, Gisela looked each way along the deserted streets, feeling her stomach tighten as she looked for any sign of Wicus. She set off, heading back towards the cellar, hopeful that what she had with her would be sufficient to meet Cyrek's demands.

Chapter Thirteen

Feeling the chill of the wind blowing through the broken pane, Dieter pulled his knees up to his chest, wrapping his arms around them. His whole body trembled, a mixture of cold, fear and fatigue, Dieter knowing he could not survive much longer. He had been interrogated twice in the past few days, each time the officer asking the same questions, each time the sergeant thinking up another way to torture him, each time, regaining consciousness in his cell. Dieter moved his hand down his chin, wincing when he touched the scab forming over the hole that had been made by the shin screws. His shoulders and back ached from the blows from the rubber tubes and the kicks from the soldiers. He was managing to get some sleep, despite the light being turned on during the night and the soldiers shouting and hammering on the cell doors and he was sure he was marking off each day as it passed on the timber lath.

Dieter forced himself to think of his wife, think of their time together, think of what he would say to her when they next met. He knew he had to retain his sanity, to fight his British torturers, to somehow survive and get out of this place. But he could not keep all of his demons at bay. He would wake with a start, covered in sweat, having just seen himself being guillotined or his legs being hacked off. Even during the day thoughts would come into his mind of what they would do to him next, making his stomach twist and turn with fear.

The sound of hobnailed boots coming along the corridor broke Dieter's train of thought. He listened intently, waiting for the key in the lock, signalling it was his turn again. His body tensed, Dieter praying they would walk past. Then he heard the key being inserted, the lock turning, his heart speeding up as the door opened. Two soldiers entered, Dieter not recognising them, shouting at him to get up and come with them. Dieter frowned, remaining where he was, huddled on the bench.

'Look at the little cretin,' one of the men said. 'The pride of Hitler's lot and look at him…shitting his pants.' His colleague grinned.

'Get up you Nazi scum!' The soldier came towards Dieter, using his rifle, painfully prodding Dieter's side.

Dieter stumbled from the bench, then fell to the floor, the pain in his feet stabbing through him. One of the soldiers kicked him hard, catching him near his kidneys, making Dieter yell out. The other one stamped on his forearm. Dieter appeared to feint.

'The little shit's out cold.' One of the soldiers bent down, grabbed Dieter's hair and pulled his head back. 'Now we'll have to drag him.'

The rough floor scrapped against Dieter's knees and the tops of his feet, Dieter hanging motionless between the two men as they dragged him along the corridor. Suddenly, somebody let out a terrible scream and burst out of a cell just ahead. Soldiers rushed out behind the man, their hobnailed boots clattering along the corridor. Dieter's men let go of him, shouting and joining in the chase. Dieter lay still for a moment or two, blinking, regaining his senses. Then he saw the metal grate, inches from him. He listened. He could hear the water flowing below the grate but there was no sound of his guards. Dieter eased himself up and placed his fingers through the grate, pulling hard, expecting the grate to be firmly wedged. He fell backwards when the grating came straight out in his hands. Dieter glanced behind him then lowered himself into the hole, feeling the icy water flowing past his feet. He moved his feet around, trying to find a ledge to stand on, feeling the edge of an archway and then a row of bricks on each side. He pushed with his feet, making sure the bricks could hold his weight. Satisfied, he lowered his head and pulled the grating back over him, hearing it fall neatly into place. Dieter tried to feel further down for a foothold, suddenly slipping and falling into the flowing water, the rough brickwork skinning his elbows. In pitched darkness, his feet touched the bottom of the tunnel and Dieter could feel that the water was almost to the top, pushing hard against his back. Taking a deep breath, he eased himself down, moving with the flow, trying to keep his head near the roof as the water forced him along. His feet slipped and he went under, fighting to regain a foothold as he was swept along. He could feel his lungs heaving, desperately hanging on to the last of the air inside them, Dieter completely disorientated, fighting against blacking out.

A feeling of suddenly falling and then splashing into a deep pool registered in Dieter's mind, forcing him to kick out. He came to the surface, gulping in air, coughing. He felt around, touching the sides, realising he was in some sort of chamber. Dieter found a handhold and waited to regain his senses, letting his eyes adjust to the dark. The water was gently flowing past him and Dieter was sure he could see a glimmer of light coming from the opposite side. He let go of the wall and floated across the chamber. When he reached the wall he could feel the water flowing past him at a faster rate, disappearing along another tunnel. Dieter knew he had to take a chance. He breathed in deeply and, ducking down into the water, started to swim as hard as he could. Again, he could feel the oxygen disappearing, again his lungs started to heave when Dieter saw the light above him. He came to the surface, gasping, seeing that he was in a large pool outside a building. He swam to the edge and pulled himself out of the water, lying on the ground, breathing heavily. Dieter looked up at the building and realised that he had escaped, that he had to move quickly and find somewhere to hide before the Tommies discovered he was missing.

'Stop crying! Please...stop crying, Heinz,' Brigitte shouted.

'I'll take him with me,' Professor Ostermann said. 'We can carry on with your English lessons later.'

Brigitte sighed. 'Are you sure?'

'Absolutely. Come on Heinz, let me put your coat on and you can come with me to get some water.' The Professor smiled at Heinz who looked back at him, slightly unsure.

Brigitte got up and went across the room, picking up Heinz's coat and helping him put it on. 'Go with Professor Ostermann and help him.' She turned to the Professor. 'I will go out and see if I can get some rations.'

Frau Eichel entered the room, nodding at the Professor as he led Heinz out. She saw Brigitte putting her coat on. 'Are you all going out?'

'Heinz is getting tetchy so the Professor suggested he go with him to get some water. I'm going to get some rations…I hope,' Brigitte replied.

'Strange how the Professor has taken such an interest in the boy since he moved in,' Frau Eichel said. 'I would never have thought a man like that would like children.'

Brigitte smiled. 'Well, without Gisela, it certainly helps, especially now Heinz is walking and getting everywhere. You can't take your eyes off him for a moment.'

'That's true. Whilst you are all out, I'll get this place cleaned up.' Frau Eichel started closing the books on the table.

Leaving the apartment, Brigitte went down the stairs, humming to herself. She thought about the day, a few weeks ago, when she had seen the Professor walking along the road, stopping to talk to him, seeing how thin and gaunt he was. She had suggested he come and live with them and he had initially refused, saying he could not impose but had soon been persuaded to change his mind. Now, Brigitte was not sure she could do without him. Every evening they would read aloud through English texts, the Professor helping and encouraging her. During the day, he would go and get the water and occasionally, he would queue for bread or vegetables, giving Brigitte time to get extra provisions from the street traders. The pangs of hunger were never far away and Brigitte knew she had to keep the supplies coming, knowing she was responsible for the two older ones and Heinz.

Heading along Hopfenstrasse, Brigitte noticed the occasional person walking past, usually pulling a cart or pushing a pram, carrying wood. People were getting ready for the winter months and she realised she had better start collecting before there was no wood left to be found. She heard the noise of a vehicle approaching from behind, carrying on walking. The Jeep passed her, then pulled up.

'Can you tell me how to get to the Atlantic,' a man's voice shouted out, as she drew level.

Brigitte momentarily studied the man looking at her, seeing his American uniform. She saw two lines on his helmet, not sure what they meant. She started to tell the man the way.

'Better get in...we'll never get there,' the man said.

Brigitte felt anxious. 'I have to get rations for my baby.'

The American lithely hopped out of the Jeep. He was tall, looking down at Brigitte. 'Get in. We'll bring you back here when we've finished.'

Brigitte thought about running back along the street, glancing behind her, seeing the driver standing at the rear of the Jeep, grinning. She got into the back, the Americans getting in and setting off. They passed St. Michaelis, Brigitte seeing the church standing tall and proud, overlooking the rubble all around it and continued, going along Alter Wall, passing the Rathaus. They soon reached the Atlantic, the Americans stopping near the front doors and getting out.

'You'd better come with us,' the shorter American said, taking a firm grip of Brigitte's elbow and leading her inside.

Brigitte was amazed that the hotel appeared to be unscathed, the foyer buzzing with people. The tall American walked across to the reception and came back with a room key. 'Here, lady, take this and let yourself in. Take a bath, whatever. We have some business to attend to then we'll join you.'

Looking at the two men, Brigitte stood motionless, not sure what to do.

'Lady, we're sitting near the doors so...don't even think about getting out,' the tall one said, almost as though he was reading her mind. 'Now...get going.' He pointed towards the stairs.

Entering the room, Brigitte noticed the large bed and the upholstered chairs standing each side of a polished table. There was glass in the windows and heavy, velvet curtains draped on each side. She walked into the bathroom, seeing the clean towels folded, soap on a dish, a pot of talcum powder standing near the hand basin. Brigitte went back into the bedroom and went to the door, opening it slowly and peeking outside, looking each way along the corridor. There was no sign of the Americans but soldiers, mostly British, were coming and going. She closed the door and walked across to one of the chairs, sitting down, debating what to do. Impatiently, she stood up and went back into the bathroom. She turned the hot tap on, feeling the water flowing over her hand, noticing that it was soon warm. Brigitte smiled and shook her head, amazed that such normality was available, here, in Hamburg. Using the plug, she turned the tap fully on, seeing the steam rising as the bath started to fill. She quickly removed her clothes, washing her underwear in the bath and hanging it over the basin. She eased herself into the water, luxuriating in its warmth. Picking up the soap she had soon lathered her hair and, standing up, soaped herself all over, feeling her skin coming alive. She lay down in the bath and turned the tap on, swirling the water with her hands, only turning the tap off when the water reached the overflow. She could barely see across the bathroom for the steam, closing her eyes, enjoying the moment.

'Room in there for another?' a voice boomed out, startling Brigitte.

Sitting up, clasping her arms across her breasts, Brigitte saw the tall American standing in the middle of the room. To her horror, she saw him remove his boots, unbutton his shirt and trousers and then strip off completely. He walked towards the bath, placing his foot in the water.

'Holy cow! That's hot.' He removed his foot, pulled the plug chain and let the water level drop before turning on the cold tap. When he was satisfied, he then got into the bath, facing Brigitte. He smiled. 'Relax honey, I ain't gonna hurt you.'

Brigitte started to stand up but the American moved quickly, grabbing her ankle. Brigitte sat back down, water spilling over the top of the bath, wetting the wooden floor. The American told her to stand up and Brigitte eased herself upright. She saw the man admiring her body, his eyes lingering on her breasts, then moving down, looking at her pubic hair. He leant forward and stroked her womanhood, his thumb circling round, pushing slowly into her. He stood up, his large penis erect, taking Brigitte's hair in his hands and pulling her towards him, kissing her on the lips. He then pushed her down into the water, forcing her to take him in her mouth. Brigitte did as he wanted, satisfying him. She spat his seed into the water, washing her mouth.

When they had both dried off, the American took Brigitte into the bedroom and forced her to lie, face down, on the bed whilst he satisfied himself again. He then started to get dressed, telling her to do the same, as it was time to go.

'You use me and then discard me like...like some worthless rag doll?' Brigitte asked, not disguising the anger in her voice.

The American smiled at her. 'We'll give you a little gift, lady...for your services to the Allied Powers.' He went across to an attaché case, carefully opening it so that Brigitte could not see what was inside. 'Put these on.' He passed her a pair of silk stockings. Brigitte went into the bathroom, shutting the door. Her underwear was still damp but she pulled it on and then got dressed, shoving the stockings into her coat pocket. When she came out the American was lounging in one of the chairs. He got up, passing her two packs of cigarettes and they left the room.

Looking along the track as he made his way through the forest, south of Salzgitter, Hartwig could hear the buzzing of the flies moments before he smelt the sickly scent of decaying bodies. He gagged, pulling a cloth from his pocket and holding it to his nose. He walked slowly forward, pushing past a low-lying branch and then he saw them, about a dozen bodies, lying to the side of the track, fully dressed in their Wehrmacht uniforms. He glanced round before stepping closer, seeing the dark stains of blood on the coats and the bullet holes through the chests, knowing they had been taken by surprise, mown down with machine guns. Hartwig

forced himself to look at the first body, gagging again as he
saw the face of a young boy, the skin shredded by birds, the
eyes missing, maggots moving around the nostrils and
mouth. Hartwig vomited, tears welling in his eyes, cursing
the madness of the world he had witnessed during the past
few years, the madness of young boys being sent to be
slaughtered. He moved forward, noticing that all of the bodies were in a similar condition, obviously killed here some
time ago. It appeared that, apart from no sign of their weapons, the bodies had not been searched. He could see the
boots on one body, relatively new and Hartwig was sure
they were about his size. He crouched down, picking at the
knot, undoing one of the boots and then pulled it off. A pile
of maggots fell at his feet, making Hartwig drop the boot,
seeing that the foot inside was virtually eaten away, the
bones red and raw. He picked the boot up and shook it, more
maggots falling out. Hartwig pushed through the nearby
bushes, looking for something, a small branch or a clump of
leaves that he could use, to clean the boot with. He saw a
small pond and pushed the boot under the water, turning
back, determined to get the other one. When he had re-
trieved the second boot, he placed it in the water before going back to the bodies. He pushed one of the bodies with his
foot, trying to turn it over but to no avail. Crouching down,
he unbuttoned the coat, swatting as more flies buzzed
around him. He saw the man's dagger, still in its sheath and
unbuckled the belt, pulling it out and placing it around himself. He carefully undid the tunic pocket and eased out the
man's Soldbuch, seeing the swastika on the cover page and
the man's name and unit details. Hartwig checked each of
the bodies, forcing himself to reach into the tunic pockets
and retrieve the contents. All the men and boys belonged to
the same unit according to their papers. Hartwig picked up
the three daggers, the small amount of cash and three part
full cigarette cartons, placing them in his coat pockets. He
went back to the pond and swilled the boots out, placing
them upside down on a tree branch, waiting for them to dry
out. He sat down against the trunk and dozed off.

The crack of a rotting branch and the hubbub of voices awoke Hartwig. For a moment he sat motionless, listening, then he got up, grabbed the boots from the branch and ran round, past the pond, pushing into the bushes and under-growth, seeking somewhere to hide. He saw a small earth bank ahead and climbed up it, sitting on the grass, behind a row of bushes. He waited, undoing his old boots and trying on the new ones, lacing them up quickly, pleased that they were a perfect fit. Shouts came from in front of him, star-tling him before he realised that the men who were ap-proaching had obviously just come across the bodies. He could clearly hear them talking and, unbelievably, laughing. Hartwig knew a little Russian but he could not make out what they were saying to each other. He was more con-cerned by the fact that they were Russians, realising that he must have strayed too far east, that he would have to turn back. Hartwig eased himself up into a crouching position and started to move carefully through the undergrowth, fur-ther into the forest, knowing his family was only a hundred miles away, to the south.

'Will you please keep still…it's only a scratch,' Han-nelore said firmly as she bathed the graze across Captain Jagger's back. 'You were lucky James, it could have been much worse.'

Jagger eased himself, straightening his back, sitting on the surgery table. 'Suppose you are right.'

'Of course I am right. You really must take more care of yourself. One of these days you're going to get seriously injured.' Hannelore finished dabbing and started to bind a bandage around Jagger's chest, admiring his physique. 'How did it happen?'

'We found the body of a young soldier amongst the ru-ins in Hamburg. He had been molested, drowned and robbed. Anyway, whilst two of my men were carrying him out to our vehicles, I saw a gang of about ten armed men, real ruffians, walking nearby and ordered them to stop. The next thing we know is that they are firing at us.' Jagger paused, taking a sip from the cup of tea Hannelore had made. 'Everyone dived for cover and we started firing back, picking them off one at a time. Eventually, the shooting stopped and we saw a couple of them stand up, holding their hands in the air, surrendering. I stood up and walked towards them, covering them with my pistol when, all of a sudden, this man leapt at me. I ducked but he hit me across the back with a bloody large piece of wood. Fortunately, one of my men stabbed the man with his bayonet. Turns out they are Poles…apparently thought we were Russians.'

'And you believed them?' Hannelore asked.

Jagger shook his head and smiled.

'So…you arrested them?' Hannelore persisted.

'They were taken into detention,' Jagger replied, his hand feeling the hem of Hannelore's skirt, touching her knee and moving up her thigh.

Hannelore stood still, smiling, looking down at Jagger. They had been lovers for a few weeks and whenever he went out, she found herself worrying about him, wanting him to return quickly, return safely. He had been gentle and considerate, letting her get use to his body, encouraging her to reach enjoyment, something she had thought would never happen again after being raped. Hannelore ruffled his blonde hair, feeling his fingers stroking the top of her leg. She pulled away, seeing the look of dismay on his face. She went across to the surgery door and slid the bolt across, turning and smiling at him. Hannelore walked across to the table and pressed herself against him, feeling his hands encircle her bottom as she kissed him. Jagger stood up and almost crushed her in his arms, returning her kisses and hoisting her skirt. He slowly turned her round and eased her across the table, entering her from behind, gently thrusting, Hannelore responding.

They left the surgery together, going up to the living room where Hannelore's mother had laid the table. Her mother called out from the kitchen, telling them she was about to serve up. They sat down.

'Why do you have that stupid red hat?' Hannelore asked, her eyes twinkling, looking at Jagger.

'Why is it stupid?' Jagger asked.

Hannelore poured water into the glasses, seeing her mother enter with two plates, steaming with stew and vegetables. 'Well, if you want someone to shoot you, it's a good colour to wear...a red hat.'

'Point taken except that I don't wear it when I'm out on patrol. I wear my helmet,' Jagger replied.

Hannelore bit into the piece of pork, chewing happily. 'So, what is the significance of the hat?' she asked, after she had swallowed.

Jagger studied her for a moment. 'If I tell you...well, you have to keep it a secret.'

Hannelore nodded, intrigued.

'It is the hat worn by officers of the Corps of Military Police...CMP for short,' Jagger said, Hannelore sensing his pride.

'Police? You are Police? What are you doing here?' Hannelore looked puzzled.

Jagger grinned. 'You know there is a thriving black market, that lawlessness prevails. It is my job to re-establish law and order in this area.'

'I couldn't feel in safer hands,' Hannelore said, giving Jagger an outrageously provocative look.

Jagger coughed. 'Just let me finish this plate and I'll show you just how safe.'

Chapter Fourteen

Checking the action of the Sten gun, Bill satisfied himself it was working perfectly. He clipped the magazine into place, checked the safety catch and put the gun on the passenger seat. Lighting another cigarette, he sat back, waiting for his contact to appear. The windscreen was starting to frost over and Bill could feel the cold penetrating his boots, pulling his coat firmly round him. He glanced at his watch, feeling the nervousness building inside. It was always the same whenever he was about to trade, always wary, even with the people he already knew, always on his guard. Bill smiled to himself, thinking about Colin's stupid and pitiful story about the Military Governor at Nienburg. Within days, Bill had visited the Governor and had suggested an arrangement whereby Bill would clear the wagons full of items that could be traded on the black market, through to Hamburg and, in return, collect a percentage of each load. Captain Blinkey had at first filibustered about handling his own shipments through to Antwerp, Bill having pointed out that it was becoming more risky without the correct documentation. The following week, Bill had tipped off the authorities about a wagon on its way and it had been stopped and the shipment impounded. Blinkey had requested a second meeting and a deal was done. This business was easy for Bill, making sure the correct paperwork was arranged and providing him with an additional income. His recent trip to Lubeck for the Americans had proven to be highly lucrative and now he was about to undertake a second run.

He saw a truck approaching, slowing down and stopping some fifty yards in front of him. Its headlights flashed once, Bill picking up a torch and flashing it twice. The truck moved forward and Bill saw Lanky at the wheel, beckoning for him to follow. Bill started the engine and swung the truck round, seeing the tail light of the truck in front. He followed the truck for at least two miles before it turned between two buildings and stopped. Bill reversed into the narrow street, backing up to the other truck. He got out and walked to the rear.

'Thought you guys were never coming,' he said, seeing Lanky and Shorty appear round the rear of their truck.

Lanky smiled. 'Had a few problems with one of our patrols this side of Osnabruck...wanted to know where we were going. Told 'em we were delivering to the British High Command.'

'You told them that!' Bill said, not disguising his concern. 'What if they check out your story? It could lead them to me.'

'Calm down Bill. How many trucks do you think travel that way every day? They don't have time to check every one,' Shorty said.

Lanky dropped the tailgate. 'Come on guys...it's too bloody cold to stand here all night.'

They started working, hauling the boxes and cartons from one truck to the other and when they had finished, all three of them were sweating. Shorty offered Bill a swig of bourbon from a flask. Whilst they smoked, Shorty handed Bill a well stuffed envelope and checked that Bill knew where to meet their contact in Lubeck. Then the Americans set off leaving Bill to drive back to Bad Oeynhausen. Feeling the envelope that was stuffed inside his tunic, Bill smiled and lit another cigarette. He would travel up to Lubeck tomorrow and, on his return, thought he would call in on Captain Blinkey. He started the engine and drove off, not noticing the man who had been standing in a doorway, watching him for some time.

Observing the village from the top of a small hill, hidden behind a thorn bush, Walbert could see smoke coming from some of the chimneys. Other than that, there were no signs of the inhabitants. He also saw four trucks and an armoured car parked at the far end of the village but at this distance, he could not make out which army they belonged to. He glanced over his shoulder.

'Ernst, come up here.'

His brother shuffled closer and lay down beside him, looking at the village. 'You're not leaving me here...not again,' he whimpered.

Walbert understood. Since the time he had fallen into the lake, avoided capture by the Russians and eventually found Ernst after two days of searching, he knew he would not leave his brother behind. Walbert remembered how he had almost given up, berating himself for losing his way, feeling full of guilt and remorse, the fear of what might have happened to Ernst overpowering his senses. He had sat crying by the edge of the lake when Ernst had crept out of a clump of reeds, throwing his arms around Walbert's neck. Since then, skirting south around the lake, they had never parted.

'You see beyond the village...that river.' Walbert pointed, Ernst nodded. 'I'm almost certain that is the River Elbe. It's the only big river I know around here and if I'm right, it means we only have to follow it to get to Hamburg.'

Ernst stifled a cough. 'Have we far to go Wally?'

'Should think less than fifty kilometers.' Walbert looked at his brother, seeing his sunken cheeks and the dark circles around his eyes. He knew they had to keep moving, that Ernst cough was getting worse and that both of them were getting weaker as each day passed. 'Trouble is Ernst, as you can see, it is so flat and there is virtually no cover. It means we will have to wait here until nightfall before walking past that village.'

Ernst coughed again. 'Can't we find something to eat? My tummy aches...it's always aching.'

Walbert put his arm around Ernst shoulders. 'Little brother, we have to be brave. We have come a long way and seen some terrible things and now we are getting close. Once we get to our Aunt's house I'm sure she will feed you until you swell up like a pumkin. We have to be determined.'

'I know…I'll try,' Ernst said. 'Could we walk down there?'

Walbert looked at where Ernst was pointing, seeing a sparse hedge and a shallow ditch. It led to the road, some hundred metres from the village. 'We could crawl along the ditch…come on, let's go.'

The boys got up and made their way back down the slope, skirting round the hillock and emerging where the hedge started. Crouching, they walked along the ditch, Walbert feeling the ground soft beneath his feet, stopping every few paces to look along the road ahead. The hedge turned sharply to the left, away from the village and they reached the corner, squatting down, both looking round.

'It's starting to get darker,' Walbert whispered, pointing at the sky. 'We'll reach the road when it's dark.'

He stepped forward, seeing that the ditch was getting slightly deeper and muddier. Then Walbert saw the bundle of rags ahead, pausing, Ernst coughing loudly behind him. He continued, constantly looking to both sides, seeing two trucks coming along the road from the village. He squatted down, beckoning Ernst to do the same. The trucks drove past, less than a hundred metres from their position, red stars painted on the cab doors. As they disappeared, Walbert moved forward, approaching the rags, hoping they could be of use, they might have food. Then he saw the hand, lifeless, protruding from the bundle, realising it was a body. He turned to prevent Ernst from seeing but he was too late. His brother stared past him, transfixed.

'Wait here…I'll look,' Walbert said. He reached the bundle and, using his foot, tried to push it over but to no avail. He bent down and used his hands, rolling the bundle over. He had to stifle a scream, retching as he stood back, looking at the girl's eyes, staring blankly back at him, her throat slashed. She looked about the same age as himself. Walbert noticed where her coat had fallen open that there were dark bruises and bite marks on her thighs. He could not prevent his tears, sobbing quietly to himself. He heard Ernst cough and realised he was next to him.

'Who could...who could do that?' Ernst asked. She's our age; she's just a girl. Why?'

Walbert squatted down and pulled the coat together, covering the girl as best he could. 'I don't know Ernst...I don't know. Only a madman could do this.'

'We'll have to bury her Wally. We can't leave her.'

'What with?' Walbert snapped. 'Anyway, I don't think she's been here very long so, whoever did this might be coming back. We have to move.'

Something tickled his nose, making Dieter sneeze. Drowsily, his hand wiped his nose, Dieter enjoying the warmth around him, the fresh smell. Then reality struck home, Dieter's body protesting as he tried to sit up. He blinked, wiping his eyes and looking round. He was lying on a rug, another one over his body, lying on a bed of hay. Through the wooden slats he could see daylight, realising he was in a hayloft. He tried to get to his feet, but the effort was too great, slumping back. He eased himself backwards, propping himself against the wall, hearing the timber creak. Then he noticed that he was wearing clean underwear. He felt the panic rise inside as he looked around, looking for his clothes but there was no sign of them. He had no recollection of getting to this place. A door creaked open below and Dieter felt his heart racing as he heard the light tread of someone moving across the barn. He heard the person start to climb the ladder, Dieter realising he was helpless, staring at the spot where the ladder reached the loft, seeing it vibrating. A head appeared and a ruddy faced woman looked sternly at him. She heaved herself up and stood, legs apart, her hands on her hips, looking down at him.

'So, you've woken up at last. Didn't think you'd make it...almost gave you up for dead.'

Dieter tried to speak, his voice croaking. 'Who are you? 'Where am I?'

The woman glared at him. 'I'm the one who ask the questions. Who are you and where do you come from?'

Dieter stared at the woman, trying to work out if she was friendly or not, could he trust her or was she working for the enemy. He was about to answer when the noise of a vehicle pulling up outside and the sound of English voices stopped him. The woman turned and made her way back down the ladder, Dieter frantically looking around, trying to see where he could hide, how he could escape. He dragged himself across to the slatted wall and peering through he could see a scout car below, three soldiers standing round, smoking. He heard the woman ask them what they wanted, the men gesticulating, indicating they wanted food. Dieter saw the woman walk into the shed opposite and soon reappear, carrying a bucket, offering them some eggs. One of the men, speaking poor German, asked her if she had seen any strangers passing during the last week. The woman shook her head, explaining that she and her husband only worked, they had no time to watch out for strangers passing. The soldier thanked her and Dieter saw them get into the scout car and drive away.

When the woman reappeared in the loft, Dieter thanked her.

'I asked you some questions,' the woman said, ignoring his thanks.

'I am Dieter Barth, Captain, Wehrmacht. I come from Hamburg.'

The woman stared at him, questioningly. 'So what were you doing in the bath house at Bad Nenndorf?'

'What do you mean?' Dieter was puzzled.

The woman folded her arms across her ample bosom. 'You were a prisoner of the British. Yes?'

Dieter nodded.

'So, why were you in Bad Nenndorf. Only Nazis and Gestapo are taken there. It is an interrogation centre.'

Dieter gave a wry grin. 'Now I understand. I was captured in April and imprisoned at Munsterlager, waiting for the British to discharge me. I happened to cross swords, so to speak, with someone I am certain was Gestapo and he falsely claimed that I was Gestapo. No matter what I said to the British, they didn't want to listen and I was taken to another place and tortured. That must be Bad Nenndorf.'

The woman eye's continued to bore into Dieter's. 'How did you escape?'

'I was lucky...through the tunnels below,' Dieter replied.

The woman nodded and went back down the ladder, Dieter again puzzled by her actions. He heard her coming back some ten minutes later, climbing back into the loft.

For the first time she smiled at him, opening a sack and taking out a large tin. She removed the lid and held it out to him. Dieter saw the chunks of pork, the cooked potatoes and the cheese. He started eating, taking small bites, forcing himself not to eat too much.

'How did I get here?' Dieter asked.

'My husband was riding back here on his motorbike when he saw you by the side of the road. You were stone cold, shaking and delirious. He was almost certain you had come from the interrogation centre, judging by the wounds on your legs and he bundled you into the sidecar and came home. Between us we managed to strip you and wash you then haul you up here. I've been up and down that ladder a dozen times a day, forcing you to take water and some thin soup, washing you as best I could and hoping you'd survive.'

Dieter smiled at the woman. 'Thank you for saving my life. How long have...'

'Two weeks,' the woman cut in. 'The British came round a couple of times the first week and asked if we'd seen anyone but we said we hadn't. They took us at our word.'

'Are we close to Bad Nenndorf?'

The woman nodded. 'About five kilometres away but we have very few visitors here. We like it that way.'

Dieter belched loudly, apologising. 'I want to get to Hamburg to...to find my wife.'

'You'll not be going anywhere until you've got your strength back,' the woman said, her stern expression returning. 'Anyway, got work to do.' She walked across to the ladder.

'How do you know I'm not Gestapo?' Dieter asked.

The woman climbed onto the ladder, just her head showing. 'You haven't got the tattoo.'

Looking up at the fleeting moon as the low clouds scudded past, Colin pulled the collar of his coat tighter around his neck. The rain continued to fall, making him even angrier that he was outside, in the middle of the night - cold, wet and feeling totally miserable. He saw the light come on in the house opposite and someone moving behind the curtain, the house where Mary had arrived earlier in the evening, accompanied by a young officer. It had taken Colin days to find out where Mary went when she left the Officers Mess, always with an officer. By standing at various points along the road leading from the Mess, Colin had finally tracked Mary down to this house, realising this was where she was billeted. After the drive to Nienburg, Colin had managed to see Mary once when she had delivered some files to the office. As it was late in the evening and they were the only ones there, Colin was able to ask her what she thought she was doing, flirting with Manson. Mary had stared at him, fury in her face, a look Colin had never seen before. She had told him to grow up, that she was not his possession and that she would do as she pleased. She had stormed out, leaving Colin speechless. They had not spoken since.

Throughout the evening, Colin had watched the house, his emotions boiling. He could not stop himself visualising what Mary was doing, kissing and caressing the man with her, letting him have her when and how he wanted. One moment he was seething with rage, the next, justifying to himself why she acted this way, the strange and unsettling circumstances they all found themselves in, wanting her. He was sure he could forgive her, tell her he understood, tell her that he still loved her.

The sound of the door opening made Colin step back, behind the trunk of the tree. He saw the officer walking away, along the road, pulling his raincoat tight. Colin waited, seeing the light go out. There was no sign of anyone on the road, hardly surprising Colin thought, only idiots like himself would be out at this time. He stepped forward, ran across the road and knocked on the door. No sound. He knocked again, harder. There was the sound of someone shuffling along, then Mary's voice asking who was there.

'It's me,' Colin said.

There was a long pause. 'Who?'

Colin felt a jolt of anger. 'Me...Colin.'

'What do you want? Do you know it's the middle of the damn night,' Mary said from behind the door.

'I know but I have to talk to you.' Colin waited, no response. 'Mary, I have to talk...please, let me in.'

After what seemed to be an age, Colin heard the lock being turned and a bolt being pulled back. He turned the doorknob and eased it open, seeing Mary walking back along the hall. He followed her into her bedroom, noticing her clothes strewn across the floor, the rumpled bedclothes and the empty wine bottles on the table. Mary, a dressing gown pulled firmly around her, sat on the bed, looking at him through sleepy eyes, her mascara smudged, her hair tousled.

'Speak then,' she said.

'I love you Mary,' Colin blurted out. 'I can't keep you out of my mind. I can't sleep, can't work, can't concentrate. I want to be...'

'For goodness sake!' Mary cut in. 'You are a mere boy. You need to grow up. Do you think you are the only person I've met since arriving here?'

Colin felt the tears welling up in his eyes. 'Mary. My darling, please...don't talk like this. I thought you...'

'Go home. You are soaked through and you will catch pneumonia if you don't change your clothes. You'll quickly get over me.' Mary nodded towards the door.

Colin stepped across the room, his temper propelling him, grabbing Mary's shoulders and squeezing hard. He pushed her back, falling on top of her, trying to kiss her, Mary starting to resist.

'Get off me! Get off and leave,' she shouted, pushing against Colin's chest.

'Just because I'm not an officer,' Colin snapped as he regained his feet. 'You only like officers.'

Mary slapped him hard across his face. Colin turned and walked out of the room, along the hall and let himself out, not noticing the two WAAF's standing at the top of the stairs watching him depart.

Chapter Fifteen

Casually propped against a stack of ammunition crates, Cyrek listened carefully to the timorous man standing, rigid, in front of him, firing questions, watching the man intently when he answered. Satisfied with the man's responses, Cyrek suddenly laughed, clapped the man around the shoulders and told him to get some food, drink and a woman. Cyrek could see the man relax as he walked across the cellar, joining his other colleagues. Wicus, sitting nearby, took another long swig from the wine bottle clutched in his hand.

'What do you think?' he asked.

Cyrek's beetle brows puckered. 'I'd certainly like to know what the Americans are shipping up here. And what the Tommy is up to, driving for them.'

'We could grab him next time he goes to Osnabruck,' Wicus said, grinning.

Cyrek shook his head. 'No. This time we need to be more careful...subtle, something you wouldn't understand my friend. We can watch his movements, follow him and, when we know who he is contacting, then is the time to act. It could be useful to us to use the same route. We have got to start shifting this stuff but we need buyers. You'd only end up killing them.'

'Your right.' Wicus glanced over his shoulder at the stacks of cartons, trunks and boxes. 'It's alright having all this stuff and trading locally but there's more money to be had if we can get it out of Germany.'

One of the men let out a raucous laugh, the others joining in. Cyrek and Wicus both looked across the cellar, seeing four of the women coming down the stairs. Cyrek watched them as they nervously came across to him, each of them placing cigarette cartons, stockings, perfume bottles and food coupons on the table.

Wicus stood up, looking at the small piles. 'No money?'

The women shook their heads.

'Get some food,' Wicus ordered, sitting down again. 'That's not much for a night's work,' he said to Cyrek.

Cyrek shrugged his powerful shoulders. He left the women to Wicus. He started to discuss his plan with Wicus, deciding when men should be sent to Osnabruck, how many, what transport they would require, debating if the men should carry weapons. During their discussions, other women came in, each coming across to the table and placing their items on it. Eventually, the young blonde Gisela came in and placed a bottle of brandy on the table, a full carton of cigarettes and a handful of crumpled notes. Cyrek grinned at her, seeing her blanch and move quickly away, joining the others. He yawned, feeling tired, realising that it was probably close to dawn. It had been a long night, overseeing the loading of two trucks for Antwerp and dealing with two British officers near St. Michaelis – a gold bar for each of them in exchange for a continuous supply of morphine, penicillin and petrol. Cyrek had seen the greed in their eyes.

Wicus got up and shouted to the women to come across to the table. Cyrek watched them gather round, seeing the tiredness in their bodies, the fear in their eyes. Wicus grabbed one of them by her hair, making her yell out in pain, demanding to know what she had been doing, pointing at the half used carton of cigarettes and a perfume bottle. Cyrek grinned, waiting for Wicus' show to start, noticing the men gathering round like a pack of wolves.

Standing in front of the trembling woman, Wicus shouted at her, telling her she was not doing enough work to warrant her keep. He slowly unbuttoned her coat, pulling it roughly off her, throwing it to the ground. He then told her to remove her blouse and skirt, the men starting to jeer. The woman did as she was told, standing in her underwear, Cyrek glancing appreciatively at her long legs. Wicus made her turn round and undid her bra, the woman pitifully clutching her bared breasts. Using his hand, he forced her to bend over the table and, with the other, he pulled her pants down, baring her bottom, all the time telling the other women they had to bring back more cigarettes and money. Wicus then forced the woman's legs apart, stroking her between the thighs, pushing his thumb into her anus. He unbuttoned his trousers, spat on his hand, stroked his erection and thrust himself into her, causing her to cry out in pain. A look of satisfaction crossed his face and he withdrew. Another man came forward and entered the woman.

Cyrek watched the other women, seeing the shock and pain in their faces. He saw Gisela staring, frozen to the spot, suddenly realising that he was becoming aroused. Cyrek walked round the table, reached past two of the men waiting to take their turn and, gripping Gisela's arm, pulled her towards him. He turned and led her across to his bed, pushing aside the rugs hanging in front of it, ignoring her pleading.

Ducking down behind the fence, Brigitte listened to the Tommies standing nearby, holding her breath, sure they had seen her approaching. They carried on talking, moving away from where she was crouching, saying something about the girls they were meeting when they had finished their sentry duty, Brigitte calming down. She eased herself up, clutching the wooden slats and peered over the top. The soldiers were walking towards the railway wagons standing at the opposite side of the goods yard and Brigitte cursed under her breath. She shuddered, feeling the cold of the night through her boots and coat, looking up at the moon, realising that she should have waited for a cloudy night, the goods yard bathed in light. But there was no turning back empty handed, Brigitte thought, she had to get to the wagons.

Easing herself over the fence, Brigitte crawled along the base, staying out of the moonlight. She studied the yard, seeing that she could crawl further along the fence then use the railtracks, standing on cinders and sleepers, to provide her with cover as she approached the wagons. She made slow progress, stopping and watching the soldiers standing on the far side, feeling the cinders painfully pressing into her palms and knees. Eventually she reached the first of the wagons and crawled underneath it, standing up in the shadows on the opposite side, brushing the dirt and dust from her coat. She stepped towards the front of the wagon and climbed onto the coupling, reaching up to the top of the wagon and pulling herself up. Brigitte smiled, seeing the glistening coal. She pulled the sacks from her belt and started to pick up lumps of coal, placing them in each sack until, feeling the weight, she was satisfied that she could manage to carry them. Brigitte climbed out of the wagon and, wedging herself between it and the wagon next to her, she lowered each sack as far as possible before letting it fall to the ground. Getting down, Brigitte took a length of rope and tied it around the neck of each sack, making a loop, which she placed around her shoulders. She could feel the hardness of the coal pressing against her hips and thighs and the weight across her back. She paused, adjusting the weight, wondering how she was going to get back to the fence without being seen.

Suddenly, she heard the footsteps of people running across the cinders, forcing her to push herself back between the two wagons, staying in the darkness. The footsteps got closer, Brigitte hearing the harsh breathing of the people. A burst of gunfire startled her and she heard people fall, others shouting, some screaming, more sporadic gunfire. She heard footsteps coming from the opposite direction, feeling the panic rise inside, crouching down and pushing herself back, under the coupling. She saw four soldiers walk past, their rifles held to their shoulders, looking straight ahead, not glancing towards her. They started shouting at the people ahead of them, Brigitte unsure how many had been killed, injured and captured. She had not dared to look out.

A hand grabbed her leg, Brigitte biting her lip, stifling a scream. She looked down and saw a boy looking up at her, his eyes pleading with her not to give him away. Brigitte placed a finger to her lips and then started to ease herself under the coupling, carefully lifting her sacks so that they did not make any noise. The boy crawled out behind her and they started walking along the side of the wagon. Brigitte knew she had to take a chance. If the soldiers were distracted by the people they had caught, she might be able to reach the fence without being seen. She set off, crouching as low as she could, her back screaming at her in protest. The boy hobbled along behind her. The fence got closer, Brigitte breathing heavily, waiting for someone to shout or worse. They reached the fence and Brigitte collapsed beside it, trying to regain her breath, perspiration running down her face. The boy stood in front of her and Brigitte pulled him down, next to her in the shadows.

'What happened?' Brigitte asked.

The boy wiped his eyes. 'We...my two brothers and I, were getting coal. Then others came along...must have been twenty or more, doing the same. We had filled our sacks and were on our way back when, all of a sudden, the Tommies were behind us.' The boy paused, stifling a sob. 'Then they started shooting.'

'They must have shouted a warning...surely?' Brigitte asked.

The boy shook his head. 'No, they just fired. That caused everyone else to panic and start running. I fell over and rolled under one of the wagons.'

'But we were only getting coal,' Brigitte said, more to herself. 'They can't kill people for that, not when we are freezing to death.' She eased herself upright and lifted her sacks over the fence, climbing over after them, the boy following her.

'What happened to your brothers?'

The boy shook his head. 'I don't know. When I fell, they were both running ahead of me.' He sobbed again.

Brigitte put her arm around his shoulders. 'I'm sure they will be all right. Do you have far to go?'

'About two kilometres...near the Binnenalster,' the boy replied. 'But I have to go back and find my brothers.'

'Look,' Brigitte said, pointing over the fence, 'see those trucks arriving and the Tommies getting out. If you go back, you will be detained in a camp for goodness knows how long. Go home.'

The boy walked slowly along the road beside the fence, Brigitte watching him until he disappeared behind a pile of rubble. When she was sure he had followed her instructions, she picked up the sacks and set of home.

Keeping to the woods and away from the roads, Hartwig had made steady progress. He had managed to find the odd rotting turnip to chew on and there was plenty of water. Having skirted Nordhausen, Hartwig knew he was close to Erfurt, close to his wife, feeling his excitement and longing bubbling inside him. He had decided, following his discovery of the dead bodies and almost bumping into the Russians that, to go westward was unnecessary, only prolonging his arrival home. Using his field craft, he knew he could take the more direct route. Apart from the frequent rain, the temperature was mild for the time of year, Hartwig grateful that he could sleep during the days and walk at night. He knew it was going to be a special Christmas, being reunited with his family.

Watching the road ahead, Hartwig could see the single pole barricade, manned by two sentries, about a hundred yards from where he crouched on the bank of the River Gera. He had deliberately chosen to approach the town from the north, using the river bank as cover and, looking along the river, he could see the Kramerbrucke, the bridge crossing the river with its closely packed buildings and the churches at each end. Hartwig could also see the two churches that dominated the town, standing side by side in the centre, the Mariendom and the Severikirche, their spires standing out in the dwindling light. His spirits soared. From his position on the outskirts he could not see any damage to the buildings, the road seemed intact and everything looked normal and peaceful, except the barricade. Hartwig was more certain than ever that his family was safe and, before the night was over, that he would be holding his wife in his arms.

As the last light of the day faded, Hartwig started to move along the bank. He had seen the occasional truck pass his position, some carrying loads of potatoes and vegetables, others soldiers. A small number of people, some pulling carts or pushing prams, laden with wood or food, had also passed, the sentries stopping everyone and checking their papers, searching their loads and taking whatever they fancied. Hartwig noticed that nobody protested. From what he had seen, Hartwig was certain that the town was probably under the control of a small Russian detachment, maybe forty men at most. A truck approached the barrier, heading out of the town and Hartwig, peering over the bank, could hear the driver talking to the sentries. Using the distraction and the noise of the engine, Hartwig moved quickly along the bank, his boots clattering on the stony ground as he approached the first house. He ducked into the shadows under the overhanging roof, breathing hard, hearing the truck move off. He waited, listening, watching the sentries who were lighting up their cigarettes, talking and laughing. Hartwig moved to the next house and paused, then darted further along the street. At the end, he looked across the square and could see the wide steps leading upwards between the two churches. There was no sign of anyone and Hartwig could feel his heart pounding, knowing he was so close to home. He only had to go up the steps and his wife's house was within sight.

With one final look around the square, Hartwig stepped forward, walking quickly, his boots clattering on the cobbles. He reached the bottom step and started the climb, glancing up at the dark windows of the Mariendom, looming over him. He paused, taking a deep breath, then continued, starting to feel nervous, wondering if his wife had changed, what he was going to say, would she recognise him. He reached the top step and saw the houses ahead, immediately looking at the door behind which his wife was waiting. He started to run.

The door beckoned him, Hartwig feeling the tears running down his cheeks. His mind barely registered the shouts coming from behind or the cocking of weapons. Hartwig was home, that's all that mattered as far as he was concerned. The deafening chatter of sub machine guns and whine of bullets ricocheting off the cobbled street, rent the night air. The first bullet hit Hartwig in the hip, another splintering his femur and a third severing the artery in his thigh, spinning him round as he crashed to the ground. Hartwig rolled onto his front, reaching out towards the door, yelling out to his wife. He could feel himself weakening and started to realise that he had been shot but he could feel no pain. He tried to move but his legs would not obey his commands. Hartwig started to cry.

The Russian looked down at Hartwig, shaking his head, wondering why this fool was out during curfew. He could see the blood gathering in a large pool around the man's legs and knew he was fatally wounded. He drew his pistol, cocked it and placed the barrel at the back of Hartwig's head. He fired once.

Captain Manson stormed into the room, everyone abruptly stopping their conversations, sitting down and waiting.

'I've just had the biggest bollocking of my life!' Manson shouted, his face flushed with anger. 'Montgomery has read the riot act to all Commission Commanders. We are not coming up to his expectations and he has declared that the 'Battle of Winter' has commenced. With the Yanks pulling back and shipping out as fast as they can, the Russkies staying put, not relinquishing any territory and saying if the German's want food, they can buy it from Poland, we've got some serious problems to sort out. We've got at least twenty million German's to feed, a couple of million POW's and God alone knows how many Displaced Persons in the British sector.' Manson paused, looked round and saw a jug of water. He poured himself a glass and drank it. He looked at the men seated in front of him, glaring.

'There are also the problems associated with the black market, looting, pilfering, false identity papers and rape. Unofficial roadblocks appear to spring up all over the place, hampering movements and often, those involved, help themselves to whatever they fancy.' Manson stopped, refilled the glass and took a sip. 'You will all get to work and sort this mess out. Our first priority has to be getting the food supplies distributed efficiently. I know there's not enough to go round but you'll have to do your best. Finally, a word of warning. If anyone in this room...anyone under my command is caught dealing in the black market, I will personally

make sure they end up being sent back home and gaoled. Do
I make myself clear?'

People nodded, Bill Thornton looked down.

'I want to see Sergeant Major Thornton and Sergeant
Patterson in my office immediately,' Manson said 'and the
rest of you...get to work!' He walked quickly out of the
room.

Bill felt his heart thump, fearing the worst, his mind
spinning, trying to work out what Manson might know, who
had snitched on him. As he stood up, he felt the beads of
sweat on his brow. Did Manson know about his truck parked
nearby and the cargo for Lubeck?

'Wonder what he wants us for?' Colin said as he approached Bill.

'What? Oh...it's you,' Bill replied. 'Don't know.'

Colin smiled, seeing the look of alarm on Bill's face.
'Probably you and the cigarettes you keep scrounging,' he
joked.

'Don't be so effing stupid!' Bill thundered. 'Let's go.'

They walked in silence to Manson's office, Bill in front
of Colin. Entering the office, they both stood to attention
and saluted Manson.

Manson did not return the salutes. 'Ser'nt Major Thornton. You are to take a convoy of trucks tomorrow from here
to Hamburg. Ser'nt Patterson will accompany you. In Hamburg you will go to the Rathaus and report to the newly appointed Burgermeister who will issue instructions for the
distribution of the rations. This will be done strictly on the
provision of ration cards by all recipients and according to
the quantity and amounts specified. Any questions?'

Bill was so relieved, he could think of nothing to say.
He shook his head.

'Right, get moving...there's plenty of organising to get
on with.' Manson started writing. Bill and Colin turned and
left the office.

A sudden flapping of wings startled Dieter as he pushed
his way through the bushes, making him stop. He saw the
owl settle on a branch nearby, its silhouette clear in the

moonlight. It hooted, waiting for an answering call. Dieter could feel the cold through his boots, thankful that the leather coat the farmer's wife had forced him to take, kept the biting wind from his body. Dieter wiped his nose on the back of his glove as he looked round, seeing the white frost covering the ground. Glancing backwards, he could see his own footprints, knowing that if any Tommies were out on patrol, it would be easy for them to find him. He knew he had to keep moving even though he felt exhausted, keep walking until daylight and then find somewhere to rest. As he was in the woods and it was such a cold night, he had to hope that the British were staying in their warm barracks. This was the fourth night since leaving the farm and Dieter had passed Fallingbostel and Soltau, seeing the large numbers of British in the area. He reckoned that he should reach Luneburg by the morning and then head for Lauenburg where he hoped he would be able to cross the River Elbe. With the moonlight it was easy to see the tracks and, taking a drink of water from his flask, Dieter continued.

Listening to his footsteps crunching on the frosty ground and seeing his breath billowing out in front of him, Dieter made good progress, thankful for the flat terrain. He thought about the farmer's wife who had nursed him back to strength, fussing over him and making him eat more each day. She had provided a full set of her husband's clothes and even though they were slightly too big for Dieter, they were most welcome. When he had finally decided he had to leave, he sensed her regret. She had provided him with two small sacks of food and flasks of water. Dieter had thanked her many times for saving his life and, when he had kissed her on the cheek, he had noticed a slight flush on her face as she waved him away in her normal, brusque manner. He never had found out their names.

Pushing past a large bush, Dieter saw the road immediately ahead. He stopped and listened. He could just hear voices, somewhere along the road. Dieter stepped forward, looking both ways along the road. He could make out the ditch on the opposite side and, sure that there was nobody within sight, he ran across the road and slid down into the ditch, feeling the ice beneath his feet. Crouching, he moved forward, carefully ducking under the low branches, hearing the voices getting louder. He stood up and looked over the top of the bank. The road forked and there were at least four vehicles parked, forming a barricade across the roads. A roaring log fire provided warmth for the several Tommies sitting round and Dieter could see the sleeping bags of others nearby. Dieter ducked down and moved on.

As Dieter approached a sharp bend in the ditch there was a sudden crashing sound as someone fell into the ditch just ahead of him, cursing and shouting. The Tommy tried to stand up but his hobnailed boots slipped on the ice, causing him to fall onto his back. Then he saw Dieter. Both men were momentarily paralysed but Dieter moved first. He picked up the soldier's rifle by the barrel and swung it, the butt hitting the soldier hard across the side of his head. Dieter paused, breathing heavily, the rifle held above his shoulder, ready to strike the soldier again but there was no movement, he was knocked out. Dieter bent down and could see that the soldier was still breathing. He noticed the two magazine clips on the soldier's belt and removed then, shoving them into his coat pocket. Dieter moved fast, keeping to the ditch for about a hundred yards then, climbing out, he ran as fast as he could along the road. He knew it would not be long before the other Tommies would find their colleague. Seeing a wide track leading back into the woods, Dieter left the road, forcing himself to run, ignoring his protesting lungs and aching legs.

After what seemed like a marathon to Dieter, but was probably only a mile or so, he saw a disused forester's hut. He went inside, slumping to the floor, fighting to get his breath back. Putting the rifle down, Dieter unbuttoned his coat and took his gloves off, wiping the sweat from his face. He undid his flask and emptied it, feeling the cold water revive him, his heartbeat starting to slow down. He picked up the rifle and undid the bolt, sliding it back, seeing a round in the breech. He pushed the bolt forward and snapped it shut then released the magazine and checked it. Satisfied, Dieter got to his feet and left the hut, taking a track that led north.

He expected to hear the noise of vehicles at any moment but there was no sound. The track ahead started to dip down and through the trees, Dieter could make out another road, hopeful that it was the road leading to Lauenburg, that he had passed Luneburg. He looked round and saw a large, tangled clump of briars and walked across, looking for a way to get inside, seeing where the briers thinned. He eased himself carefully forward, wriggling on his stomach until he was satisfied that nobody could see him. Dieter was about to place his head on his arms and go to sleep when he heard the vehicles approaching. He waited. The vehicles, a mixture of trucks and jeeps, drove past his position. Dieter momentarily wondered what they were carrying before he fell asleep, exhausted.

Chapter Sixteen

Colin could not understand why Bill was in such a foul mood. When they had left Manson's office he had tagged along, trying to find out from Bill what he could do. Having spent the past few weeks trying to get over Mary's rejection, Colin was only too pleased to be given a task other than the dreary filling out of forms and filing countless documents. But as soon as they had left the building, Bill had rounded on him, yelling at him to bugger off and be ready the following morning.

At six o'clock sharp, the convoy had left Bad Oeynhausen, taking the road for Hannover. There were twelve vehicles in total, mainly Leyland Hippo's with a couple of Opel Blitz and Daimler Dingo scout cars at the front and rear. Bill had instructed the lead scout car which route to take and the convoy had made good progress. They had passed through Hannover and then turned north, passing through Fallingbostel and Soltau. When they reached the village of Evendorf, instead of taking the road for Hamburg, as Colin had expected, they had continued, heading for Luneburg. When he had asked Bill why, he only got told to mind his own business. There were quite a lot of people on the road as they proceeded, mainly groups of German's, Colin assumed, making their way homewards, pulling a variety of carts and wagons. Bill smashed his fist on the horn whenever he saw people ahead, not slowing down, Colin thankful that they got out of the way. As they had approached Luneburg, they had been forced to stop at a road block covering a fork in the road and Bill had sworn, jumping down and yelling at the officer in charge. The officer had threatened Bill with insubordination and had insisted on looking through the travel documents and ordering his men to search two of the vehicles, despite Bill ranting on about the Control Commission and its rights. To make matters worse, the officer had an injured man, suffering from concussion, which he insisted had to be taken to Hamburg. Bill had reluctantly agreed and eventually, the convoy had continued.

Passing through Luneburg, Colin had again wondered why the scout car in front took the road north rather than turning left towards Hamburg. This time he did not ask, he studied the map on his lap. The town of Lauenburg appeared ahead on the opposite bank of the River Elbe and as soon as they had crossed the bridge, Bill blew his horn, indicating to the scout car to stop. Bill jumped down from the cab and spoke to the driver, Colin unable to make out what he was saying due to the noise of the truck engine. Bill came back, got in and moved forward, suddenly taking the road north.

'But the scout car is going straight on,' Colin shouted. He pointed at the vehicle continuing along the road as Bill came to a halt. Then Colin saw the rest of the convoy following, the driver of the rear scout car waving as he passed. 'What is going on?'

Bill lit another cigarette. 'We've got a special delivery to make. We'll be joining up with the others later.'

'What delivery? Manson never said anything about it.'

'He told me last night,' Bill replied. 'Now, you've got the map...make sure we take the right road to Lubeck.' Bill slammed the truck into gear and lurched forward, climbing the hill as they left Lauenburg, Colin noticing the old, partly timber constructed houses and the disinterested people as they passed.

'What are we delivering?' Colin asked.

Bill glanced across. 'Special consignment of medical supplies. You're German might come in useful.' He continued to concentrate on the road ahead.

They turned right in Schwarzenbek and were soon approaching Lubeck. As they entered the town, Bill pulled up. He took a document from the inside of his tunic and studied it, Colin making out that it was a hand drawn map. Bill moved forward and, taking various streets, eventually pulled up outside a tailor's shop. He instructed Colin to wait inside the cab as he got out and went into the shop. Within minutes, Bill was back, starting the engine and driving off, still not saying anything to Colin. They turned at the end of the street and then reversed along an alleyway that ran behind the shop. Bill stopped and told Colin to get out.

Colin was relieved to stretch his legs as he walked to the rear of the truck. He saw three men waiting for them, two rather powerful, dark types and a thin man wearing a hat and suit. He spoke to them in German and the thin man replied, telling him to unload the cargo and pass it to his men. Colin started to undo the tail flap and Bill joined him. They lowered the tailgate and proceeded to drag the crates to the rear of the truck, the men carrying them into the shop.

'Christ! These crates are damn heavy Bill. What's in them?' Colin asked, wiping his sleeve across his brow.

'Told you...medical stuff,' Bill snapped.

Colin bent over and grabbed the handle of the next crate, dragging it along the floor. He was trying to work out what medical equipment could be inside that weighed so much. It was obvious that either Bill did not know or, if he did, he was not going to tell. Colin watched as the two men carried the last crate into the shop, Bill then telling him to get back into the cab. Colin got down and made his way forward, getting up into the cab and shutting the door. He reached down and grabbed his water bottle, unscrewing the cap and taking a long drink. Movement in the door mirror caught his eye as he leant forward to place the bottle down and he saw Bill taking a large brown envelop from the man and stuff it inside his tunic.

Bill got back into the cab, started the engine, lit a cigarette and then set off. 'When we get to Hamburg you are to say nothing to the others as to where we've been...understand?'

Colin frowned. 'Sure. But what do I say if they ask?'

'Special consignment as requested by Captain Manson to a field hospital. You don't have to say where,' Bill replied.

'That's what puzzles me,' Colin said. 'I didn't see any of our men around and can't understand why we are delivering medical supplies here rather than Hamburg.'

Bill chuckled. 'Listen son, we do as we are told. It's not our place to ask questions.'

They drove along in silence, Bill yelling out of the window at the various people cluttering the road, Colin seeing the bedraggled men, women and children, pitying them.

'Look, there's Hamburg ahead.' Bill pointed through the windscreen.

Pulling the blanket tightly round her shoulders, Hannelore turned onto her side, away from James. She had enjoyed their love making but it was obvious to her that James' mind was elsewhere. He had, in his usual considerate way, satisfied her but she knew he was troubled. Perhaps it was the loss of one of his men a few days ago when they had tried to apprehend a group of smugglers and there had been vicious hand to hand fighting. They had captured three men, two Polish and one Russian, the rest had escaped. Hannelore had patched up the men with minor injuries but she had two with serious wounds who were sleeping in the front living room. She knew James was carrying out a dangerous task, never certain who the enemy might be. She realised it was probably worse than when the war was raging. At least then you knew who you were fighting against. Now, as James had told her, you could not trust anyone, not even your own countrymen. Every time he went out, Hannelore found it difficult to concentrate on her duties, becoming more anxious as each hour passed. James had told her not to be so foolish, that he was well protected by his men.

James turned and placed his hand across Hannelore's belly. 'Are you all right?'

'Of course I am,' Hannelore replied, 'but I know you are troubled. Is there anything I can do to help?'

'Make sure those two next door are up and running as quickly as possible,' James replied.

Hannelore could tell he was smiling. 'That's not what I meant and you know it.'

James reached out and turned the lamp on, sitting up in the bed. 'You're right. We know there is a major black market operation going on in Hamburg, centred on the Hotel Atlantic and in the western suburbs. The trouble is it involves everybody. The Americans are involved, the British, some of the locals and the crowd we bumped into the other day. I need a lot more men to overcome it but I suspect that...well, that there are some highly placed officers involved.'

'You mean British?' Hannelore asked.

'Quite probably.' James folded his arms across his chest.

'What will you do?'

James grinned. 'I have to proceed with care. Information is the key. My men and I will be watching and listening and when we know a shipment is about to move, then we will act.'

'Why do you have to stop the trading? You know yourself that it is only because of the black market, people can feed themselves and get the odd luxury,' Hannelore stated.

'The black market encourages the theft of food shipments, the pilfering of all types of supplies and prevents people getting back to normal. Unscrupulous individuals and gangs are taking everything they can get their hands on that has any value and trading it for incredible profits, damaging an economy that is already desperate. That is why I and others are trying to curtail such activity.'

'I understand James but promise me you will take great care.' Hannelore eased herself up and placed her arms around James' neck, kissing him.

Peering through the shattered frame of the window and watching the people walking past, Walbert was not sure what to do next. He could see that the people were all dressed in old clothes, all looked as hungry as himself and Ernst, their faces drawn, their eyes sunken. Some were carrying pails of water, some staggering along with bundles of wood over their shoulders. An old woman was dragging a battered pram, two of its wheels missing, piled with rags and clothes and two boys, about his age, were pulling a small cart made from a wooden box with small wheels attached. Walbert rested his head against the wall, wishing the dull throbbing that had started a few days ago, would go away. He knew he could not continue for much longer, that he had run out of energy and that Ernst was seriously ill, coughing all the time. The walk along the bank of the Elbe had been much further than he had thought and he was thankful that at last, they had reached the outskirts of Hamburg. He knew their journey was almost over, that he had to remain strong, that he had to save his brother.

A fit of coughing from behind him, made Walbert look round, seeing Ernst huddled inside his coat, wiping the blood from his mouth.

'Ernst, we're almost there. We've just got to find our Aunt and then we will be looked after.' Walbert stepped across to his brother and squatted down beside him. 'If you stay here, I'll go and find her and then we can come back for you.'

Ernst slowly shook his head. 'Don't leave me, Wally...please, don't leave me.'

'I'd be quicker on my own, Ernst. Then I can bring help... you need a doctor.'

Ernst coughed, his pale face creased in pain. 'Be quick, Wally.'

Walbert stood up. He looked through the window and decided it was now time to risk walking on the street. With all the people moving around, he thought he should be safe. Since passing Lauenburg, he had not seen any Russkies. He had seen the British soldiers and was sure Hamburg was under their control, not that he trusted them either. It had been a very long walk and he had got this close. Now, with Ernst ailing, he had to find his Aunt quickly.

He looked down at his brother. 'I'll be back very soon Ernst.' Walbert then climbed through the window and walked out, onto the road. He had no idea where his Aunt lived but he could see the copper dome of the large church in the distance and decided to head towards it, keeping the river on his left side. The blisters on his heels sent stabs of pain up his legs but Walbert forced himself to walk, avoiding looking at those people passing him, keeping his head down. He could feel the biting wind, chilling him to the bone but he did not care. He had to get to his Aunt, had to get help for his brother. Pulling his glove off, he reached inside his coat pocket and withdrew the piece of card, looking at the address. The sudden noise of vehicles approaching made Walbert run into the derelict building nearest to him, ducking down behind the wall. He listened, waiting, hoping they would not stop. The vehicles roared past. He stood up and looked out, seeing the vehicles passing the large church at the end of the street. Walbert continued, reaching the church and stopping, wondering which way to go. He fought the panic rising inside him as he looked round, seeing an old woman approaching. He walked towards her, noticing that she was watching him, seeing the suspicion on her face. He asked if she knew the way to Erichstrasse and she pointed, past the church, telling him to walk about a kilometre and then turn right along Davidstrasse. Erichstrasse was on the left. Walbert thanked her and set off.

The wind caught Walbert's breath but he forced himself on, knowing he was almost at his destination. Nothing was going to stop him now. The street ahead was long and straight, the buildings on either side nothing more than piles of rubble, the odd smoke blackened wall standing out of the debris. Walbert wondered if his Aunt's building was still standing. He reached the street to the right and turned the corner, seeing that the buildings were badly damaged, but that most were standing and there were more people here. He walked along, keeping his head down, turning into Erichstrasse. He stopped outside a damaged building, looking up at it, seeing that most of the windows had cardboard and rugs over them. He walked inside and wearily climbed the stairs. He found the door with Frau Eichel's name on it and knocked.

'Who is it?' a woman's voice asked.

Walbert paused. The door did not open. 'I am Walbert Keller. I am looking for Frau Eichel...my Great Aunt.'

The door opened and a young woman appeared, looking down at him. 'Good grief! You'd better come in,' she said, standing to one side as Walbert edged past. 'My name is Brigitte and I live here with your Aunt. She's out at the moment but please…please come into the living room.'

Walbert staggered along the hall and entered the room, seeing a small child staring up at him, a piece of wood in its hand. An old man was asleep in a scruffy chair, his head back and mouth open.

'Please sit down,' Brigitte said, pointing towards another upholstered chair. Walbert did as she asked. 'Can I get you something to eat and drink?'

'Water please.' Walbert saw the damaged walls and the cardboard covering the window. He glanced across at the open grate, the fire glowing, the first warmth he had felt for months. He suddenly felt overwhelmingly tired.

Brigitte came back from the kitchen, a glass and jug in her hand. She poured water into the glass and passed it to Walbert.

'Thank you.' Walbert drank it straight down, passing the glass back. 'I have to…have to get…get my bro…' He fell asleep.

Feeling the warmth of the man next to her, Gisela turned towards him, placing her arm across his belly. She looked at his face, seeing the stubble on his chin, his dark hair lying across his forehead. She lent closer and kissed his cheek. Spending the night with him was something Gisela looked forward to, something that gave her hope that she would eventually escape from the nightmare that surrounded her, the demands of Cyrek, taking her whenever he felt inclined and Wicus, always insisting that she brought back more cigarettes, alcohol, scent and money. The British soldier was often away but whenever he was going to be in the apartment he would leave a message at the Atlantic. Gisela checked every night, disappointed on most occasions. It meant another night letting men abuse her, taking her however they wanted, forcing her to satisfy their needs. With her limited ability to speak and understand English, the men could easily tease her but this man did not. She had established that his name was Wilf and that he was nineteen years old. He had only shown her kindness and consideration.

A grin formed on Wilf's face and Gisela slipped her hand down lower, feeling his erection. 'You are waking?' she asked.

Wilf turned slightly towards her, kissing her. 'That's nice.'

Gisela slipped down the bed, taking him in her mouth, hearing him groan. She moved forwards and lowered herself onto him, feeling him fill her, feeling her spasms rush through her, shrieking with delight as Wilf joined her in that moment of mutual ecstasy.

'Wow!' Wilf exclaimed. 'It just gets better and better.'

Gisela slid off Wilf and lay beside him, breathing hard. She started to cry.

'What's the matter?' Wilf leant over her, concern creasing his forehead.

Gisela looked away. 'It is so...so good with you. I wish it could be always.'

'What do you mean?'

'I only want you,' Gisela said. 'I...Ich liebe dich.'

Wilf smiled and, taking her face in his hands, kissed her gently and lovingly. 'I think I know what you just said. You love me. Well, I'm rather keen on you.'

Gisela frowned.

'Ich love de,' Wilf said, seeing Gisela giggle and then she threw her arms around his neck.

Gisela lay back, staring at Wilf. 'Can we leave here?'

'I'm not sure...why?' Wilf asked.

'I have to get out of Hamburg. It is not safe for me here,' Gisela replied.

Wilf slumped back against the pillow. 'Suppose I could set something up. Could take me a bit of time but you're safe with me.'

Frowning, Gisela was not sure what Wilf had said. 'I'm safe when you are here, yes but when you are not?'

'All right. I'll see what I can do. I've got some mates billeted out at Pineberg. I'll talk to them.' Wilf eased Gisela over onto her stomach, stroking her back and kissing her shoulders.

Gisela sighed, knowing what was coming.

Twice weekly, Colin had accompanied the convoy to Hamburg, passing on Captain Manson's instructions to the Burgermeister and noting down his requests, informing Manson on his return. He was starting to like the Burgermeister, Herr Schreiner; a tall, upright man in his forties who was obviously very capable at organising the distribution of the rations. Herr Schreiner was always polite and courteous, precise in how he reported what was happening and making his requests. It was always the severe shortage of rations that concerned him and he was obviously concerned for the people under his jurisdiction but he never overstated his requirements, never pleaded. As the weeks passed, Colin found himself getting more involved, trying as best he could to secure what Herr Schreiner wanted, ignoring Bill Thornton's comments and sarcasm, telling him he was wasting his time. At least Bill seemed to have come out of his nasty mood and the trip to Lubeck, every other Thursday, always seemed to please him. He refused to discuss with Colin what they were delivering to the tailor's shop, the routine the same each time they went, Colin wondering what was inside the plump envelope Bill always received.

Getting up from his desk, Colin stretched, looking at the figures on the sheet in his hand. According to the Food Committee, a working man should get 2,650 calories a day and others at least 1,550. Given what was being delivered to Hamburg and assuming the Burgermeister had provided accurate figures for the number of adults and children in Hamburg, Colin had calculated that what was being received amounted to less than 1,000 calories per day – this was slow starvation. Colin went to Captain Manson's office and knocking on the door, walked in.

Manson looked up at him, disinterestedly. 'What do you want Ser'nt Patterson?'

Colin saluted. 'Sir, I would like you to look at these calculations I have made.' He handed Manson the piece of paper, seeing him glance down it.

'And what, Patterson, do you think I can do about it?' Manson stared at him.

'Well Sir, if we don't start shipping more food into Hamburg, thousands are going to die. They can't live on the rations we are providing, especially now that winter has set in.'

Manson shook his head. 'I can't get enough food for our entire region, let alone Hamburg. I'm struggling to maintain food to our own people...you included. There is just not enough being produced. The Russkies won't supply anything from Prussia, now Poland and the Yanks can't ship food over fast enough.'

'There has to be an answer,' Colin said, his frustration obvious.

Manson snorted. 'Too many people in our sector. Anyway, it'll teach the Jerries what it's like to go hungry...they had no mercy on the sodding Jews.'

'That's not the point Sir,' Colin stormed, 'we are talking mainly about women and children. And why are we shipping medical supplies every other week to Lubeck? I don't know of any hospitals in that area.'

Manson frowned. 'What medical supplies? And why Lubeck?'

Colin flushed, realising he had blurted out information that could get Bill into trouble. 'Nothing Sir.'

'Oh yes there is,' Manson said, standing up behind his desk. 'What have you been doing?'

'Every other week we take one truck of medical supplies to Lubeck and then continue on to Hamburg,' Colin replied.

'Who's we?' Manson came around his desk, his eyes boring into Colin's.

'Sergeant Major Thornton and myself...Sir.'

Unexpectedly, Manson smiled. 'Sit down Patterson and tell me about these shipments.'

Colin sat, waiting for Manson to return to his chair and then he recounted what had happened. When he had finished, Manson thanked him and asked him to keep him informed as to when the next shipments were going to take place. Manson also told Colin to keep this conversation to himself, Manson's threat being obvious - Bill was not to be informed.

Leaving Manson's office, Colin could feel his anger rising. Bill had obviously lied to him. He went to his office, grabbed his coat and went outside, walking in the cool air, mulling over what had just happened. A blast from a vehicle horn made him jump to the side of the road and Colin saw Mary drive past at speed, grinning at him, adding to Colin's dark mood.

Chapter Seventeen

Frau Eichel had been amazed when she first saw Walbert, sleeping in the chair, telling Brigitte that he was just like her nephew, his father. The boy had slept solidly, even when Brigitte and the Professor had lifted him up and placed him on the sofa. He had not come to until the middle of the following day, tossing and turning in his sleep, screaming out and mumbling incoherently, obviously what he had seen, playing on his mind. Brigitte had sat near him throughout the night, occasionally bathing his brow. Frau Eichel had boiled up porridge from the small amount of wheat she had and they had watched as Walbert had devoured it, his eyes darting between them, still suspicious. Then he had started crying, telling them between sobs, that his brother, Ernst, was waiting for him. He had struggled to stand up, letting out a scream and collapsing back onto the sofa. Brigitte had unlaced his boots and, despite his protests, she had eased them off, smelling and seeing the raw, puss filled blisters on his heels and toes, telling him he could not walk for some time. Frau Eichel had found a basin and filled it with water, placing his feet into it, trying to bathe them. All the time, Walbert kept on pleading for them to save his brother. Brigitte had calmed him down, asking him where his brother was, Walbert telling her where they had come from and giving her vague directions. She had set off, with the Professor, and they had walked to the area described by Walbert, calling out Ernst name but with no reply. They had searched through countless derelict buildings, asking people if they had seen a young boy, but to no avail - there were hundreds of children without parents, meandering through the debris, living in small groups underground. When it had turned dark, they had returned.

That night, they had failed to comfort Walbert. He had cried through the night, occasionally drifting off into a disturbed sleep. Brigitte had realised that they had no chance of finding the boy without Walbert and the following morning she had gone out and managed to convince two boys with a small cart to lend it to her. She had returned and managed, with the Professor's help, to carry Walbert down the stairs and place him on the cart. They had set off, Walbert managing to recognise the streets he had walked along. Eventually, they had come to a long block of damaged houses and, at Walbert's insistence, started to search the ground floors. There had been no sign of Ernst and they had moved on, starting on the next street. Brigitte had pushed her way through a door, attached by one hinge, into a house and had found Ernst. The small boy was sitting against the rear wall, his head forward. Brigitte had approached him, leaning forward and touching his shoulder, then she had screamed as the boy toppled over, his blank eyes staring into space, his colourless face unmarked. She had returned to the cart and told Walbert to wait, taking the Professor by the arm, leading him back inside. The Professor had lifted the boy and placed him over his shoulder, taking him outside. Brigitte had gone to Walbert and clutched him to her, telling him that Ernst was dead, Walbert sobbing in her arms. They had made their way back to Frau Eichel's, the Professor carrying Ernst the whole way and they had buried him in the garden behind the apartment.

For the following week, Walbert had been inconsolable, the adults taking it in turns to sit with him throughout the nights, seeing him toss and turn, frequently sitting up and screaming. It was obvious he had given up the will to live, barely touching the food he was given. His feet had healed up and Frau Eichel had managed to cut and sow a pair of trousers and a shirt donated by the Professor. Brigitte decided it may help if she took Walbert with her, despite Frau Eichel's concern that he may run away. Brigitte forced Walbert to dress and put his boots on, taking him firmly by the hand and forcing him to go with her. They set of for the butcher's shop two streets away.

Queuing, as usual, Brigitte tried to get Walbert to talk but he just stood beside her, his head down, not saying a word. Brigitte got her rations and set off, heading for a small shop near St. Michaelis where she knew the pack of cigarettes she had in her coat pocket would get the identity and ration papers Walbert needed. She walked quickly along Seewartenstrasse, noticing the army truck parked ahead, Tommies standing round, smoking.

'Stop! Let's see your papers,' a powerful looking corporal said, as Brigitte and Walbert approached.

Brigitte felt Walbert pulling on her hand, gripping him tighter, pulling him to her side. Handing her papers across to the corporal she smiled. 'I know I have been stupid but I've left my nephew's papers at home. They're in his other coat.'

The corporal shook his head. 'You know the law. Should arrest you. You always have to carry your identity with you...and that includes children.'

'I know...I know. Sorry, I won't do it again.' Brigitte maintained her smile.

'Get going,' the corporal replied, 'and don't let me catch you again.'

Brigitte continued, feeling her heart banging inside her chest. 'That was close Wally. We were lucky.' Walbert did not respond. They reached the shop and went inside, Brigitte obtaining the papers she wanted after wrangling for more than an hour, the shop keeper eventually settling for twelve cigarettes.

Heading home, Brigitte decided to take a different route to avoid the soldiers. Taking well worn tracks through the debris, she had reached Kastanienallee, stepping out onto the street. A scream from the building opposite caused her to pause, at the same instance Walbert snatched his hand out of hers and ran across the street. Despite shouting after him, Walbert disappeared inside the building. Brigitte followed. She could hear shouts and curses and people fighting. Brigitte entered a room and saw, to her amazement, Walbert grappling with two other boys on the floor, both considerably bigger than him. Brigitte shouted for them to stop but they took no notice. She leant forward, grabbing one of the boys by his arm, trying to pull him off. The boy swung his boot, catching Brigitte on the shin, causing her to cry out. Brigitte saw a piece of wood and, picking it up, she brought it down hard, across the boy's back. He rolled away, grimacing. She lashed out at the second boy, hitting him hard across his arm. He shouted out and started to get to his feet. Walbert brought both of his legs up and kicked out, hitting the boy in the crotch. The boy fell down, groaning.

'What is going on?' Brigitte said.

'He saved me,' a voice said from the shadows, Brigitte turning and seeing a girl of Walbert's age emerging, her dress torn. She had blisters on her face, her hair was filthy and tangled and she was emaciated. 'Those two attacked me when I came in here looking for wood.'

Brigitte shook her head. 'Where do you live?'

'Wherever I can find a sheltered spot...a cellar, a room,' the girl replied.

'But...where are your parents?' Brigitte asked.

The girl lowered her head. 'They're dead. All my family...my parents, my sister, my grandmother. Killed by a bomb.'

'You poor child.' Brigitte walked over to the girl, ignoring the two boys who had regained their feet and shot out of the room. 'You'd better come with me...you need some food.'

'Please...please come with us,' Walbert said as he stood up.

Brigitte suppressed the surprise on her face. She looked at Walbert, seeing the bruise forming below his eye and the cut on his cheek. 'Wally and I would like you to come and have some food and maybe...maybe we can find you a good coat.'

The girl smiled, holding out her hand, Brigitte taking it in hers.

It was time to make a move, Dieter decided. He had watched the bridge across to Lauenberg for the past three days and had seen vehicles and people crossing, noticing that the British had set up a guard post at the far end, nearest to the town. As each day passed, Dieter felt colder and colder, his food had run out and he knew he could not wait any longer. He had seen a group of around twenty men coming across the bridge each morning and returning in the evening, each carrying sacks and faggots of wood, assuming that they were working the land nearby. He waited patiently for their return, making a large faggot and tying it up with some wire he had found. Reluctantly, he had dropped the rifle and magazines into a ditch.

The tramping of feet on the road alerted Dieter and he peered round the tree trunk, seeing the men approaching. He let the group pass and then walked out onto the road, walking just behind the last man. The faggot of wood, carried across his shoulders forced his head forward, making it difficult for anyone to see his face. The group soon reached the bridge and started across it. They were nearing the guard post and, glancing up, Dieter could see two soldiers watching them approach. Then he heard a vehicle coming along the road behind him, driving onto the bridge. It was coming fast and a loud blast on its horn made Dieter step towards the parapet. A truck passed close to him, stopping when it reached the guards. The men in front of Dieter continued walking, passing the truck, the two guards talking and laughing with the driver. Dieter passed them, breathing a sigh of relief, maintaining his steady pace. He walked away from the bridge and started the slow climb along the main road. He could see the men in front taking different directions as they headed for their homes, Dieter pausing, unsure what to do. He could see the road running along the side of the river, heading towards Hamburg but he knew it would be busy with troops and others. He continued along the high street, the faggot pressing into his back. Seeing a small road forking off to the left, Dieter took it, passing the old, wooden houses, not seeing anyone around. He started to relax as he left the town behind, noticing the light fading, thankful that he had got across the bridge.

Dieter threw the faggot into the ditch, relieved to get rid of the weight. He glanced to each side, looking for a shed or barn for the night and rounded a bend, the hedgerow masking the road ahead. Dieter stopped, seeing the jeep parked on the roadside. A Tommy was looking straight at him, unshouldering his rifle in the same instance.

'Halt! Papier bitte.' The soldier stepped forward, another appearing from the hedge, buttoning up his trousers.

For a moment, Dieter thought about turning and running. His training prevented him, knowing the Tommy would shoot him in the back before he had taken more than half a dozen steps. Dieter stepped forward, forcing himself to grin. 'I'm sorry. Been out in the fields all day and left my papers behind...don't usually need them out here.'

'Papier bitte!' The Tommy did not understand.

Dieter shook his head, realising he was going to be in serious trouble. He spoke again, using limited English.

'Sorry, mate...no papers, we've got to take you in,' the Tommy replied.

'But my wife...she is expecting our first born any day now,' Dieter pleaded. 'Please, let me go home...please.'

The Tommy smiled. 'Go on then, mate.'

Dieter thanked him and stepped forward.

'Wait!' the other Tommy shouted as he approached, Dieter noticing the new sergeant's stripes on the man's tunic. 'Where's he going?' he said to his colleague.

'Got a wife expecting...said he could go Serge', forgot his papers,' the soldier replied.

'No he can't,' the Sergeant shouted, 'search him and then stick him in the back of the jeep. You never know who these Jerries are...could be a war criminal. Hasn't got his papers has he? So, how do you know who he is, where he lives?'

The soldier looked apologetically at Dieter, telling him to raise his arms, quickly searching him. He produced a set of handcuffs and placed them on Dieter's wrists. 'Get in the back.'

Dieter walked across to the jeep and got in. His mind was racing but he knew it would be foolish to try and escape. Even if he were capable of getting away from these two, they would soon raise the alarm and there was very lit-

tle cover as far as he could see. The men got in and the sergeant started the engine, setting off towards Lauenburg.

Terrified, the man tried to scrabble across the floor, trying to get away as Wicus kicked him hard in the ribs, causing him to scream out in pain. Looking down at him, Wicus
kicked out again, his steel capped boot catching the man in
the face, breaking his cheek bone. Wicus grinned. He
walked across the small cellar and looked at the steel cabinet, smashing the lock with the butt of his pistol. Pulling the
door open, his eyes widened, seeing the bundles of
Reichsmarks stacked inside. He glanced over his shoulder,
seeing the man still huddled on the floor.

'Where did you get all this money from?' Wicus asked.

The man mumbled something inaudible. Wicus walked
across to him and crouched down beside him. 'Where
from?' he repeated.

'I've been saving,' the man mumbled.

Wicus admired the man's obstinacy, even though he
thought, given the circumstances, it was foolish. His men
had been watching this man for the past two weeks, logging
the visits he had, establishing that he was the major forger in
Hamburg, capable of producing any type of document re-
quired. Behind the façade of a tailor's shop, this man was
making considerable sums of money. Now Wicus had seen
the proof.

'I don't want to kill you,' Walbert said in his usual
quiet manner, 'but unless you tell me what the Americans
use you for, I will be forced to.' Wicus stood up, lashing out
with his boot, kicking the man's buttocks. If it was his decision, Wicus thought, he would kill the man immediately but
Cyrek had sent him to convince the man to work for them,
that he was useful. Wicus still could not understand Cyrek's
interest in documents. Gold, diamonds, drugs, money –
Wicus could understand that. Documents, works of art and
antiques left him cold.

The man lay still, moaning. Wicus crouched down
again, grabbed the man's hair and yanked his head back,

drawing his dagger and placing it across the man's throat. 'Tell me what you supply the Americans.'

'Identity papers, travel documents, cargo manifests...and shipping documents,' the man stammered.

'What are they shipping?' Wicus asked, exerting more pressure with his dagger.

The man urinated. 'I don't know...please.'

'What are they shipping?' Wicus repeated, seeing a trickle of blood running down the man's neck.

'Medical supplies to Russia, diamonds to America,' the man gasped.

Wicus removed his dagger and let go of the man's hair. 'From now on you will tell us when you are producing these documents. My men will visit each day.' Wicus stood up and then kicked the man hard in the ribs, hearing the sound of a bone breaking. 'If you say anything, I will kill you. Do you understand?'

Turning towards the cabinet, Wicus did not expect a reply. He stuffed as many bundles of notes into his pockets as he could and then left the cellar. When he reached the rear door, he stepped out, into the back alley and nodded to the two men lounging against the far wall. He walked along the alley, coming out onto Herrengraben and seeing the kubelwagen parked ahead, its exhaust smoking. As he approached the car, Cyrek clambered out, his large frame dwarfing the car.

'That took you time,' Cyrek said. 'Did he take a little persuasion?'

Wicus grinned and nodded.

'He's still alive...willing to do as he is told?' Cyrek asked, one bushy eyebrow rising.

'Of course,' Wicus replied. 'Now, can we go to the Atlantic...I've a feeling it could be to our advantage.'

The two men got back into the car and set off, taking little notice of the four men in scruffy clothes, stacking bricks onto a truck.

Glancing at the departing car, Captain James Jagger smiled to himself, nodding at his men who stopped loading bricks.

Ignoring the man who was asking her what she wanted for her services, Gisela continued to walk slowly round the hotel foyer. She had been instructed by Wicus to look for two American officers – one tall, one short. She had checked with the reception desk and Wilf had left a message, causing Gisela to flush with excitement, desperate to go to him straight away. But she knew Wicus' command took precedence. She would continue to look for the Americans, feeling herself becoming excited as she thought of Wilf.

Turning towards the entrance, Gisela felt her heart miss a beat. Walking in were two American officers, one tall and one short. The taller one walked towards the reception desk, the shorter one headed towards the bar. Gisela knew what she had to do. She started to approach the American at the reception desk, then froze. A woman had touched his arm and spoken to him, smiling at him. The American lowered his head and kissed her on the cheek. Gisela stepped behind a pillar, confused. The woman was Brigitte. What was she doing here, Gisela thought. How could she know him, the same American she had been told to seduce and try and get information from. Gisela left the hotel, glancing nervously over her shoulder, looking for Wicus.

Tapping the door, Gisela was relieved when Wilf opened it, falling into his arms, clutching him tightly to her body. He kissed her and eased her arms from around his back.

'I've got some news for you,' he said, smiling. 'Sit down.' Gisela did as she was told, Wilf sitting on the floor beside her, leaning against the chair and placing his hand on her knee. He passed her a glass of wine. 'When do you want to go to Pineberg?'

Gisela could not stop herself from gasping, throwing her arms around Wilf's neck, kissing the top of his head. 'When! We go now?'

'Suppose we could,' Wilf said. 'Me mates have found me a spare room and it's got an enormous bed!' He laughed, his hand sliding along the inside of Gisela's thigh.

Gisela thought she understood what he had said. 'Yes, we go now?'

'Not just yet...' Wilf eased Gisela's legs apart, pulling at her pants, Gisela easing herself up. She slid down the chair, straddling Wilf, feeling him slide into her, gasping as she gripped his hair, pressing his head against her chest.

'Time to go,' Wilf said, standing up and fastening his trousers.

Gisela pulled her pants on and straightened her dress. She buttoned her coat and waited for Wilf. They left the apartment, Wilf's arm around Gisela's waist and stepped outside, turning along the street.

Wilf glanced at his watch. 'There's a truck going to Pineberg in about ten minutes...it's near the station.' Kissing Gisela's ear, they walked along, Gisela realising she was about to be free at last. Tears ran down her cheeks.

Rumbling towards them was an old truck and, at the last moment, Gisela recognised it. She wrenched herself from Wilf's arm, turning round, seeing the kubelwagen stopping behind them. She shouted out to Wilf, telling him to run, Wilf standing still, nonplussed. Gisela grabbed his hand, pulling him across the debris, trying to climb the pile in front of them. Wilf stopped her and turned.

'What do you want?' he said, looking at the men surrounding them.

'The girl,' Wicus replied, grinning in his usual, threatening way. 'We take the girl, you can go.'

Wilf glared back. 'I'm a British soldier and I don't take orders from the likes of you. Now, I suggest you get going before I have you all arrested.' Gisela, standing behind Wilf, shook with fear.

Wicus slowly looked each way along the street and then burst out laughing. 'I don't see your troops.'

'We are the Military Authority and this girl is under my protection,' Wilf said forcefully. 'You will obey my command...go, before you get into serious trouble.'

Wicus shrugged. He then raised his sub machine gun and fired. The short burst hit Wilf across the chest, killing him before he hit the ground. Gisela collapsed beside him, sobbing uncontrollably. She felt strong arms gripping hers, lifting her up and taking her to the truck, throwing her into the back. Men climbed in and the truck set off. The men ripped her clothes off, taking her in turns, forcing her to do whatever they wanted.

Chapter Eighteen

It had been a busy couple of months for Bill, organising the convoys to Hamburg and planning his own lucrative business dealings around the journeys. At first he had been annoyed with Manson's orders but, with his ability to write up his own movement documents, the Hamburg trips provided him with the ideal cover for his illegal trading. Bill had considered dropping his weekly collection of cigarettes, alcohol, chocolates and other items from the officers and men around Bad Oeynhausen but when he had mentioned this to Lanky, the American had told him not to be so foolish, that this activity was accepted, that it distracted anyone from finding out what else Bill was up to. Bill had agreed, even though the money he made was only small compared to what he was now getting out of his Lubeck and Nienburg connections. God alone knew how Captain Blinkey was getting hold of so much stuff but, every week, Bill had taken two truck loads of antiques, pictures, jewels, carpets and other items out of Nienburg, each delivery to the Americans netting him at least five hundred pounds. As Nienburg was now on his return route from Hamburg, it was easy to arrange. When Colin had first questioned the route, Bill had told him it was safer to use the back roads as there was less chance of meeting marauding bands of Poles, Russians, Italians, French and others who were still travelling across the region. Bill had remained calm when Colin had asked him why they stopped at Blinkey's, explaining that what Blinkey provided were items for other officers. Colin had gone quiet. The only problem Bill had struggled to resolve was getting his money transferred home. He had managed to expand the number of field cashiers he could use, from Hamburg to Bad Oeynhausen and this enabled him to obtain sufficient money orders to send home without arousing suspicion.

Seeing the barrier ahead, Bill smiled, slowing the truck and stopping. He leant out of the window and threw a pack of cigarettes towards the corporal standing at the side, the corporal catching it, swearing at Bill and raising the barrier. The men on guard were so use to seeing Bill and his truck, they always let him through, knowing Bill had something extra for them. Bill lit a cigarette and started singing to himself. He soon reached the butcher's shop, pulling up outside and strolling in, nodding at the butcher and walking through the rear door.

'Hi guys,' Bill said, 'got a beer for a thirsty mate?'

Shorty stood up. 'Hi Bill.'

Bill sensed his subdued mood. 'Where's Lanky?'

'We've got a problem Bill. Rob...I mean Lanky, is trying to get it sorted out,' Shorty said as he came round the table, passing Bill a bottle of beer.

'What sort of problem...not with the shipments?' Bill asked, realising for the first time that Shorty had just call Lanky by his real name.

Shorty leant against the table, taking a long swig from his bottle. 'Yes and no. We've been told that we're about to embark for home and demob.'

'Christ!' Bill's heart missed a beat.

'Yea...that's what we thought,' Shorty said, reading Bill's mind. 'Our lucrative arrangements are under threat.'

Bill grabbed a chair and slumped down, lighting a cigarette. 'But there must be something we can do?'

'Difficult. We've got the contacts in the south; you've got movement in the north. If we are ruled out then...that's it,' Shorty said, shrugging his shoulders.

Bill saw his business disappearing before his eyes. 'Christ! There's got to be an alternative.'

'We are working on it.' Shorty stood up and walked slowly round the table, sitting down opposite Bill, staring at him. 'We're trying to get shifted to another unit...one that's sticking around for a bit longer. Trouble is, it may be a bit more difficult to meet up as frequently...shipments may be more erratic.'

'That'll cause me a lot of bloody problems,' Bill said. 'It's difficult enough arranging the right documents as it is. And I've got to coordinate these shipments with others.'

Shorty nodded. 'I know...don't think we don't appreciate what you do already Bill.'

'You could let me have your contact details and I could set up something with them direct,' Bill said. 'I could...'

'No chance!' Shorty cut in. 'Where would that leave us? No disrespect Bill but this thing only works because each of us does our bit...so to speak. Anyway, we have to protect our contacts...they wouldn't appreciate you or anyone else finding out about them.'

Bill took a swig of beer and lit another cigarette. 'Well, you'd better make sure Lanky manages to get you transferred. Don't think our man in Lubeck's going to take kindly to this if he finds out.'

'Suggest you keep this quiet for the time being Bill...wait till we see you next time.' Shorty stood up. 'Let's get the trucks sorted.'

Bill followed Shorty out, through the shop. They moved their trucks to the rear and swapped the cargos, Bill setting off after Shorty had handed him his usual envelope. On the drive back to Bad Oeynhausen, Bill's mind worked overtime, trying to work out alternatives, how much money would be lost, how to replace the Americans, what he could offer the man in Lubeck. Driving hard, Bill turned into a bend, only seeing at the last moment a woman with two children. He heard the thump and felt the truck lurch as it hit one of the children and ran over it, the mother's scream penetrating the noise of the engine. Bill carried on, cursing.

Spots of rain started to land on Dieter's face, causing him to turn his head, open his eyes, seeing the man's face next to his. He tried to ease away from the man but could not move, feeling like a sardine, wedged between a man on each side. The only way everyone in the open compound could keep warm at night and get some sleep was to lie against each other, the outer men getting up when they were too cold to sleep and forcing themselves into the middle of the huddle. Dieter eased himself into a sitting position then he stood up and carefully stepped away from the sleeping bodies, walking across to the barbed wire fence. He thought it would not be long before daylight. The rain continued to fall, Dieter pulling the collar of his leather coat tighter round his neck. He reckoned he had been held in this compound for at least a week since the men in the jeep had arrested him. Nobody had questioned him and talking to others being held, it appeared that nobody was interested in them. The compound, just along the Elbe from Lauenburg, was obviously temporary, consisting of a barbed wire fence and nothing else. There was no shelter, no ablutions, no water supply. A small number of Tommies took turns patrolling the perimeter and, once a day, a truck would reverse up to the one, small gate and a barrel of water would be pushed into the compound along with some sacks of bread. The conditions were even worse, Dieter thought, than Munsterlager. He stretched and stamped his feet, trying to get his circulation going, feeling the familiar gnawing in his stomach, the need for food dominating his thoughts.

The noise of trucks pulling up outside caused Dieter to walk towards the gate, others joining him. Even stale bread was better than nothing, Dieter thought, as he approached the gate. He saw soldiers getting out of the trucks, wondering why there were so many.

'Schnell! Schnell!' a sergeant called out. 'Get into the trucks.' He waved his sub machine gun threateningly. Dieter told those around him what the sergeant wanted and he walked through the gate, seeing the Tommies forming two lines, making sure the men walked straight to the trucks. Dieter walked along to the furthest truck and climbed into the back, others following him. When the compound was empty, the Tommies carrying the last dozen or so injured and weak prisoners to the trucks, the convoy set off. With a bitter irony, Dieter noticed they were heading for Luneburg, passing the fork in the road where he had hit the British soldier.

Stopping outside the railway station, the sergeant started yelling out orders, telling everyone to go to the train and get on board. Dieter wondered where they were being taken, ruling out Munsterlager as that was only twenty five kilometres away. The trucks could have driven that far. It was obvious they were going a lot further and Dieter felt the emptiness swell inside him. He had spent all this time trying to get to Hamburg and now, he was going to be taken to goodness knew where. A shove in his back pushed him along, Dieter seeing the cattle wagons, their ramps down, men walking up and into them. He noticed the sidings on the opposite side of the wagons.

As he reached the ramp, Dieter shoved the two men in front of him hard in their backs, forcing them to do likewise, men falling over each other. Dieter stepped sideways and fell to his knees, crawling quickly forward, under the wagon, hearing people shouting behind him. When he reached the other side he got up and ran, zigzagging his way towards the wagons in the sidings. He heard shouts and then firing, seeing the cinders spurting up in front of him. His breath came in rasps as he forced himself forward, his thighs aching. Suddenly, he fell, unsure what had happened, then realising he had been hit. Dieter forced himself to his feet, his heart pounding and stepped forward, the nearest wagon only feet away. He dived underneath it, using his knees and elbows to drag himself across the lines and out the opposite side, ignoring the pain that was coming from his calf. He stood up and glanced each way, ducking under the coupling of the wagons in front of him. He saw the guards van and hobbled towards it, thinking he could hide inside, realising that it would be the first place to be searched. He ducked under another wagon and paused. He could hear boots running across the cinders, men shouting, knowing he only had moments before he was discovered. He looked up then, grabbing the axle, he eased himself over the top of it, squeezing himself through the gap at the top, wedged against the underside of the floor. He moved himself sideways, getting his legs up onto the axle. He lay still, feeling the dampness of his blood soaking into his trousers, gritting his teeth as the pain shot through him. He could hear footsteps approaching, then stopping. His heart beat faster.

'I want that Nazi shit,' a voice hissed. 'Search every ef-fing wagon...he can't have got far.'

'Right Serge...come on you lot, search these wagons.'

Men started walking along the wagons, Dieter hearing some climbing up, checking inside. He could see the boots of the Sergeant, standing just in front of him, hearing the strike of a match as the man lit a cigarette. 'We know he's injured,' the Sergeant shouted out. 'If we don't find him, good chance he'll die.'

As the train swayed along, Brigitte clutched the girl around the waist, making sure she did not fall off. Trying to make sure Wally was all right and hang on herself, Brigitte knew they could not reach the station quickly enough. Thankfully, she had managed to tie the four small sacks of potatoes and vegetables on the running board. The journey to and from Itzehoe had taken all day and Brigitte could tell the children were very tired. At least they had managed to obtain some food, Brigitte thought, the biting wind cutting through her woollen gloves and coat.

Since the fight in the basement, the girl Frieda and Wally had become inseparable. Brigitte had smiled on many occasions; Frieda obviously enamoured with her hero, Wally happy to have someone of his own age to talk to, distracting his mind from dwelling on the death of his brother and the guilt he felt for leaving him behind. Both of them had been very helpful, playing with Heinz, taking him into the garden at the rear and helping him to practice his walking, helping Frau Eichel and joining Brigitte whenever she went out to obtain rations. Brigitte managed to make sure there was suf-ficient food - entertaining men when necessary to obtain cigarettes and money - to feed everyone and Frieda had started to regain some weight and colour.

As the train started slowing down, Brigitte saw the sta-tion emerging from the gloom. She helped Frieda and Wally down and then joined them, quickly untying the sacks. They set off for home, jostling amongst others, doing likewise. The people ahead started to stop, Brigitte feeling the pushing of people behind her. She craned her neck to see what was happening, seeing a line of Tommies at the front, checking each person as they passed. The crowd edged forward, Brigitte trying to prevent the children from being crushed and stop anyone taking one of her sacks. As she got nearer to the front, Brigitte could see what was happening, the Tommies were confiscating everything people were carrying and throwing bags and sacks of food, buckets of coal, bundles of wood and rags, onto a growing heap behind them. Brigitte elbowed her way backwards, pulling the children with her.

'Open that sack Wally and start putting whatever you can into your pockets,' Brigitte said as she started untying the sack at her feet. 'Frieda...do the same...use Wally's sack.'

The children obeyed, watching Brigitte as she filled her pockets, even stuffing potatoes into her pants and down her trouser legs. They copied her. Two sacks disappeared and Brigitte picked up the other two sacks and placed them over her shoulders. They moved forward, Brigitte pleased to see that it was not too obvious want they had done, the large coats disguising their figures. The light was fading and as they reached the first soldier, he reached out, Brigitte handing him the two sacks. She walked forward, the Tommies busy taking items from other people. They left the station and, as soon as they had turned into a side street, Brigitte let out a long sigh. She pulled the empty sacks from her belt.

'Now, let's get this food out of our clothes. Wally turn your back...I have to lower my trousers,' Brigitte said, giggling. The food was soon in the sacks and they set off.

'Why did the Tommies do that?' Wally asked. 'They don't need the food.'

'We are the one's starving...not them,' Frieda added.

Brigitte shrugged. 'I don't know. Probably told to confiscate our food to stop us going to the countryside and getting it. Anyway, we kept at least half of ours...didn't we?'

The children laughed. 'We beat the Tommies,' Wally said, starting to chant the phrase as they carried on walking.

Sitting at the bar, Colin watched the two girls on the dance floor, taken by the blond one. She was tall and slender, her breasts straining against the tight fit of her dress, her long, wavy hair hanging down her back. He took another sip from the tankard of beer, feeling slightly woozy, wondering why he had not seen her before. Then she looked across at him, smiling and beckoning to him. Colin felt the flush in his cheeks as he got off the stool and, almost mesmerised, walked towards her.

'Would you like to dance?' the girl shouted, above the noise of the music.

Colin nodded, realising he still had the tankard in his hand. He looked round and put it down on the nearest table, walking back to the girl. Someone else came across and asked her friend to dance, leaving Colin facing the girl, swaying to the music, looking into his eyes. Colin knew he was blushing, not sure what to say.

The girl placed her arm around his waist, taking his hand in hers. She said something but Colin could not hear what, shaking his head. She giggled and started to dance, Colin sure it was a jive, joining in. He felt the sweat on his brow, both of them gasping when the music stopped.

'Wow! You're a good dancer,' the girl said. 'I really enjoyed that. What's your name?'

Colin took his handkerchief from his pocket, mopping his brow. 'Colin...Colin Forsyth-Patterson,' he replied, 'and your name?'

'Victoria Hughes but everyone calls me Vicky.'

'I haven't seen you before...just arrived?' Colin asked.

Vicky nodded. 'Got here yesterday. Fantastic place and there seems to be lots going on.'

Colin smiled. 'You can say that again!'

The band struck up and they started dancing, Colin feeling his confidence returning. When the band stopped, he felt exhausted, perspiring profusely.

'Can I get you a drink?' he asked, breathing heavily. 'You certainly know these new dances but I need a rest...shall we go next door?'

Vicky grabbed his hand, nodding. They left the dance floor and went through, into the anteroom. Colin beckoned to the steward and ordered drinks, sitting down next to Vicky, noticing her long legs as she elegantly crossed them, seeing her light up a cigarette.

'With the Commission?' Vicky asked.

Colin nodded. 'And you?'

'Yes...secretary and a bit of interpretation but my German's not up to much,' Vicky replied.

They continued talking for the next hour, the drinks flowing, Colin establishing that Vicky was twenty-six, had married halfway through the war but her husband had been killed during a bombing mission and that she had then signed up with the Commission. They left the mess, Colin escorting Vicky back to her billet, agreeing to see each other the next evening. Colin found it difficult getting to sleep and was startled when his alarm went off, jumping out of bed and getting ready for his next trip to Hamburg.

'Had a hard night?' Bill asked when Colin got into the cab beside him.

Colin nodded, shifting in the seat, trying to get comfortable. During the drive to Lubeck, Colin cat-knapped most of the way, waking up when Bill started reversing the truck along the alley. They got out and Colin undid the rear canvas sheet, dropped the tailboard and climbed into the back. Bill joined him and they started unloading the wooden crates, the usual two brutes taking them into the shop, the thin man watching. They were almost finished, Colin watching as the men pulled a crate from the truck when suddenly, the rope handle at one end gave way, the crate smashing to the floor, the wood splintering. Its contents clattered across the ground, Colin's eyes bulging. He had never seen gold ingots before. The thin man yelled out, the men scrabbling to pick up the ingots, taking them inside.

'You'll say nothing,' Bill hissed, his arm across Colin's neck. 'I'll see you alright...do you understand?' Colin nodded.

Bill took the envelope from the thin man, stuffing it inside his tunic, telling Colin to get into the cab. As he walked along the side of the truck, Colin heard Bill assuring the man he would take care of any problems, wondering what he meant.

As they drove in silence to Hamburg, realisation started to dawn on Colin. He knew what Bill was up to and, furthermore, he was now the problem Bill had referred to. Colin could feel the panic rising inside him, glancing surreptitiously at Bill, seeing the Webley in its holster on Bill's belt, wondering if the sub machine gun Bill always carried was under his seat. Bill smoked constantly, glowering through the windscreen, deep in thought. When Colin saw the other trucks lined up outside the Rathaus, he breathed a sigh of relief, getting out as soon as the truck stopped.

The river bank provided cover and enabled Dieter to rest. He had managed to get out of the goods yard but only after staying hidden above the axle for the entire night. When he had tried to move, his body had protested. He was stiff all over and his leg was causing him pain and concern. He had hobbled to the wooden fence and somehow managed to scale it, falling heavily, thankful it was a grass bank on the opposite side. He had looked at his leg, seeing the congealed blood and realising that the bullet had passed through his calf. He had managed to find a branch, snapping it off and using it as a crutch, keeping his foot off the ground. Ignoring the pain, Dieter had walked, crouched and crawled his way out of the town, heading off across the fields, vowing to himself that he would never allow himself to be captured again. For three days, Dieter managed to move slowly and cautiously forward.

Cupping his hands, he drank from the water and then looked each way along the river, certain it was the River Luthe. If he remembered correctly, it meant he was less than thirty kilometres from Hamburg. He made his way along the bank, knowing there had to be a bridge not far away, the lie of the land shielding him from any roads. He followed the bank, the river meandering back and forth, for about two kilometres and then he saw the bridge ahead. Dieter edged his way closer, using the scrub along the river bank as cover.

When he was within fifty meters, he settled down, listening and watching. He could see that the bridge was old and narrow, a single track road passing over the top. Dieter wiped his eyes, trying to clear his vision which was becoming blurred. There was no sound other than the squawk of a pair of magpies, playing with each other on the parapet. Dieter moved forward, feeling slightly dizzy, reaching the bridge. He looked along the road and saw smoke curling into the sky from a fire some distance away. Then he heard voices coming from the opposite side of the road, ducking back down, flattening himself to the ground. He waited, hearing the sound of boots stepping onto the road then walking away from the bridge. Dieter eased himself up and moved forward, breathing a sigh of relief when he saw two youths walking away from him, their fishing rods slung across their shoulders. He stepped onto the road and hobbled across the bridge, stumbling down the bank and setting off, across a field. He walked as fast as he could, dizziness affecting him and as he reached a hedge he heard a vehicle approaching. Dieter squatted down, seeing a jeep driving along the road, crossing the bridge and disappearing. Dieter found a gap and climbed through the hedge, maintaining his walk westwards.

With the light fading, Dieter was relieved to see a village ahead. He shivered, feeling the chill pass through his body and he knew his leg was festering, knew he had to get proper attention. The walking throughout the day had weakened him mentally and physically to the point where he knew he could easily become careless, missing vital clues as to the enemy's whereabouts. Dieter assumed there would be a large number of British troops around and inside Hamburg. He knew he had to stay alert but, as each hour passed, he found it more difficult. He hobbled towards the first house, standing beside it and looking round the corner, studying the main street. He wiped his sleeve across his brow, wondering why he was perspiring so heavily, blinking and trying to clear his vision. He could see at least four vehicles parked along the road, all military. He felt his spirits sag. He knew it was the British. Suddenly Dieter felt his balance going, grabbing the corner of the building with his hands, trying to support himself. He slid down the wall, breathing heavily. Then he saw the child looking at him, Dieter trying to focus on the child's face, trying to make out the features before unconsciousness overcame him.

Weighing the carton in his hand, Cyrek knew the British officers were not trying to fool him. He glanced at the cargo and then shouted orders to his men, watching them as they quickly unloaded the truck. He noticed the two officers standing nearby, nervously pulling on their cigarettes, obviously wanting to get away as soon as possible. Cyrek smiled to himself, thinking his gold bar had produced a handsome return. The insulin and other drugs were worth ten times the amount he had paid out and this was the fourth truck load the British had delivered. When the unloading was completed, the British left, Cyrek going down into the cellar and checking that the goods were stacked carefully, locking the room as he left. He waved goodnight to his men and walked out, into the street, heading for the large apartment he had now taken over, two streets away.

Letting himself in, he shut the door behind him, hardly noticing the thick rug in the hall, the expensive furnishings or the gilt framed pictures on the wall. He unbuttoned his coat, took it off and threw it across a leather chair, then entered the living room. A tall, willowy blonde got to her feet and walked across to him, placing her arms around his neck and kissing him. Cyrek pushed her away, asking for a drink. He slumped down on the settee, picking up the needle lying on a plate, flicking it and then, rolling up his sleeve, he found a vein and injected himself, waiting for the elation of the opium to swamp over him. He felt the drug relaxing him, watching the blonde as she filled a glass with malt whisky, a drink Cyrek particularly enjoyed. He noticed the silk stockings, hearing them rub against each other, the bare flesh above them, approving of the girl's figure, encased in a Basque corset. She walked across and handed him a drink, Cyrek seeing the watchfulness in her eyes despite her smile. She sat on the floor between his legs, looking up at him, her hands sliding up his thighs, resting on his crotch. Cyrek smiled and shifted himself further down on the settee, the girl unbuttoning his trousers. Cyrek ruffled her hair, taking a long sip of his whisky, feeling the girl's mouth wrap around his manhood, resting his head on the back of the settee and closing his eyes. As soon as she had satisfied him, he fell asleep.

'Wake up!'

Cyrek felt someone kick his foot, opening his eyes, waiting for them to focus then seeing Wicus standing in front of him. 'What. What's the time…what's the matter?'

Wicus grinned. 'Obviously she gave you a good time…never seen you this dozy before.'

'What is the problem?' Cyrek asked as he eased himself upright, getting to his feet.

Wicus shouted out and two men came through the door, carrying a bloodied man between them. 'Seems one of our men thought he'd carry on a little business of his own. Trouble is, he's been using our stuff to do it…you know, the odd thousand cigarettes, a few bundles of notes here and there.' Wicus walked across to the man, grabbing his hair and yanking his head backwards.

Cyrek could see the man's one eye staring at him, his other eye closed where someone had hit it, the lids cut and swollen. His nose was dripping blood onto the floor. Cyrek recognised the man, one of his Polish colleagues who had been with him since they first escaped from the camp. 'Why? Why have you betrayed us like this?'

The man said nothing. Wicus smashed his fist into the man's stomach.

'Take him to the cellar,' Cyrek ordered. 'Wicus…I want him alive.'

Wicus nodded, the men departing, Cyrek following. They arrived at the cellar and Cyrek had the man stripped and then strung up by his thumbs, hanging from a beam, his toes only just touching the floor. Cyrek told the men watching what had happened. He then approached the man, his dagger slashing across the man's bare chest, blood oozing through the skin. The man pleaded with Cyrek, begging for mercy, saying he would never steal from Cyrek again. Cyrek looked at the man's open eye, stony faced. He reached down and grabbed the man's scrotum, cruelly squeezing his testicles. The man yelled out in agony, his legs bending as he drew his knees up, all his weight pulling on his thumbs. Cyrek sliced open the scrotum and castrated the man before severing his penis, letting the man's blood pour down his legs, spreading across the floor. The man died slowly, his screams filling the cellar. His former colleagues watched, mesmerised and shocked, knowing what Cyrek meant by his actions. Cyrek wiped his hands on a cloth and walked out.

Chapter Nineteen

Scratching her palms, Gisela eased herself up, into a sitting position on the bed. She looked round the small cubicle, seeing the two girls in the double bed next to hers, asleep, wrapped around each other, like lovers in an embrace. Gisela got out of the bed, pulling the rug hanging across the entrance to one side and making her way through the cellar to the makeshift washroom, noticing that most of the men had already gone out. She squatted over a pail, urinating, feeling the pain inside and around her vagina. Carefully, she touched herself, feeling the sores around her vaginal lips and anus, wincing. She looked at her hands, seeing that the rash on them had got worse. She could not understand why it was there. It had started a few weeks ago and it was getting worse. She knew she was not interested in food even though she felt hunger pangs, believing it was due to the savage murder of Wilf. Since his death, Wicus had been particularly hard to please, never satisfied with whatever she brought back, letting the men have her whenever they wanted. Cyrek had ignored her. Gisela went across to the bowl on the table and poured some water into it, washing herself as best she could. Pulling her coat on, she walked back to her cubicle and dressed, then made her way out of the cellar, wishing her headache would go away.

The day was chilly but that was to be expected in February and Gisela pulled her coat tightly around herself. The pale sun was shining directly towards her and she continued towards St. Michaelis. Since her failure to escape from Wicus' clutches and the death of Wilf, Gisela had lost interest in what happened to her, oblivious to whatever was done to her, passing each day almost trancelike, not caring. She queued outside the bakers, ignoring those around her, eventually getting two small rolls and, disinterestedly, taking a couple of bites, the bread going round her mouth, Gisela eventually swallowing. Her headache was getting worse and she thought she ought to get a drink, queuing near a stand-pipe, waiting her turn. When she reached the front, she moved the lever back and forth, cupping her other hand and drinking, feeling slightly better. She walked to St. Michaelis, standing near to the imposing church, waiting. When she saw two Tommies walking towards her, she pulled the flap of her coat back, revealing her thigh. One of them stopped, asked the usual question – how much and then, nudging his mate, they walked each side of Gisela, turning into a narrow alley. Gisela let one of them kiss her, shoving her roughly up against the wall, ignoring his rank breath and his clammy hands pushing her skirt up. He quickly satisfied himself then swapped places with his mate, who had been standing at the entrance, watching the street. The Tommy crouched down in front of Gisela, his fingers prodding into her, suddenly standing up and slapping her hard across the face.

'You filthy bitch!' he shouted at her. 'Hey, mate...you've been frattin with a right little whore.'

The other soldier came across. 'What you mean?'

'She's pox ridden, mate.' He laughed. 'Reckon you'll get a right dose of clap, mate.'

The soldier stood motionless, looking between his colleague and Gisela. 'You gotta be joking,' he said, half heartedly.

'Nope...she's got it, mate...syphilis, seen it before,' his colleague replied. 'Tell you...if you don't see the medics...you're pecker will drop off.'

'Bitch!' The soldier pushed passed his colleague, slamming his fist into Gisela's midriff. Gisela screamed, falling to the ground. The soldier kicked her in the face and continued kicking her as she squirmed on the ground, yelling bitch at her with every kick. When he finally stopped, breathless, he leant against the wall.

'Bloody hell, mate!' his colleague said, bending over the motionless figure of Gisela. 'Think you've effing killed her you stupid bugger. Come on, let's get away from here.'

The two soldiers ran out of the alley and set off along the street.

Colin and Vicky were in a meadow, lying under the canopy of a willow tree, a stream gurgling past nearby. He was looking at Vicky's naked body, stretched out in front of him, stroking her breasts. She was lying with her arms folded under her head, her eyes closed, murmuring to him, encouraging him. Then she parted her legs, inviting him. Suddenly, Colin's alarm shattered his dream. Colin turned over in his bed, feeling warm and aroused, trying to ignore the blast from his alarm clock. He slowly opened his eyes, the room was pitch black, Colin wishing he could stay where he was. Damn the alarm, he thought, as he forced himself out of bed, walking across to the light switch and flicking it on. He squinted as the harsh light hit him. Grabbing his dressing gown and sponge bag, he left his room, walking down the corridor to the bathroom. He quickly washed and shaved, returning to his room and dressing.

After breakfast in the mess, Colin went to the office, thinking about Vicky, trying to blot out what he knew he had to do, another day of boring administration. He walked into his office and sat down behind his desk, pulling the nearest file towards him, opening it and looking at the contents. He did not look up when someone entered the room, continuing to read the delivery schedules typed neatly on the page in front of him. Suddenly, an envelope landed on top of the file, Colin looking up, surprised.

'Just a small token of my appreciation, lad,' Bill Thornton said, standing with his back against the door. 'There'll be more to follow...just keep your trap shut...understand?'

Colin nodded.

Bill started to turn. 'See you Thursday then.' He opened the door and walked out. Colin sat staring after him then looked down at the envelope. He picked it up and carefully opened it, glancing inside, seeing the bundle of notes. He took them out and flicked through them. Then he counted them, stuffing them back inside the envelope and shoving it inside his tunic. A hundred pounds, almost a year's salary.

Colin stood up, pacing the room, his mind in turmoil. A knock on the door stopped him, Colin looking across and seeing a woman peeking round the door.

'You're wanted by the Captain,' she said.

'When?' Colin asked.

'Now...he said come immediately.' The woman disappeared. Colin could feel his heartbeat quickening as he put his coat on and walked across to Manson's office. The captain's secretary made him wait whilst she tapped the captain's door and went into the office, Colin feeling as he used to when he was at school, waiting outside the headmaster's study, his nerves jangling as his apprehension rose. The secretary ushered him in.

Colin saluted, standing to attention, seeing Manson talking to another officer.

'Stand at ease Sern't Patterson,' Manson said, turning towards him. 'This is Captain Jagger of the Military Provost Branch. He's here to listen to what you've got to say about the trips to Lubeck.

Colin felt the blood drain from his face, the fear tightening in his belly. He did not look at Jagger or Manson, he stared at the wall behind Manson's head. They knew. He knew they knew about Bill's activities and the bribe. 'Nothing to report Sir...just delivering medical supplies,' Colin stammered.

'Look at me Sergeant,' Jagger said, his voice quiet, persuasive.

Colin looked across at the captain, seeing his blond hair across his forehead, the fierce look in his eyes.

'As Captain Manson ordered, tell me about your journeys to Lubeck.'

Colin explained the trips, Jagger asking lots of questions, wanting details of frequency, routes, times. He seemed particularly interested in the descriptions of the thin man and his accomplices.

'And you still think you are delivering medical supplies?' Jagger asked, when Colin had finished answering his last question.

There was a long pause, Colin looking back at the wall, eventually lowering his head. 'No Sir.' He unbuttoned his tunic and pulled the envelope out, placing it on the desk. Jagger leant across and picked it up, glancing inside.

'Last week, one of the cases was dropped and it split open,' Colin continued. 'What looked like gold bars scattered across the ground.' Colin looked at Jagger but the captain just stared back, unnerving him. 'Sergeant Major Thornton came into my office this morning and gave me the envelope, telling me to keep my mouth shut and that I would get more.'

'How convenient,' Jagger said sarcastically. 'You expect me to believe that you did not know what was going on all this time and then, suddenly, on the very day I arrive, you receive your first payment. Sergeant Patterson...you'll have to do better than that.'

'It's true! Honestly Sir...I...I knew something was wrong but I didn't know what,' Colin blurted out. 'If the Sergeant Major knows what I have told you he will...he will kill me. I know he will...he told the thin man he would take care of me.'

Jagger looked across at Manson and nodded. 'Take a seat Sergeant and calm yourself. I've already had your pay receipts and the amount of money you have transferred home checked. I happen to believe you. Now, I want your help.'

Trying to break the tangled metal, moving it backwards and forwards with the help of two other women, caused Brigitte to breath heavily, feeling the coldness of the metal through her gloves. It was almost midday and she had been on the site clearing bricks since daylight. The metal gave way, one of the women letting out a short shout of triumph, Brigitte wiping her arm across her brow, smiling. Now they could get on with passing more bricks along the line. It was hard, tedious work but it meant Brigitte could obtain extra rations and with Heinz growing quickly, she always struggled to provide enough food. This work, clearing the mounds of debris and salvaging as much useful material as possible, combined with her occasional evening activities when she obtained tradable items for her black market purchases, had enabled her to provide sufficient food to keep Frau Eichel and the others from starving. Brigitte did not mind, knowing that Heinz was well cared for when she was out, the Professor taking charge of water carrying and Frau Eichel running the apartment, cooking for all.

Bending down and pulling at the bricks around her feet, Brigitte was looking forward to hearing the whistle, signifying a fifteen minute break for lunch. She had a slice of brown bread, smeared with honey, which Frau Eichel had pushed into her hand as she left the apartment. Standing straight, Brigitte glanced down the long line of women, hearing a few singing as they passed the bricks along. She was about to pick up more bricks when she saw Wally waving to her. She told the women around her, asking if she could go across to him and they agreed, another woman taking Brigitte's place. Brigitte scrabbled across the piles of debris, reaching the road, seeing Freida joining Wally, both of them smiling up at her.

'What are you two doing here?' she asked.

Freida looked conspiratorially at Wally. 'We've got you something.'

Brigitte raised her eyebrow. 'Is it a...'

The crump of an explosion, instantly followed by the rush of air smashing into Brigitte's back, knocking her on top of the children and flattening them under her body, took them all by surprise. Wood, bricks and dust flew past them, a brick smashing into Brigitte's wrist, breaking it. Then it rained debris down on top of them.

There was a sudden, eerie silence, punctuated by the last bits of debris hitting the ground. Freida started screaming followed by others around them. Brigitte tried to get to her feet, yelling out as the pain shot through her wrist. She grabbed it with her other hand as she tried to get to her knees. Freida looked at her, blood running down her face, a cut across her forehead. Wally sighed, Brigitte staggering to her feet, seeing him lying partially underneath her, his knee-cap split open. Brigitte looked round, gasping. The pile of debris that she had just run across had disappeared, what was left covered with women's bodies; broken, ripped to pieces, some still alive. Brigitte cried out, staggering towards them, others joining her, trying to help the survivors. The sight of so many maimed bodies made Brigitte vomit. She was barely aware of the sirens approaching, her tears running down her cheeks. Then Brigitte heard shouting, turning and seeing the Tommies running towards them. For a moment she felt the fear rise inside her, then she realised they were shouting out warnings, yelling at people to get away, that a bomb had gone off, that it may trigger other unexploded bombs. Brigitte started running back towards Freida and Wally.

She knelt down beside Wally. 'Can you walk?'

'Help me to stand up,' Wally said, trying not to grimace.

Freida helped Brigitte get Wally onto his feet, ignoring the blood running down her face.

'Are you all right?' a man's voice bellowed.

Brigitte turned and saw a large Tommy approaching them. 'I think we can manage,' she replied.

'Orderly! Orderly...over here,' the man yelled. He looked back at Brigitte and gently lifted her arm, noticing her wince. 'It's broken...your wrist...kaputt.' He tried to demonstrate what he meant, causing Brigitte to smile and nod, even though she was in pain. The man smiled back as a young soldier approached, a red cross on his armband signifying what he was. He quickly looked at Brigitte's wrist, carefully turning her arm over and then binding it tightly. A bandage was soon applied to Freida's head and one to Wally's knee, then he was gone.

'Do you live nearby?' the Tommy asked.

'Not far,' Brigitte replied. 'We will be all right.'

The Tommy nodded, smiled and then walked across to where the soldiers were treating the many other wounded; some who could walk being helped to the road, some being taken away on stretchers, some being covered with blankets. Brigitte put her arms around the children's shoulders, hugging them to her. She saw, for the first time, how the Tommies were trying to help the injured, their compassion and consideration. It surprised her.

Withdrawing the hypodermic syringe from the man's arm, Hannelore looked down at him, lying on the bed, seeing his thick beard and mop of dark brown hair. The man was barely conscious, his eyes flickering and closing, but Hannelore was certain she had saved him. The ethylenediaminetetraacetic acid and dimercaprol she had been injecting him with, doing their job, overcoming the poisoning she had originally diagnosed. She left the living room and went down the stairs, going into the surgery.

Her mother tapped the door and entered, placing a cup of coffee on the table. 'How is the patient?'

'He'll survive...I'm sure of it,' Hannelore replied. 'Mind, it was fortunate the child found him and came to get us and even more fortunate that two of Captain Jagger's men were here. You and I couldn't have carried him from the other end of the village. If he'd been left out for the night, he would have died. His leg injury was the cause, even though the bullet passed clean through his calf. Unusually, it turned sceptic very quickly and he somehow contracted lead poisoning.'

He's one of ours,' Hannelore's mother said, lowering her voice.

'Does that make any difference?' Hannelore snapped, regretting her reply immediately as she saw her mother flush. 'Sorry Mother...but I am a Doctor. I don't take sides.'

'I just meant...we have lost too many men,' her mother mumbled.

Hannelore walked across to her mother and put her arm around her shoulders. 'I know Mother. He'll live...I'll make sure he does. Goodness knows where he came from but I'm sure Captain Jagger will find out when he talks to him.'

'You'll report him?' Her mother pulled away from her, staring at her.

'Mother...I am not reporting anybody. He's here and Captain Jagger is bound to return before he is fit enough to get up. What am I suppose to do...hide him?'

'Hide whom, Fraulein Doctor?'

Hannelore almost choked on her coffee, both her and her mother looking towards the door. 'James! I mean...Captain Jagger, we didn't hear you come in.'

'Obviously,' Jagger replied as he walked into the surgery. He smiled and nodded towards Hannelore's mother as she quickly left the room. He walked across to Hannelore and placed his arms around her waist, kissing her affectionately. 'Hide whom?'

'There's a wounded man upstairs,' Hannelore replied, kissing James, unable to stop herself smiling, delighted Jagger was back. 'He was found at the far end of the village, suffering from a leg wound and lead poisoning.'

Jagger let Hannelore go, stepping backwards, a frown on his face. 'What sort of wound?'

'Bullet wound...passed clean through his calf.'

'Recent?' Jagger asked.

Hannelore looked at the man she loved, realising he was doing his job. 'I'd say within the past week.'

Suddenly, there was the sound of someone falling above them. They both ran out of the surgery and up the stairs, Hannelore leading the way. As she entered the living room, she saw her mother pulling at one of the man's arms, the man on the floor, groaning. 'Mother! What are you doing?'

Jagger stepped past her and placed his arms under the man's armpits, lifting him back onto the bed. The man was mumbling incoherently, Hannelore checking his pulse.

'Frau Gerber. Any further attempts by you to help this man escape will result in dire consequences,' Jagger said. Hannelore translated, her mother lowering her head, then leaving the room.

Jagger closed the door and turned round, smiling. Hannelore smiled back, then she walked over to him and they embraced, kissing each other long and hard.

Agitatedly, Bill thumped the steering wheel. He knew the shipment he had brought to Osnabruck this time was full of antiques supplied by Captain Blinkey and that meant his cut was not worth a lot, not worth the risks he was taking. Carting a load of furniture around was always risky and certainly not easy to explain to any zealous sergeant at a road block. Fortunately, he had not been stopped, waived through as usual but now, having arrived and gone into the building, he had found out that the Americans had not arrived. Parked in the alley, Bill lit another cigarette, inhaling deeply, nervously glancing at his watch. He had been here for more than an hour and was beginning to wonder what had happened. Had the Yanks been sent home already? What would he do with the furniture? Would Colin keep his mouth shut? How could he maintain his income? Bill could not stop asking himself questions. He suddenly saw two soldiers turn into the alley, coming towards him, feeling the sweat bead on his forehead.

'Got a light, mate?' one of them asked, as they reached the truck.

Bill passed his lighter across to the man who lit up, thanking him.

'What are you doing here?' the man asked.

Bill forced himself to smile. 'Just waiting for orders.'

'You to? We're all waiting for bloody orders,' the man replied. 'What have you got on the load?'

'Rations and such like,' Bill answered.

The man grinned. 'Anything we could use…if you get my drift?'

Bill smiled. 'If sacks of corn and cement are any use to you…well, be a bit difficult carrying that stuff away, wouldn't it?'

'You're right, mate,' the man replied, shrugging. 'Suppose we'd better get back on patrol…never know who's creeping round. See you, mate.' The two soldiers walked slowly back along the alley, Bill breathing a sigh of relief.

'Who were they?'

Bill jumped in his seat, looking across at the passenger door, seeing Shorty looking in. 'Where the hell have you been?'

'We got waylaid,' Shorty replied. 'Anyway, what did they want?'

'Just a foot patrol wanting a light.' Bill opened his door and climbed down. He followed Shorty into the rear room and helped himself to a bottle of beer, Lanky coming in.

'Hi, Bill. What've you got for us?' Lanky asked, picking up a bottle.

'Antiques,' Bill replied, 'but what I want to know is what is happening to you two?'

Lanky glanced quickly at Shorty. 'We think we've managed to get a transfer...not confirmed yet but we should know soon,' Shorty said.

'What's more important buddy is that we have a big shipment coming through in a couple of week's time,' Lanky said. He paused. 'Can you get a bigger truck?'

Bill frowned. 'What's wrong with the Bedford?'

'Ain't big enough,' Shorty replied. 'You need something like a Hippo. Can you get one?'

'A Hippo? You gotta be bleeding joking!' Bill sat down at the table. 'Where am I supposed to get one of those from?'

Lanky shrugged his shoulders. 'Bill, buddy...you're the expert there. Gotta be plenty up at your HQ. Bribe somebody. To carry the next shipment, you need a bigger truck.'

'Any problems with our man in Lubeck?' Shorty asked.

'Not with him. Problems yes but...well, I can take care of them,' Bill replied.

Lanky stepped forward. 'What sort of problems, buddy?'

'Just the young lad who comes with me,' Bill replied, feeling uncomfortable, wishing he had not said so much.

'Why's he a problem?' Shorty asked.

Bill told the Americans what had happened during the last delivery, assuring them he had got it covered, that Colin would not say anything.

'You gotta be bleeding joking Bill,' Lanky said. 'The less people know what we are up to, the safer we all are. You're going to have to...have to arrange an accident. The kid's gotta be silenced...for good.'

Bill looked at Lanky, then at Shorty, seeing that they were both staring at him. 'You mean...you mean kill him?'

The Americans nodded in unison.

'I can't do that. He's one of ours,' Bill protested.

'Listen up buddy,' Shorty said tersely. 'You get well paid for what you do and there's a lot more riding on this next shipment. Enough to make you rich for the rest of your life. Get rid of the kid, understand me?'

Bill nodded.

Chapter Twenty

Squinting, Dieter eased opened his eyes, adjusting to the daylight. He looked slowly around, realising he was in a living room, wondering where he might be. He eased himself up, onto his elbows, feeling dizzy. Dieter moved his legs, the slight pain in his calf reminding him of what had happened. He placed his feet on the floor and tried to stand up. A wave of nausea hit him and suddenly, Dieter was kneeling on the floor, vomiting. He was aware that somebody had entered the room and, wiping his arm across his mouth, he glanced up, seeing a tall, elegant woman leaning against the door jamb, studying him.

'If you want to continue vomiting, please continue trying to stand up,' she said, humour in her voice.

Dieter slumped back onto the bed, pulling a blanket around him.

The woman approached him. 'I'd prefer it if you stayed where you are. I don't really enjoy cleaning up your mess.'

'I apologise for that,' Dieter croaked. 'Where am I?'

'You're in Buckholz,' the woman replied as she started to mop up Dieter's vomit.

'Who are you?' Dieter asked.

The woman looked at Dieter. 'Doctor Gerber.' She carried on cleaning.

Dieter lay back and closed his eyes. 'What was wrong with me?'

'Lead poisoning,' the Doctor answered, matter of factly.

Dieter groaned. 'How did I get here?'

'The British brought you here,' the Doctor answered.

Dieter tried to move, his foot catching the Doctor on her back. 'I'm sorry...I have to go...now.'

'Go where?' a man asked.

Dieter looked at the doorway and saw a man in military uniform, a red hat tucked under one arm – a British Army officer. Dieter slumped back on the bed, cursing under his breath, wondering how many more times he was going to be captured by the British. He knew he was not in a fit state to escape and if the doctor was telling the truth, lead poisoning could take a little while to fully recover from.

'You're not well enough to go anywhere,' the Doctor said, looking down at him. 'I am still administering medication and that is what is causing you to feel nauseous.' She repeated what she had just said to the officer.

'Ask him for his name, rank and service number,' the officer said. 'He has to have served in the military during the war.'

After the doctor had asked him, Deiter gave the information, thinking of how he could escape later.

'He's Gestapo,' the officer said. 'Probably on the run for war crimes.'

'Ich bin nicht Gestapo! Ich bin Wehrmacht,' Dieter replied. He realised his mistake.

The officer walked across to the bed and leant forward, his blond hair falling forward. 'So. You understand English?' He smiled, sitting down on the side of the bed. 'How did you get wounded?'

A wave of dizziness caused Dieter to close his eyes. He waited, then opened them, the officer staring at him. 'Escaping.'

'From whom?' the officer asked.

'You...the British.' Dieter glanced across at the doctor. She smiled back.

'Who tortured you?' the officer asked, his voice quiet but persuasive.

Dieter was surprised by the question. 'What do you mean?'

The officer looked at him. 'You have been tortured with shin screws...the marks are still on your legs. Where did that happen?'

'You British tortured me,' Dieter said, defiance in his voice. 'At a place called Bad Nenndorf.'

The officer stood up and walked across to a table, pouring himself a glass of water. He turned round. 'To be there you must have something in your past that is unsavoury. You are not Gestapo but…you must have been a prison guard or a Nazi Party member…something you are not telling me.'

Dieter could not explain why but he started to tell the officer everything, starting with the day his brigade had surrendered to the Americans.

'I can check your story,' the officer said, when Dieter had finished.

Dieter nodded.

'In the meantime, I suggest you let the good Doctor here help you back to full recovery.' The officer stepped towards the door, then turned. 'You can escape but what will that achieve? Do you want to stay on the run? I think I can help you if what you have told me is the truth.' He left the room.

'Would you like to come in?' Vicky asked.

Colin nodded, glancing each way along the street. He knew it was forbidden to visit the women's billets after dark but he was sure nobody had seen them. He had taken Vicky to a film evening in the mess and she had seemed to thoroughly enjoy it. On the walk back, she had stopped him twice, throwing her arms around his neck and kissing him long and hard. They had been seeing each other for the past three weeks, going dancing on a number of occasions and, every time, when Colin had walked Vicky home, he had wanted to go to bed with her. This was the first time she had invited him in. Colin could feel himself becoming aroused as he stepped inside. Further down the street, in a doorway on the opposite side, Bill Thornton smiled to himself, lit a cigarette and walked away.

After Vicky had quietly closed the door, Colin felt her hand in his, guiding him along the darkened hallway, leading him towards a room at the rear. Vicky opened the door and they went into the room, closing the door behind them. Colin felt Vicky pressing her body against his, seeking his lips, Colin responding. They clung to each other, moving slowly backwards, Vicky stopping when her bottom touched the table. Colin felt her hands undoing his tunic and shirt, moving across his chest, caressing him. He started to fumble with the buttons on her coat, reaching inside and unbuttoning her blouse. Vicky now had his trouser belt undone and quickly unbuttoned his flies, his trousers dropping to his ankles. Her hands pushed his underpants down and she gently started to stroke his erection. Colin undid Vicky's skirt, letting it drop, his hands pulling her petticoat up, then feeling her bottom. They continued kissing, their tongues exploring each other's mouths. Vicky turned her head away, moaning, pulling her pants down. She eased herself onto the table, placing her legs around Colin's thighs, pulling him towards her, her hand guiding him into her. She lay back on the table, letting out a loud moan then started to thrust her pelvis against Colin's, the pair in unison. Colin placed his hands around her hips, pulling her tighter against him, thrusting slowly and deeply into her. He knew he was about to explode, hearing Vicky moaning. Then she let out a loud wail, Colin feeling the pulses inside her as he reached his own climax. Neither of them moved for what seemed like an eternity then Vicky sat up, kissing Colin.

'That was wonderful,' she said, 'you are fantastic.'

Colin withdrew, his erection still quite firm. 'But…but I didn't take precautions.'

Vicky laughed. 'Frightened I might give you something?' she joked.

'No. More the other way round,' Colin replied. 'You might get pregnant.'

'Don't worry about that…wrong time of the month.'

Colin was perplexed. He never could understand how women worked this out. He stepped back and pulled his pants and trousers up, buttoning them and refastening his belt. Vicky eased herself off the table and walked across the room, turning the light on, her pants in her hand. Colin blinked, seeing her standing almost naked then, looking round, he could see that they were in the kitchen. Vicky asked him if he would like a cup of tea, buttoning up her blouse and fixing her skirt. Colin nodded and watched her as she filled the kettle and placed it on the stove. He sat down.

'Can I tell you a secret?' he asked.

Vicky smiled at him. 'If you think you can trust me to keep it.'

Colin frowned and Vicky walked over to him, placing her arm across his shoulders.

'You don't have to tell me...I won't mind,' she said.

'It's not that. It's just that it's dangerous,' Colin said.

Vicky stepped away, made the tea and placed a cup in front of Colin. She then sat down. 'You're really worried, aren't you?'

'It's all to do with the black market,' Colin said. 'I've been questioned by the Military Provost Branch.'

'Are you in trouble? Have you been a naughty boy?' Vicky asked, trying to suppress a smile. 'I don't want to go out with a criminal.'

Colin grinned. 'It's not funny. I'm not the criminal but...I know who is and I think he might try to kill me.'

'No!' Vicky stopped smiling and sat upright. 'You must report him.'

'That's the problem...I already have but he doesn't know that,' Colin said. 'You know I'm off to Hamburg next Thursday? Well, I'm going with him to Lubeck with another shipment.'

'Shipment of what?' Vicky asked.

'Gold.'

Vicky stared at Colin, knowing that he was incapable of telling a lie. 'My goodness. Who is this man?'

Colin hesitated. 'I'm only telling you this so that, if anything happens, you can tell Captain Manson. It's Sergeant Major Bill Thornton.'

'How do you know you can trust Manson?'

'He's trustworthy. He called in the Provost chap,' Colin replied. 'They want me to carry on as usual, just tell them what happens. Suppose they are laying a trap.'

Vicky smiled and reached out, taking Colin's hands in hers. 'Sounds exciting but do be careful.'

'I intend to be,' Colin replied. He stood up and eased Vicky from her chair, holding her round the waist. He lowered his face to hers, kissing her, Vicky responding.

In the cellar, the noise of people chatting and laughing made it difficult for Brigitte to hear what the man was saying to her. She could feel the oppressive heat, the air thick with cigarette smoke, stinging her eyes. Bodies were crammed together, sweating and smelling. And the drink flowed. Everyone seemed to be drowning in a sea of alcohol. Brigitte could feel her bound up wrist throbbing, knowing it would take a little longer to heal. The man facing her handed her a glass, the pale liquid burning Brigitte's throat as she swallowed. Brigitte wished she had not come here. Some of the women she worked with had told her it was a good place to meet the Tommies and get cigarettes, perfume and other items for offering her company. Brigitte knew what they meant and, as her stock of food was now getting very low and she had almost run out of cigarettes to barter with, she had decided to try the cellar, euphemistically called a night club.

The man grinned at Brigitte, his beery breath making her turn her head. The musicians started and he put his arm round her waist, trying to dance, stumbling forward and standing on Brigitte's foot. She yelped out, hopping on one leg as she clasped her foot in her hand. The man's grin widened as he pushed forward through the crowd, pulling Brigitte by the hand. They reached the wall and he pushed Brigitte's back against it, shouting in her ear, saying he was not any good at dancing. The man left her standing there, Brigitte seeing him getting a bottle of drink from another man nearby and returning to her. He opened the bottle and started to drink from it, burping and wiping his sleeve across his mouth, offering Brigitte a drink. Brigitte declined. The man drank his way through the bottle. He then faced Brigitte, pushing against her. She felt his hand groping at her crutch, pushing it to the side. The man grinned, trying to kiss her, a hand squeezing one of her breasts. Brigitte just wanted to go home. She nodded towards the door, the man following her gaze. Taking her by the hand he led her out of the cellar.

Stumbling up the stairs, Brigitte found herself helping the man, trying to steady him as he rocked on his feet. She led him into the street and then he placed his arm over her shoulder, Brigitte partly holding him up. They walked a short distance then Brigitte saw the entrance to a bombed out building. She helped the man inside.

'You have cigarettes or money,' Brigitte asked.

The man nodded, still grinning. 'Yea darlin', you good fratin?'

Brigitte nodded, forcing herself to smile. 'Show me the cigarettes,'

'Show you somethin' else darlin'...you'll like this.' The man started to unbutton his trousers, struggling with his coordination. Suddenly, he fell forward, flat on his face. Brigitte stared at the motionless form. She stepped forward and crouched down beside the man. He was alive but, as far as Brigitte could tell, unconscious. She stood up and went outside, checking the street, going back to the man. He still had not moved. Brigitte put her hand inside his coat pocket, pulling out a large wad of notes. She tried the other pocket and found the same. Despite her wrist protesting, Brigitte managed to turn the man over, going through the pockets inside his coat, finding more wads. Brigitte stuffed the money into her own pockets, looked at the man one last time and left.

Lying beside the railway track, Wicus placed his ear on the rail, hearing the approaching train. He looked along the track, satisfied that the spot he had chosen was ideal; it provided the train driver with sufficient time to stop, especially as the train would be travelling slowly up the steep gradient. He shuffled backwards and slid down the embankment, nodding towards Cyrek.

'It's coming,' he said.

Cyrek indicated to his men, watching a group of them struggle to drag a tree trunk across the tracks. He turned to

Wicus. 'You are sure your forger has given us the correct details?'

Wicus grinned. 'He wouldn't dare lie to me. He told me when the train would be passing and he'd heard that it was carrying a large consignment of dollars and other foreign currencies from Bavaria up to Kiel where it would be transferred to a ship sailing for America. He was sure it had been stolen from secret caches in the mountains.'

Did he say how much?' Cyrek asked.

Wicus shook his head. 'Not exactly…but he thought it was more than one million dollars in total.'

'Did you find out if the train is carrying armed men?' Cyrek asked.

Wicus again shook his head. 'Bound to be a few…isn't there?'

'Shit! Wicus, when will you learn? You've dragged me out here on this mad idea, not telling me anything until we get here and now, when I ask you two simple questions, you haven't got the answers.' Cyrek looked away in disgust.

Wicus felt a slight shiver pass down his spine. With the amount of opium Cyrek was taking, he had not been able to tell him what he had planned. It was only when they arrived that Cyrek appeared to be his normal self. 'A million dollars. It's worth having a go…isn't it?'

They could hear the train coming round the bend, straining to maintain its momentum. Within seconds, they heard the distinctive squeal of wheels locking as the driver applied the brakes. The train stopped some fifty feet from the trunk. Cyrek blew once on his whistle, standing and running up the embankment, Wicus by his side. His men were emerging from their positions along the track and Cyrek could see the frantic look on the driver's face. Suddenly, gun fire rent the air, Cyrek throwing himself across the tracks. Soldiers piled out of the train, firing almost point blank at Cyrek's men, cutting a number down before they could turn and run. Cyrek opened fire, aiming for the driver, his bullets ricocheting off the cab. Then the train started to move backwards as the driver released the brakes, gathering speed, the soldiers scrabbling to get back on board. The train disappeared round the bend as Cyrek got to his feet. He looked round and saw Wicus helping an injured man to his feet.

'What a total balls up!' Cyrek yelled out. 'If I didn't know you so well, I'd be thinking it was a set up.' He stood, staring at Wicus. 'There must have been at least fifty men on that train. We could have been wiped out.'

'Wait till I get my hands on that effing forger,' Wicus replied. 'He must've known.'

'You won't kill him,' Cyrek stated. 'I want him kept alive…do you understand?'

Wicus nodded.

'Come on, let's get back to the truck. Leave the dead behind.' Cyrek set off down the embankment, heading for the trees.

Thanks to the doctor's care and her mother's insistence that he should eat a meal three times a day, Dieter had recovered quicker than the doctor had anticipated. He had enjoyed the cleanliness of his washed clothes, the cutting of his hair and removal of his beard. He had forced himself to walk round the room each day with the aid of a crutch, stopping his leg from stiffening up as the bullet wound healed. He had sat, talking to Frau Gerber, the doctor's mother, for hours at a time. The old lady had told him about the suffering of the local people and had answered, as best she could, his questions about the state of Hamburg. She had eventually told him what they had endured when the Polish had forced themselves upon them. Dieter had already realised that the doctor was in love with the British officer, at first feeling revolted but now, understanding and respecting her. Frau Gerber had suggested to him that, as soon as he could, he should escape, that she could help him, that the British were not to be trusted.

As he awoke, Dieter glanced across at the window, seeing the sunlight. He eased himself out of the bed and walked across to the table, helping himself to a glass of water. The door opened and Dieter saw the doctor enter, carrying a small tray.

'Good morning Dieter. I see my patient is looking healthier by the day,' Hannelore said.

Dieter smiled. 'Thanks to you, Fraulien Doctor.'

'Hannelore...please. Now, on the bed and let me take a look at the leg.'

Doing as he was asked, Dieter sat on the edge of the bed as Hannelore knelt down and undid the bandage around his calf. He looked down at her, seeing her long, brown hair tied in a neat bun at the base of her neck, noticing her long fingers gently massage his calf.

'Is there any pain?' she asked.

'No,' Dieter replied. 'It feels stiff but no pain.'

'That is good. I think we will leave it unbound...let the air get to it,' Hannelore said, standing up. 'You should go for a walk, it is pleasant outside and the exercise will do you good.'

Dieter nodded. 'Do you have my leather coat?'

'It's downstairs, in the hall.' Hannelore crossed the room and went into the kitchen, returning with a basket of bread and a plate of cold meat. Dieter joined her at the table and they talked about the future of Germany, Hannelore telling him that the Russians had not moved back from the River Elbe and, from what she could gather, they would not be forced to. Dieter questioned what would happen to the eastern part of Germany if the Russians stayed where they were, both of them wondering what the Americans and British had in mind. When the breakfast was finished, Dieter, with the help of Hannelore, made his way down the stairs.

Stepping outside, Dieter took some deep breaths, looking along the street and seeing a number of people queuing outside a small butcher's shop. Even with the sun shining, Dieter felt the chill of the wind on his face, pleased that he still had his leather coat. He set off along the street, gingerly at first then, as the stiffness eased from his calf, he forced himself to walk faster. He saw a jeep parked outside a house ahead of him and as he approached, four Tommies came out and got into it, driving off, ignoring him. Dieter soon reached the edge of the village and he glanced over his shoulder. Nobody was watching him. He climbed over a gate and walked into a field, quickly reaching a copse on the far side. Breathing heavily, he sat down. It was obvious to him that he could easily escape - do it now, before the officer returned.

Sitting down, Dieter considered his options. He could walk to Hamburg and find his wife. However, without papers, he would have to stay in hiding, fearful of being arrested and carted off to a detention camp. He could stay in the countryside until the British left but that could be for two years or more and, again, he could be captured at any time. He could walk back to the village and take his chances with the British officer, despite Frau Gerber's reservations. Dieter dozed off.

Chapter Twenty One

Putting his penknife into his pocket, Bill walked from the back of the truck, kicking its tyres. He climbed into the cab, cursing the rain, cursing the truck, cursing Colin. He lit a cigarette, inhaling deeply, cursing the ruling that Montgomery had applied to the field post offices. He could no longer purchase money orders for more than he was paid. This limited him to one hundred and fifty pound orders, meaning he would have to spend more time visiting field offices, assuming he could find a sufficient number to transfer what he wanted to each month. Bill knew this would not be possible – he would have to start shipping goods and money home. At least he had his contact in Lubeck, he thought.

'Morning,' Colin said, as he opened the passenger door and climbed in.

Bill looked across. 'Don't like these early mornings do you, lad?' He started the engine and set off, the other trucks following.

Peering through the windscreen, the wipers struggling to clear the rain and the headlights barely showing the road, Colin thought Bill was driving to fast, as usual. He said nothing, his hand moving to his side, feeling the pistol in its holster, under his coat.

'How you gettin' along with that WAAF?' Bill asked.

Colin looked surprised. 'What do you mean?'

Bill grinned briefly at him. 'That leggy blonde you've been frattin with.'

'For God's sake, Bill...,' Colin protested, 'you're so bloody crude. Anyway, it's none of your business.'

'It is when it interferes with your job, lad. Staying up all night and then turning up knackered...you can start making mistakes, accidents can happen,' Bill replied.

Colin stared through the windscreen, wondering how Bill had found out, knowing Bill had seen him staying at Vicky's billet. He kept quiet.

Crossing over the river into Lauenburg, they were waved through the road block and, shortly after, Bill turned the truck northwards, the others driving west to Hamburg. With the daylight, Colin could see through the trees that they were skirting a large lake, dropping down into a shallow gully. Bill changed down as the truck started to climb out the other side, suddenly stopping.

'What's wrong?' Colin asked.

Bill frowned. 'She's not right. Maybe a puncture. Stay there, I'll take a look.' He got out and Colin watched him in the wing mirror, seeing Bill crouch down near the back wheel. Colin got out and walked round the front.

'Bloody flat,' Bill said, standing up. 'Come on, let's get the jack and spare out.'

Colin helped, turning the jack handle, eventually seeing the rear wheel lift off the ground as Bill loosened the nuts. Bill changed the wheel and asked Colin to tighten the nuts, standing behind him as he bent down.

Looking both ways along the road, Bill picked up a large spanner. He looked at the back of Colin's head, knowing one good blow would be sufficient. He stepped closer, raising his arm. The discharge of a pistol caused Bill to turn, Colin to look behind him, seeing Bill clutching a spanner in his hand, then seeing an approaching vehicle roaring towards them, the jeep skidding to a stop next to them. Bill cursed under his breath, looking at the Military Provost Branch officer, a sergeant sitting next to him.

'Got a problem?' the officer asked.

Bill saluted. 'No Sir. Just a puncture...soon be on our way.'

Colin stood, staring in disbelief, his mouth open.

'And where are you heading for?' the officer asked.

'Hamburg, Sir,' Bill replied.

The officer raised an eyebrow. 'Bit out of your way...isn't it?'

Bill smiled at the officer. 'Have to be careful, Sir. The main routes into the city are full of unsavoury characters and I've been told by colleagues about unofficial road blocks, supplies being robbed, even lives being threatened.'

'What are you carrying?' the officer did not smile back.

'Just some medical supplies, Sir.'

The officer nodded towards his sergeant. 'Take a look Sergeant.'

Bill watched the sergeant go to the rear of the truck, heard him unfasten the tail-flap and then climb inside. Bill could feel the sweat prickling his skin. The sergeant jumped down to the ground, looked at the officer and nodded.

'Let me see your papers,' the officer said, Bill fumbling with his tunic pocket, pulling a sheaf of papers out and handing them across. The officer glanced at the papers, handing them back. 'Right Sergeant Major, all seems to be in order.' The officer slammed the jeep into gear and roared off.

Bill watched them disappear. 'Bloody police! Right, let's get going if you've finished tightening that wheel,' he shouted at Colin.

They got into the cab and set off.

'How come that sergeant didn't find anything?' Colin asked.

Bill pulled on his cigarette. 'Because, lad, I made sure the last three cartons did have medical supplies in them. Thank God they were in a hurry and he didn't have time to start looking through everything. Otherwise, we'd have been in trouble.'

Colin looked out of the side window, wondering why Captain Jagger had not carried out a full search.

'Get down!' Brigitte hissed, pushing Walbert to the ground. She watched the two Tommies walk past, hoping Frieda remained still, lying in the grass on the opposite side of the track. It had been foolish, Brigitte thought to herself, to have let Frieda come with her but Walbert had pleaded with her and she had eventually given in, knowing the children would be able to help her carry the sacks home. The

Tommies disappeared and Brigitte eased herself to her feet, checking each way along the track. Walbert got up beside her, complaining that his clothes were wet and it was getting cold. Frieda appeared, Walbert immediately stopping his moaning.

'We have to walk about another kilometre, then we are there,' Brigitte said. She took their hands and they walked along the track, heading for the farmhouse Brigitte had been told could supply as much pork and chicken as she wanted.

Frieda pointed ahead. 'Is that it?'

'Should be,' Brigitte replied. 'I want you both to hide over there,' she added, pointing at a clump of shrubs. 'Wait until I come and get you...understand?' She saw both of them nod, then walked up to the front door, tapping it with her fist.

The door opened slowly, just enough for Brigitte to see a small woman peering inquisitively at her, asking her what she wanted at this late hour.

'I've been told you can supply me with meat,' Brigitte replied, smiling.

The woman eyed her up and down. 'Depends what you got to offer.'

Brigitte pulled a bundle of notes from her coat pocket, seeing the woman's eyes widen. The door eased open and the woman invited her in, leading the way along a narrow, unlit corridor, entering a large kitchen at the rear. The woman immediately asked Brigitte what she wanted, Brigitte telling her. The woman yelled out a name, her husband appearing, his clothes filthy and ragged. He went out again, shortly returning with a side of pork and two dead chickens. Brigitte started counting out the notes, the woman complaining that it was not enough, Brigitte adding a few more to the pile. Satisfied, the woman nodded, her husband placing the pork over Brigitte's shoulder, then passing her the chickens. The woman and Brigitte set off along the corridor. The sound of vehicles stopping, feet pounding on the loose stones and gravel, shouting and then thumping on the front door, had caused the women to stop, Brigitte turning and heading back to the kitchen.

'Is there a back door?' Brigitte asked.

The woman nodded and pointed. 'Out there...don't get caught.'

Brigitte walked through a scullery, the woman's husband holding the back door open.

'Go across to the barn and then turn right...leads you to a ditch,' he said.

Brigitte set off, feeling the weight of the pork, determined she was not going to lose it. She reached the barn, turned and found the ditch, sliding down the side. Her feet sank into the mud, the cold water reaching her crotch. Brigitte waded along, worried her boots would be sucked off her feet. The ditch seemed to be getting deeper as the cold water reached her waist, Brigitte breathing heavily. She heard a vehicle approaching, unsure how close to the ditch it could get. Then the beams of a searchlight pierced the dusk, flitting towards where she stood. Brigitte took the pork off her shoulder and pushed it behind some reeds, doing the same with the chickens, the beam getting closer. Just as the beam was about to reach her, Brigitte took a deep breath and lowered herself under the water. She looked up, through the murk, seeing the beam above her, sweeping back and forth, praying it would go away before she ran out of oxygen. The beam swept away, Brigitte rising, gulping in air. The squeal of a pig in pain came from the barn, followed by gunfire and men's voices. Then she heard the vehicle moving away, the beam being played across the field. Retrieving the pork and the chickens, Brigitte started to walk back the way she had come, eventually reaching the barn, shivering in the cold water, listening for the men. There was no sound, just an unnatural stillness. She got out of the ditch, her clothes heavy and dripping, making her way quickly passed the barn and across an orchard, circling round the house. She saw men getting back into the vehicles then driving off. She made her way across to the shrubs.

'Are you there?' she whispered. No reply. Brigitte walked through the shrubs but there was no sign of Frieda and Walbert. Panic started to rise inside her, wondering where they might be or worse, they had been taken by the men. She called out, walking round, still no sign. Then she noticed the door to the house was wide open. Brigitte walked towards it, seeing that it had been splintered. She put the side of pork and chickens down, walking cautiously along the corridor, the complete silence amplifying the sound of her beating heart. She peeked round the door and gasped. The woman was lying on the floor, blood pouring from her head. Brigitte moved quickly across the room, crouching down beside the woman, seeing that she was dead. A noise behind her made her whirl round, the husband staggering towards her, holding his belly, his hands covered in blood. Brigitte stood up, grabbing a chair and helping him to sit down.

'What happened? Did the Tommies do this to you?'

The man shook his head. 'They just…they just hit her,' he mumbled. 'When I came out one of them stuck his bayonet into me.'

'Who were they?' Brigitte asked.

'Don't know. Think they might have been Russians.'

Brigitte looked round the kitchen, seeing a bundle of cloth on a chair. She quickly found a soiled sheet and went back to the man. 'Not British?'

The man shook his head. 'Don't think so…they've been here before. This lot sounded different.' He grimaced as Brigitte eased his shirt off, pulling his vest up. 'Think they've taken the pigs and hens. Is she…is she..?'

Brigitte glanced across at the woman. She took the farmer's hand in hers, looking at him. 'Yes…your wife is dead.'

The man looked down at his belly, his frame shaking, the sobs building. Brigitte started to bind the sheet around him as best she could. 'You have to get this seen to. Do you have a doctor nearby?'

'Why? They didn't have to kill her. They could just take what they wanted,' he mumbled, almost incoherently. 'Why?'

'Do you have a doctor nearby?' Brigitte said, more forcefully.

The man nodded. 'End of our road, lives in the big house to the left. Why did they do this?'

'I've got to go,' Brigitte said. 'I will ask the doctor to come as soon as possible.'

Walking back along the corridor, Brigitte felt the anger inside, knowing there was no answer to the man's question. It was all so senseless. The war was over but this thievery and murdering was still a regular occurrence. There were too many people, of all nationalities, trying to make their way somewhere; some for home, some to evade capture, some to disappear anonymously, some to escape from oppression. The gangs of various nationals were the worst, living off the countryside, pillaging, raping and murdering. She stepped outside and slung the pork over her shoulder, picking up the chickens, feeling her body shivering as the light wind blew through her wet clothes. She had to get home quickly but she knew she had to find the children first. Brigitte started calling out their names and continued as she walked slowly along the track leading away from the farm.

Walking up to the door of the large house, Brigitte was trembling all over. She placed the pig and chickens behind a bush and then knocked the door. There was no sound. She bashed her fist on the door, shouting out. Eventually, she heard someone unbolting the door and an old man, his grey hair dishevelled, peered at her through thick glasses. Brigitte quickly told him about the farmer and his wife.

'But you are soaked. You'll catch your death if you don't come in and get out of those clothes,' the man said, pulling the door fully open. He ignored Brigitte's protests, leading the way into the kitchen. 'I'll go and see what I can find. Meanwhile, there's a towel over there. Get out of those things and dry yourself.'

Brigitte watched the old man hobble out of the kitchen. She quickly removed her clothes, drying herself and tying the towel around her.

'Here, try these on,' the man said, as he hobbled back into the kitchen. 'My wife was a petite woman, bit shorter than you but they should fit. I can see you haven't got much weight on you.'

Brigitte flushed, conscious that the towel barely covered her. Reading her thoughts the old man laughed and turned away from her. 'I am...was a doctor,' he said. 'I'll go and get my case ready.' He hobbled out and Brigitte let the towel drop, picking up the pants and pulling them on, feeling the silk against her skin. The doctor's wife had certainly only bought good quality clothes, Brigitte thought as she buttoned the skirt up, fitting her waist perfectly. She felt much better and had stopped shivering. The old man came back in.

'Herr Doctor. Thank you so much for your kindness. I will return your wife's clothes as soon as I can.'

The old man waved his hand dismissively. 'No need. I can't wear them! Anyway, they look a good fit to me and I'm sure they will help you. There are coats in the hall. Take one...you'll need it. Now, I'd better get off and see how my neighbour is faring.'

They walked out together, Brigitte taking a thick woollen coat from the hallstand. On the road, she thanked the old man again and set off. When she had walked about fifty metres, Brigitte paused and turned round. The old man was nowhere in sight. Brigitte ran back to the house and collected the pig and chickens. She walked back to the road and then turned, heading back towards the farm. As she walked along, she saw a large elm tree overhanging the track and she placed the pig and chickens behind the trunk. She continued, calling out the children's names as quietly as possible, hearing the noise of running water in a stream nearby. Brigitte headed towards it, reaching a small bridge and pausing on it, peering into the darkness, assuming there must be a field in front of her. She called out again.

A sudden splashing came from beneath Brigitte, startling her. She looked over the low parapet and saw the muddy face of Walbert looking up at her.

'Wally! Thank God! Where is Frieda?' Brigitte scrambled down the side of the stream, reaching out for Walbert, his arms wrapping tightly around her waist. He started to sob.

Easing him gently away from her, Brigitte looked down at Walbert. 'Where is Frieda?'

Walbert shook his head. 'Don't know. We ran off when the men came and...and we lost each other in the dark. Oh, I thought you were dead...I didn't know what to do.'

'We have to find Frieda...come on.' Brigitte took Walbert's hand and they climbed the bank, crossing the bridge and walking to the track. 'She can't have gone far on her own,' Brigitte said, hopefully. They soon reached the farm, calling out for Frieda as they walked, Wally starting to shiver in his wet clothes. Brigitte led him into the house, calling out and walking into the kitchen. The doctor was sitting at the table, opposite the farmer, both men looking slightly surprised, Brigitte noticing that the woman's body had been removed.

Brigitte explained to them that she was looking for Frieda and that Walbert had to get out of his clothes. The farmer told her where she might find some clothes and Brigitte soon returned, Walbert stripping and putting them on. The doctor and Brigitte tried not to laugh, the farmer's clothes being far too big for Walbert. Brigitte rolled the sleeves and trouser legs up. At least Walbert was dry. Thanking the farmer, they left, setting off back along the track, calling out.

'We will have to go home soon Wally,' Brigitte said, 'before the dawn. We can't carry a pig through the streets in daylight. We would either be arrested or robbed. I'll come back tomorrow and find Frieda.'

Wally suddenly stopped. 'I'm not going without Frieda. I'm staying here until I find her.'

Brigitte looked at Walbert. She knew it was pointless arguing. He had lost his brother; he was not going to lose Frieda. They walked on, stopping at the elm tree. Brigitte felt the weariness in her legs, suggesting they sit down and wait for the light. She walked behind the trunk and slumped against the tree. The rustle of bushes nearby startled her, Frieda emerging. Brigitte threw her arms around the girl, hugging her tightly, Walbert joining them.

'Knew you would come back here for the pig,' Frieda said, tears running down her cheeks.

'But...how did you know I had the pig?' Brigitte asked.

'Saw you leave the farmhouse with it over your shoulder,' Frieda replied, squeezing Walbert's hand.

'Why didn't you call out to me?' Brigitte asked.

Frieda looked down. 'I wasn't sure all the men had gone. I didn't...didn't want to get caught. Then, when I thought it was safe to come out from where I was hiding, it was too late, you'd disappeared.'

Brigitte hugged Frieda and laughed. 'Let's get home.'

Wielding the pick-axe, Dieter felt the dampness of the sweat on his back, his shoulders aching. He paused, standing up straight and stretching, glancing across the street, seeing four men disappearing into the cellar entrance. Dieter looked at his watch, noting the time. He raised the pick-axe and brought it down, cracking the stone. Others around him were picking up the stones, bricks and fire-blackened debris, loading hand carts and hauling them away. The German overseer blew his whistle, signifying a break for fifteen minutes. Dieter slumped down on the ground, those around him doing the same. The man next to him passed a pale of water to him, Dieter cupping his hands and taking a few mouthfuls, then passing it on.

Dieter did not join in the conversation that started, concentrating on the cellar entrance, thinking about Jagger's instructions. He thought back to when he had suddenly woken up in the copse, walking determinedly back to Hannelore's house, his mind made up. Later that day, the captain had returned and they had sat each side of the table, drinking a glass of beer. The captain had then slid a package across to Dieter, smiling, telling him to open it. Dieter had been amazed. It was a full set of papers. His identity card, discharge papers, rations card and a bundle of Reichsmarks. When he had asked why, the captain had told him that he had checked Dieter's story and that he was satisfied Dieter was who he said he was. He then continued, asking Dieter if he would like to work for him. He explained to Dieter that, with his perfect German and English, Dieter could help him to catch the black marketers and help Germany to recover. It had only taken a moments thought before Dieter agreed, shaking the captain's hand, both men enjoying some more beer.

Wearing shabby clothes, Dieter had been placed by Jagger in this working group, observing the comings and goings from the cellar. When the whistle sounded there were loud groans all round, Dieter easing himself to his feet, feeling a slight twinge in his calf. He started breaking stones and worked at a steady pace for the next hour, a man taking the pick-axe from him, Dieter then picking up bricks and stones and passing them down the line. He saw three men come out of the cellar, looking cautiously each way along the street, barely glancing across at the men and women clearing the debris. Dieter scrabbled down the opposite side of the mound, ignoring the shouts of the overseer, running along, parallel with the street. He had seen the short, wiry man between the two others and Jagger wanted this man followed. Dieter reached the end of the track through the debris and ran across the road, into a bombed out building. He was already breathing heavily, knowing he was not yet fully recovered. He peered round the corner of the wall and saw the three men approaching, ducking back and squatting down. The men walked passed. Dieter waited, watching them proceed along Seewartenstrasse, stepping out and following them at a safe distance, thankful that there were a number of people walking in both directions, enabling him to remain inconspicuous. The men passed St. Michaelis, turning into Herrengraben, then stopping outside a tailor's shop. The short, wiry man and one of the others walked on, turning into an alley, leaving the other man outside. Dieter was not sure what to do next. He paused at the corner.

Talking quietly amongst themselves, a group of women passed Dieter and headed along the street, Dieter tagging on at the rear of the group, passing the man outside the tailor's. He saw the entrance to the alley, seeing a man standing halfway along, the wiry man nowhere in sight. Dieter continued, turning into the next alley. He noticed an empty beer bottle lying on the floor, giving him an idea. He picked the bottle up, wiped round the top and staggered back into the street, weaving from side to side, bumping into people. He turned along the alley, grinning and raising the bottle to his lips before collapsing against the wall. Cursing to himself and slurring his voice, he staggered unsteadily to his feet, seeing the man watching him. He walked forward, almost reaching where the man was standing, before falling against the wall again, placing the bottle to his lips then, disgustedly, holding it upside down, mumbling and cursing to himself. He asked the man if he could spare some coins to get another beer, the man spitting at him, telling him to go away. Dieter was about to ask again when the wiry man came out, into the alley. He looked down at Dieter.

'What's he doing here?' Wicus asked.

The other man moved away from the wall. 'Just a drunk. Asking for money,' he replied.

Wicus bent down, looking at Dieter who grinned back at him gormlessly. 'Effing shit! Bugger off!' He stood up and kicked Dieter hard, Dieter taking the blow on the back of his thigh. Wicus and the man walked away, disappearing into the street. Dieter stood up quickly, rubbing his thigh and made his way through the door the wiry man had emerged from, seeing a small yard and an open door in front of him. He listened and, not hearing anyone, walked cautiously into the building, going down the stairs leading to the cellar. Letting his eyes adjust to the gloom, Dieter could start to make out the small printing press, engraving plates stacked on a table and a steel cabinet, its doors open, bundles of notes stacked inside. Then he heard a loud moan, making him spin round, seeing a man huddled in one corner. Dieter slowly approached the man who put his arms up, protecting his face.

'What happened to you?' Dieter asked, seeing the smear of blood on the floor. 'Did the man who just left rob you?'

The man mumbled something. Dieter gently took hold of his wrists and eased them away from the man's face.

'Good God! Did he do this to you?'

The man nodded slowly.

Dieter looked at the man's bloody face, bleeding from cuts on the eyebrow, cheek and top lip, his nose broken. He helped the man to his feet and, seeing a chair, sat him down. Dieter went upstairs and found a bowl, filling it with water and returning to the cellar. He picked up a piece of cloth and carefully bathed the man's face, hearing him moan and feeling him flinch. 'Why did he do this to you?'

The man shook his head. 'He wanted money.'

'He beat you up this badly for money?' Dieter asked. 'How did he know you had money?'

The man shrugged. 'Don't know.'

'Perhaps it's because he has been here before,' Dieter suggested.

Looking away, the man spat a globule of blood onto the floor. 'Please…please go. Leave me. If he finds out you've been here he will…will…'

'Kill you?' Dieter cut in.

The man's shoulders drooped and his head slumped forward. 'Yes.'

Dieter stood up and picked up an engraved plate, looking at it closely. 'I can see you are a skilled printer,' he said, 'this is fine workmanship. Are you forging documents for him?'

'Don't know what you mean,' the man replied.

'He's Polish isn't he?' Dieter asked. 'He shouldn't be here. I can protect you if you'll let me.'

'How?' The man looked up at Dieter.

'Tell me what you are doing for him and I'll arrange for you to get out of the city for a while.'

The man looked at Dieter for a long time. Then he started to tell Dieter what Wicus wanted, the shipping documents he forged and when the next shipment was due. Dieter listened, nodding encouragement, realising that he could not take the man with him, it would cut off a good source of information.

'I know you can't let me leave here,' the man finished, 'it would alert the Pole.'

Dieter nodded. 'Can you put that money somewhere else? It will stop encouraging him to beat you up.'

'It wasn't the money, the man replied. 'I gave him some information about a train. It resulted in him losing a number of his men because I didn't tell him it would have guards on board.'

Dieter looked at the man. 'Will you tell me what you tell the Pole?'

The man nodded.

'Also, if you give him documents, will you tell me what they are for?'

'Yes.' The man looked away.

'I will keep an eye on you…you have my word,' Dieter said. He made for the door.

Chapter Twenty Two

Falling to the floor, Colin looked up at Vicky standing over him, her legs apart, breasts heaving, smiling down at him.

Breathing heavily, Colin raised himself onto his elbows. 'Thank God the music's stopped…never thought it would end. This jazz…it's incredible!' He sat forward and, holding out his hand, let Vicky help him to stand up. 'I always thought I was fit,' Colin said, 'but my legs feel like jelly.'

'You're getting better at dancing every time we come,' Vicky replied, wiping the sweat from his brow. 'Let's get a drink and go outside.'

They went to the table and Colin bought two beers, placing his arm around Vicky's waist and escorting her to the door. They stepped outside, the cold air welcoming and walked to the corner of the building, going along the side. Colin took Vicky's beer from her hand and put the two glasses down. He took her in his arms and kissed her, feeling her tongue darting in and out of his mouth. Colin placed his hand on Vicky's breast, feeling her nipple through the material. He moved his hand down, stroking her crotch, Vicky moaning. She pulled out of his embrace and knelt down, unbuttoning his flies and taking his manhood out, licking and nipping the end with her teeth, taking it into her mouth. Colin held her head, the sensation driving him wild, feeling himself coming, trying to pull away, Vicky taking his seed in her mouth.

Colin helped Vicky to her feet, doing up his flies and then picking up the glasses. They both took a long drink. 'You are the most amazing woman I have ever met.' Colin kissed her on the cheek.

'So, you've had plenty before me?' Vicky replied, jocularly.

'No! No, I didn't mean that,' Colin protested. It's just that…'

Vicky placed a finger on Colin's lips. 'Let's get back inside, it's too cold out here.'

They walked, arms around each others waists, back along the building and turned the corner.

'Well, well…the love birds return,' Bill said, lounging against the front doorway. 'Hope you didn't get too cold round there. Mind, from what I saw, don't think the temperature got in the way.'

Colin flushed. 'Sod off, Bill, it's none of your business.'

Vicky walked up to Bill. 'What are you…a dirty old man, getting your kicks from spying on others? Can't you find your own woman or, more like, they wouldn't go out with you. You disgust me.'

'Watch your tongue, my girl. I could have you charged,' Bill replied, slightly taken aback.

Vicky laughed. 'What with? We'd deny anything you'd say and, what would others think of your snooping around?'

'I'm going to keep an eye on you and when I get the chance, I'm going to have you sent home,' Bill fumed, turning and walking away.

Colin grabbed Vicky and took her back inside. 'You shouldn't have upset him. He's not one to cross and I wouldn't trust him an inch.'

'He's just irritating,' Vicky replied. 'Pompous little sod…thinks he's boss just because he's given a complimentary rank in the Commission. So, we have to be careful not to let him catch us but he doesn't frighten me.'

'I don't think I can dance,' Colin said. 'I'm too weak.'

Vicky playfully thumped him in his stomach. 'Well, what would you suggest we do?' She widened her eyes and smiled. Colin went to get their coats.

Carrying a full pale in each hand, Walbert had to stop and put them down, his shoulders and hands aching. He was halfway back to the apartment and he was determined to take back more water than the Professor did, his pale's full to the rim. He turned round and saw Frieda bent over, dragging a small door along the road, piled with wood they had found.

'Come on Frieda, we haven't got all day,' Walbert joked.

Breathless, Frieda stopped next to Walbert. She unwrapped the scarf around her head. 'What did you say?'

Walbert waved his hand. 'Doesn't matter, we've got to keep going.'

'It's hard, pulling that along,' Frieda said, 'you don't realise how heavy it is with all that wood on it.'

'I'm sure Frau Eichel and Brigitte will be impressed when we get home,' Walbert answered. 'Right, get going and I will follow you.' He watched as Frieda set off, not wanting her to notice that he was struggling with the pales.

They were approaching the end of Wexstrasse and Frieda started crossing the road, Walbert struggling behind, feeling as though the pales were pulling his arms off. He heard the noise of vehicles approaching and in the next instance, saw a Dingo scout car hurtle round the corner followed almost immediately by a truck, heading straight at Frieda. Walbert screamed out, dropping the pales and running towards her, Frieda, with her head down, only looking up at the last minute. A cloud of smoke emerged from the scout car's tyres as the driver hit the brakes, swerving but unable to avoid Frieda. Walbert could see the vehicle closing in, hitting Frieda and spinning her up, into the air, then running over the wood. Walbert flung himself onto the pavement, the scout car coming to a stop just past him.

Then Walbert saw the truck, its front wheels locked, sliding at speed towards where he lay. He got up and ran back past the scout car, hearing the screech as the truck hit the scout car and the ripping of metal and shattering of glass. Walbert stopped and turned. The truck was half buried inside a shop, the scout car lay on its side. There were bodies everywhere; Tommies lying on the road, hanging out of the back of the truck, some staggering around, trying to help others; civilians trapped under the wreckage, lying on the pavement. Walbert ran past the mayhem, looking for Frieda, calling out her name. He saw the small bundle of rags lying on the opposite pavement. He knew it was Frieda, blinking to clear his vision as his tears ran down his cheeks. He ran. He kept on running, unaware of where he was going. He ran until he could run no longer, collapsing where he stopped. His chest heaved, his tears poured down his face and then he retched and retched.

Enjoying the meal Frau Gerber had placed in front of them, Hannelore and Dieter were discussing the coming year and what might happen to Germany, how long the British would remain now that the Americans seemed to be withdrawing, who would take over the ruling of the country.

Hannelore studied Dieter, noticing his mannerisms and how much he had changed since they had first met. His bright, green eyes looked back at her, a smile forming around his mouth.

'What are you going to do when you have finished working with the British?' Hannelore asked.

'My first priority is to find my wife...assuming...'

'She's alive,' Hannelore cut in, 'and you will find her. I know James is making enquiries on your behalf and he is extremely resourceful. He will find her.'

Dieter pushed his plate away and took a sip of wine. 'I hope you are right. But Hamburg took a hell of a pounding...have you seen the decimation, the destruction the Allies caused?'

Hannelore nodded. She could see the pain in his eyes. She could understand how hard it must be for him to not know for sure if his wife was alive or dead. She reached across the table and placed her hand on top of his. 'Dieter, I'm sure you will find her.'

'Have you any idea when the Captain will return?' Dieter asked. 'I have information for him.'

Hannelore withdrew her hand, looking down at the table. 'I never know when he will suddenly appear. Sometimes he is away for a few hours, sometimes for two weeks.'

'You are...you care for him a great deal, don't you?' Dieter asked.

Hannelore stood up, feeling herself flush, starting to tidy the table. 'I do like him. Is it wrong?' She looked at Dieter, seeing him smiling back.

'Of course not! If you are in love with the man then...enjoy it,' Dieter said. 'After what we've all been through, we deserve some happiness...surely?'

'You're right,' Hannelore replied, smiling. 'I do love him and I think...'

'You think what?' a familiar voice said from the doorway.

Hannelore dropped the plate in her hand, smashing as it hit the floor. She turned and saw James lounging against the doorframe, a broad grin on his face. Hannelore felt her heart leap as she ran across to him, throwing her arms around his neck and kissing him. She felt Jagger respond and then he gently broke away.

'We have others present,' he said, trying to look sternly at Hannelore.

Dieter chuckled. 'Don't take any notice of me.'

'You must be hungry. I will get you some food,' Hannelore said, turning and going into the kitchen.

Jagger sat at the table facing Dieter. 'Sorry I have been some time but I've been rather busy. I don't want to raise your spirits too much but I think your wife is alive.'

'You've seen her, met her, what?' Dieter asked.

Jagger raised one of his hands. 'Not quiet. I've been to the Rathaus and had the records checked. There is a woman of the same name and age as your wife on the labouring roll but...'

'But what?' Dieter cut in.

'But she is not at the address...well location, a cellar, that she gave when she first registered. I've been there and it is full of people, young and old but...not your wife.' Jagger helped himself to a tumbler of wine.

'When can I go in search of her?' Dieter asked.

'Hopefully as soon as possible. Tell me what you've discovered,' Jagger replied.

Dieter told him about the Poles and the forger, Hannelore coming in and placing a plate of food in front of Jagger and then clearing up the pieces and mess from the broken plate.

'That sounds horrible,' Hannelore said, listening as Dieter told Jagger about the way the forger had been treated.

'Those Poles are ruthless,' Jagger said. 'I believe they are running the biggest racket in Hamburg. That's why I really need your help Dieter. I have been informed that a large shipment of gold has mysteriously gone missing...somewhere near Munich. It was under the control of the Americans and...this is strictly between us, it is pretty certain that some of the Americans are involved in the disappearance. I am certain that some of this gold will pass through Hamburg and that's why I need your help.'

Dieter sighed. 'Is there a reward?' he joked.

Jagger laughed out loud. 'Actually, there may well be...hadn't thought about it but I think there should be.' He took another mouthful of food. 'I promise you Dieter, if you can keep on with your observations, when we have dealt with the Poles, I will put all of my resources into finding your wife. Unless you are extremely lucky, searching on your own could take months.'

Dieter nodded. He knew Jagger was right. He had already been to the house where his wife had lived and seen the pile of debris and smoke charred ruins. 'I'll get off early tomorrow morning and keep an eye on the forger.'

Hannelore watched as Dieter left the room, hearing him join her mother in the kitchen. She walked across to Jagger and eased herself onto his lap, kissing him and stroking his face.

'Let me just finish this and then we can go to bed,' Jagger mumbled.

As the coldness of the night penetrated Brigitte's clothes, she was becoming increasingly frantic, running and walking along the streets, trying to find Wally and Frieda. She knew she was exhausted having only slept for an hour or so the previous night when they had not returned home. She knew something had happened to them, fighting to keep the worst thoughts from her mind. With Heinz being tetchy

and taking more and more of her time, Brigitte was thankful
that the Professor had taken him out with him for the day,
covering the west side of the city.

Turning into Jungfernstieg, she could see the Binnenalster, the water on the lake choppy. Then she saw a small figure, huddled on the side of the lake and ran forward, shouting out. Slowly, the person turned towards her and Brigitte
recognised Walbert, seeing his puffed eyes and colourless
face.

'Oh Wally! Where have you been? I've been searching
for you for the past two days,' Brigitte said as she knelt
down beside him, pulling him to her. 'Where is Frieda?
What happened?'

Walbert sobbed quietly, his body shaking against
Brigitte's.

'You are so cold...we have to get home and get you
warm,' Brigitte said, instinctively knowing that something
dreadful had happened. 'Come on, let me help you up.'

Brigitte took Walbert's hand and they walked away
from the lake.

'It was terrible,' Walbert mumbled. 'They killed her.'

During the walk home, Brigitte slowly and carefully
coaxed out of Walbert what had happened, aghast at what
she heard. She placed her arm around Walbert and hugged
him to her. They entered the apartment and the Professor
looked up, Heinz pushing to get off his lap.

'Thank God we've found you,' the Professor said as he
struggled to stand up. What happ...'

'Get out of those clothes and change immediately
Wally,' Brigitte cut in, placing a finger on her lips, the Professor nodding.

Frau Eichel came in from the kitchen and saw them
standing round the table. 'My poor boy! Where have you
been?'

'Frau Eichel, could you help Wally get out of his wet
clothes and put on clean ones?' Brigitte asked. She watched
Frau Eichel take Walbert through to the kitchen, turning towards the Professor and telling him what had happened.

'Poor, poor girl,' the Professor said, slumping back into the chair, shaking his head. 'And there is absolutely nothing we can do about it…is there?'

Brigitte pulled a chair out and sat down, resting her elbows on the table. 'All we can do is help Wally. It must have been horrendous for him, seeing…' Brigitte wiped the tears from her cheeks, picking Heinz up and placing him on her lap. 'I will have to go out and get our rations…there should be some tinned meat available today.'

'You look very tired,' the Professor said, 'could I go?'

Brigitte smiled. 'You can look after this young man…I'll be quicker.'

Dieter watched the two men walk out of the alley, the wiry man was not with them. He stayed in the doorway of the building, waiting for some time and, when he was sure the wiry man was not around, he sauntered across the road, glancing along the alley. Nobody was in sight and Dieter walked quickly along, going into the rear of the shop. He saw the man sitting at the table, mending a jacket. He glanced up as Dieter came in.

'I saw the Poles leave,' Dieter said. 'Do you have any news?'

The man put the jacket on the table and slowly, got to his feet. He walked across to the steel cabinet and picked up some documents, passing them to Dieter. 'I made copies.'

Dieter read the shipping notes and manifest. 'How come medical equipment weighs so much?'

The man grinned for a moment. 'Let you work that out.'

'Did you tell the Poles anything…something you may have heard?'

The man studied Dieter, remaining silent for some time. 'Rumour has it that a lot of gold has gone missing.'

'You told the Poles that?' Dieter asked.

The man nodded. 'Don't want that lunatic coming back here and beating me to within inches of my life.'

Dieter nodded, thanked the man and left. He had to get back to Captain Jagger as fast as possible. The shipment was moving tomorrow. Dieter walked quickly along the street and turned into a damaged building, relieved to see that his bicycle was still where he had left it. He set of, peddling as fast as he could, feeling his calf protest, heading for the bridge. He shouted out as a woman almost stepped in front of him, barely glancing as he passed.

Standing on the pavement, watching him cycle away, Brigitte was thankful she had stepped back off the road, thankful it was only a cyclist, not a vehicle. She thought of Frieda.

Forcing the gear lever into third, Bill cursed, hearing the gearbox screeching in protest. The Hippo truck had cost him a small fortune in cigarettes to get the driver to let him borrow it for two days and, as far as Bill was concerned, it was little better than scrap. The radiator leaked, the tyres had virtually no tread on them and the gearbox had a mind of its own. Also, the seat was stuffed with cardboard, the driver's door did not shut properly and the bottom half of the driver's windscreen was missing. Bill could feel the cold air blasting at him, cursing again as he tried to light a cigarette. He started slowing down as he approached the roadblock ahead, seeing at least four soldiers watching him approach. As he came to a stop, Bill, opened the cab door and leaned out.

'What's all this then…looking for someone?' he joked as the nearest soldier approached him. Then he saw the officer approaching, the distinctive red hat denoting his regiment, the same officer he had met the previous week.

'We'll take a look in the back,' the officer said, taking the documents Bill passed to him and scrutinising them. One of his men came from the back of the truck, telling the officer that it was empty. 'So Sergeant Major, you're going to Osnabruck to collect a consignment of medical supplies?'

Bill nodded.

'Big wagon?' the officer said.

'Only one I could get,' Bill replied. 'Gotta take whatever is available Sir.'

The officer nodded, handing the documents back to Bill. 'On your way, Sergeant Major.'

Finding first gear, Bill moved slowly forwards, letting out a deep breath. He lit another cigarette, thinking about the return trip, deciding that he would take the Melle road back and then cut across country on the back roads, avoiding the roadblock. He reached the town and was soon reversing into the yard, relieved he had reached his first destination without the truck breaking down.

'What kept you Bill?'

Bill turned, seeing Lanky approaching him. 'Took longer than I thought in this bloody truck.'

Lanky looked at the vehicle. 'See what you mean. Any way, let's get goin', got a lot of stuff to shift.'

Joined by Shorty, the three men worked for the next hour, transferring the loads from the two American trucks into the Hippo. They went into the back room and Bill accepted the beer offered by Lanky, drinking it down quickly.

'That's one hell of a shipment,' Bill said, burping.

'That's why we needed the larger truck,' Shorty replied, picking up a sub machine gun and checking it.

Bill watched him. Then he saw Lanky picking up a kit bag and a rifle. 'What's going on?'

'You don't think we're letting you drive off on your own?' Shorty said.

'We're coming with you,' Lanky added, 'ridin' shotgun.'

Bill's eyes widened. 'You've got to be effing joking! What about the roadblocks? What if someone sees you?'

'Relax, Bill. You won't even know we are with you,' Lanky said, grinning. 'We'll hide in the back and...I'm sure you know how to avoid the checkpoints.'

Sighing, Bill knew there was nothing he could do. 'Where's my cut?'

Shorty passed a thick envelope across to him, Bill stuffing it inside his tunic. They went out to the truck and the Americans got into the back, Bill securing the tail flap. He climbed into the cab and started the engine.

Chapter Twenty Three

As the opium kicked in, Cyrek felt his body floating, felt good, felt himself relaxing. He lay back on the settee, letting the girl pull his trousers and pants off, play with him, then mount him, thrusting her hips backwards and forwards, screaming out as she satisfied herself. She got off, Cyrek grabbing her round the wrist, insisting she satisfy him. The girl grinned at Cyrek, the large amount of alcohol she had consumed earlier, obliterating her fear of him. Half heartedly, she played with his erection, placing it in her mouth, stopping and giggling. Cyrek reached down and, taking a handful of her hair, yanked hard, causing the girl to scream out in pain. He pulled her up to him, taking one of her nipples in his mouth and biting hard. The girl screamed again, struggling to get away from him, Cyrek tasting her blood. He threw her to the floor and got up, went across to the chair the girl had placed his trousers on and, removing the belt, walked back to the cowering girl. He brought the belt down, hard across her buttocks and continued thrashing her in a frenzy, ignoring her screams. Breathing heavily, he bent down, noticing the blood running from the cuts on her back and buttocks, forcing her over the settee and forcing himself into her rear, feeling his orgasm pulsing through him. He got to his feet and walked into the bathroom, pouring a jug of water down his belly, washing the smears of blood from his skin, then towelling himself dry.

Dressing himself, Cyrek heard the knock at the door, Wicus calling out. He opened the door. 'What do you want at this time of night?'

'It's on!' Wicus said, 'just as the forger told us, the truck's left Osnabruck…it's on its way. We've got to go.'

Cyrek shrugged. 'What's the hurry? He will stay at Lubbecke overnight…may not go for a couple of days.'

'Can we count on that?' Wicus asked. Then he saw the girl. 'Christ! What the bloody hell happened...she attack you?'

Cyrek glanced across at the girl. 'She needed a lesson in...manners.'

'Well, are we going?' Wicus asked.

Grabbing his coat, Cyrek nodded, the two of them leaving the girl moaning on the floor. They quickly reached the cellar, Wicus kicking men awake, ordering them to get their weapons and get into the trucks. One of the men, still drunk and half asleep, told Wicus to sod off. Wicus placed the tip of his dagger on the man's exposed stomach and started to push, the man yelling out, trying to sit up, terror on his face. Wicus withdrew the dagger, spitting into the man's face. The man staggered to his feet, grabbing his trousers, dressing as quickly as he could.

Cyrek came across, standing beside Wicus. 'Did your forger tell you if there's going to be an escort this time?'

'He's never had one before...just him and a younger bloke,' Wicus replied. 'As they are both in on whatever scam he's been up to, hardly likely to want to tell others...is he?'

'Suppose you could be right.' Cyrek looked round the cellar. He felt good. If Wicus' information was correct, this could be the opportunity he had been waiting for, the opportunity to become very wealthy.

A few miles away, in Buchholz, Captain Jagger was briefing his men on the operation ahead. He instructed two groups, consisting of two BMW R75 motor bikes and sidecars, a radio and four men with weapons, to head for Luneburg. Jagger pointed to the map, indicating the side roads he was certain Bill Thornton would be driving along, telling the men to watch out for a small convoy or possibly, a single truck, reporting immediately back to him using the radio. Jagger then detailed four men to drive to the bridge at Lauenburg, using an M3A1 scout car and wait out of sight, near the road block, again reporting to him when the trucks had passed. When Jagger was certain Bill Thornton had been identified, all groups were to follow at a distance whereby they could not be seen by the truck. Jagger answered questions and then told the men to be ready to leave at four o'clock in the morning, ignoring the groans.

'How do you feel?' Jagger asked as he walked towards Dieter.

Dieter looked up, frowning. 'I just hope I've learnt enough to use this,' he replied, pointing at the wireless set.

'It's a number sixty-eight...very reliable if you don't drop it,' Jagger said. 'Anyway, you look rather smart in your uniform.'

Dieter smiled, looking down at his tunic and trousers. 'Never thought I'd end up dressed like a Tommy.'

'When the shooting starts, don't want you being killed by one of my men,' Jagger said. 'Have you practiced with the Webley?'

Dieter leant across and picked up a Luger pistol, snapping the magazine in. 'I'd rather use this...more familiar and, I know I can hit something with it.'

Jagger chuckled. 'Lucky we had a couple spare. You're right, the Webley is not the easiest of pistols to use. You'll need a sub machine gun...any preference?'

'The Schmeisser,' Dieter replied.

'Thought that might be the case.' Jagger looked round, seeing that all his men had left the room. 'You're coming with me Dieter. We're setting off in about ten minutes so, get your kit together and make sure you have plenty of ammo.' Jagger turned and walked out.

Vicky moved, throwing her arm across Colin's chest and her leg over his. Colin listened, hearing her steady breathing, knowing she was fast asleep. He dare not move for fear of disturbing her, smelling the scent in her hair, feeling her breasts pressing against his side. Before they had fallen asleep, they had made love abandonly, the bed creaking, both of them giggling, certain that they must be keeping Vicky's colleagues in the other rooms awake. Vicky did not seem to care, yelling out in ecstasy, despite Colin's efforts to keep her quiet. Now, Colin lay still, knowing it would soon be time to get up. Today he was off to Lubeck with Bill and he was certain Bill would attempt to get rid of him. He felt the fear knotting in his stomach, felt the sweat bead on his forehead. He slowly eased himself out of Vicky's embrace, sliding out of the side of the bed. He felt around in the dark room, finding his clothes and carrying them to the door, letting himself out, into the corridor. Colin found the light switch and turned the light on, quickly dressing himself. He crept out of the house, hoping the scuff of his boots on the wood floor would not wake anyone.

Reaching his own billet, Colin let himself in, closing the door to his room and turning the light on. He stripped down to his underwear, washed and shaved and put his uniform on. Colin then checked his Webley pistol, working the mechanism, cocking and firing, loading the chamber. He put the pistol back in its holster and fastened the flap. Colin then walked across to the small, wooden chest of drawers and pulled the bottom drawer out. He tipped the clothes on the bed and removed the envelope, partly tucked into the back, opened it and counted the wad of notes. This was the envelope Bill had last given him and he had decided, for the time being, not to hand it to Captain Manson. Colin frowned. There was five hundred pounds in new notes, enough to purchase a house, a car, whatever he wanted when he returned home. Colin placed the notes back in the envelope and wedged it into the back of the drawer, placing his clothes on top and sliding it back into the chest. He would consider what to do with the money later. Colin checked his watch, seeing it was coming up for six o'clock, time for him to go.

Splashing through the mud, Bill approached the truck, the torch beam flickering, throwing a dull light in front of him. Bill coughed a couple of times and spat the phlegm from his mouth. He reached the back of the truck and lit a cigarette.

'You two all right?' he whispered. He heard someone move, just behind the flap.

'Yeah Bill...just get this show on the road, we're effing freezing in here.'

Bill recognised Lanky's voice. 'You're choice... could've found you somewhere to sleep.'

'Just get us to Lubeck,' Lanky replied.

Bill shrugged and walked round the truck, relieved to see that the tyres were all inflated and pleased that he had filled the radiator up the night before. He walked towards the truck parked ahead, seeing torch beams flashing through the darkness, other men coming. Bill started shouting out orders, men going to their trucks, engines grinding slowly into life. Bill walked back to the Hippo, seeing Colin standing in front of it.

'Glad to see you managed to get away from your floozy,' Bill said, disparagingly. Colin did not reply.

'Get in,' Bill said as he went to the driver's door.

'What's this?' Colin asked.

'What d'ya mean?'

Colin pointed at the truck. 'Why are we going in this? It looks cream crackered.'

'Just get in,' Bill snapped. He climbed into the cab and started the engine, relieved when it rumbled into life after the third attempt. Turning the lights on, Bill moved slowly forward, taking up his position at the front of the convoy.

'Is it essential for you to go out?' Frau Eichel asked, looking disapprovingly across the table.

Brigitte looked at Frau Eichel. They had never talked about Brigitte's activities but Frau Eichel knew what Brigitte had to do to obtain additional food and other essential items such as soap, cooking oil, flour and grain, needed to keep everyone from starving and maintain a level of hygiene. Brigitte smiled. She knew Frau Eichel had come to rely on her and appreciated what she brought home but, every time she put on her best frock and some lipstick, Frau Eichel gave her a disapproving look. 'We've only got a few packs of cigarettes remaining and I will need those and more to go to the market today,' Brigitte replied.

'I think Wally is starting to sleep better,' Frau Eichel said, changing the subject.

Brigitte chuckled. 'He's got a long way to go to catch up with Heinz.'

'I've never known a youngster like him,' Frau Eichel exclaimed, 'when he is put to bed you never hear him again until seven o'clock the next day.'

'Must mean he's not hungry. Well, I'd better be on my way.' Brigitte emptied the glass of water.

'It's barely light outside but, no doubt, you know what you are doing. Take care my dear,' Frau Eichel said as Brigitte stood up and put her coat on.

As Brigitte left the building, heading for the cellar club, she wished she could stay in the warm apartment, talking with the Professor and Frau Eichel, play with Heinz, anything other than what she was about to do. The Reichsmarks she had taken from the man the last time she had visited had quickly been spent, proving to be almost worthless, nobody wanted them; everyone was happier with cigarettes and Brigitte had seen young children outside the Hotel Atlantis picking up the butt ends on the pavement and in the gutter, removing the tobacco and rolling new cigarettes, making enough to survive on.

She soon reached the cellar, going down the steps and passing her coat to a girl who was sitting behind a table, half awake. Taking a deep breath of air, Brigitte opened the door and entered the club, making her way to the far end and sitting on a stool beside the counter. She asked for a glass of water and looked round, noticing that there were not many people present, a few other women and girls. Brigitte smiled to herself, seeing the variety of clothing the women wore; some wore evening dresses, some frocks, some skirts of varying lengths with an assortment of blouses. She picked out the legs covered by stockings, those with painted lines down the rear of the calf and those left completely bare. Where everyone obtained their clothes from never ceased to amaze her. She sipped at her water, debating whether to leave and head for the Hotel Atlantis. At this early hour, the chances of meeting someone were limited; most of the men would be sleeping off the excesses of the previous night.

'Don't know why I come to a place like this…it's a meat market,' a deep voice said, startling Brigitte.

She turned round and saw a tall, handsome man standing behind her, smiling. 'Perhaps it's to watch people making fools of themselves,' Brigitte replied.

The man nodded. 'Could be…I'm Pat.' He held out his hand, Brigitte feeling the firm grip as she shook hands. 'Can I get you a drink?'

'A coffee would be nice…thank you.' Brigitte noticed his dark eyes boring into hers, disconcerting her. She could not define why; it was just something about him. He started talking, explaining that he had only recently arrived in Hamburg having been with Montgomery's army, stopping the Russians before Lubeck. Brigitte started to relax.

Pulling his scarf tighter round his face, Dieter was thankful Jagger had supplied him with a pair of goggles and gloves. The night air had chilled him to the point where he could not feel his feet inside the sidecar. They had driven from Buchholz, through Rotenburg and on to Nienburg and Minden, Jagger expertly handling the powerful BMW R75, travelling at speeds which Dieter, begrudgingly, had found exhilarating. They had pulled off the road and hidden the bike, Dieter lying some two hundred metres from where Jagger lay, each watching the two roads into Minden that Jagger was certain the convoy would come along. A couple of hours had passed before Dieter, fighting to stay awake, had heard Jagger yelling at him, seeing him running into the bushes where the bike was, thankful it was daybreak. Dieter had got up and, despite the stiffness in his legs, had run and joined Jagger, jumping into the sidecar, Jagger immediately setting off, yelling at him that the convoy had just passed, heading into the town.

The bike slowed to a stop. 'Where the hell are they going?' Jagger asked as the convoy turned north, taking the road towards Nienburg. 'They're going the way we came.'

'Should I radio the others?' Dieter asked.

'Don't waste the batteries…we're well out of range,' Jagger said, setting off again.

Waving his arm out of the window, Cyrek indicated to the Opel truck behind his that he was pulling over. The two trucks stopped, just on the outskirts of Lauenburg, where the road forked. Cyrek climbed out and walked back to the other truck, Wicus opening the driver's door. Cyrek looked round, observing the lie of the land.

'What do you think?' he asked Wicus.

'Difficult. There's no cover for miles.'

Cyrek nodded. 'We're sure he will come out this side of the town...aren't we?'

Wicus coughed and spat. 'He has to go this way to get to Lubeck. Well, one of these two roads.'

'There's also that track over there,' Cyrek said, pointing across the field. He walked back, past his truck and viewed the road ahead, seeing an old barn. Wicus joined him. 'Let's take a look at that.' Cyrek walked towards the barn and stopped in front of it. He walked up to the opening, paused, then walked in.

'We can just about get the trucks in here.'

Wicus nodded. 'Yeah. Then, when he turns up we can take him.'

'Don't be so bloody stupid!' Cyrek responded. 'We're less than a mile from the roadblock across the bridge. Any gunfire and they will hear it. Do you know how many men are down there?'

Wicus looked down. 'Suppose you're right. So, when do we take him?'

'We have to let him pass then take him when we are well out in the countryside. Meanwhile, let's get the trucks and get them out of sight.' Cyrek set off.

Within minutes, they had driven the trucks to the barn and reversed them in. Cyrek told his men they were to wait until he returned, that he was going to walk back into the town to watch out for the convoy. The men made themselves as comfortable as they could inside the trucks.

As he left the building, Cyrek turned to Wicus. 'No, I want you to stay here, keep your eyes open but don't stop anyone passing.' Cyrek looked at Wicus, making sure he understood.

'What are you doing here?'

Cyrek and Wicus both turned round and looked at the young man, hobbling with difficulty on crutches, his left leg missing, coming towards them. A young woman was by his side.

Cyrek grinned. 'We are taking shelter. Who are you?'

'I own that building...part of the farm,' the young man replied. 'Don't see why you need to shelter, it's not that cold.'

Shrugging his shoulders, Cyrek looked towards the truck just inside the doorway. 'We've got a problem with the truck...engine needs fixing.'

'What sort of problem?' the young man asked as he looked at the truck.

'It keeps cutting out,' Wicus said.

The young man hobbled past them, the woman beside him, Cyrek and Wicus following. 'Use to be with the motor pool...I'll have a look, see if I can fix it,' the young man said.

As he and the woman reached the truck, Cyrek glanced each way along the road. He drew his dagger and, placing his arm around the young man's neck, thrust sharply upwards, the dagger going in below the rib cage, the young man gasping, Cyrek letting him drop to the floor. The woman turned, letting out a scream before Wicus placed his hand over her mouth. Cyrek bent down, seeing the blood coming from the young man's mouth, hearing his breath rasping. Cyrek straightened up, knowing the man would soon be dead.

'Play with the girl Wicus...she'll keep you occupied,' Cyrek said, as he walked out of the barn. He paused and looked back. 'Don't let her get away.'

Climbing the third flight of stairs, Brigitte felt the man's hand touch her lightly on her back. They reached the landing and she waited whilst he unlocked a door, welcoming her into his room. Brigitte stepped inside and gasped.

There were boxes and cartons stacked against one of the walls, bottles of alcohol on a table and a long rack of women's clothes.

'What do you think?' the man asked. 'Aladdin's cave?'

Brigitte shook her head. 'What's in the boxes?'

'Cigarettes, perfume, alcohol, drugs...all the things one needs to trade in this city,' the man replied, taking Brigitte's coat. 'Would you like a coffee or..?'

'A coffee would be fine,' Brigitte replied, sitting down in a large leather chair. She saw the man walk into the kitchen. Brigitte smiled to herself. When the man had first started talking to her, she was unsure about him but they had spent the past hour in the cellar talking, the man telling her about his war exploits and what he was going to do once he was demobbed. He seemed genuine and was very courteous. He had told her about his billet and asked if she would like to see it, Brigitte accepting, not concerned, especially as it was early morning.

The man came into the room, carrying two steaming mugs of coffee and handed one to Brigitte. He walked over to a box and undid the flap, taking out a carton of cigarettes and walked back to Brigitte, handing it to her. 'That should help you get whatever it is you want.' He pulled another chair closer to Brigitte's and sat down, sipping his coffee, looking at her over the rim.

'Thank you so much,' Brigitte said, 'but I have nothing I can offer you in return.'

The man smiled. 'Oh, don't know about that. I enjoy your company. Tell me all about yourself.'

Brigitte started to tell him, sipping her coffee, noticing the slightly bitter taste.

As Bill grated the gears, Colin clenched his teeth. The wind coming through the missing window pane in front of Bill, forced Colin to keep his coat tightly buttoned up and his gloves on. For the entire journey, Bill had not stopped complaining and swearing about the truck. They had driven along at a slow speed, every slight incline forcing Bill to change down as the truck struggled. Colin had told him that it must be because he had put too much in the back, Bill shouting back that it was the truck that was the problem, not the load. Colin had asked Bill why he had continued north before Rohrsen instead of turning right. Bill had shouted at him, telling him it was necessary to take different routes to avoid being robbed, an answer that confused Colin. They had eventually turned right in Verden, continuing through Soltau, heading towards Luneburg.

'Should that be doing that?' Colin asked, pointing at the steam pouring from the top of the radiator.

Bill glared at him. 'You stupid bugger! Course it's not...we'll have to stop when we see some water.'

Colin looked through the windscreen. 'Think I can see a stream or ditch up ahead.' He pointed, Bill looking.

Bill stopped the truck next to a gateway and got out, Colin doing the same, relieved to get out of the cab. Colin started flapping his arms, trying to get his circulation going.

'What the 'ell do you think you're doing?' Bill rasped. 'Use your jacket and get the radiator cap open.'

'I'll get a bucket or whatever...must be something in the back,' Colin replied.

Bill stepped in front of him, pushing him in the chest. 'Radiator cap. I'll find the bucket.' Bill walked to the rear of the truck, Colin hearing him shouting at the driver of the following truck, explaining what was happening. Colin managed to find a foothold, pulling himself up and unclipping the radiator cap, a hiss of steam gushing out. He saw Bill appear, carrying a petrol can.

'Get down, lad and fill this,' Bill said, passing the can to Colin. Colin soon filled the can, returning to the truck and passing it up to Bill. It took five cans to fill the radiator, Bill taking the can from Colin and going to the back of the truck. Colin started to get in when he heard a cough from inside the truck.

'Did you hear that?' Colin said to Bill, seeing him climbing in the opposite side.

'What?'

'Someone coughing in the back,' Colin replied.

Bill started the engine, looking across at Colin. 'Asked one of the lads to ride in the back.' Bill slammed the truck into gear and they lurched forward.

Leaning on the handlebars with binoculars to his eyes, Jagger watched the convoy ahead. 'It's the lead truck...having problems I think.' He turned to Dieter, passing him the binoculars and then getting off the bike.

Dieter raised them to his eyes and looked. 'Might explain why they are moving so slowly.' Dieter put the binoculars down and hopped out of the sidecar. He stood by the side of the road and unbuttoned his trousers, relieving himself, Jagger doing the same. It had been hours since they started following the convoy, taking an unusual route, moving forward slowly and, all the time, trying to stay far enough behind so as not to be spotted.

'Try the radio,' Jagger said, buttoning up his trousers and remounting the bike. 'It's certain he's going to cross at Lauenburg...only place he can.'

Dieter switched the radio on, waiting for it to warm up. He then started transmitting, getting a reply and passing the handset across to Jagger. Dieter listened to Jagger issuing instructions, telling one of the motorbike groups to go across the river and stop in the town, out of sight. He told the other motorbike group to stop at the roadblock and watch the convoy pass but not to interfere. Jagger turned to Dieter when he had finished. 'Should make him sweat a bit, seeing two of our bikes at the roadblock.'

'Shouldn't we take him at that point?' Dieter asked. 'He can't move forward and, with the rest of the convoy behind him, he can't get back across the bridge.'

'Had crossed my mind but I want him to lead us to his contacts in Lubeck,' Jagger said, 'and, I don't want the others in the convoy exposed if it comes down to a shooting match.'

'Look!' Dieter pointed, seeing the convoy starting to move forward.

Jagger started the bike.

Chapter Twenty Four

Coming to and feeling cold, Brigitte felt as though her head was splitting in half. She tried to move her arm but it would not budge. Blinking and squinting, she slowly opened her eyes, realising she was lying on a bed, looking up at a cracked ceiling. She tried to move, feeling the pain of the restraints around her wrists and ankles. Slowly, Brigitte raised her head, seeing her naked body spread-eagled on the bed then realising someone had molested her, a numb throbbing coming from between her legs. She lay back, closing her eyes, remembering talking to the man, drinking a coffee then, nothing. Brigitte knew she had been drugged, her mouth completely dry, her stomach aching. She tentatively tried each of the bindings, feeling the rope secure and tight. She listened, hearing someone moving in the adjoining room, determined not to call out. Then she heard footsteps approaching, the floor boards squeaking.

The cold water on her face surprised Brigitte, forcing her to splutter and open her eyes, seeing the man standing above her, looking at her.

'Thought you'd be awake by now,' he said. He sat down on the bed, his hand caressing Brigitte's breast, playing with her nipple.

'What do you think you are doing?' Brigitte rasped, forcing herself to speak.

'Have some water...think you need it,' the man said, placing his hand behind Brigitte's head, raising it and placing a glass of water to her lips. Brigitte drank the whole glass, the man refilling it and offering her another.

'What have you done to me?' Brigitte asked, her eyes flashing with anger.

The man stood up. 'I think you look so...so marvellous like that. Helpless, exposed, vulnerable. I just find it so...so arousing.' He stepped towards the foot of the bed, his hand caressing Brigitte's belly and pubis.

Brigitte struggled, letting out a groan as the ropes cut into her. 'You are mad! You can't do this! Let me go!'

'Ssh...ssh...don't struggle. You'll only upset yourself,' the man said, sitting down on the bed and leaning across, kissing the inside of Brigitte's thighs.

Brigitte lay back, breathing heavily, feeling the fear climb through her belly, up into her stomach. It was pointless struggling. 'Could you please release the bindings...they are too tight.' She felt the man draw his nail up the bottom of her foot, twitching involuntarily.

'Don't think there is a problem. Your circulation is fine, you have feeling in both feet and your hands look fine to me,' the man replied.

Brigitte looked at him. 'I'm terribly stiff, lying in this position. Can you please let me get up?'

The man smiled, his thumb playing teasingly round the entrance to Brigitte's vagina. 'Maybe...but later.'

Relieved to have reached the bridge at Lauenburg, Bill started to slow down as he approached the roadblock. As long as this truck got him to Lubeck, that was all that mattered. Bill saw the two sentries watching him as he came to a stop at the barrier. He reached into his tunic pocket and pulled the documents out, opening the door and getting down. He handed the documents to the sergeant who had appeared from the hut.

'Nice day,' Bill said, smiling.

The sergeant scrutinised the documents, not responding.

'As you can see, usual convoy on our way to Hamburg.' Bill nodded to the sentry standing nearby. 'Like a pack of fags?'

'Don't offer items...you know it is against orders,' the sergeant said.

'Sorry...mean't no offence...just a few fags in the packet, that's all,' Bill replied, trying to look upset.

'Wait here,' the sergeant ordered, walking past the hut.

Bill shrugged. 'Haven't got all day. There's plenty of starvin' people waiting for us.' Then Bill noticed the two motorbike and sidecar combinations nudging forward from behind the hut. He didn't like the look of the men watching him, seeing a sergeant on one of the bikes looking closely at his documents. Bill wiped his arm across his forehead.

'Seem in order...raise the barrier,' the sergeant shouted out, stepping towards Bill and handing him the documents.

Bill climbed into the cab, praying the engine would start, relieved when it did. He moved slowly forward and took his usual route, stopping in the town when he reached the fork in the road. He waved as the rest of the convoy went passed, then set off, turning towards Lubeck. Suddenly, he swung left, onto a narrow track.

'Where are we going?' Colin asked, surprised.

Bill lit a cigarette, glancing across at Colin. 'Just being cautious...varying our route.

'Shit! Cyrek had seen the truck turn off. He climbed over the wall and ran along the road, yelling and waving at Wicus, standing at the entrance to the barn. Cyrek pointed across the field, indicating the truck, Wicus suddenly comprehending what was happening. The two trucks came out of the barn, Cyrek jumping in beside Wicus. 'That track takes him to Schwarzenbek. We'll follow him and then take him when he's five or so kilometres out of the village.'

'Bloody stupid way to go,' Wicus replied , as he turned the truck onto the track.

Cyrek smiled and thumped Wicus on the arm. 'Not so stupid. Where can we pass him?'

'Hadn't thought of that.' Wicus grinned. 'How're we going to stop him then?'

Cyrek reached behind his seat and pulled out a Panzerfaust, placing it between his knees. 'When we see the right place, I'll blast the back off the truck with this. Now, slow down! We don't need to get too close…don't want to alarm him.'

Rubbing his knees, Dieter had at first wondered what Jagger was doing, slamming on the brakes, the bike sliding to a stop. They had watched the convoy clear the bridge from the far side and had then raced across, Dieter giving orders over the radio, the sentries raising the barrier. They had seen the Hippo truck set off on its own and Jagger had started following, the other bikes and scout car behind. Suddenly, Jagger had seen the man vault over a wall and run down the road towards a barn, the two trucks roaring out. Fortunately, Jagger had stopped quickly enough to ease the bike back behind the wall of a house, keeping out of sight.

'Well, well. This is getting interesting,' Jagger said, partly to himself.

Dieter looked across at him. 'What do you mean?'

'That chap running down the road. He's the leader of the Polish group that have been causing all sorts of problems in Hamburg.' Jagger watched as the two Opel trucks disappeared. 'Must have found out from our forger,' Jagger mused.

Dieter was also watching the trucks. 'Are you sure?'

'Know that big bugger anywhere. His mate, the thin, wiry one, is the man you've been watching. Both unsavoury characters.' Jagger started the bike and, waving his arm, set off, following the other vehicles. He shouted across to Dieter, telling him they would stay well back, out of sight.

Slapping the horsewhip across his hand, the man approached Brigitte. He had removed his clothes, except for his pants, but they did not disguise his erection. He drew the tip of the whip along Brigitte's body, the soft leather almost comforting. Smiling, he looked down at her, Brigitte glaring at him.

'Tut, tut…I'm going to have to teach you not to be so defiant,' the man said.

Brigitte gasped, letting out a low groan as the whip stung her breasts. The man flicked it down again, Brigitte wincing, waiting for this torment to finish. There was a pause and Brigitte looked across at the man, seeing him playing with himself. He moved back to the bed and raised his arm, stopping as they both heard the tapping on the door. The man looked round, dropping the whip and picking up Brigitte's stocking, leaning over her and forcing it into her mouth. He grabbed his trousers and left the room.

Hearing the apartment door being unbolted and opened, Brigitte heard muted voices, desperately trying to push the stocking out of her mouth. She stopped when the man entered the room, followed by a woman.

'Oh, you naughty man,' the woman exclaimed as she saw Brigitte. 'Think we can have some fun with her.' The woman removed her coat, revealing her expensive silk blouse and skirt, open to mid thigh. She walked across to Brigitte and grinned at her. 'Attractive. You certainly know how to pick them.' She turned to the man, walked across to him and placed her arms around his neck, kissing him. 'Shall we have a drink first? Then we can enjoy her.' They left the room, Brigitte's momentary hopes fading.

Watching the uneven road ahead, Colin was pleased the land was relatively flat, allowing the truck to move faster. He would be glad when they had got rid of whatever Bill had in the back and reached Hamburg. Every bone in his body ached from the constant jostling inside the cab. They had passed through the village of Schwarzenbek and Colin had kept quiet, noticing that Bill was taking a variety of small roads, wondering how Bill knew the way. He glanced across at Bill, hunched over the steering wheel, a cigarette hanging from his mouth.

'Have you seen them?' Bill asked.

'Seen whom?' Colin replied.

Bill removed the cigarette from his mouth. 'Look in your wing mirror.'

Colin looked at the cracked mirror. Then he saw it, a truck some hundred yards behind them. 'You mean the truck behind?'

'Been following us since Schwarzenbek and followed us every time we have taken a turning,' Bill replied.

'Might just be coincidence,' Colin said.

Bill glared at him. 'Coincidence! No effing chance... they're following us!'

'What're you going to do?' Colin asked.

'Keep bloody going! They can't pass us on these roads,' Bill replied. 'Look, this is Labenz so we haven't far to go.'

Colin saw the half a dozen or so houses lining the road as the drove through the village.

Slowing down as he approached the village, Cyrek saw the driver of the truck behind frantically waving out of his window. Cyrek frowned, telling Wicus to stop the truck. He jumped down as the other truck pulled up behind, running to the driver's door. The driver told him about the two motor-bikes behind him, staying well back. He had seen the sun reflecting off them and they had been following for some time. Cyrek gave the driver instructions and ran back to his truck, ordering Wicus to move across, climbing in and set-ting off.

'What was that about?' Wicus asked.

Cyrek looked at Wicus. 'We're being followed...two bikes with sidecars.'

'Shit! Can we lose them?' Wicus spat through the open window.

Cyrek grinned. 'It's been taken care of.'

As they approached the village, Dieter saw an old man come out of a house, glancing at them, a schaferhund by his side. The large dog saw them approaching and bound to-wards them, barking. Dieter drew his Luger as Jagger swore, slamming the brakes on. The dog stopped a few feet away, barking as Dieter pointed his pistol at it. Suddenly, the dog yelped, falling to the ground, blood pouring from its

smashed jaw. Dieter saw bullets slamming into the road surface, jumping out of the sidecar and darting into a doorway.
He looked across at Jagger and saw him crawling towards
the house opposite. Automatic fire rent the air, bullets ricocheting off the wall near Dieter's head, the dust and grit
stinging his eyes. The men in the scout car were returning
fire and Dieter saw others lying, dead and wounded on the
road. He could see a man firing from the window of the end
house and when the man ducked back inside to reload, Dieter moved, sprinting along to the next doorway. He pressed
himself tightly against the door, waiting. The man reappeared, looking towards the scout car and Dieter, gripping
his pistol with both hands, raised his arms and fired. The
man fell backwards, Dieter darting forward. He dived behind a large concrete water trough as a hail of bullets
slammed into the road around him. Flat on his belly, he
peeked round the corner of the trough, seeing at least four
men lying underneath a truck. Dieter fired his pistol, seeing
the men scrabbling to get out, one of them yelling as a bullet
caught him in the leg, another slumped where he lay. Dieter
jumped up and ran for the truck, firing as he went. He saw a
rifle lying on the ground and picked it up, working the bolt,
slamming a round into the breech. Leaning against the front
wheel, Dieter looked round the front of the truck and saw a
group of men, behind a large tree trunk, firing along the
street, pinning Jagger and his men down. He glanced back at
the man under the truck and scrabbled across to him, seeing
the vacant eyes. Dieter pulled the man out and saw two hand
grenades on the man's belt. Taking them, Dieter moved back
to the front of the truck. He pulled the pin from one grenade,
held it for a few seconds then threw it, ducking back and
pulling the second pin. The blast shattered the air, shrapnel
whizzing past and pinging off the truck, Dieter throwing the
second grenade. After the explosion, Dieter peeked round
the front of the truck, seeing the dismembered and bloody
bodies of the men behind the trunk. He stood up. There was
no further gunfire. Dieter waved towards Jagger and walked
across to the men near the trunk. One man lay on his back,
gripping his intestines. Dieter drew his Luger, cocked it and

placed the barrel beside the man's head, pulling the trigger. He looked round, checking there were no others.

'Jesus! That was a close run thing,' Jagger said as he arrived beside Dieter. 'Thanks to you, most of my men and myself, are still alive. What you did was very brave.'

Dieter grinned. 'Not really. I wasn't going to die at the hands of this lot...had to do something.'

'Yep, this is one of the Poles trucks. Means they were told to stop us.' Jagger said, as he climbed into the cab and started the engine. 'We've got to get going...we'll take this. Get the radio and some more ammunition.' Jagger jumped out and started shouting orders to his men, detailing two to stay with the wounded.

Dieter ran back to the sidecar and pulled the radio out, seeing a bullet hole through the middle. He threw it back and ran to the upturned sidecar behind, pulling the radio from it and slinging it over his shoulder. Dieter glanced across at the scout car, seeing both front tyres flat, a man hanging from the side, his belt caught on a metal flange, his face missing. He ran back to the Opel truck, other men doing the same. Jagger set off, a single motorbike and sidecar following them.

Shivering from cold and fear, Brigitte could hear the man and woman next door, laughing and talking, the pouring of liquid and the clinking of glasses. She could not move, her wrists starting to bleed where the rope had cut into them. Brigitte tried to blot out thoughts of what they might do to her next. Then she heard them approaching, seeing them enter the room. They looked at Brigitte, the woman stumbling against the man who caught her round the waist, she responding by feeling his crotch. She swayed, obviously drunk, giggling, pressing her lips to the man's mouth. He pushed her away, telling her he would deal with her later. The man approached the bed.

'You still look defiant, my dear. I'm going to have to teach you to smile.' He went to a chair and picked up the horse whip, returning to the bed and stroking the tip across

Brigitte's thighs. 'I don't like inflicting pain...it hurts me but, you must obey my commands.'

The woman giggled behind him. 'You are so handsome,' she slurred, trying to place her arm around his waist. The man pushed her away, sending her staggering towards the door. He faced the bed and flicked the horse whip, Brigitte flinching and clenching her teeth, feeling a burning sensation across the top of her thighs. The man brought the whip down across her belly, then her stomach. He raised his arm, aiming for her breasts. Brigitte closed her eyes. The sudden booming noise as a bedpan hit the man on the back of his head, startled Brigitte. Then she felt the man collapse on top of her. Brigitte could see the woman standing beside the bed, her eyes clear, a look of hatred on her face. She swung the bedpan again, smashing it down on the man's head, Brigitte flinching.

Slamming the brakes on, Cyrek stopped the truck, looking through Wicus's window. 'There he is!' he yelled, ramming the truck into reverse. 'Why didn't you see him?'

Wicus rubbed his knees where they had hit the anti-tank weapon held between them. He looked across the fields at the Hippo, driving slowly along, taking a road parallel to the one they were on. 'Only just seen him...must've been the same time as you.'

'We're lucky it's so flat around here,' Cyrek said. He reached the turning in the road and stopped the truck. 'You drive. I'll take the Panzerfaust.' He jumped out of the truck and ran round the front, Wicus getting across to the driver's seat. Cyrek climbed in. 'Let's go!'

'We've got to stop for water soon,' Colin said, seeing the steam coming out of the radiator cap.

Bill nodded, looking in his wing mirror. 'Keep your eyes open for some water then.' He lit another cigarette, coughing as he inhaled, spitting through the door window. He had not seen any sign of the Opel trucks for a few miles and was starting to relax, thinking he had been too cautious, putting it down to the load he was carrying. 'As long as this effing truck get's us to Lubeck, I don't care if it never starts again.'

Colin pointed ahead. 'See the road, it dips into a slight valley. Bet there's a stream or bridge at the bottom.'

Bill nodded. 'Suppose it won't hurt if we pull over for a couple of minutes.' He glanced in his mirror, immediately pushing hard on the accelerator pedal, the truck barely responding. 'Shit!'

'What's the matter?' Colin asked, looking across at Bill tensing over the steering wheel.

'It's the effing Opel...he's only hundred yards or so behind us,' Bill replied.

The truck started to gather speed as they dropped down the shallow descent, Colin seeing the bridge ahead. Colin looked in his mirror, trying to make out the Opel truck behind. As they closed on the bridge, Colin thought he could make out the shape of a man hanging from the side of the truck. He saw a flash, wondering what it was when, suddenly, the Hippo almost left the road. There was an almighty explosion and the truck bucked and slewed sideways, its rear slamming into the bridge wall, Bill fighting to keep the truck on the road, Colin bracing himself as he felt the truck starting to topple. The truck stopped and Colin saw Bill jump out of the driver's door. Colin opened his door and got down, about to walk around the front of the hissing truck when bullets started pinging around his feet. He jumped over the bridge wall, rolling down the bank and into the water. Colin heard men shouting and more gunfire. He drew his pistol and cocked it, standing under the bridge, the water up to his waist. He heard Bill shouting and saw someone slither down the opposite bank, a rifle in his hand. Colin hadn't seen the man before. The man started firing, aiming back along the road, yelling out for Bill, his American accent obvious.

'Lanky's bought it...shot before he could get out,' the American yelled.

'The bastards have shot the arse-end off the truck,' Bill yelled back. 'Shorty...think we should make a run for it.'

Bullets ripped up the turf around the American, making him duck down. 'No bloody chance. Give those bastards what we've got?'

On the opposite side of the bridge, a grenade exploded, causing Colin to lower himself into the water. He could not understand what was happening, was wondering where the American had come from. He saw the American raising his hands in surrender, the gunfire ceasing, the American clambering up the bank and disappearing. For a few moments, there was not a sound then Colin heard a vehicle slowly approaching. Colin waited, hearing boots running along the road and onto the bridge. Then he heard someone shouting orders, his German not perfect, switching to another language, Colin thought it might be Czech or Polish. He heard the American talking in German, trying to negotiate with whoever had attacked them.

Dragging the man's body off the bed and quickly untying the ropes, the woman had left Brigitte to get dressed, going into the kitchen and making her a mug of coffee. Brigitte had rested on the side of the bed, hardly capable of moving, her body so stiff and sore from where the whip had landed. She grimaced as she forced herself to stand, unsteadily, then walked slowly towards a table, picking up a jug of water, pouring some into a bowl. She picked up a flannel and gently washed the blood from her wrists and ankles, turning the water in the bowl pink. With a determined effort, she managed to dress herself, welcoming the warmth returning to her body. Brigitte walked across to a chair and sat down, taking the mug of coffee and quickly drinking it. She stared at the man lying on the floor.

'I've wanted to get that animal for the past two months,' the woman said, as she came into the room. 'I knew I would have to wait until he had someone else tied down. Sorry luv, but you were the first chance to get my revenge.'

Brigitte shook her head. 'Drugged you?'

The woman nodded. 'Then he did this.' She pulled her blouse up, exposing her stomach, the scars from the whip lashing she had endured, vivid against the white skin.

'Why? He seemed such a nice man,' Brigitte said. 'He's good-looking, tall, well-built. Why does he do this?'

'God alone knows why. He's sick,' the woman said. 'Anyway luv, can you give me a hand.'

Brigitte put the mug down. 'What are you going to do?'

'Grab his feet,' the woman said, bending and taking hold of the man's wrists. Between them, they could not lift the man, Brigitte joining the woman and both of them lifting the man by his arms. Struggling, they managed to get him onto the bed. The woman told Brigitte what to do.

Jumping into the back of the truck, it's rear axle smashed where Cyrek had hit it with the anti-tank shell, Wicus leant down and grabbed the dead man's collar, pulling him out and dumping him on the road. He looked at the boxes, some splintered, a couple open, their contents flashing in the light. He stooped and picked up a gold ingot, kissing it.

'What've we got?' Cyrek said, standing at the tailboard.

Wicus turned, grinning from ear to ear, tossing the ingot, Cyrek catching it.

Cyrek stared at it for a few minutes. 'Shit! Is there a load more?'

'Far as I can see, there's boxes of 'em,' Wicus replied.

'Let's get moving.' Cyrek shouted to his men, getting the Opel turned round and backed up. Men started moving the boxes, grunting and cursing, from the wrecked Hippo, into the back of the Opel.

Cyrek walked across to the man who had surrendered, covered by two of Cyrek's men, listening to him suggesting a share of the spoils, that he could help Cyrek with contacts. Cyrek's German was not good enough to understand everything Shorty was saying to him and he was becoming bored. Cyrek looked at the man and drew his pistol. He checked that it was loaded, cocked it and aimed at the man's chest. The man fell to his knees, pleading with Cyrek. Cyrek stepped closer and placed the barrel close to the man's head, firing once. He told his men to throw the body over the bridge wall.

As Shorty's body hit the water, Colin felt the fear in his belly rise. He had heard the American suggest a share out and heard him when he pleaded for his life. Whoever had attacked them had shot the American in cold blood. He knew, if they found him, he would suffer the same fate. He also wondered what had happened to Bill.

Chapter Twenty Five

'Oh Lord!' Jagger lowered his head, passing the binoculars to Dieter. 'They've just executed the prisoner.'

Dieter looked at the two trucks backed up to each other, men transferring the load, a big, powerful man sitting on the bridge parapet, watching proceedings. Then he saw the thin, wiry man approach the big man, gesticulating and talking. Dieter heard Jagger giving orders, the men spreading out along the ridge.

'Right! Let's go!' Jagger shouted, running back to the bike, Dieter behind him. Jagger started the bike as Dieter got into the sidecar, picking up and cocking his Schmeisser. Jagger waved his arm and the bike lurched forward, Jagger's men getting up and charging down the hill towards the bridge. The men on the bridge looked up in surprise, running for their weapons. Dieter fired off a magazine of bullets, seeing men diving for cover. He did not expect to hit anyone as the bike and sidecar bounced and weaved down the road but he hoped it would give Jagger's men enough time to close in and start firing.

Reloading his weapon, Dieter sprayed bullets at the truck, seeing men being hit. He saw the big man running towards the Opel cab, diving inside, then reappearing, levelling a Panzerfaust at him and Jagger. Dieter yelled out a warning, standing up and jumping from the sidecar, Jagger veering violently away, jumping off the bike as it somersaulted into the air. A whoosh, followed by an explosion behind him, showered Dieter in earth. Dieter jumped up, running towards the trucks, firing his weapon. Other men were closing in, the men on the bridge falling under the assault. Dieter rolled across the road, standing behind a tree trunk and reloading. He glanced back along the road, seeing Jagger lying motionless.

Bullets thumped into the tree, Dieter ducking down. He waited, then ran out firing, seeing the big man stumble and drop his gun as bullets tore into his shoulder and arm. Jagger's men were close to Dieter and the survivors around the bridge started shouting, throwing down their weapons. Dieter stopped, breathing heavily. He walked forward slowly, watching as the big man slowly stepped backwards then falling down the bank, disappearing from view. Dieter shouted out to the survivors to come out, seeing Jagger's men covering them as they emerged, nobody seeing Wicus slip away from the Hippo, an ingot in each hand.

He saw the bodies of dead and injured men lying on the road, some inside the trucks, others underneath. Dieter looked across at the seven men standing beside the road, their arms above their heads, Jagger's men searching them. Dieter looked into the back of the Opal truck and saw a dozen or more boxes. He turned and looked inside the Hippo, climbed up and walked towards a splintered box, seeing its contents protruding through the side. Dieter pulled an ingot out and looked at it. He turned and hopped back down to the ground.

Freezing in the water, Colin heard someone sliding down the bank. He lowered himself until the water level reached his mouth, holding his arm up, clenching his pistol. He saw a wiry man slip into the water, an ingot in each hand. Colin's eyes widened, his heart beating faster, watching as the man turned away and started to slowly and quietly make his way along the stream, keeping his head below the embankment. The man soon disappeared where the stream turned. Colin let out a sigh of relief. Suddenly, a loud splashing behind him made him turn. There was an enormous man with glaring eyes and thick eyebrows staring at him, blood oozing from his chest and arm. The man stumbled towards him, Colin aiming his pistol, his hand shaking uncontrollably. The man grinned at him, still coming forward, Colin edging backwards. When the man was almost upon him, reaching out to take the pistol, Colin pulled the trigger. The retort was deafening under the bridge. Colin saw the big man's eyes widen, saw him grin, then watched as he slowly sank into the water.

'Drop your gun!' someone shouted out behind Colin.

Colin yelled out. 'I'm English...I'm English, don't shoot. My name's Colin Patterson.' As Colin raised his arms above his head, he dropped the pistol with a loud splash. He cringed, waiting for the man behind him to shoot him, knowing he was going to die.

'At least the Hitler Youth taught us to tie knots securely,' the woman said, as she gave the last knot a final pull. 'He won't get out of those easily.'

Brigitte looked up and smiled. 'No doubt about that.' She looked at the man lying naked on the bed. She then watched as the woman picked up the jug of water.

'Time for him to wake up,' the woman said as she slowly poured the water over the man's head. The man groaned, moved his head to the side, then coughed. Slowly, he opened his eyes, looking firstly at the woman, then at Brigitte. His forehead creased, the man realising that he was now at their mercy.

'I...I didn't mean you harm,' he spluttered. 'Just a bit of fun.'

Brigitte turned away.

The woman laughed and walked across to the chair, picking up the whip. 'Let's see how much you laugh.' She walked back to the bed and brought the whip down as hard as she could, across the man's crotch. He yelled out in pain. The woman continued, Brigitte standing nearby, mesmerised.

'Turn round,' Dieter ordered, watching the Tommy in front of him turn slowly. Then he recognised the young lad who had been an interpreter at the internment camp. 'What are you doing here?'

Colin stared back. 'I...I'm with the Commission. Who are you?'

'Doesn't matter who I am, how did you get mixed up in this?' Dieter asked.

'I was told by a Captain Jagger to continue with Sergeant Major Thornton, accompanying him to Lubeck and reporting back to him,' Colin replied.

Dieter smiled. 'Put your arms down. You look frozen...better get out of this water.' He waded towards the floating body of Cyrek, telling Colin to get the other body, Shorty's body. They pulled the bodies along, out the other side of the bridge. Colin got out of the water and pulled, Dieter pushing from below, easing the bodies onto the top of the embankment. Dieter heard Colin vomit as he reached him. 'First time you've seen a body blown apart by a hand grenade?'

Colin nodded, wiping his mouth. What remained of Bill Thornton lay on the grass in front of him. Colin looked at Dieter. 'I saw a man disappear along the stream. He was carrying an ingot in each hand.'

'Thin...wiry man?' Dieter asked.

Colin nodded.

Dieter bent down and looked at Shorty's body, the man's identity tags around his neck glinting in the sun. He pulled them off, noticing that the man was a colonel in the American army.

Rummaging through the cartons, Brigitte and the woman could hardly believe their eyes. There were cartons of cigarettes, boxes of alcohol, a box full of packs of stockings and boxes of perfume. Brigitte opened another box, full of cameras.

'He told me he had only just arrived in Hamburg,' Brigitte said, picking up a camera. 'He must have been collecting this stuff for months.'

'Said the same to me when I first met him,' the woman replied, 'lying scoundrel.' She pulled out a pair of stockings and started to put them on. 'These are silk...aren't they?'

Brigitte walked across and felt the stockings, nodding. 'Well, I'm going to take some of this.'

'We can share it between us,' the woman said.

Brigitte nodded towards the bedroom door. 'What about him?'

'What about him. He can stay there 'til he rots,' the woman replied. 'What do you think he was going to do to you, luv? Let you go?'

Brigitte shrugged. She went to the bedroom door and glanced across at the bed. The man was moaning, his body streaked in blood. She turned and walked across to a large carton, tipping its contents onto the floor. Brigitte then started to fill it again, selecting various items, packing the carton until it was almost full. 'I'm going to take this now and return later.'

The woman nodded. 'Think I'll do the same.'

'Thank you. Thank you for coming to my rescue,' Brigitte said,

The woman smiled.

Kneeling down, Dieter eased Jagger's head onto his lap. He could see he was in pain, holding his side. Dieter opened his water bottle and helped Jagger take a few sips. 'I'm going to get you back to Hannelore. She'll patch you up.'

'Thanks for saving my life,' Jagger said. 'Did we get them and the gold?'

Dieter nodded. 'The big fellow is dead and what's left of them have surrendered. There's a young bloke who claims he was working for you.'

'Is he called Colin Patterson?' Jagger asked.

Dieter grinned. 'Yes...he did shout out his name just before I was about to put a bullet in his back.'

Jagger looked up at Dieter. 'Thank God you didn't! He can lead us to the contact.'

'Not in your condition,' Dieter said. 'We've got to get you back first.'

'No! You must find that other Pole. He's dangerous and cunning.' Jagger tried to ease himself up, grimacing. 'Get the men to take the gold back to Buchholz along with the prisoners. I'll come with you.'

'You're going with the men,' Dieter replied. 'I'll take the young lad with me.' Dieter shouted out to the men, giving orders and getting two of them to carry Jagger to the Opel truck. He watched as the last box was transferred, the prisoners bundled on board and the men got into the truck. Dieter went across to the wrecked Hippo and picked up an ammunition belt and rucksack, called to Colin who joined him, going to the upturned bike. They managed to right it and Dieter tried to start it, hearing the engine roar into life. He told Colin to get in, throwing the rucksack in the foot-well.

The clattering of the car coming along the road alerted Wicus and he climbed out of the ditch, his wet clothes sticking to him. He waved as the car approached, standing in the middle of the road, seeing an old man behind the wheel. The car slowed and stopped in front of Wicus and he walked to the driver's door, smiling. The old man opened the door, asking him what he wanted and Wicus explained that he had foolishly crashed his car into the ditch further along the road and that he was hoping he could get a lift to Hamburg. The old man indicated for him to get in.

They drove along in silence, the old man eventually looking across at Wicus. 'Haven't seen your car yet.'

'You wouldn't, it's hidden from the road,' Wicus replied.

The old man nodded. 'You're not German.'

'Polish.' Wicus looked ahead.

Slowing the car down, the old man stared at Wicus. 'What are you doing out here? Doesn't seem right. Surely you should be home now. Or are you up to no good?'

Wicus looked at the old man and grinned. His right arm moved fast, the ingot in his hand smashing into the old man's forehead, splitting the skull. The car started to move forward, Wicus placing his foot on the brake pedal, the engine stalling. He leaned across and opened the driver's door, pushing the old man out, moving across into the driver's seat. Wicus started the engine and set off, knowing he was only a few kilometres from Hamburg. Wicus was pleased. The car would come in useful.

Struggling along the street, Brigitte knew she would not be able to pull the heavy carton all the way home. She started looking for somewhere to hide it safely until she could return with Walbert, hopefully with a cart, to transport the contents. Brigitte turned into a narrow street, noticing that most of the buildings were bomb damaged, piles of debris partly obstructing the street. She tugged at the carton, moving slowly forward. Then she saw a small gap in a wall where a doorway had been, making her way towards it. She stopped at the wall, peering cautiously through the gap, seeing the debris behind. There was nobody in sight and Brigitte pulled the carton through the gap. Looking round, she started to move a pile of bricks, soon creating a hole, large enough to take the carton. Brigitte removed a carton of cigarettes and, with difficulty, pushed the carton into the hole, soon replacing the bricks, covering it. She inspected her work, satisfied the carton was completely hidden and that the bricks looked as though they had not been disturbed. Brigitte tucked the cigarettes inside her coat and set off, knowing Frau Eichel would be anxiously waiting for her.

Fighting to keep the bike on the road, its front wheel slightly buckled, Dieter drove as fast as he dare. He could hear Colin in the sidecar, urging him to slow down but he knew they had to get to Hamburg, get to the cellar, before the Pole turned up. He saw the goose too late, feeling the sidecar judder as it disappeared underneath it, heard Colin shout out and looked across, laughing to himself at the sight of Colin brushing goose feathers from his face and hair. Dieter opened the throttle.

Pulling up along Hopfenstrasse, Dieter jumped off the bike.

'You're a maniac!' Colin said, as he scrambled out of the sidecar. 'You could have killed us.'

'Quick...help me with the bike,' Dieter replied. They pushed it into a building and Dieter checked his pistol, telling Colin to do the same. Dieter took his Schmeisser and clipped a full magazine into place. 'Let's go.'

Running along the street, the light fading, Dieter crossed into Erichstrasse and continued to the end. He paused when he reached Balduinstrasse, Colin right behind him. Dieter could see the entrance to the cellar, wondering if the wiry man had got back, sure he would come. Dieter looked each way along the street, seeing various people walking, nobody looking suspicious. He made his decision and started running towards the cellar entrance. Taken by surprise, Colin was left behind, watching Dieter disappear down the steps.

Listening intently, all his senses alert, Dieter stepped slowly down. He saw the main entrance door, slightly ajar, certain someone was inside. Dieter moved silently forward, easing himself round the door, peering into the dim light. He saw a movement ahead of him and the flicker of a lamp. Dieter waited, seeing a man rummaging through a steel cabinet, stuffing something into his pockets. Then Dieter recognised the wiry man. Dieter looked round, no sign of anyone else in the cellar.

'Don't move! Put your hands up!' Dieter shouted, seeing the man freeze. The man suddenly turned and fired, bullets splattering the wall near to Dieter. The man dived to the floor, out of Dieter's view and fired at the lamp, extinguishing it. Dieter remained motionless, the only sound he could hear was his own breathing, his eyes adjusting to the gloom. Dieter crouched and slowly inched his way soundlessly, towards the door. He could sense the other man moving but could not determine where he was.

'Are you all right? Where are you?'

Dieter gritted his teeth. He recognised Colin's voice, hearing him coming down the stairs. Then he saw Colin's outline in the doorway. 'Get Down!'

Bullets hit the door, ricocheting off the steel, Dieter dropping to the floor. He waited, hearing the man stepping lightly towards the door. Suddenly, the beam of a torch blinded Dieter. He rolled across the floor, bumping into a chair, the impact knocking his Schmeisser from his hands.

'Get up!' Wicus yelled. 'Hands up, where I can see them.'

Dieter got to his feet and raised his arms, the beam playing on his face. He knew he was trapped, any sudden movement and the man would shoot. He saw the man walk towards him.

'What are you doing here?' Wicus asked.

'Looking for you,' Dieter replied. He heard the man snort.

'Put down your weapon,' Colin said.

Wicus froze, feeling the muzzle prodding into his back. He lowered his gun and started to lower the torch. Then he turned fast, his hand knocking the pistol away from him, the roar of the gun deafening. Wicus used his other hand, bunched into a fist and smashing into Colin's face. Wicus started to step towards the doorway.

Dieter moved fast, picking up the Schmeisser, illuminated by the torch light and raised it. He fired one shot, hitting Wicus in the shoulder, spinning him round as he fell to the ground. Dieter picked the torch up and shone it towards Wicus, seeing him clutching his shoulder, seeing Colin lying on the ground, holding his nose, blood flowing across his hand. Dieter stepped across to Wicus and kicked him hard in his ribcage. He heard Wicus groan, then bent down and removed the dagger from its sheath. Dieter kicked Wicus again, aiming for his ribcage, feeling the impact of his boot. He turned and shone the torch on Colin.

'Thanks,' Dieter said as he helped Colin get to his feet. 'You certainly saved me there. Can you help me get this man outside?'

Before Colin could answer, Dieter turned, seeing Wicus raising a pistol. Dieter fired, bullets ripping through Wicus' body. Dieter stood, looking down at Wicus. He seemed to be grinning, then he coughed once and died.

Dieter walked to the rear of the cellar and found what he was looking for; the two gold ingots were inside a back pack, along with bundles of American dollars. Dieter buckled the back pack and slung it over his shoulder. He walked back to Colin. 'Let's go. Captain Jagger will be waiting.'

Turning into Erichstrasse, Brigitte was relieved. She would be with Frau Eichel in minutes. She quickened her step. Just before she reached the entrance to the apartment building, she stopped, staring at the two Tommies walking towards her. She felt her heart miss a beat, felt herself almost overcome, placing her arm out, bracing herself against the wall. The two men were almost upon her.

'Dieter?'

The man with the back pack stopped and stared at her, his mouth open, moving, but saying nothing.

'Dieter? Is it you?' Brigitte stammered.

Dieter dropped the back pack and passed his weapon to the young man beside him. 'Brigitte?'

Brigitte flung her arms around Dieter's neck, bursting into tears. 'Oh my God! I never thought I would see you again.'

Colin stood still, amazed, seeing Dieter clinging to the woman, both of them crying.

THE END